DISCARD

Keep
Reading!
™ & © DSE

AMELIA RULES!™

When the PAST IS A PRESENT

Atheneum Books for Young Readers
New York London Toronto Sydney

MEET THE GANG

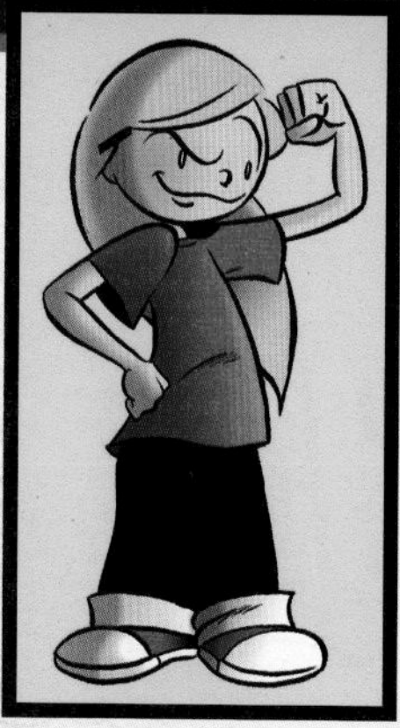

Amelia Louise McBride:
Our heroine. Wise cracking, yet sweet. She spends her time hanging out with friends and her aunt Tanner.

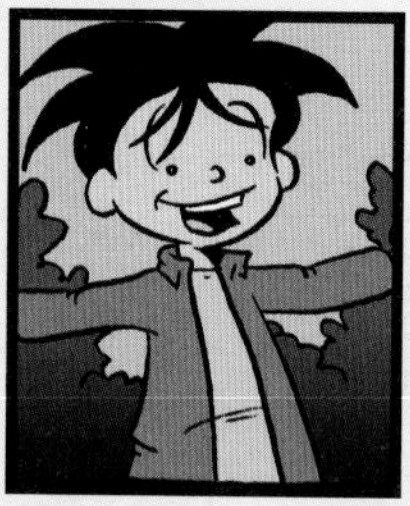

Reggie Grabinsky:
A.k.a. Captain Amazing. Founder of G.A.S.P., which he forces . . . er, encourages, his friends to join.

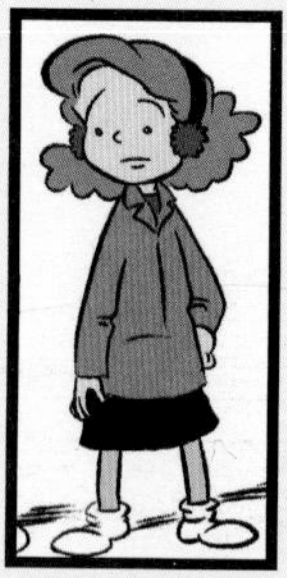

Rhonda Bleenie:
Smart, stubborn, and loud. She wears her heart on her sleeve and it's filled with love for Reggie.

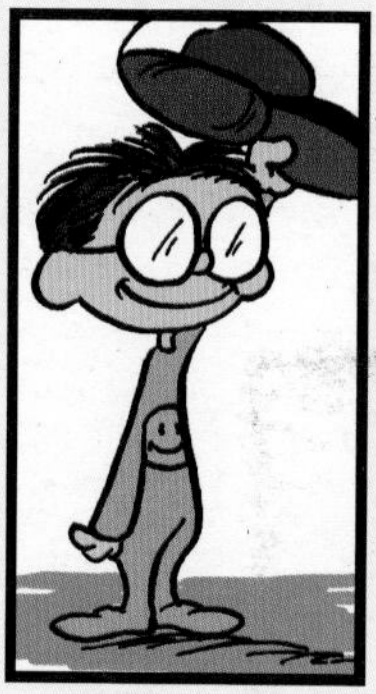

Pajamaman:
Never speaks. Always cool. His feetie jammies tell you what's on his mind.

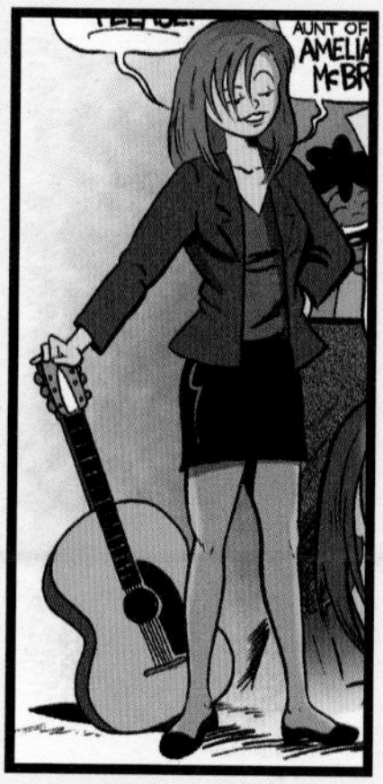
AUNT OF
AMELIA
McBR

Tanner:
Amelia's aunt and a former rock 'n' roll superstar.

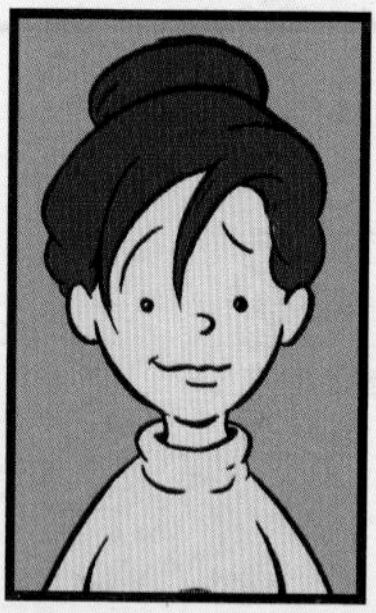

Amelia's Mom (Mary):
Starting a new life in Pennsylvania with Amelia after the divorce.

Amelia's Dad:
Still lives in New York, and misses Amelia terribly.

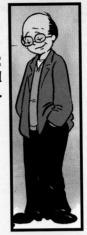

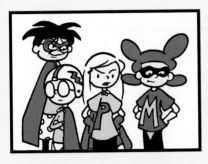

G.A.S.P.
Gathering Of Awesome Super Pals. The superhero club Reggie founded.

Park View Terrace Ninjas:
Club across town and nemesis to G.A.S.P.

NINJA KYLE

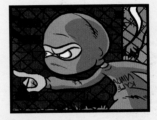

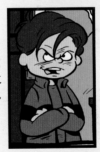

Kyle:
The main ninja. Kind of a jerk but not without charm.

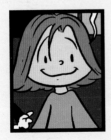

Joan:
Former Park View Terrace Ninja (nemesis of G.A.S.P.), now friends with Amelia and company.

Tweenie Zeenie:
A local kid-run magazine and Web site.

tweeniezeenie.com

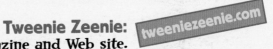

ATHENEUM BOOKS FOR YOUNG READERS

An imprint of Simon & Schuster Children's Publishing Division

1230 Avenue of the Americas, New York, New York 10020

ATHENEUM BOOKS FOR YOUNG READERS is a registered trademark of Simon & Schuster, Inc.

For information about special discounts for bulk purchases, please contact Simon & Schuster Special Sales at 1-866-506-1949 or business@simonandschuster.com.

The Simon & Schuster Speakers Bureau can bring authors to your live event. For more information or to book an event, contact the Simon & Schuster Speakers Bureau at 1-866-248-3049 or visit our website at www.simonspeakers.com.

Book design by Sonia Chaghatzbanian

The text for this book is hand-lettered.

The illustrations for this book are digitally rendered.

Manufactured in China

0711 GFC

First Atheneum Books for Young Readers hardcover edition October 2011

2 4 6 8 10 9 7 5 3 1

The Library of Congress has cataloged the paperback edition as follows:

Jimmy Gownley.

When the past is a present / [Jimmy Gownley].—1st ed.

p. cm.—(Jimmy Gownley's Amelia rules! ; 4)

Summary: When her Aunt Tanner brings out a box of mementos, ten-year-old Amelia Louise McBride learns things about her family history that help her deal with such current issues as her first date and the deployment of a friend's father to Iraq.

ISBN 978-1-4169-8607-2 (pbk)

1. Graphic novels. [1. Graphic novels. 2. Families—Fiction. 3. Friendship—Fiction. 4. Dating (Social customs)—Fiction] I. Title.

PZ7.7.G69 Whe 2010

741.5'973—dc23   2009051222

ISBN 978-1-4424-4541-3 (hc)

These comics were originally published individually by Renaissance Press.

This book is for:

Kerensa Bartlett, Hailey Cook, Ethan Gourlay,
James Elmour, Frances Cooke, and everyone at
Small Pond Productions. And especially to
Kasey Perkins, who brought Amelia McBride
to life before my very eyes.

That's what magic is.

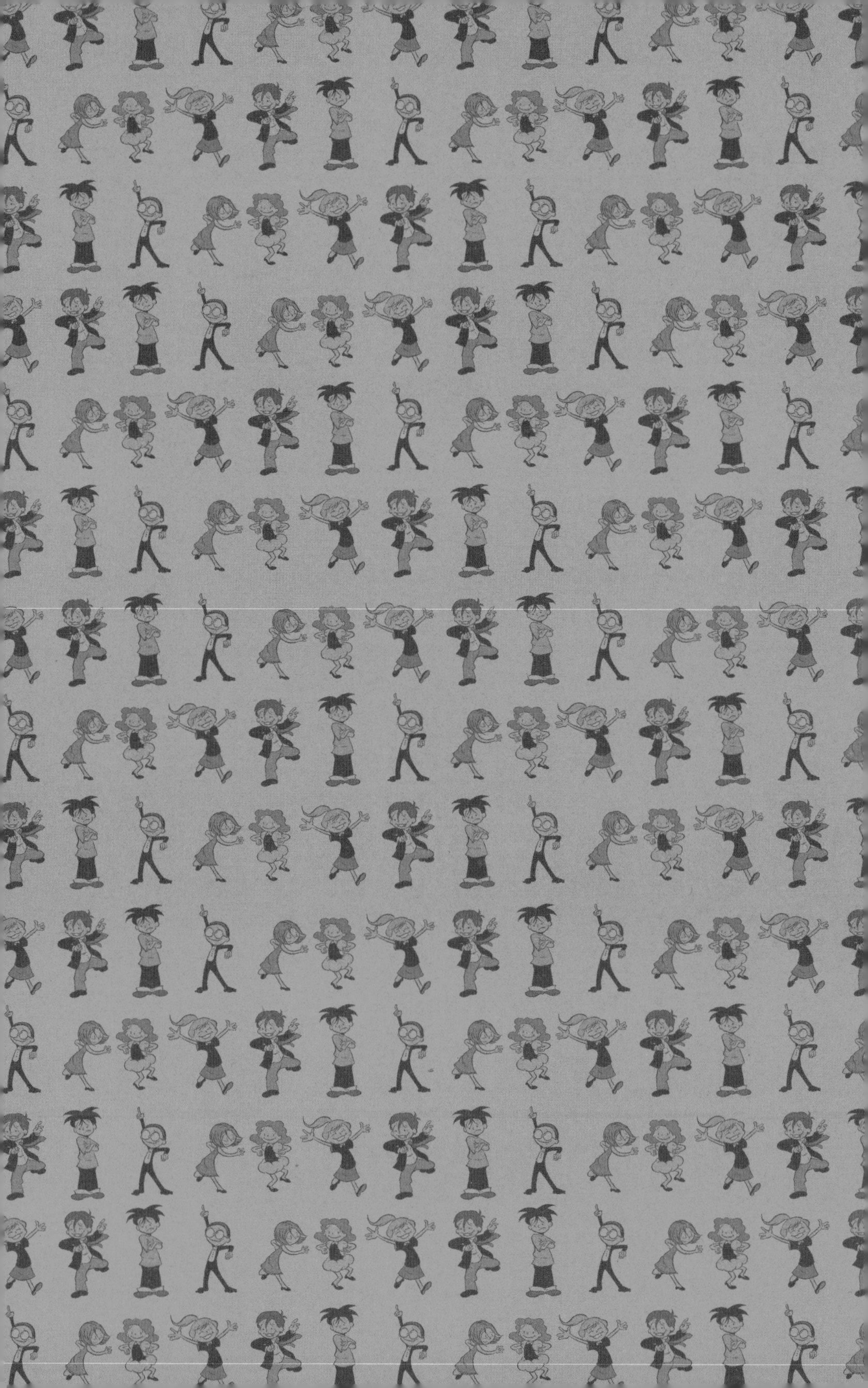

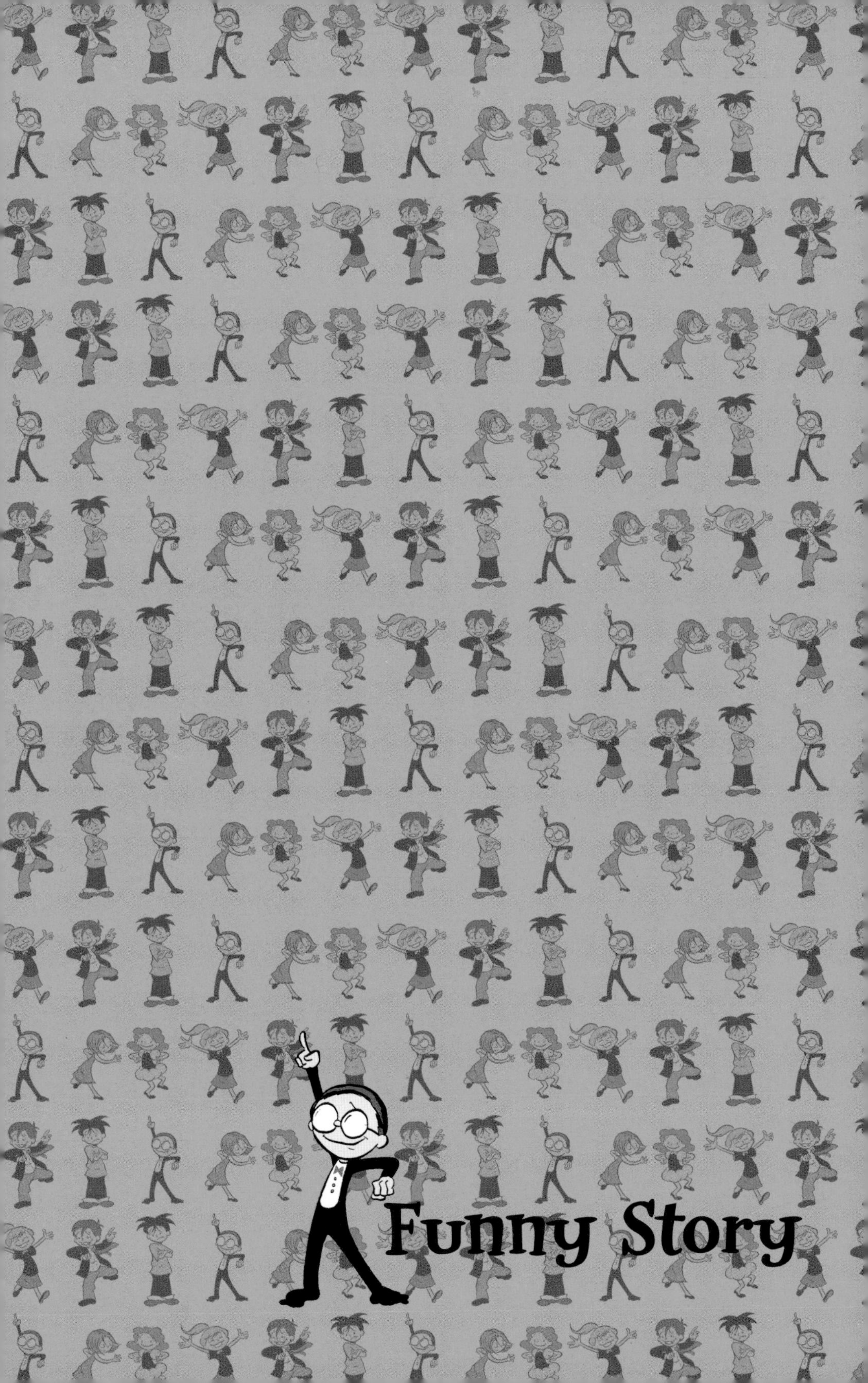

Funny Story

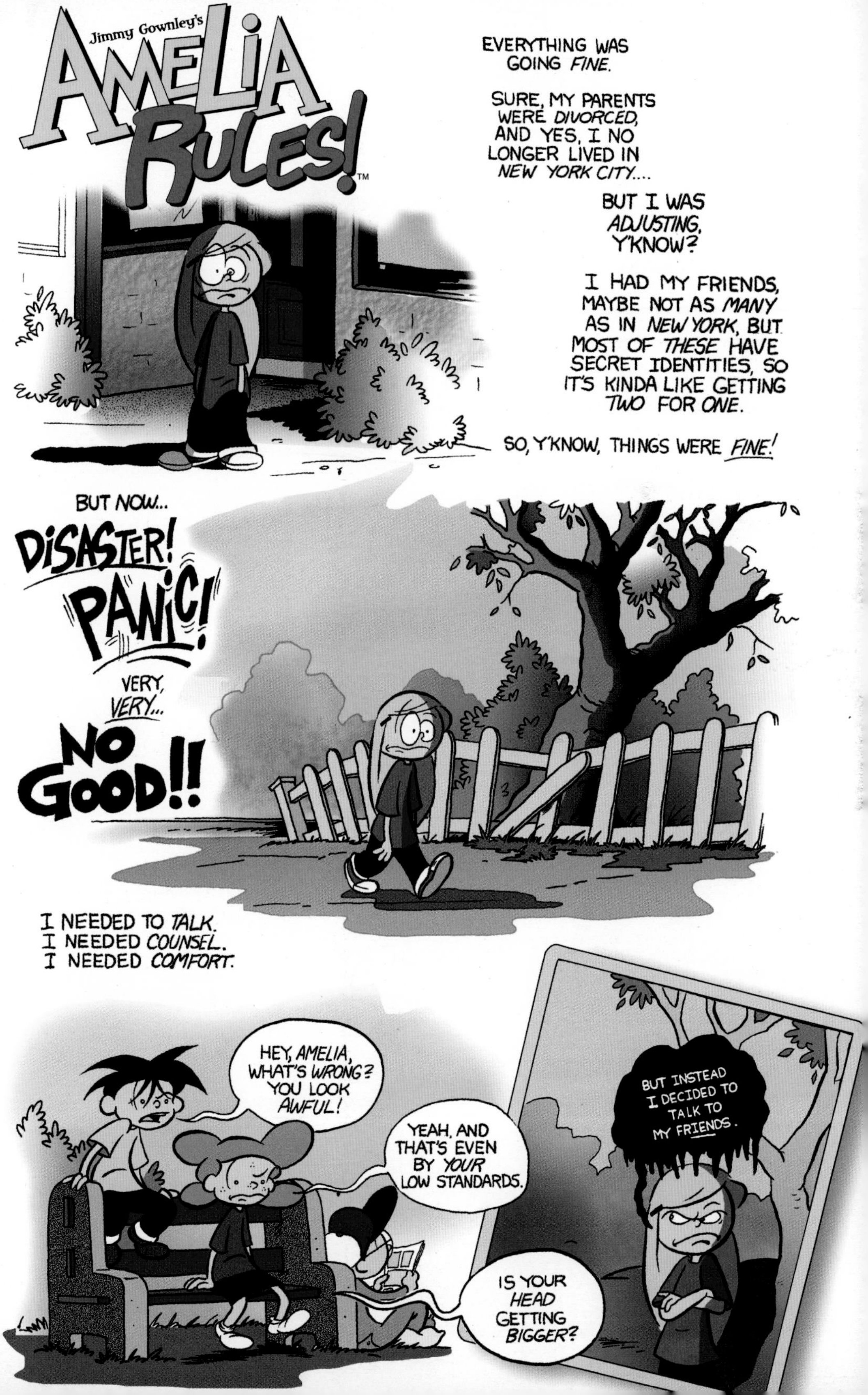

Jimmy Gownley's
AMELIA RULES!™
EVERYTHING WAS GOING FINE.
SURE, MY PARENTS WERE DIVORCED, AND YES, I NO LONGER LIVED IN NEW YORK CITY....
BUT I WAS ADJUSTING, Y'KNOW?
I HAD MY FRIENDS, MAYBE NOT AS MANY AS IN NEW YORK, BUT MOST OF THESE HAVE SECRET IDENTITIES, SO IT'S KINDA LIKE GETTING TWO FOR ONE.
SO, Y'KNOW, THINGS WERE FINE!
BUT NOW...
DISASTER!
PANIC!
VERY, VERY...
NO GOOD!!
I NEEDED TO TALK. I NEEDED COUNSEL. I NEEDED COMFORT.
HEY, AMELIA, WHAT'S WRONG? YOU LOOK AWFUL!
YEAH, AND THAT'S EVEN BY YOUR LOW STANDARDS.
IS YOUR HEAD GETTING BIGGER?
BUT INSTEAD I DECIDED TO TALK TO MY FRIENDS.

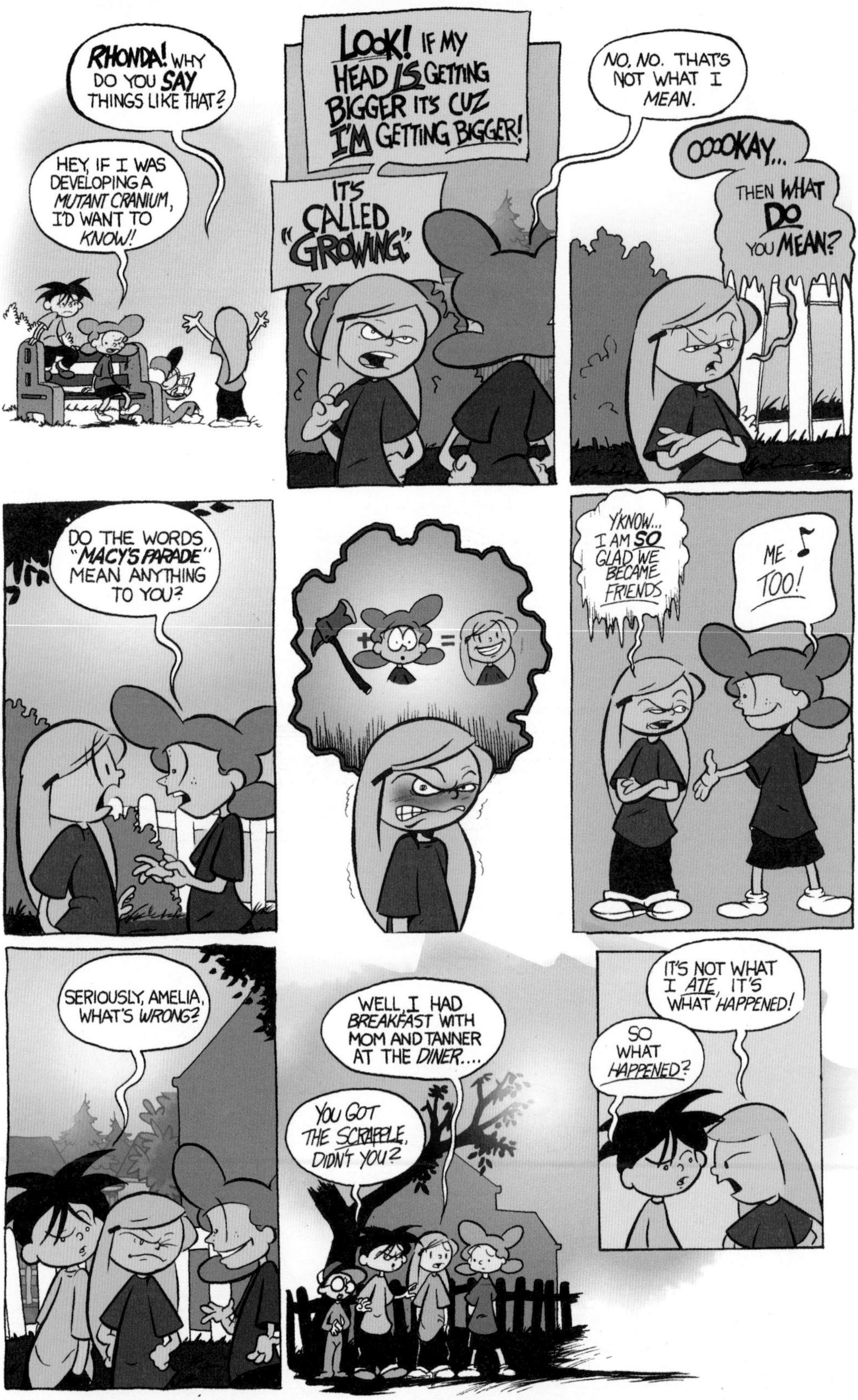
RHONDA! WHY DO YOU SAY THINGS LIKE THAT?
HEY, IF I WAS DEVELOPING A MUTANT CRANIUM, I'D WANT TO KNOW!
LOOK! IF MY HEAD IS GETTING BIGGER IT'S CUZ I'M GETTING BIGGER!
IT'S CALLED "GROWING."
NO, NO. THAT'S NOT WHAT I MEAN.
OOOOKAY...
THEN WHAT DO YOU MEAN?
DO THE WORDS "MACY'S PARADE" MEAN ANYTHING TO YOU?
Y'KNOW... I AM SO GLAD WE BECAME FRIENDS
ME TOO!
SERIOUSLY, AMELIA, WHAT'S WRONG?
WELL, I HAD BREAKFAST WITH MOM AND TANNER AT THE DINER....
YOU GOT THE SCRAPPLE, DIDN'T YOU?
IT'S NOT WHAT I ATE, IT'S WHAT HAPPENED!
SO WHAT HAPPENED?

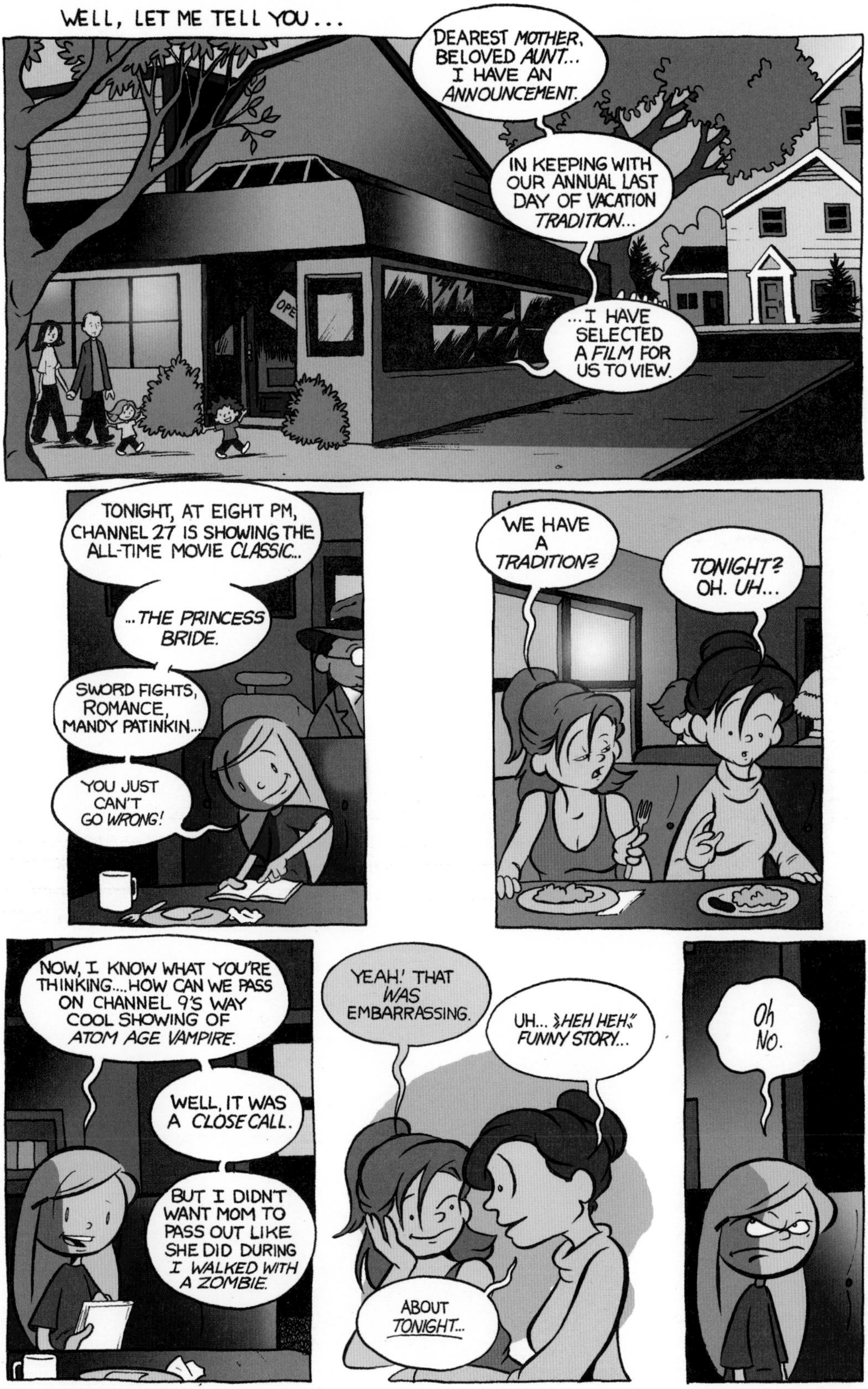
WELL, LET ME TELL YOU...
DEAREST MOTHER, BELOVED AUNT... I HAVE AN ANNOUNCEMENT.
IN KEEPING WITH OUR ANNUAL LAST DAY OF VACATION TRADITION...
...I HAVE SELECTED A FILM FOR US TO VIEW.
OPE
TONIGHT, AT EIGHT PM, CHANNEL 27 IS SHOWING THE ALL-TIME MOVIE CLASSIC...
...THE PRINCESS BRIDE.
SWORD FIGHTS, ROMANCE, MANDY PATINKIN...
YOU JUST CAN'T GO WRONG!
WE HAVE A TRADITION?
TONIGHT? OH. UH...
NOW, I KNOW WHAT YOU'RE THINKING....HOW CAN WE PASS ON CHANNEL 9'S WAY COOL SHOWING OF ATOM AGE VAMPIRE.
WELL, IT WAS A CLOSE CALL.
BUT I DIDN'T WANT MOM TO PASS OUT LIKE SHE DID DURING I WALKED WITH A ZOMBIE.
YEAH! THAT WAS EMBARRASSING.
UH... "HEH HEH." FUNNY STORY...
ABOUT TONIGHT...
Oh No.

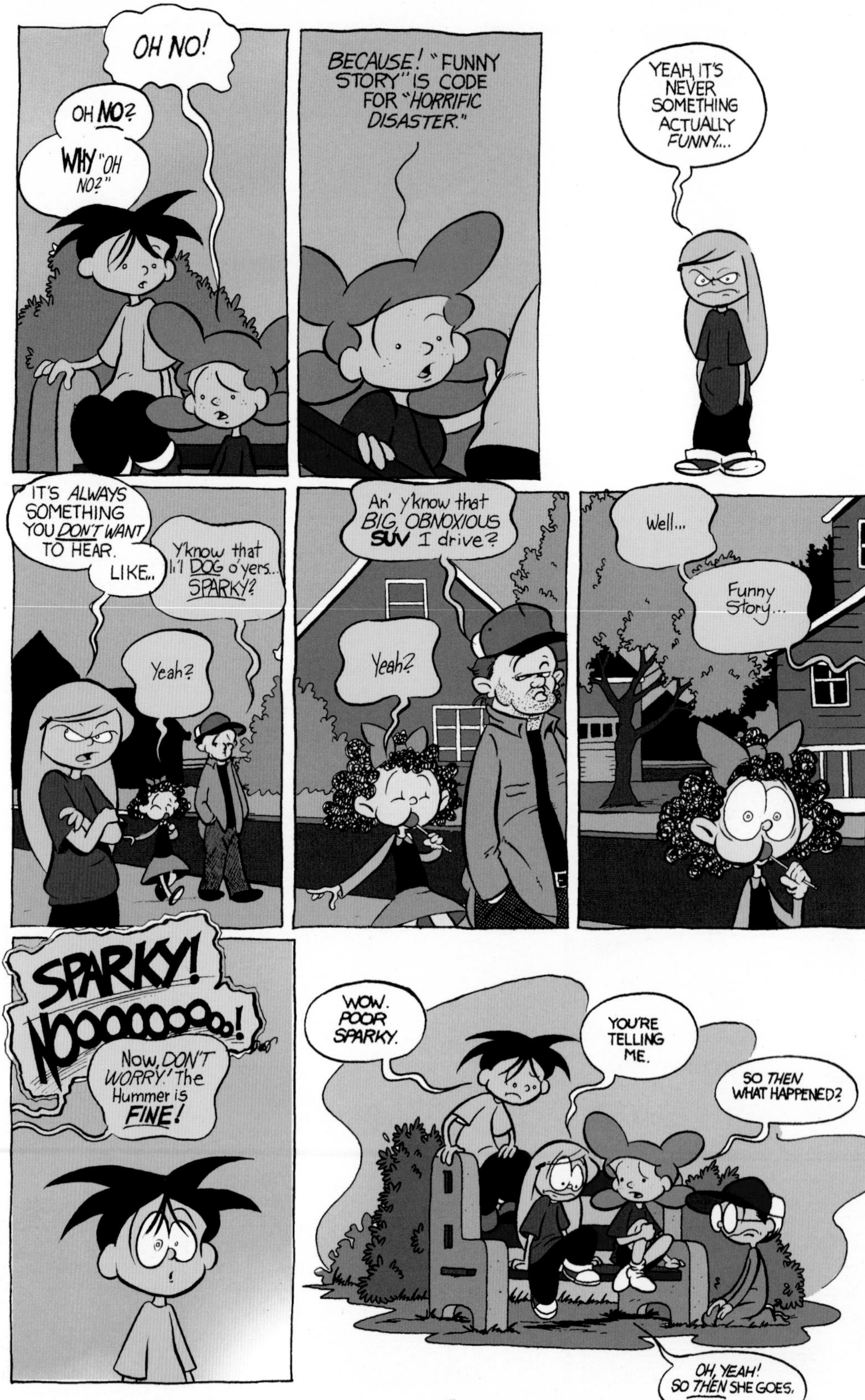
OH NO!
OH NO?
WHY "OH NO?"
BECAUSE! "FUNNY STORY" IS CODE FOR "HORRIFIC DISASTER."
YEAH, IT'S NEVER SOMETHING ACTUALLY FUNNY...
IT'S ALWAYS SOMETHING YOU DON'T WANT TO HEAR.
LIKE...
Y'know that li'l DOG o'yers... SPARKY?
Yeah?
An' y'know that BIG, OBNOXIOUS SUV I drive?
Yeah?
Well...
Funny Story...
SPARKY! NOOOOOOOOo!
Now, DON'T WORRY! The Hummer is FINE!
WOW. POOR SPARKY.
YOU'RE TELLING ME.
SO THEN WHAT HAPPENED?
OH, YEAH! SO THEN SHE GOES,

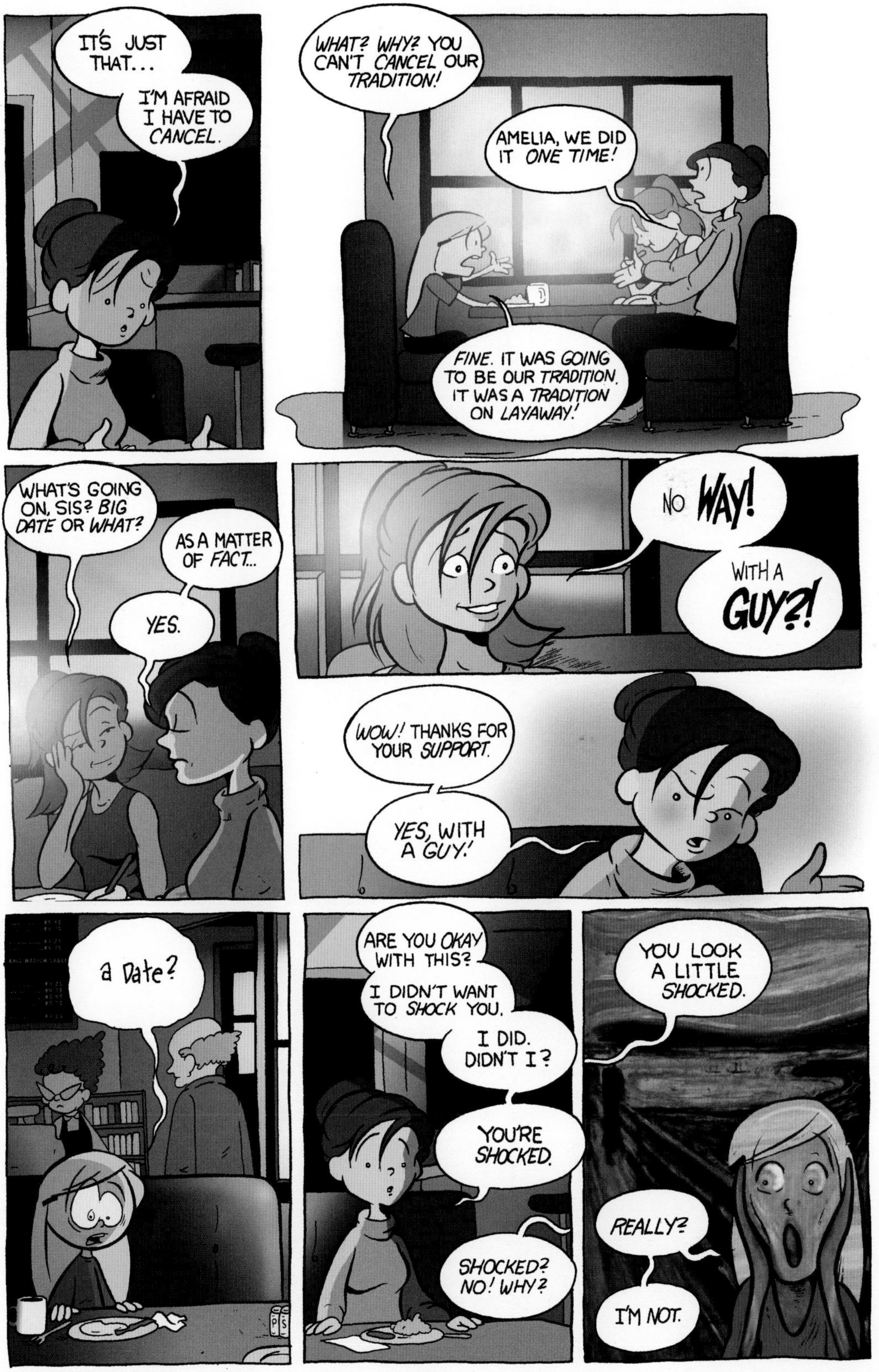
IT'S JUST THAT...
I'M AFRAID I HAVE TO CANCEL.
WHAT? WHY? YOU CAN'T CANCEL OUR TRADITION!
AMELIA, WE DID IT ONE TIME!
FINE. IT WAS GOING TO BE OUR TRADITION. IT WAS A TRADITION ON LAYAWAY!
WHAT'S GOING ON, SIS? BIG DATE OR WHAT?
AS A MATTER OF FACT...
YES.
NO WAY!
WITH A GUY?!
WOW! THANKS FOR YOUR SUPPORT.
YES, WITH A GUY!
a Date?
ARE YOU OKAY WITH THIS?
I DIDN'T WANT TO SHOCK YOU.
I DID. DIDN'T I?
YOU'RE SHOCKED.
SHOCKED? NO! WHY?
YOU LOOK A LITTLE SHOCKED.
REALLY?
I'M NOT.

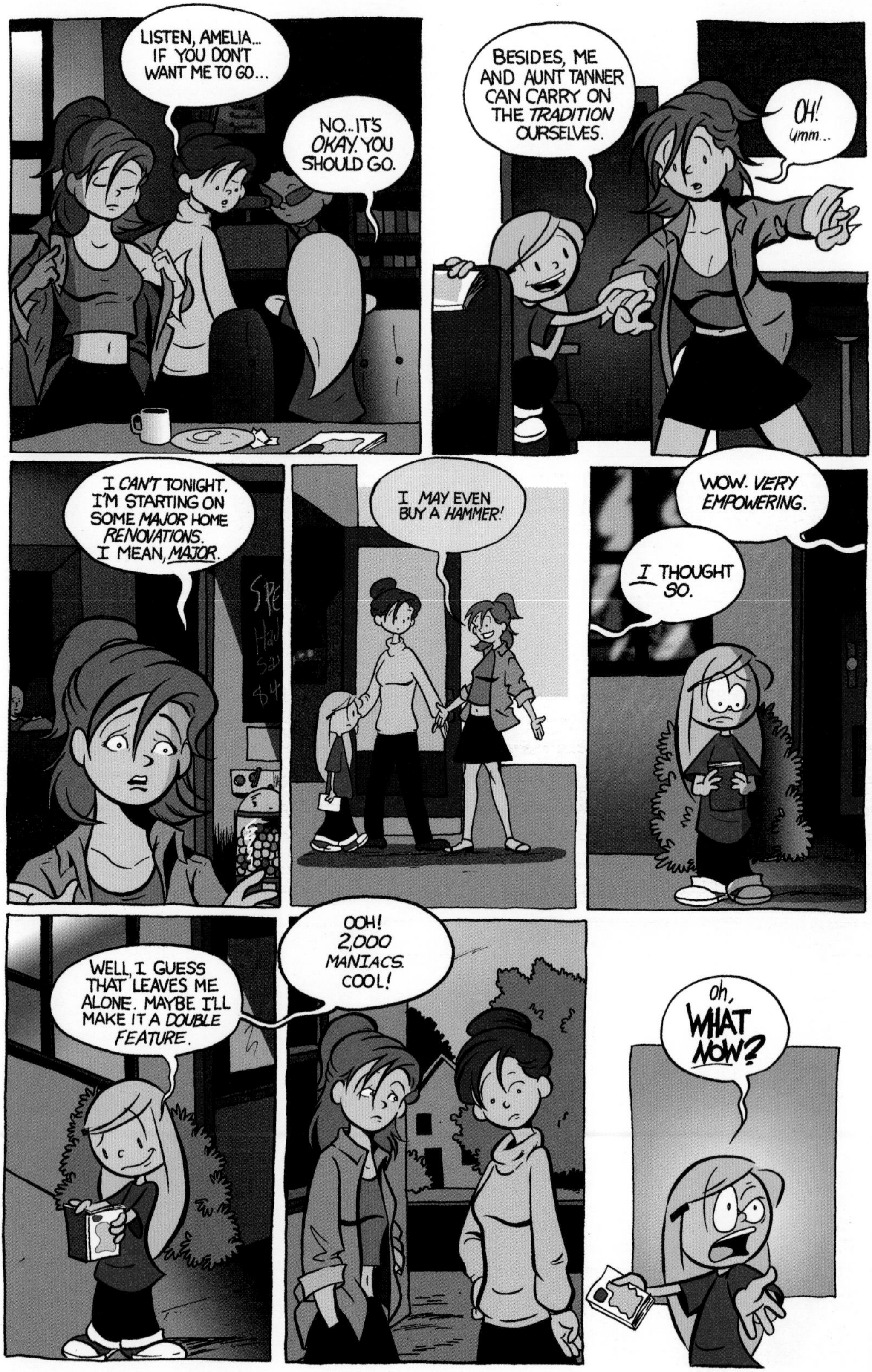
LISTEN, AMELIA... IF YOU DON'T WANT ME TO GO...
NO...IT'S OKAY. YOU SHOULD GO.
BESIDES, ME AND AUNT TANNER CAN CARRY ON THE TRADITION OURSELVES.
OH! umm...
I CAN'T TONIGHT. I'M STARTING ON SOME MAJOR HOME RENOVATIONS. I MEAN, MAJOR.
I MAY EVEN BUY A HAMMER!
WOW. VERY EMPOWERING.
I THOUGHT SO.
WELL, I GUESS THAT LEAVES ME ALONE. MAYBE I'LL MAKE IT A DOUBLE FEATURE.
OOH! 2,000 MANIACS. COOL!
oh, WHAT NOW?

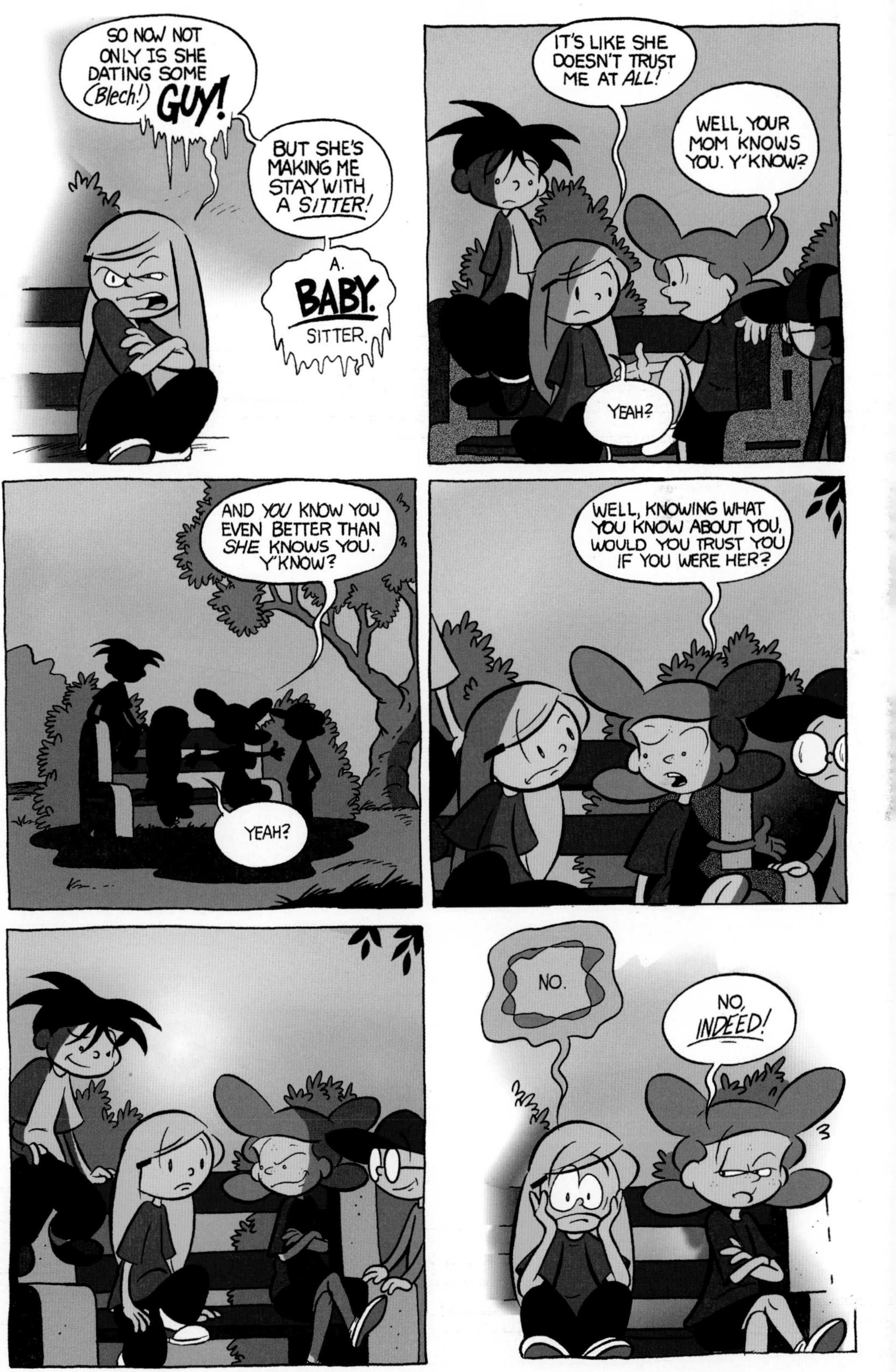

SO NOW NOT ONLY IS SHE DATING SOME (Blech!) GUY!
BUT SHE'S MAKING ME STAY WITH A SITTER!
A. BABY. SITTER.
IT'S LIKE SHE DOESN'T TRUST ME AT ALL!
WELL, YOUR MOM KNOWS YOU. Y'KNOW?
YEAH?
AND YOU KNOW YOU EVEN BETTER THAN SHE KNOWS YOU. Y'KNOW?
YEAH?
WELL, KNOWING WHAT YOU KNOW ABOUT YOU, WOULD YOU TRUST YOU IF YOU WERE HER?
NO.
NO, INDEED!

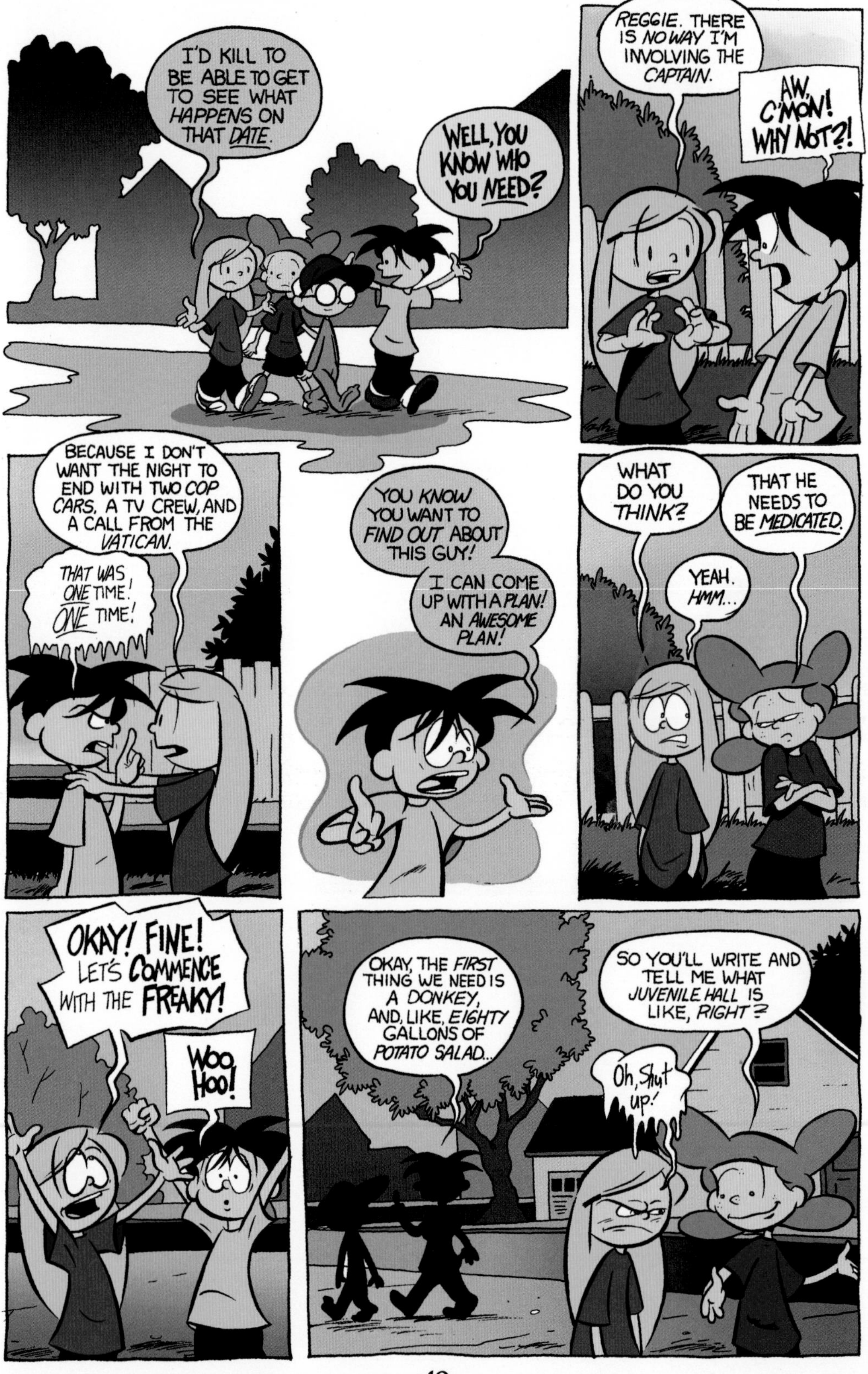
I'D KILL TO BE ABLE TO GET TO SEE WHAT HAPPENS ON THAT DATE.
WELL, YOU KNOW WHO YOU NEED?
REGGIE. THERE IS NO WAY I'M INVOLVING THE CAPTAIN.
AW, C'MON! WHY NOT?!
BECAUSE I DON'T WANT THE NIGHT TO END WITH TWO COP CARS, A TV CREW, AND A CALL FROM THE VATICAN.
THAT WAS ONE TIME! ONE TIME!
YOU KNOW YOU WANT TO FIND OUT ABOUT THIS GUY!
I CAN COME UP WITH A PLAN! AN AWESOME PLAN!
WHAT DO YOU THINK?
THAT HE NEEDS TO BE MEDICATED.
YEAH. HMM...
OKAY! FINE! LET'S COMMENCE WITH THE FREAKY!
WOO HOO!
OKAY, THE FIRST THING WE NEED IS A DONKEY, AND, LIKE, EIGHTY GALLONS OF POTATO SALAD...
SO YOU'LL WRITE AND TELL ME WHAT JUVENILE HALL IS LIKE, RIGHT?
Oh, Shut up!

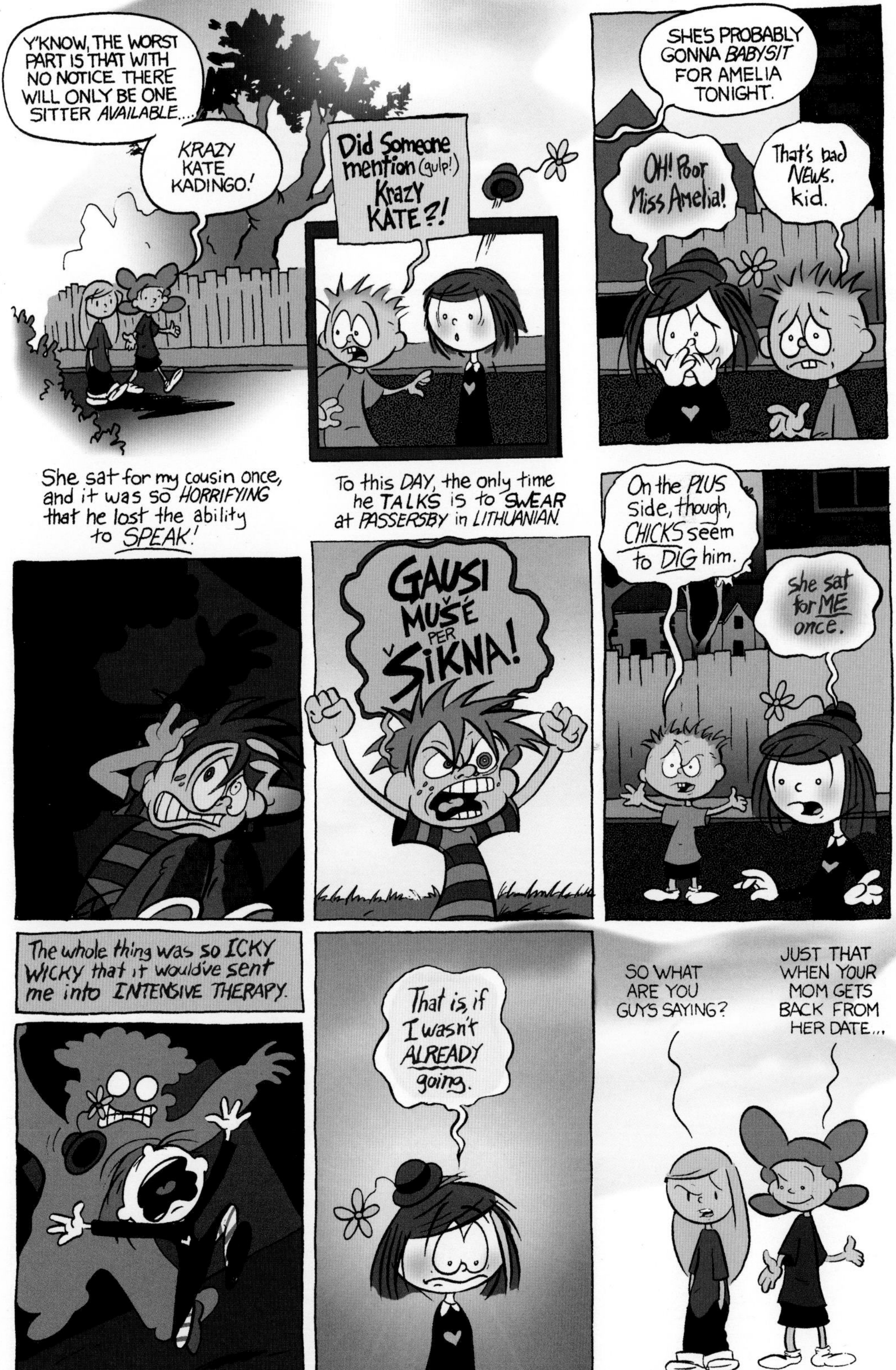

Y'KNOW, THE WORST PART IS THAT WITH NO NOTICE THERE WILL ONLY BE ONE SITTER AVAILABLE....
KRAZY KATE KADINGO!
Did Someone mention (gulp!) Krazy KATE?!
SHE'S PROBABLY GONNA BABYSIT FOR AMELIA TONIGHT.
OH! Poor Miss Amelia!
That's bad NEWS, kid.
She sat for my cousin once, and it was so HORRIFYING that he lost the ability to SPEAK!
To this DAY, the only time he TALKS is to SWEAR at PASSERSBY in LITHUANIAN.
GAUSI MUŠĖ PER ŠIKNA!
On the PLUS side, though, CHICKS seem to DIG him.
She sat for ME once.
The whole thing was so ICKY WICKY that it would've sent me into INTENSIVE THERAPY.
That is, if I wasn't ALREADY going.
SO WHAT ARE YOU GUYS SAYING?
JUST THAT WHEN YOUR MOM GETS BACK FROM HER DATE...

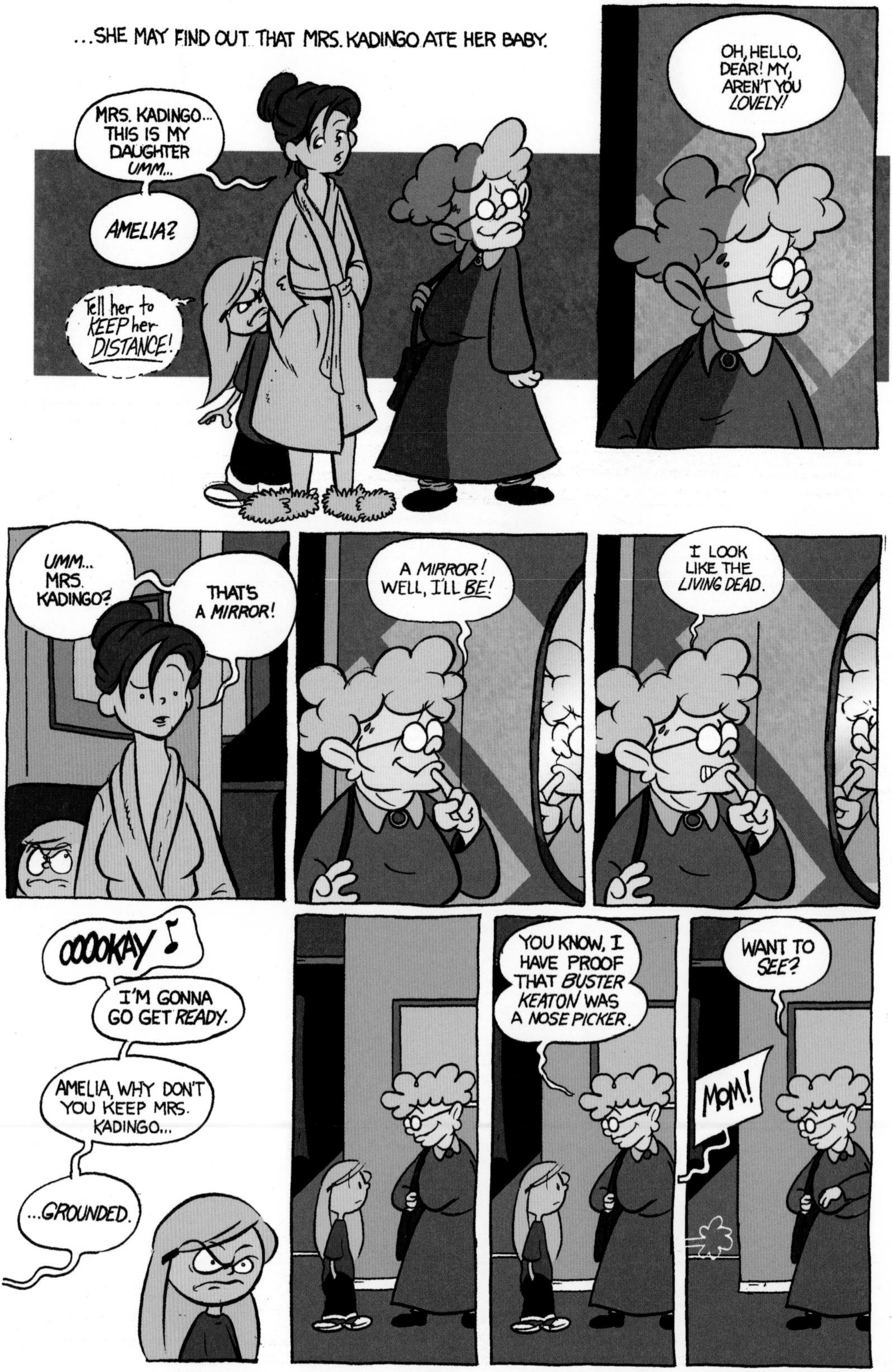
...SHE MAY FIND OUT THAT MRS. KADINGO ATE HER BABY.
MRS. KADINGO... THIS IS MY DAUGHTER UMM...
AMELIA?
Tell her to KEEP her DISTANCE!
OH, HELLO, DEAR! MY, AREN'T YOU LOVELY!
UMM... MRS. KADINGO?
THAT'S A MIRROR!
A MIRROR! WELL, I'LL BE!
I LOOK LIKE THE LIVING DEAD.
OOOOKAY
I'M GONNA GO GET READY.
AMELIA, WHY DON'T YOU KEEP MRS. KADINGO...
...GROUNDED.
YOU KNOW, I HAVE PROOF THAT BUSTER KEATON WAS A NOSE PICKER.
WANT TO SEE?
MOM!

SO, BEING TOTALLY ***GROSSED OUT***, I WENT UPSTAIRS TO WATCH MOM GET READY. LOOKING IN THE MIRROR, I DIDN'T SEE THE ***LIVING DEAD***, BUT I FELT LIKE THE ***WALKING WOUNDED***.

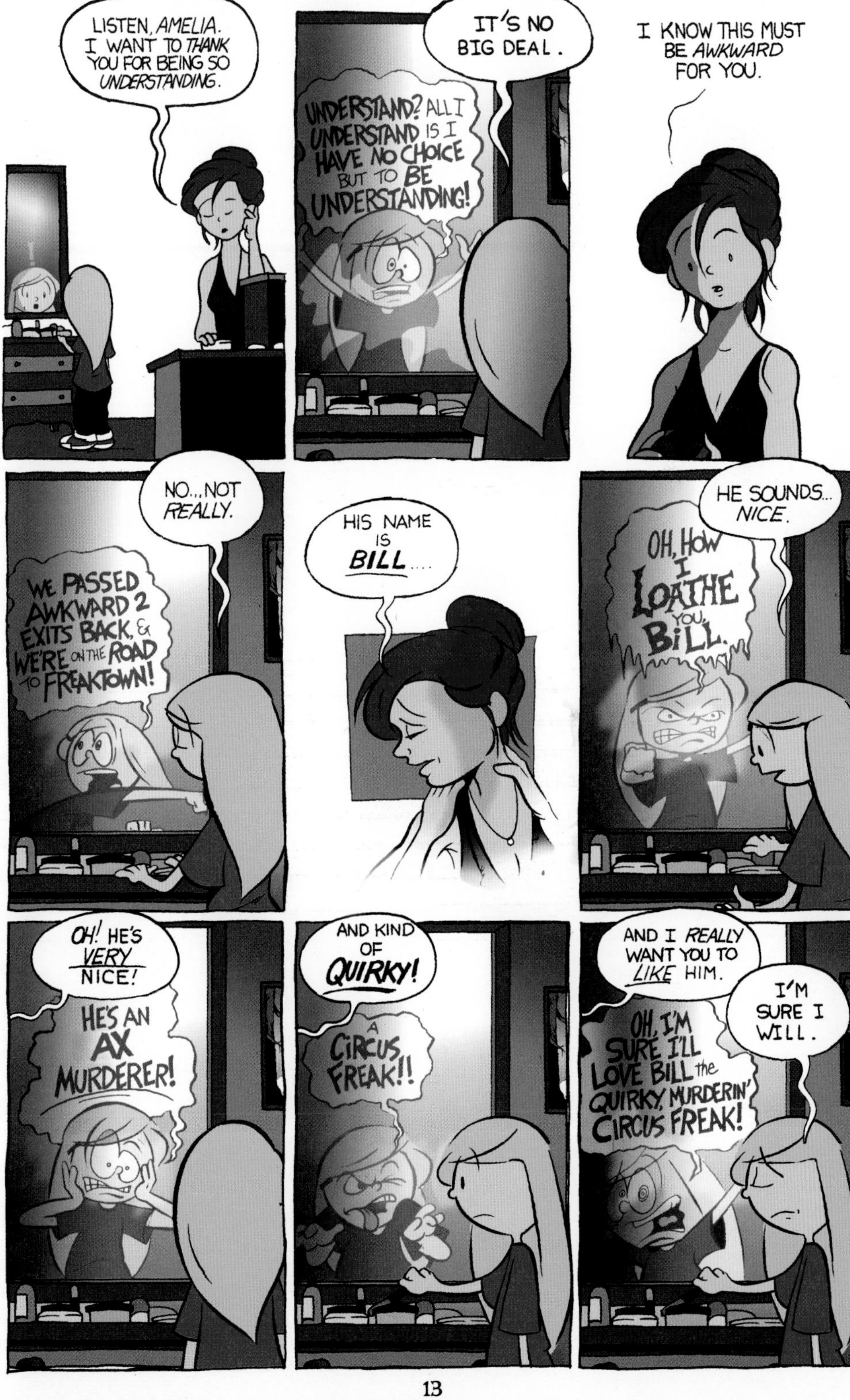

LISTEN, AMELIA. I WANT TO THANK YOU FOR BEING SO UNDERSTANDING.
IT'S NO BIG DEAL.
UNDERSTAND? ALL I UNDERSTAND IS I HAVE NO CHOICE BUT TO BE UNDERSTANDING!
I KNOW THIS MUST BE AWKWARD FOR YOU.
NO... NOT REALLY.
WE PASSED AWKWARD 2 EXITS BACK, & WE'RE ON THE ROAD TO FREAKTOWN!
HIS NAME IS BILL....
HE SOUNDS... NICE.
OH, HOW I LOATHE YOU, BILL.
OH! HE'S VERY NICE!
HE'S AN AX MURDERER!
AND KIND OF QUIRKY!
A CIRCUS FREAK!!
AND I REALLY WANT YOU TO LIKE HIM.
OH, I'M SURE I'LL LOVE BILL the QUIRKY, MURDERIN' CIRCUS FREAK!
I'M SURE I WILL.

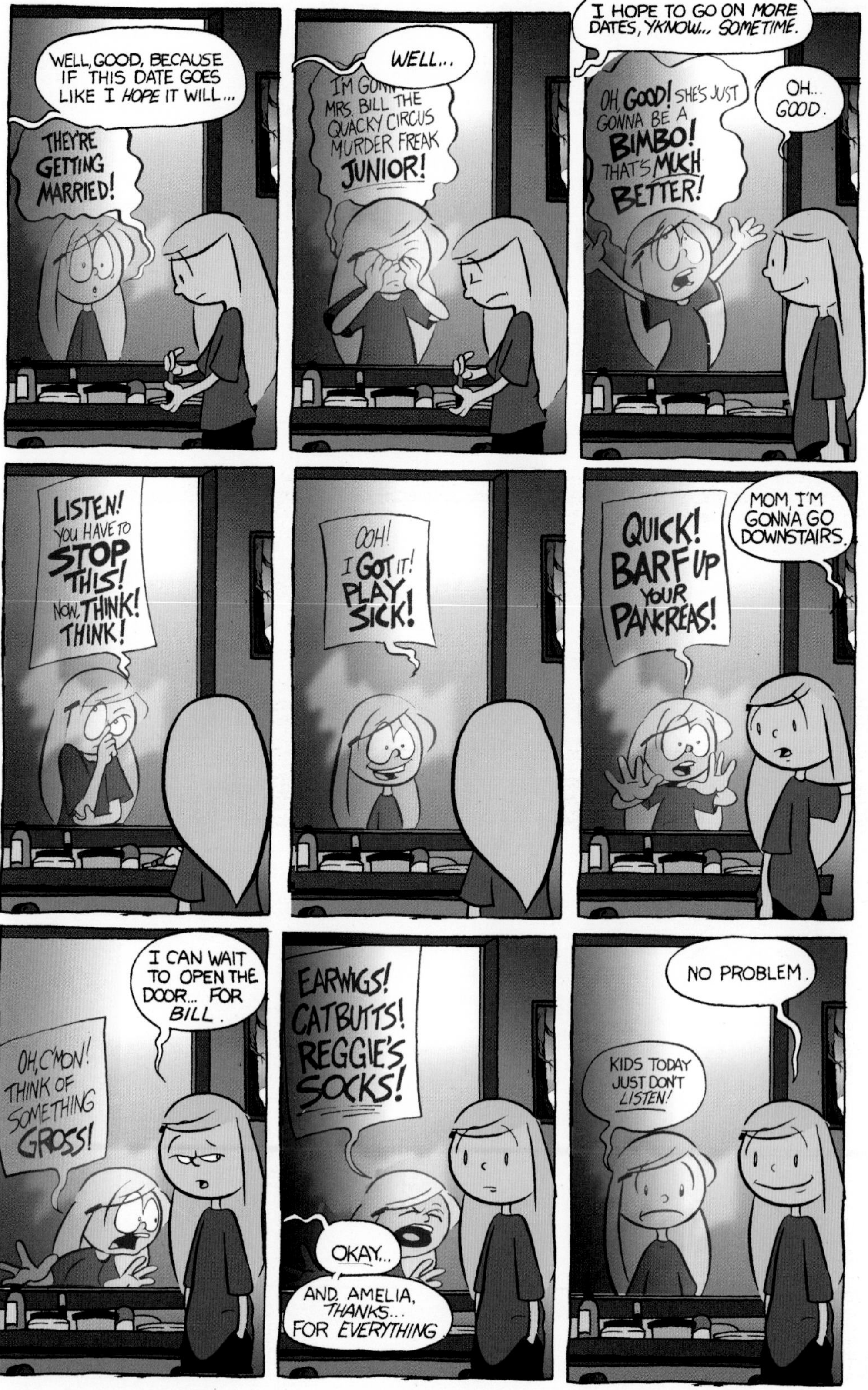
WELL, GOOD, BECAUSE IF THIS DATE GOES LIKE I HOPE IT WILL...
THEY'RE GETTING MARRIED!
WELL...
I'M GONNA ... MRS. BILL THE QUACKY CIRCUS MURDER FREAK JUNIOR!
I HOPE TO GO ON MORE DATES, Y'KNOW.., SOMETIME.
OH, GOOD! SHE'S JUST GONNA BE A BIMBO! THAT'S MUCH BETTER!
OH... GOOD.
LISTEN! YOU HAVE TO STOP THIS! NOW, THINK! THINK!
OOH! I GOT IT! PLAY SICK!
QUICK! BARF UP YOUR PANCREAS!
MOM, I'M GONNA GO DOWNSTAIRS.
I CAN WAIT TO OPEN THE DOOR... FOR BILL.
OH, C'MON! THINK OF SOMETHING GROSS!
EARWIGS! CATBUTTS! REGGIE'S SOCKS!
OKAY...
AND, AMELIA, THANKS... FOR EVERYTHING.
NO PROBLEM.
KIDS TODAY JUST DON'T LISTEN!

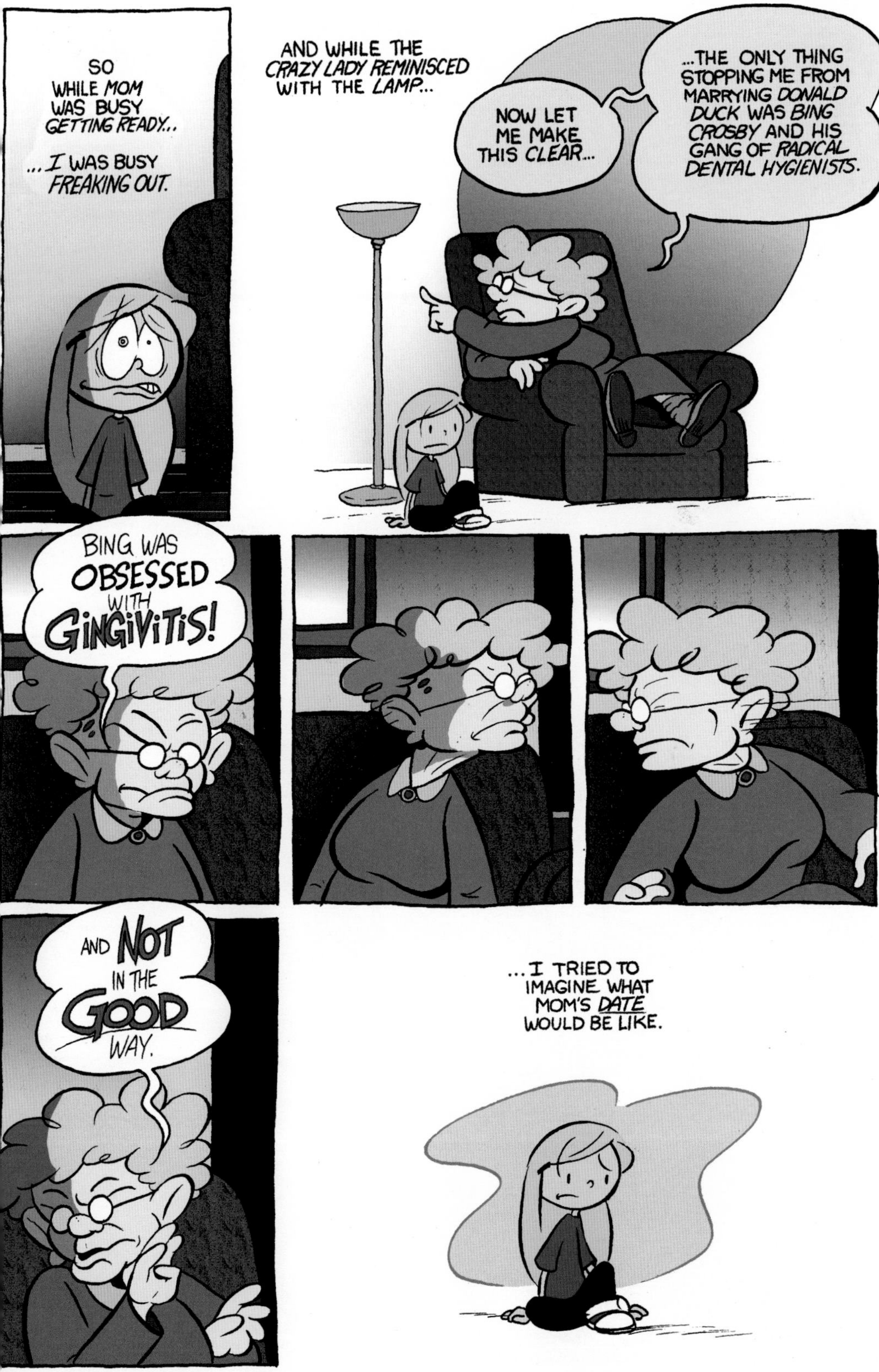
SO WHILE MOM WAS BUSY GETTING READY...
...I WAS BUSY FREAKING OUT.
AND WHILE THE CRAZY LADY REMINISCED WITH THE LAMP...
NOW LET ME MAKE THIS CLEAR...
...THE ONLY THING STOPPING ME FROM MARRYING DONALD DUCK WAS BING CROSBY AND HIS GANG OF RADICAL DENTAL HYGIENISTS.
BING WAS OBSESSED WITH GINGIVITIS!
AND NOT IN THE GOOD WAY.
...I TRIED TO IMAGINE WHAT MOM'S DATE WOULD BE LIKE.

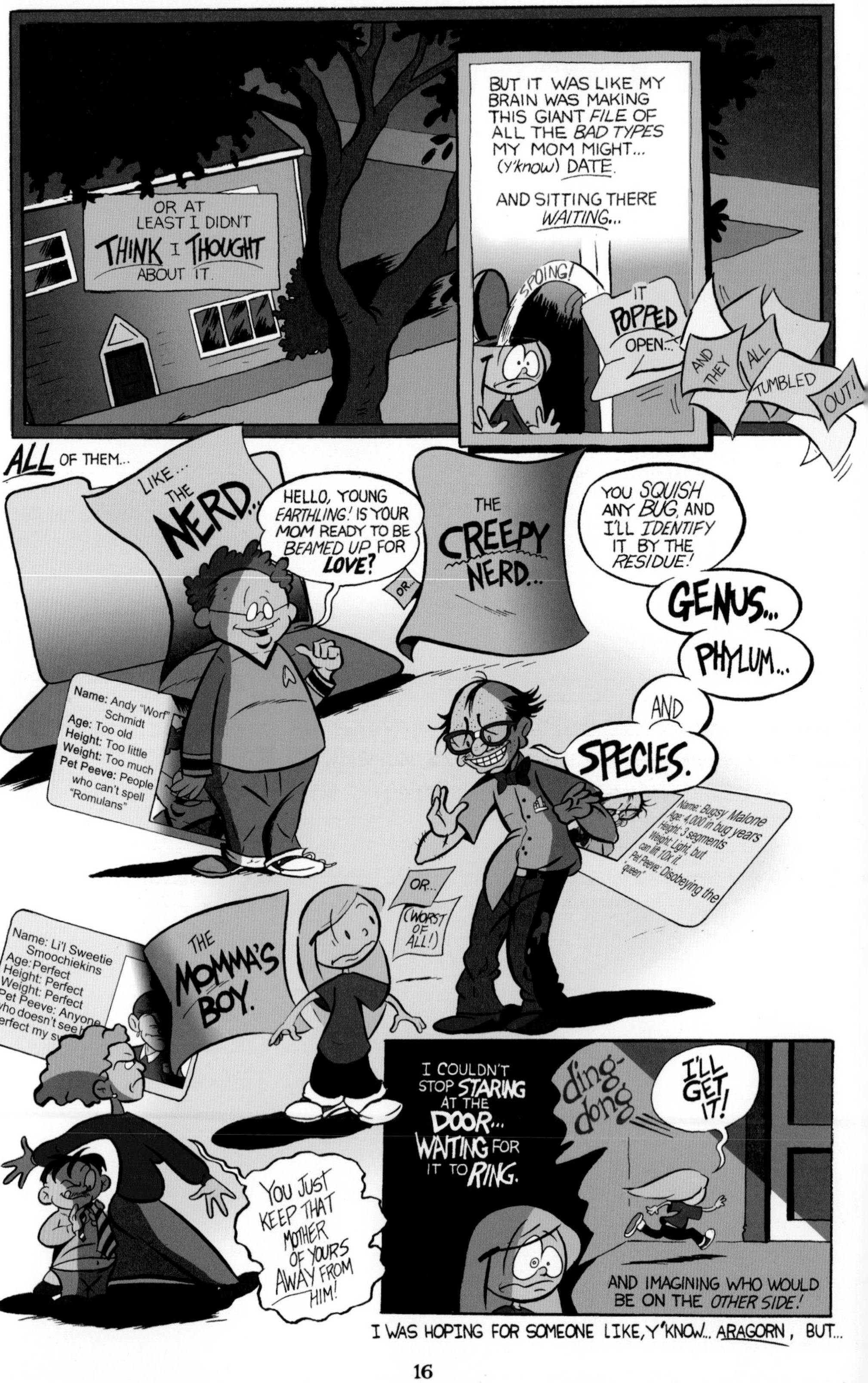
OR AT LEAST I DIDN'T THINK I THOUGHT ABOUT IT.
BUT IT WAS LIKE MY BRAIN WAS MAKING THIS GIANT FILE OF ALL THE BAD TYPES MY MOM MIGHT... (Y'know) DATE.
AND SITTING THERE WAITING...
SPOING!
IT POPPED OPEN...
AND THEY ALL TUMBLED OUT!
ALL OF THEM...
LIKE... THE NERD...
HELLO, YOUNG EARTHLING! IS YOUR MOM READY TO BE BEAMED UP FOR LOVE?
Name: Andy "Worf" Schmidt
Age: Too old
Height: Too little
Weight: Too much
Pet Peeve: People who can't spell "Romulans"
OR...
THE CREEPY NERD...
YOU SQUISH ANY BUG, AND I'LL IDENTIFY IT BY THE RESIDUE!
GENUS...
PHYLUM...
AND SPECIES.
Name: Bugsy Malone
Age: 4,000 in bug years
Height: 3 segments
Weight: Light, but can lift 10x it.
Pet Peeve: Disobeying the "queen"
OR... (WORST OF ALL!)
THE MOMMA'S BOY.
Name: Li'l Sweetie Smoochiekins
Age: Perfect
Height: Perfect
Weight: Perfect
Pet Peeve: Anyone who doesn't see
perfect my s
YOU JUST KEEP THAT MOTHER OF YOURS AWAY FROM HIM!
I COULDN'T STOP STARING AT THE DOOR... WAITING FOR IT TO RING.
ding-dong
I'LL GET IT!
AND IMAGINING WHO WOULD BE ON THE OTHER SIDE!
I WAS HOPING FOR SOMEONE LIKE, Y'KNOW... ARAGORN, BUT...

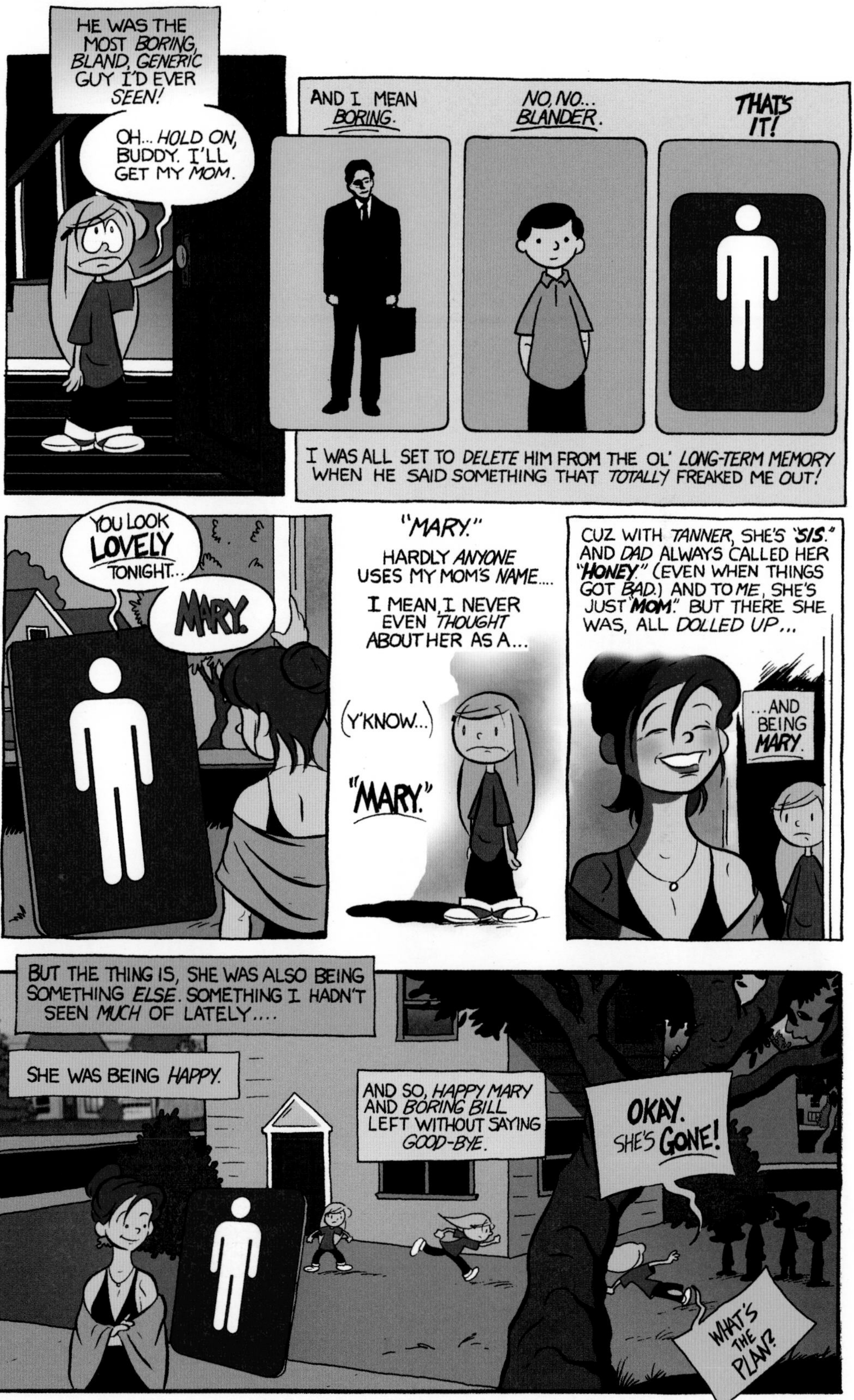
HE WAS THE MOST BORING, BLAND, GENERIC GUY I'D EVER SEEN!
OH... HOLD ON, BUDDY. I'LL GET MY MOM.
AND I MEAN BORING.
NO, NO... BLANDER.
THAT'S IT!
I WAS ALL SET TO DELETE HIM FROM THE OL' LONG-TERM MEMORY WHEN HE SAID SOMETHING THAT TOTALLY FREAKED ME OUT!
YOU LOOK LOVELY TONIGHT...
MARY.
"MARY."
HARDLY ANYONE USES MY MOM'S NAME....
I MEAN, I NEVER EVEN THOUGHT ABOUT HER AS A...
(Y'KNOW...)
"MARY."
CUZ WITH TANNER, SHE'S "SIS." AND DAD ALWAYS CALLED HER "HONEY." (EVEN WHEN THINGS GOT BAD.) AND TO ME, SHE'S JUST "MOM." BUT THERE SHE WAS, ALL DOLLED UP...
...AND BEING MARY.
BUT THE THING IS, SHE WAS ALSO BEING SOMETHING ELSE. SOMETHING I HADN'T SEEN MUCH OF LATELY....
SHE WAS BEING HAPPY.
AND SO, HAPPY MARY AND BORING BILL LEFT WITHOUT SAYING GOOD-BYE.
OKAY. SHE'S GONE!
WHAT'S THE PLAN?

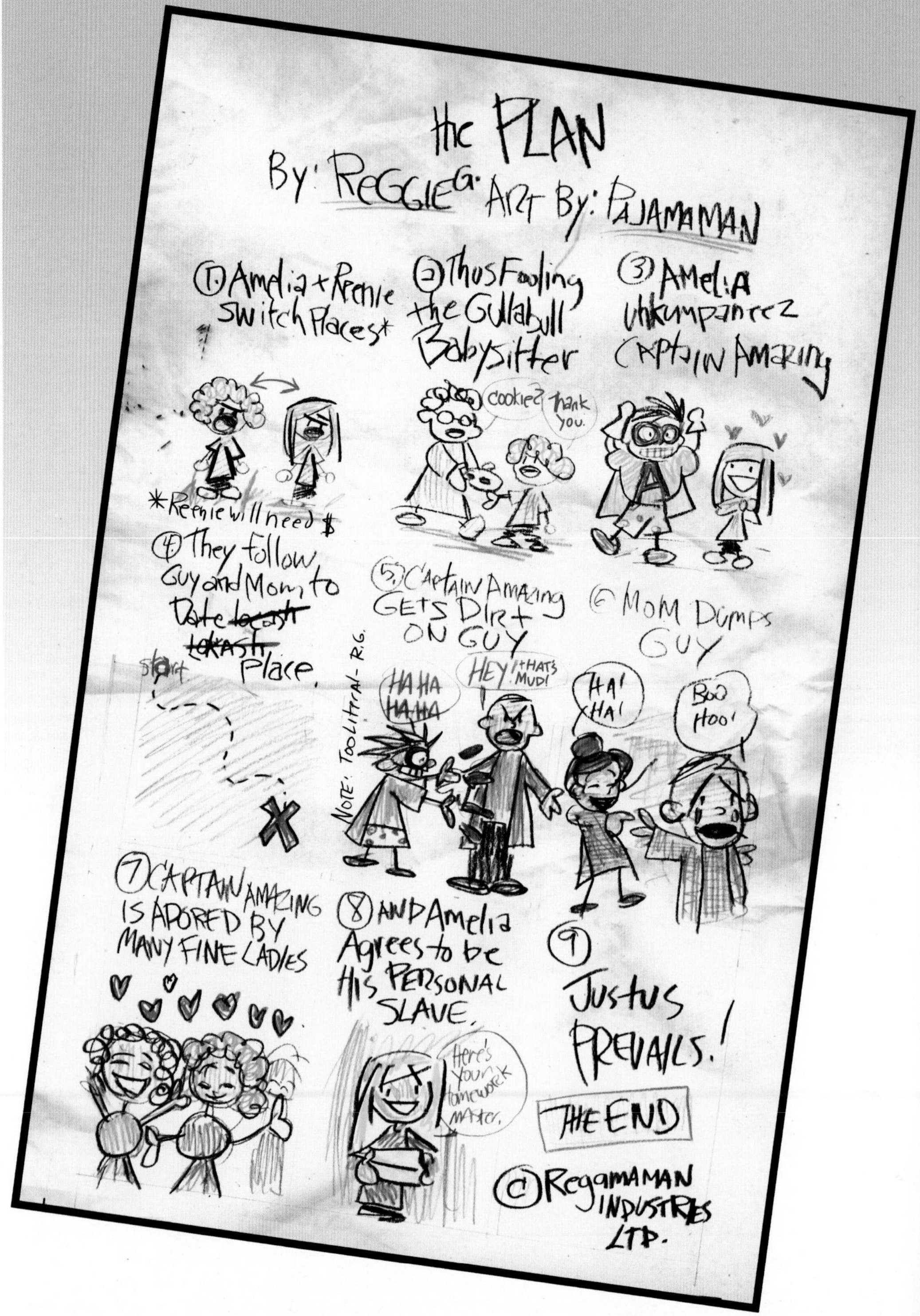
the PLAN
By: ReGGIE G. Art By: PAJAMAMAN
(1) Amelia + Reenie Switch Places*
*Reenie will need $
(2) Thus Fooling the Gullabull Babysitter
cookie?
thank you.
(3) Amelia Uhkumpaneez Captain Amazing
(4) They follow Guy and Mom to Date lokash lokash Place.
start
(5) Captain Amazing Gets Dirt ON GUY
NOTE: TOO LITERAL - R.G.
HA HA HA HA
HEY! THAT'S MUD!
(6) MOM Dumps GUY
HA! HA!
Boo Hoo!
(7) CAPTAIN AMAZING IS ADORED BY MANY FINE LADIES
(8) AND Amelia Agrees to be His PERSONAL SLAVE.
Here's your homework master.
(9) Justus PREVAILS!
THE END
© Regamaman INDUSTRIES LTD.

OKAY, SO MAYBE IT WAS A DUMB PLAN, BUT SINCE I HAD NO DESIRE TO BE "SAT" BY "KRAZY KATE," I TRADED SHIRTS WITH RHONDA'S SISTER AND SENT HER INSIDE, LEAVING ME FREE TO CAVORT WITH THE INFAMOUS CAPTAIN AMAZING.

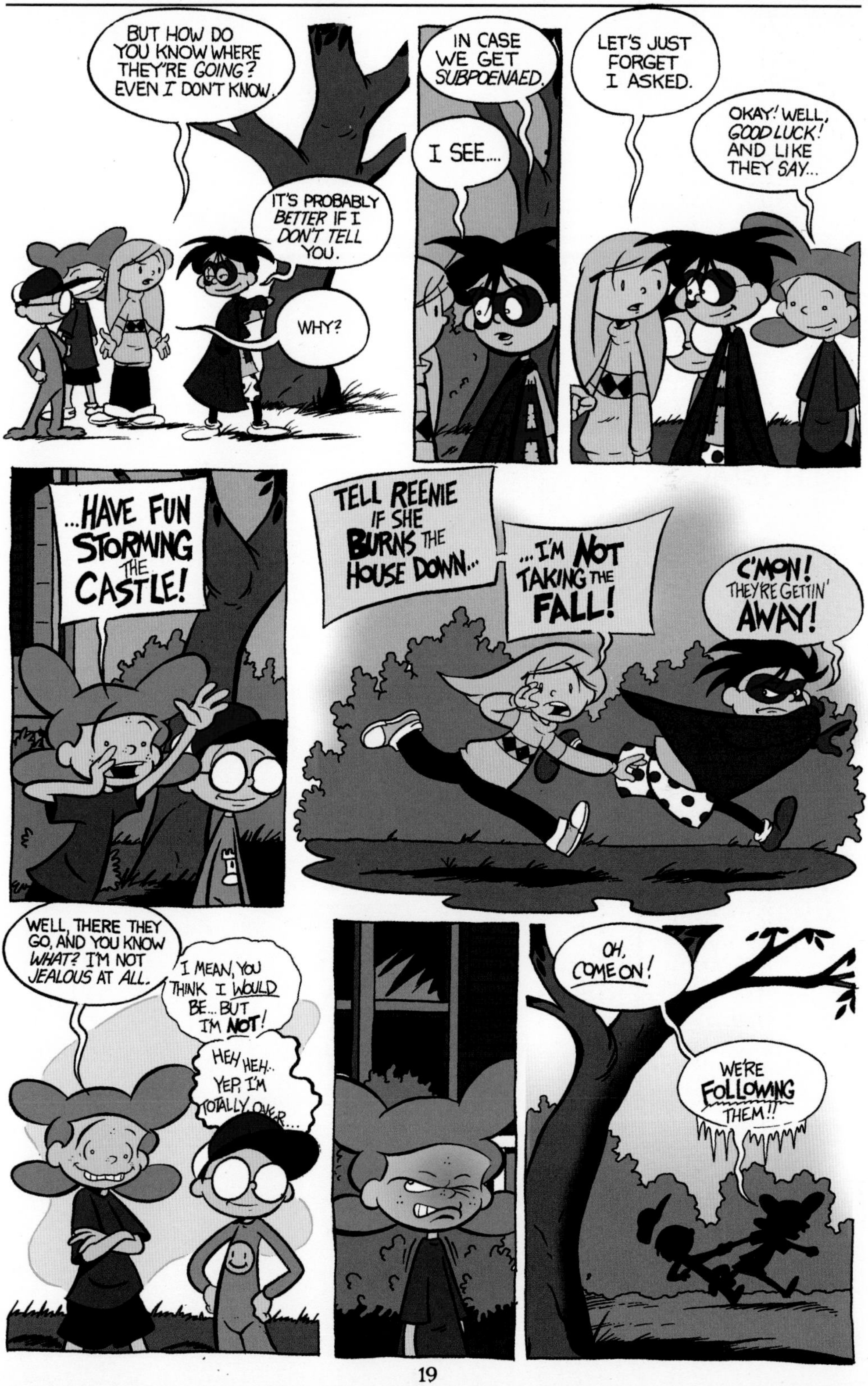

BUT HOW DO YOU KNOW WHERE THEY'RE *GOING*? EVEN *I* DON'T KNOW.
IT'S PROBABLY *BETTER* IF I *DON'T TELL* YOU.
WHY?
IN CASE WE GET *SUBPOENAED*.
I SEE....
LET'S JUST FORGET I ASKED.
OKAY! WELL, *GOOD LUCK!* AND LIKE THEY *SAY*...
...HAVE FUN STORMING THE CASTLE!
TELL REENIE IF SHE BURNS THE HOUSE DOWN...
...I'M NOT TAKING THE FALL!
C'MON! THEY'RE GETTIN' AWAY!
WELL, THERE THEY GO, AND YOU KNOW *WHAT?* I'M NOT *JEALOUS* AT *ALL*.
I MEAN, YOU THINK I WOULD BE... BUT I'M NOT!
HEH HEH.. YEP, I'M TOTALLY OVER...
OH, COME ON!
WE'RE FOLLOWING THEM!!

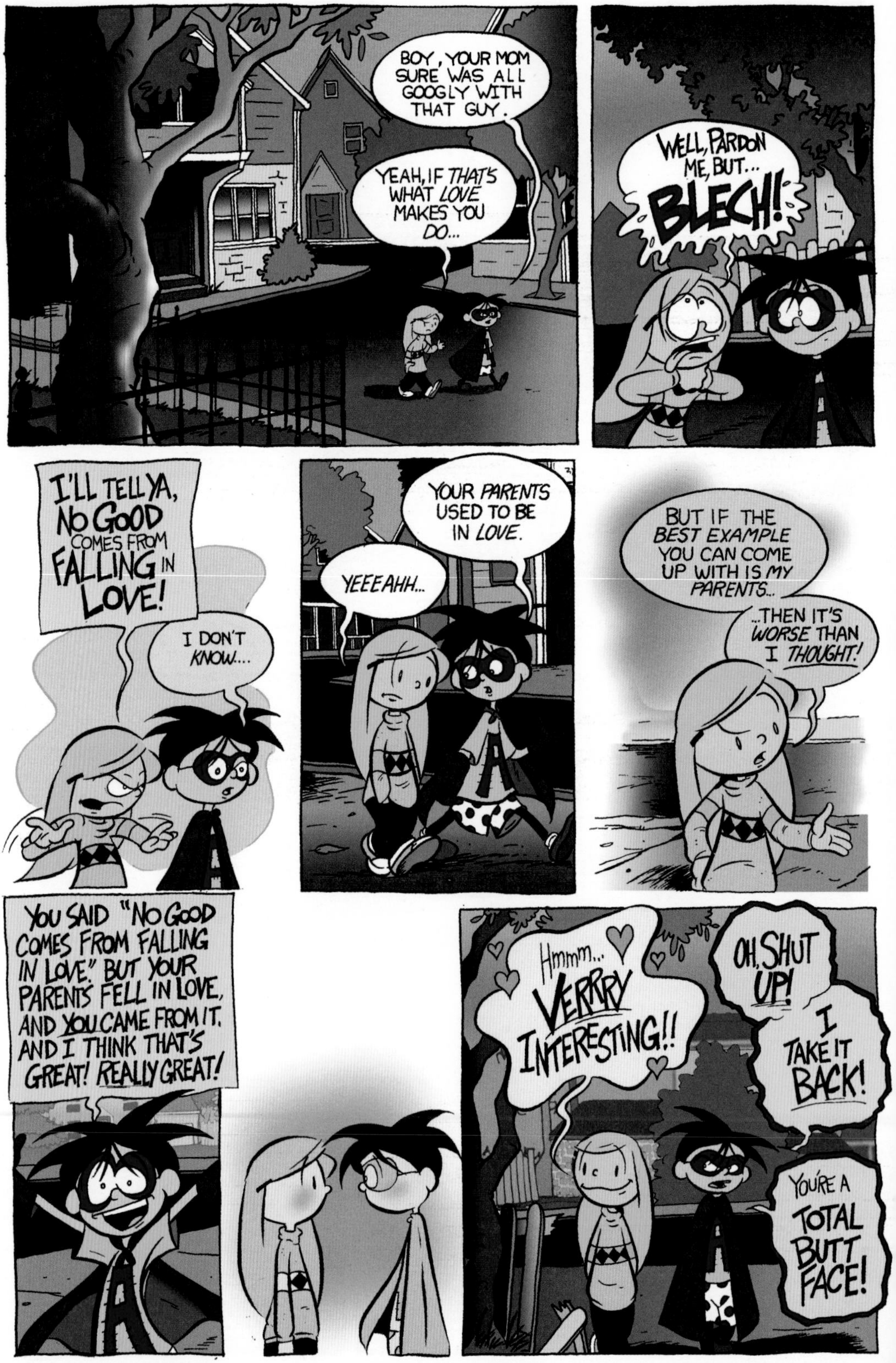
BOY, YOUR MOM SURE WAS ALL GOOGLY WITH THAT GUY.
YEAH, IF THAT'S WHAT LOVE MAKES YOU DO...
WELL, PARDON ME, BUT...
BLECH!
I'LL TELL YA, NO GOOD COMES FROM FALLING IN LOVE!
I DON'T KNOW....
YOUR PARENTS USED TO BE IN LOVE.
YEEEAHH...
BUT IF THE BEST EXAMPLE YOU CAN COME UP WITH IS MY PARENTS...
...THEN IT'S WORSE THAN I THOUGHT!
YOU SAID "NO GOOD COMES FROM FALLING IN LOVE." BUT YOUR PARENTS FELL IN LOVE, AND YOU CAME FROM IT. AND I THINK THAT'S GREAT! REALLY GREAT!
Hmmm... VERRRY INTERESTING!!
OH, SHUT UP!
I TAKE IT BACK!
YOU'RE A TOTAL BUTT FACE!

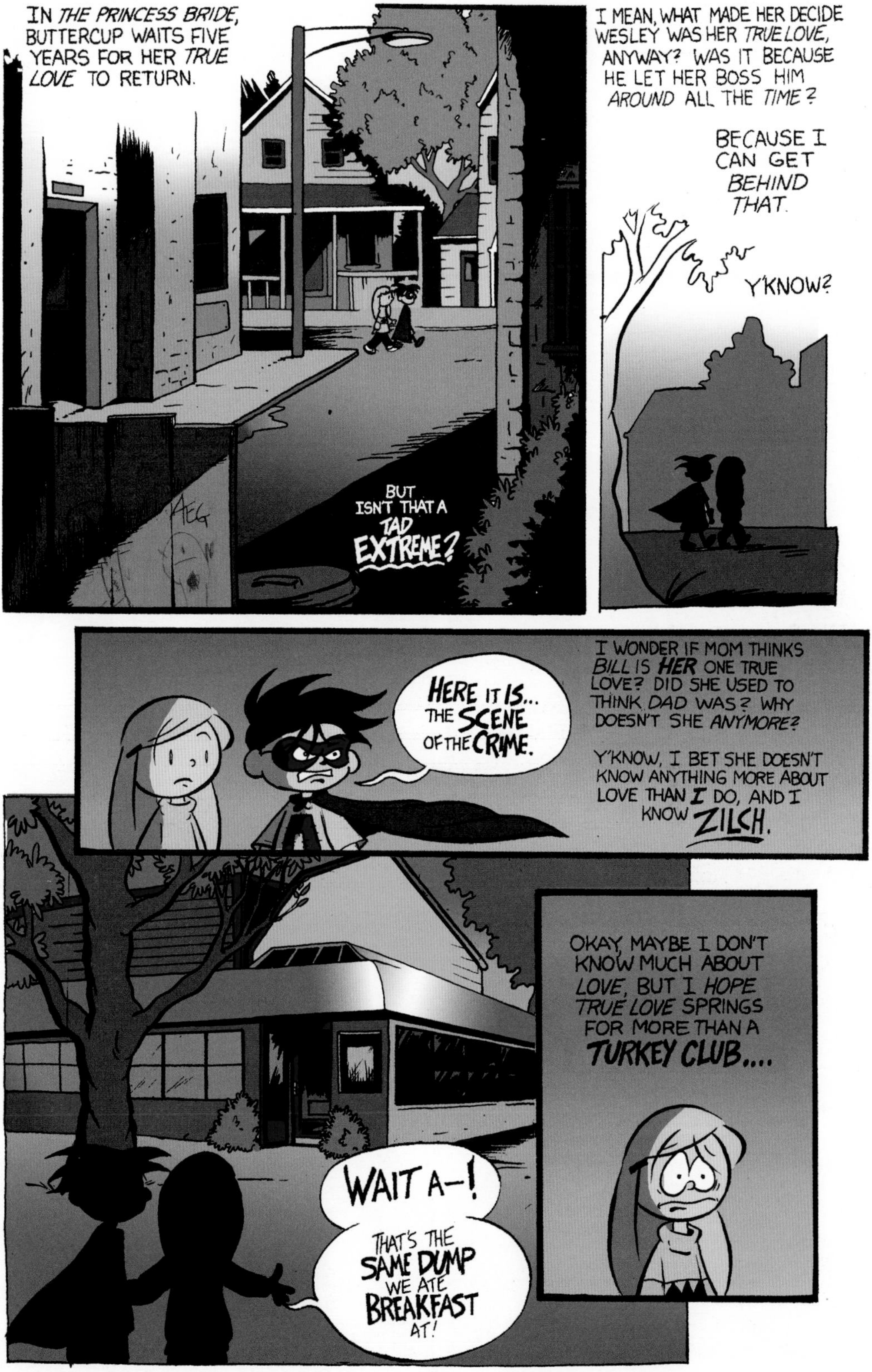
IN THE PRINCESS BRIDE, BUTTERCUP WAITS FIVE YEARS FOR HER TRUE LOVE TO RETURN.
BUT ISN'T THAT A TAD EXTREME?
I MEAN, WHAT MADE HER DECIDE WESLEY WAS HER TRUE LOVE, ANYWAY? WAS IT BECAUSE HE LET HER BOSS HIM AROUND ALL THE TIME?
BECAUSE I CAN GET BEHIND THAT.
Y'KNOW?
HERE IT IS... THE SCENE OF THE CRIME.
I WONDER IF MOM THINKS BILL IS HER ONE TRUE LOVE? DID SHE USED TO THINK DAD WAS? WHY DOESN'T SHE ANYMORE?
Y'KNOW, I BET SHE DOESN'T KNOW ANYTHING MORE ABOUT LOVE THAN I DO, AND I KNOW ZILCH.
WAIT A-!
THAT'S THE SAME DUMP WE ATE BREAKFAST AT!
OKAY, MAYBE I DON'T KNOW MUCH ABOUT LOVE, BUT I HOPE TRUE LOVE SPRINGS FOR MORE THAN A TURKEY CLUB....

OTHERWISE, WHY IS EVERYBODY TRYING SO HARD TO FIND IT?

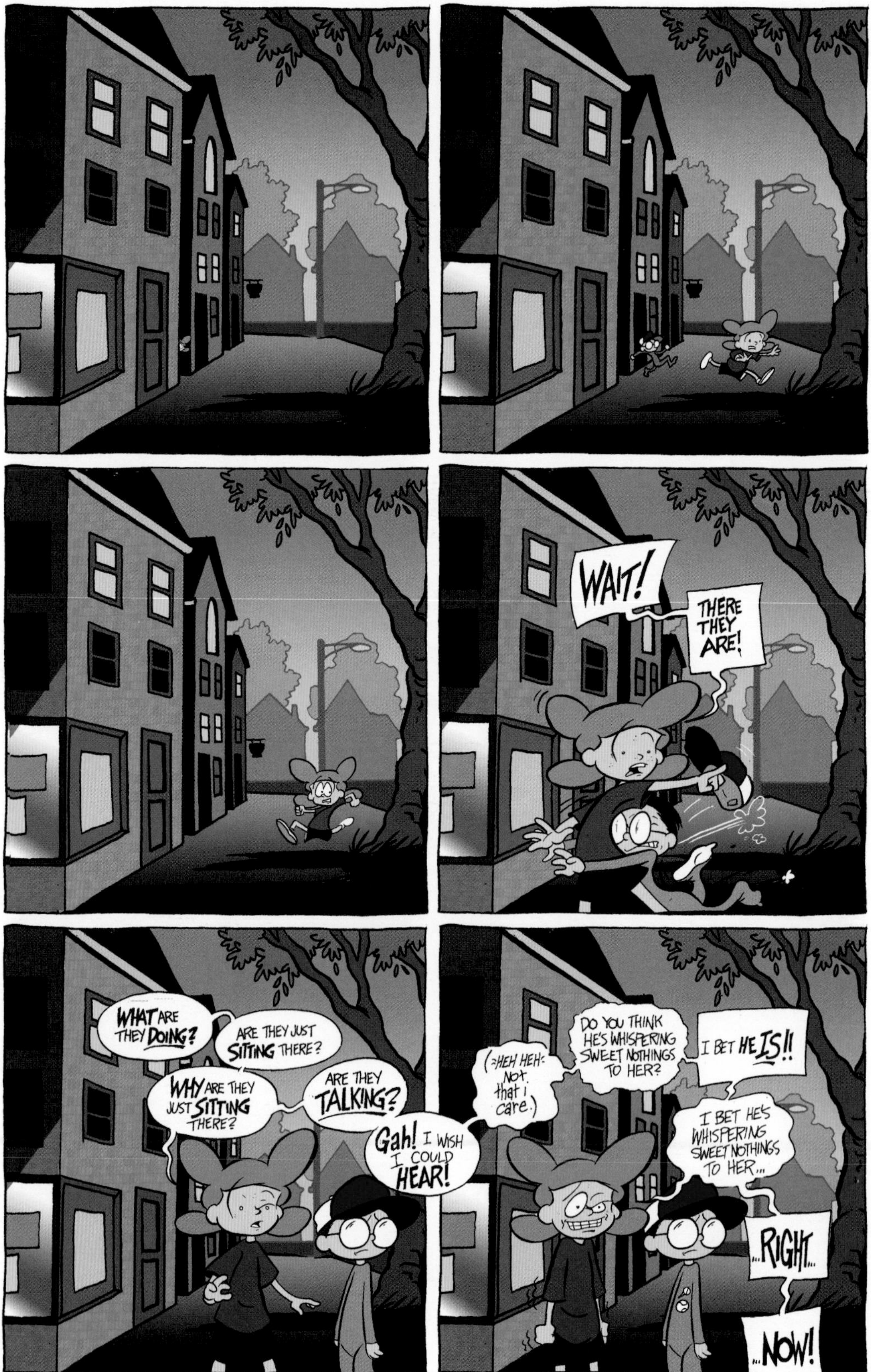
WAIT!
THERE THEY ARE!
WHAT ARE THEY DOING?
ARE THEY JUST SITTING THERE?
WHY ARE THEY JUST SITTING THERE?
ARE THEY TALKING?
Gah! I WISH I COULD HEAR!
(HEH HEH. Not that i care.)
DO YOU THINK HE'S WHISPERING SWEET NOTHINGS TO HER?
I BET HE IS!!
I BET HE'S WHISPERING SWEET NOTHINGS TO HER...
...RIGHT...
...NOW!

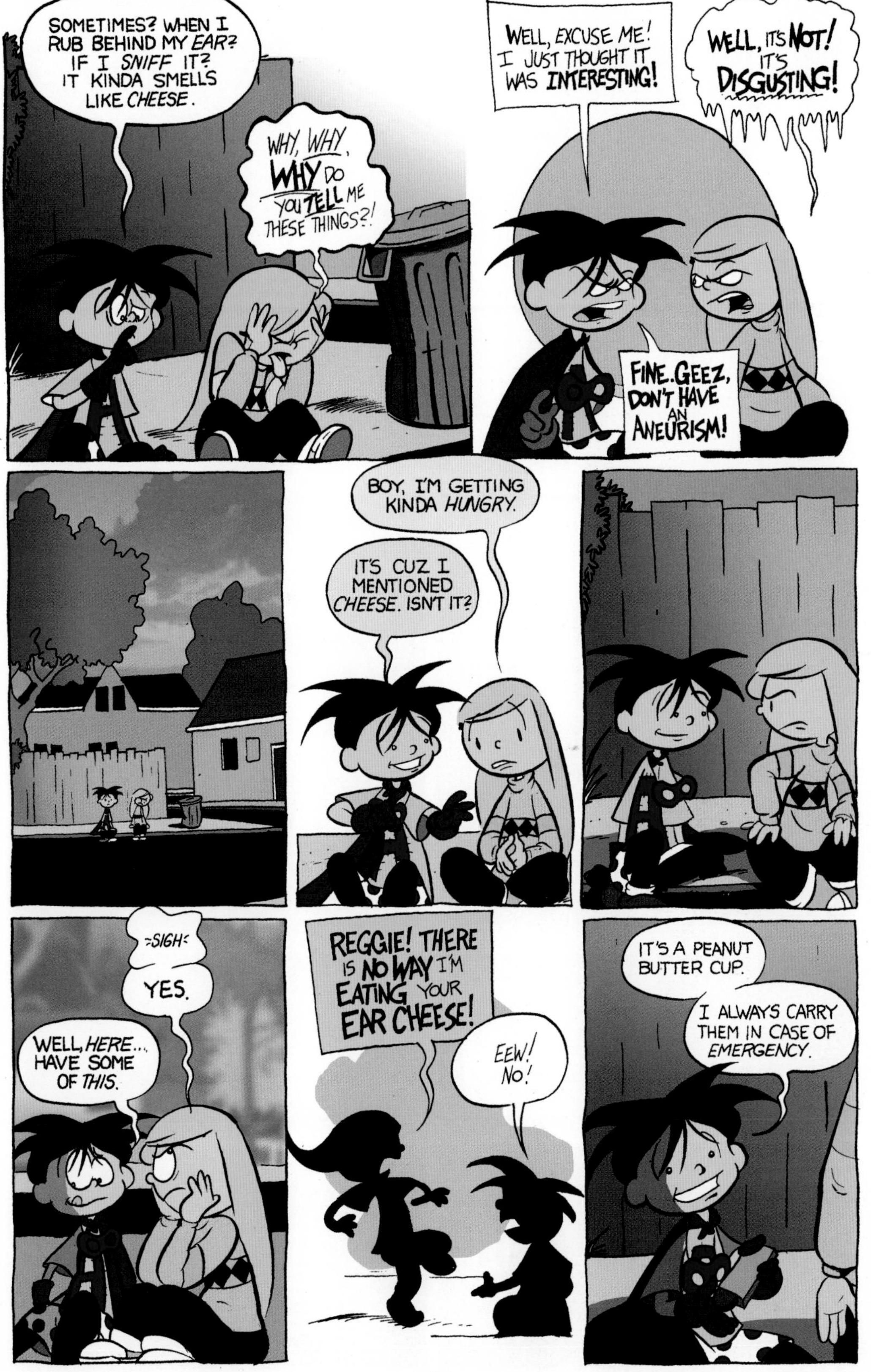
SOMETIMES? WHEN I RUB BEHIND MY EAR? IF I SNIFF IT? IT KINDA SMELLS LIKE CHEESE.
WHY, WHY, WHY DO YOU TELL ME THESE THINGS?!
WELL, EXCUSE ME! I JUST THOUGHT IT WAS INTERESTING!
WELL, IT'S NOT! IT'S DISGUSTING!
FINE. GEEZ, DON'T HAVE AN ANEURISM!
BOY, I'M GETTING KINDA HUNGRY.
IT'S CUZ I MENTIONED CHEESE. ISN'T IT?
≈SIGH≈
YES.
WELL, HERE... HAVE SOME OF THIS.
REGGIE! THERE IS NO WAY I'M EATING YOUR EAR CHEESE!
EEW! NO!
IT'S A PEANUT BUTTER CUP.
I ALWAYS CARRY THEM IN CASE OF EMERGENCY.

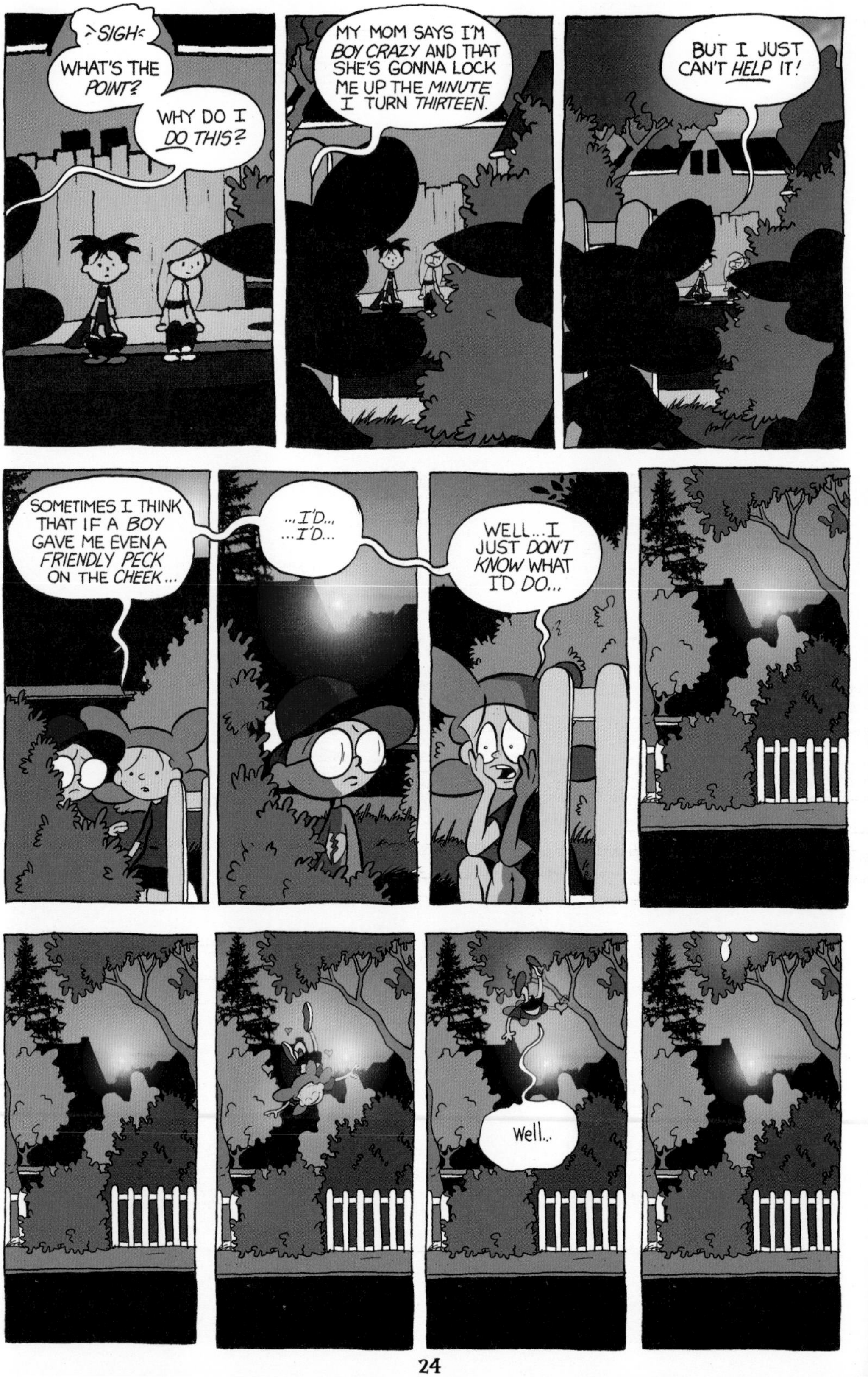
~SIGH~
WHAT'S THE POINT?
WHY DO I DO THIS?
MY MOM SAYS I'M BOY CRAZY AND THAT SHE'S GONNA LOCK ME UP THE MINUTE I TURN THIRTEEN.
BUT I JUST CAN'T HELP IT!
SOMETIMES I THINK THAT IF A BOY GAVE ME EVEN A FRIENDLY PECK ON THE CHEEK...
...I'D... ...I'D...
WELL...I JUST DON'T KNOW WHAT I'D DO...
Well...

THAT ANSWERS **THAT** QUESTION.

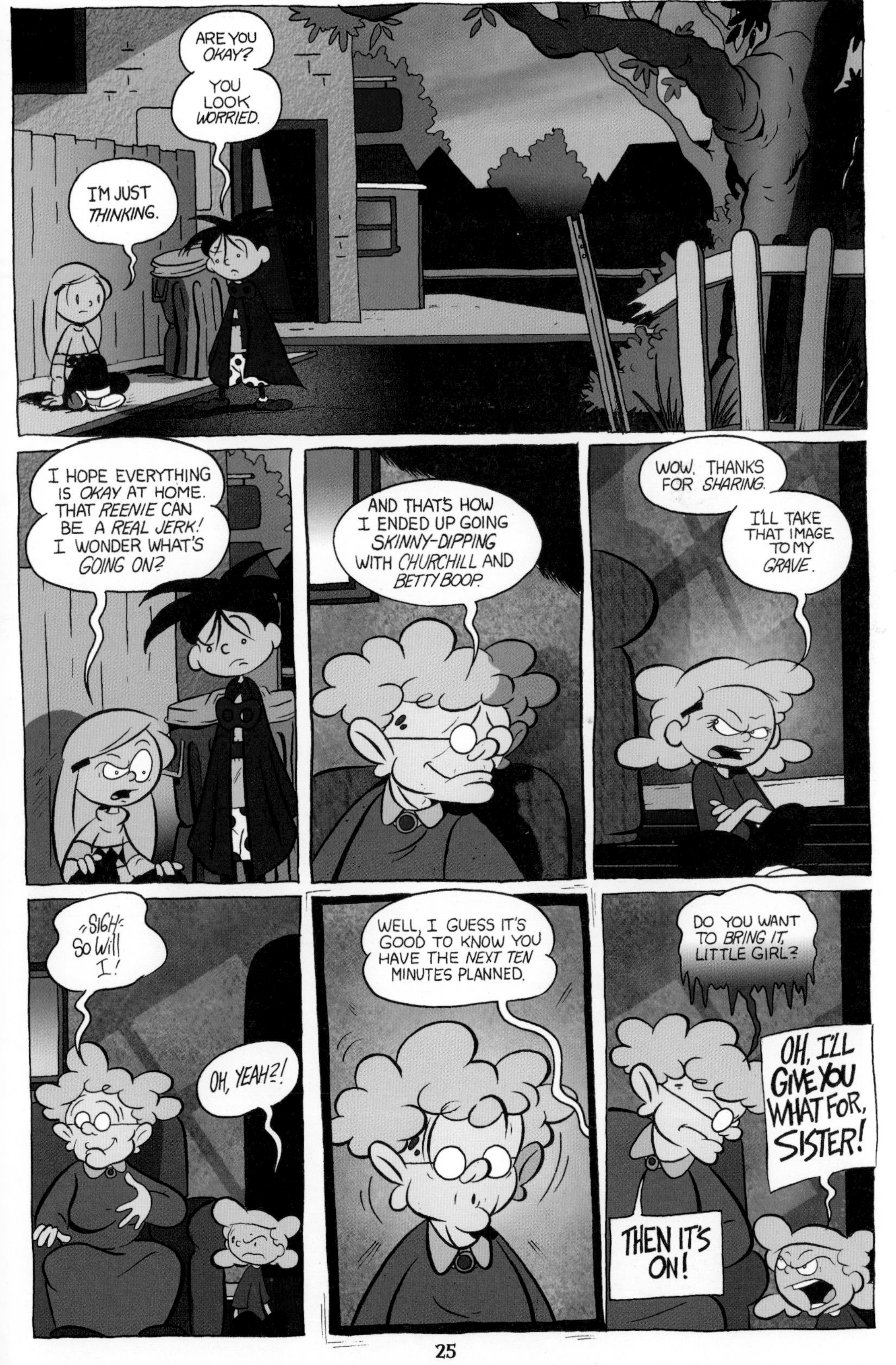
ARE YOU OKAY?
YOU LOOK WORRIED.
I'M JUST THINKING.
I HOPE EVERYTHING IS OKAY AT HOME. THAT REENIE CAN BE A REAL JERK! I WONDER WHAT'S GOING ON?
AND THAT'S HOW I ENDED UP GOING SKINNY-DIPPING WITH CHURCHILL AND BETTY BOOP.
WOW. THANKS FOR SHARING.
I'LL TAKE THAT IMAGE TO MY GRAVE.
-SIGH- So will I!
OH, YEAH?!
WELL, I GUESS IT'S GOOD TO KNOW YOU HAVE THE NEXT TEN MINUTES PLANNED.
DO YOU WANT TO BRING IT, LITTLE GIRL?
OH, I'LL GIVE YOU WHAT FOR, SISTER!
THEN IT'S ON!

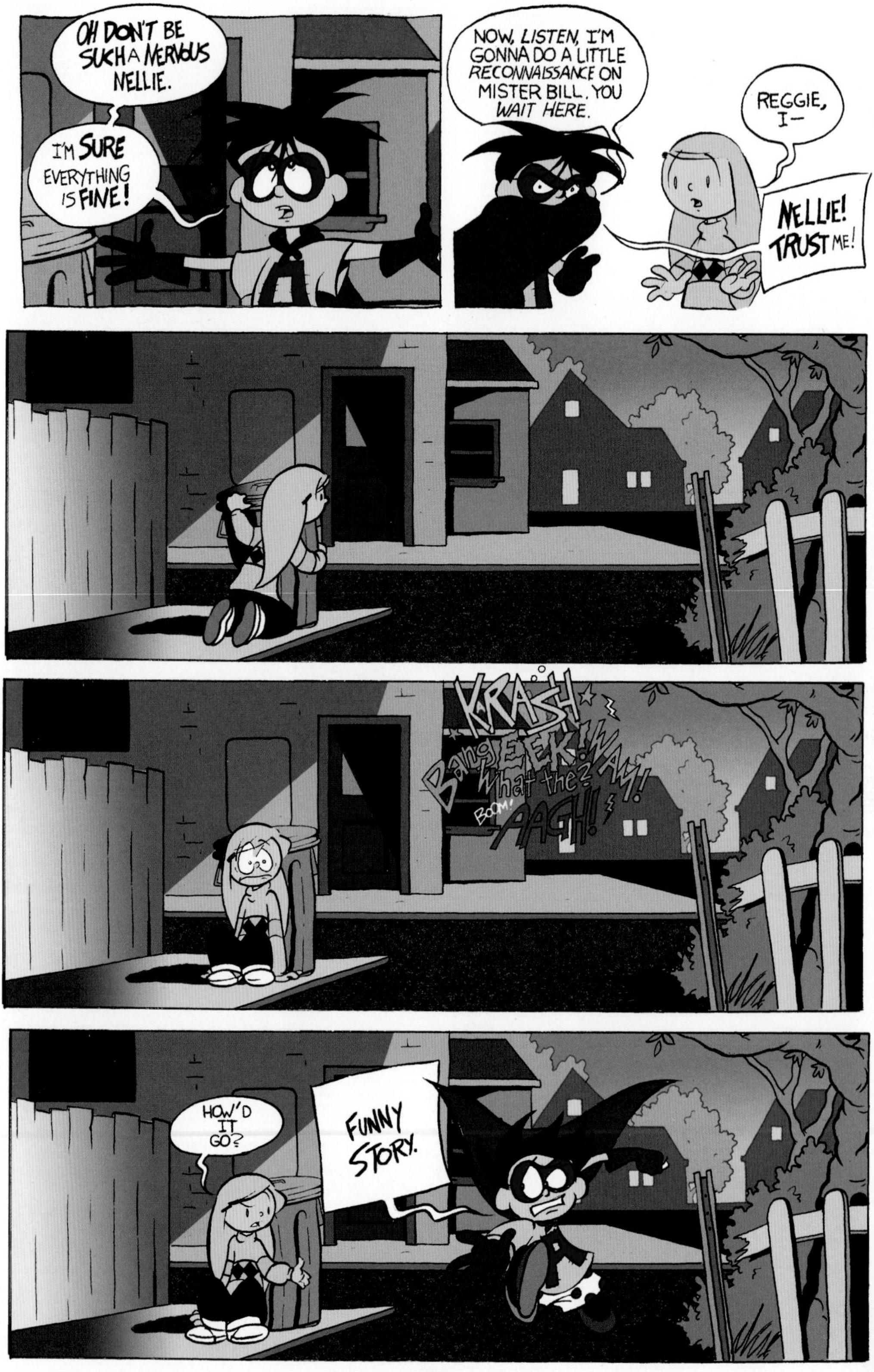
OH DON'T BE SUCH A NERVOUS NELLIE.
I'M SURE EVERYTHING IS FINE!
NOW, LISTEN, I'M GONNA DO A LITTLE RECONNAISSANCE ON MISTER BILL. YOU WAIT HERE.
REGGIE, I—
NELLIE! TRUST ME!
KRASH
BANG
EEK!
WAM!
What the?
BOOM!
AAGH!
HOW'D IT GO?
FUNNY STORY.

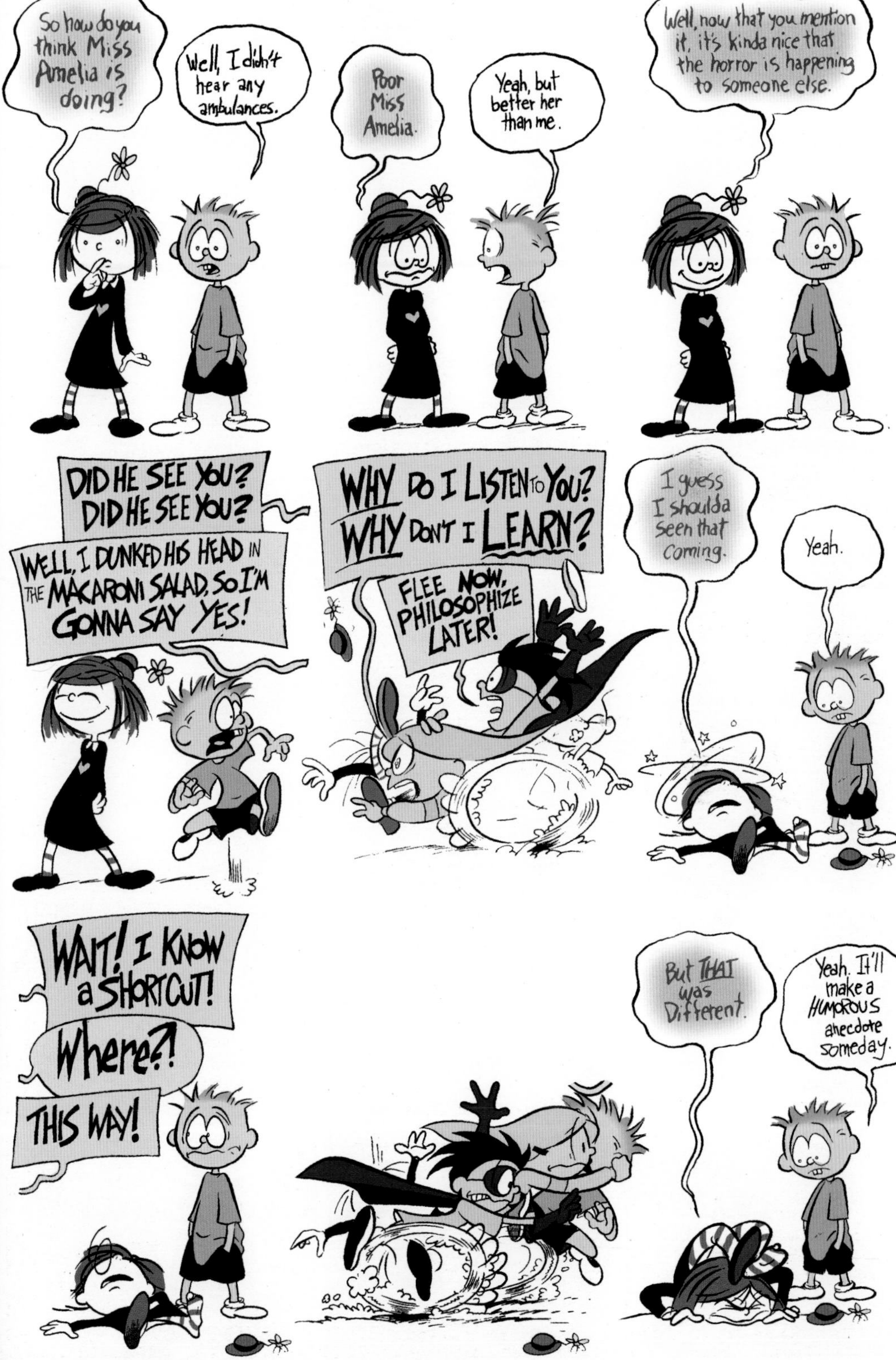
So how do you think Miss Amelia is doing?
Well, I didn't hear any ambulances.
Poor Miss Amelia.
Yeah, but better her than me.
Well, now that you mention it, it's kinda nice that the horror is happening to someone else.
DID HE SEE YOU? DID HE SEE YOU?
WELL, I DUNKED HIS HEAD IN THE MACARONI SALAD, SO I'M GONNA SAY YES!
WHY DO I LISTEN TO YOU? WHY DON'T I LEARN?
FLEE NOW, PHILOSOPHIZE LATER!
I guess I shoulda seen that coming.
Yeah.
WAIT! I KNOW a SHORTCUT!
Where?!
THIS WAY!
But THAT was Different.
Yeah. It'll make a HUMOROUS anecdote someday.

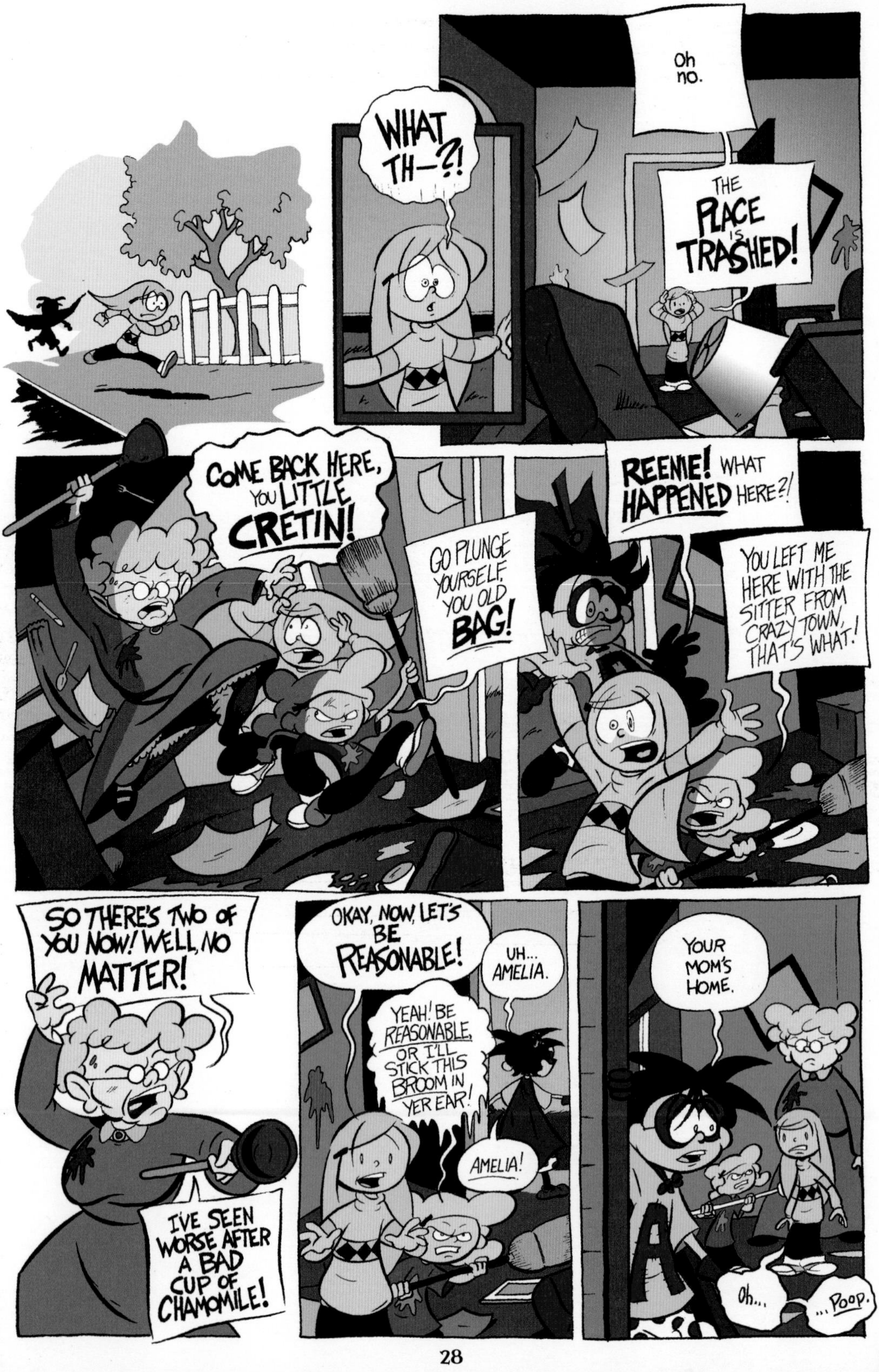
WHAT TH—?!
Oh no.
THE PLACE IS TRASHED!
COME BACK HERE, YOU LITTLE CRETIN!
GO PLUNGE YOURSELF, YOU OLD BAG!
REENIE! WHAT HAPPENED HERE?!
YOU LEFT ME HERE WITH THE SITTER FROM CRAZY TOWN, THAT'S WHAT!
SO THERE'S TWO OF YOU NOW! WELL, NO MATTER!
I'VE SEEN WORSE AFTER A BAD CUP OF CHAMOMILE!
OKAY, NOW, LET'S BE REASONABLE!
YEAH! BE REASONABLE, OR I'LL STICK THIS BROOM IN YER EAR!
UH... AMELIA.
AMELIA!
YOUR MOM'S HOME.
Oh...
...Poop.

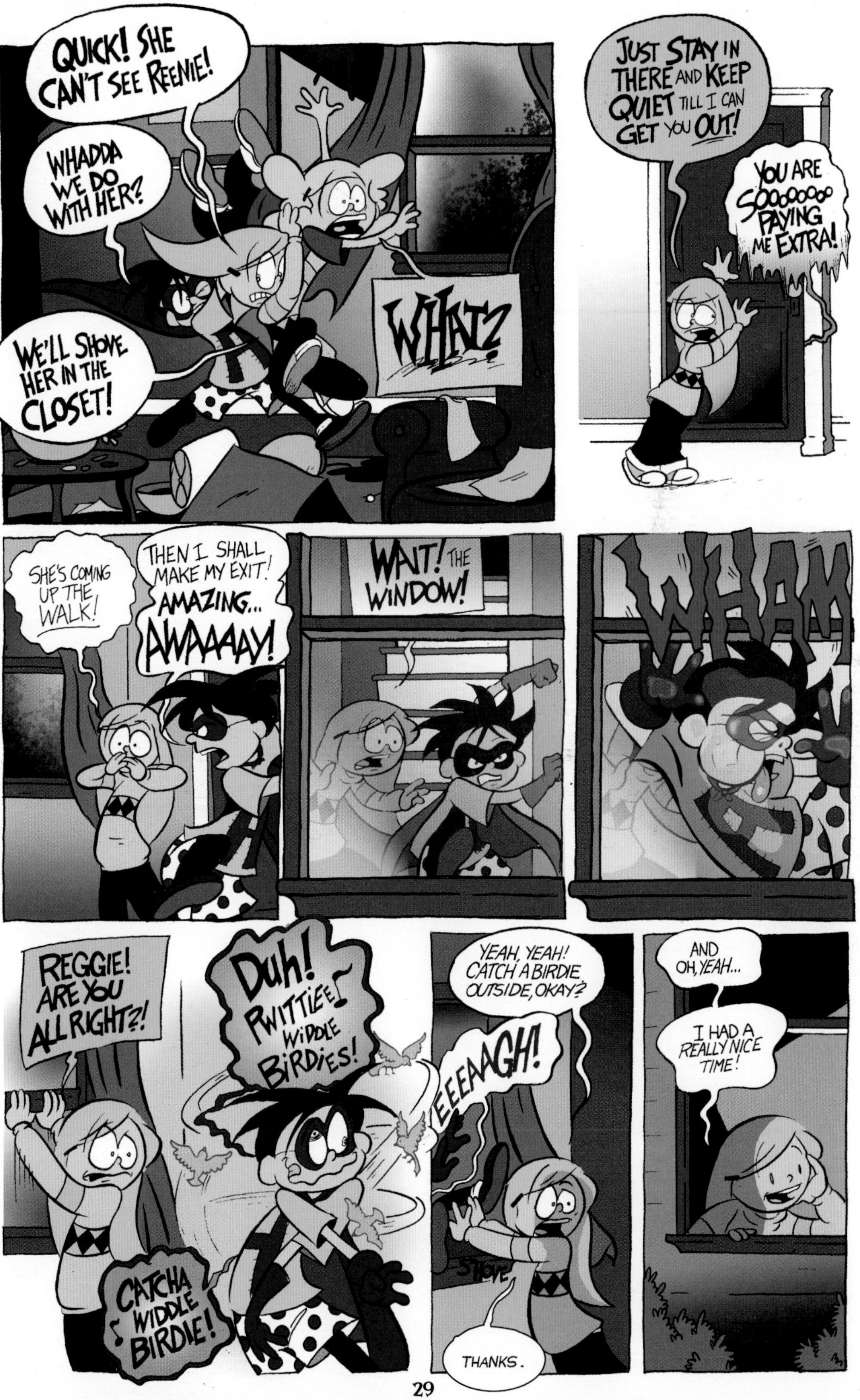

QUICK! SHE CAN'T SEE REENIE!
WHADDA WE DO WITH HER?
WE'LL SHOVE HER IN THE CLOSET!
WHAT?
JUST STAY IN THERE AND KEEP QUIET TILL I CAN GET YOU OUT!
YOU ARE SOOOOOOOO PAYING ME EXTRA!
SHE'S COMING UP THE WALK!
THEN I SHALL MAKE MY EXIT! AMAZING... AWAAAAY!
WAIT! THE WINDOW!
WHAM
REGGIE! ARE YOU ALL RIGHT?!
Duh! PWITTIEEE! WIDDLE BIRDIES!
CATCHA WIDDLE BIRDIE!
YEAH, YEAH! CATCH A BIRDIE OUTSIDE, OKAY?
EEEAAGH!
SHOVE
THANKS.
AND OH, YEAH...
I HAD A REALLY NICE TIME!

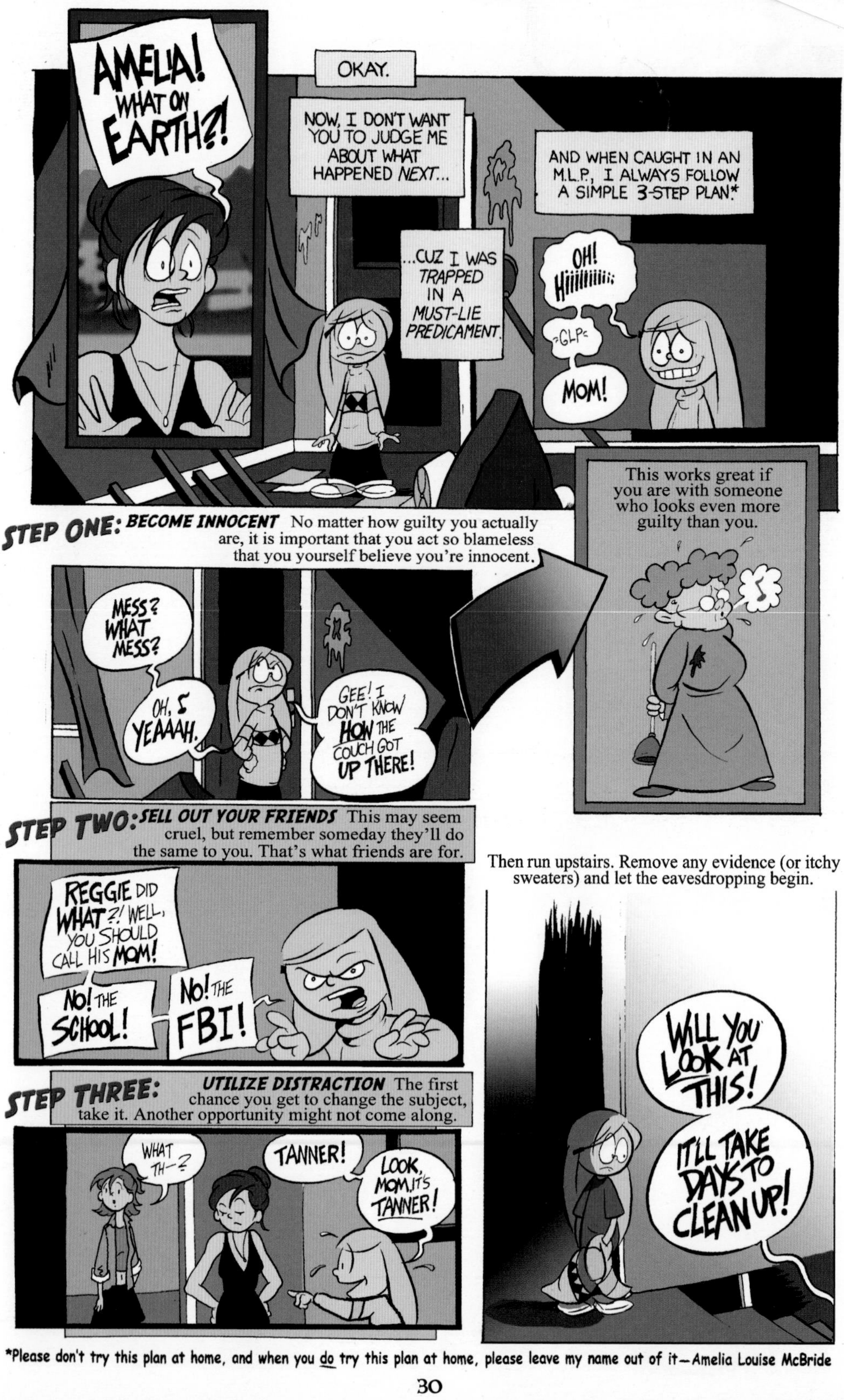
AMELIA! WHAT ON EARTH?!
OKAY.
NOW, I DON'T WANT YOU TO JUDGE ME ABOUT WHAT HAPPENED NEXT...
...CUZ I WAS TRAPPED IN A MUST-LIE PREDICAMENT.
AND WHEN CAUGHT IN AN M.L.P., I ALWAYS FOLLOW A SIMPLE 3-STEP PLAN.*
OH! Hiiiiiiiii
GLP
MOM!
STEP ONE: BECOME INNOCENT No matter how guilty you actually are, it is important that you act so blameless that you yourself believe you're innocent.
MESS? WHAT MESS?
OH, YEAAAH.
GEE! I DON'T KNOW HOW THE COUCH GOT UP THERE!
This works great if you are with someone who looks even more guilty than you.
STEP TWO: SELL OUT YOUR FRIENDS This may seem cruel, but remember someday they'll do the same to you. That's what friends are for.
REGGIE DID WHAT?! WELL, YOU SHOULD CALL HIS MOM!
NO! THE SCHOOL!
NO! THE FBI!
STEP THREE: UTILIZE DISTRACTION The first chance you get to change the subject, take it. Another opportunity might not come along.
WHAT TH–?
TANNER!
LOOK, MOM, IT'S TANNER!
Then run upstairs. Remove any evidence (or itchy sweaters) and let the eavesdropping begin.
WILL YOU LOOK AT THIS!
IT'LL TAKE DAYS TO CLEAN UP!

*Please don't try this plan at home, and when you do try this plan at home, please leave my name out of it—Amelia Louise McBride

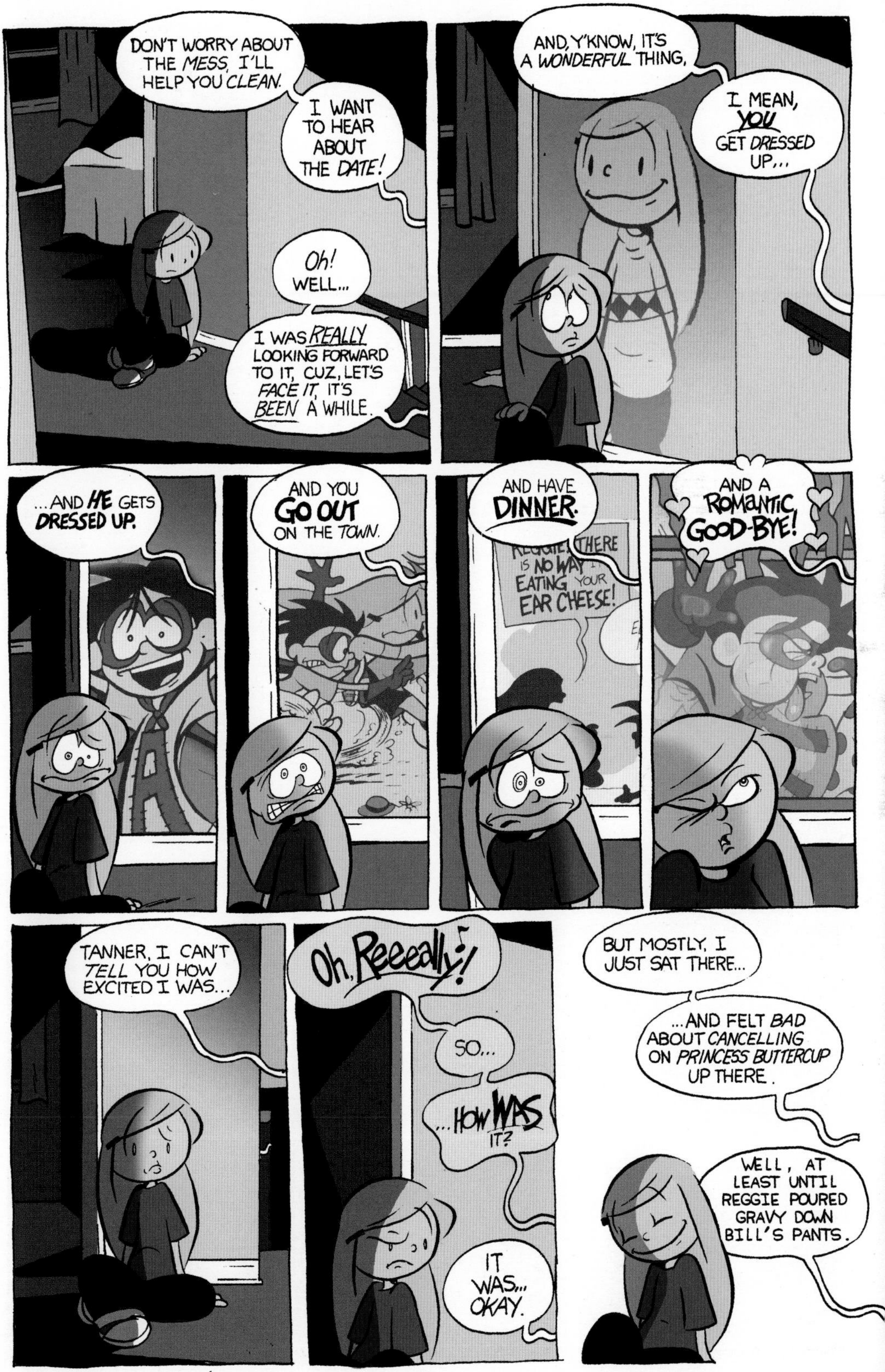
DON'T WORRY ABOUT THE MESS, I'LL HELP YOU CLEAN.
I WANT TO HEAR ABOUT THE DATE!
Oh! WELL...
I WAS REALLY LOOKING FORWARD TO IT, CUZ, LET'S FACE IT, IT'S BEEN A WHILE.
AND, Y'KNOW, IT'S A WONDERFUL THING.
I MEAN, YOU GET DRESSED UP...
...AND HE GETS DRESSED UP.
AND YOU GO OUT ON THE TOWN.
AND HAVE DINNER.
REGGIE! THERE IS NO WAY I ... EATING YOUR EAR CHEESE!
AND A ROMANTIC GOOD-BYE!
TANNER, I CAN'T TELL YOU HOW EXCITED I WAS...
Oh, Reeeally!
SO...
...HOW WAS IT?
IT WAS... OKAY.
BUT MOSTLY, I JUST SAT THERE...
...AND FELT BAD ABOUT CANCELLING ON PRINCESS BUTTERCUP UP THERE.
WELL, AT LEAST UNTIL REGGIE POURED GRAVY DOWN BILL'S PANTS.

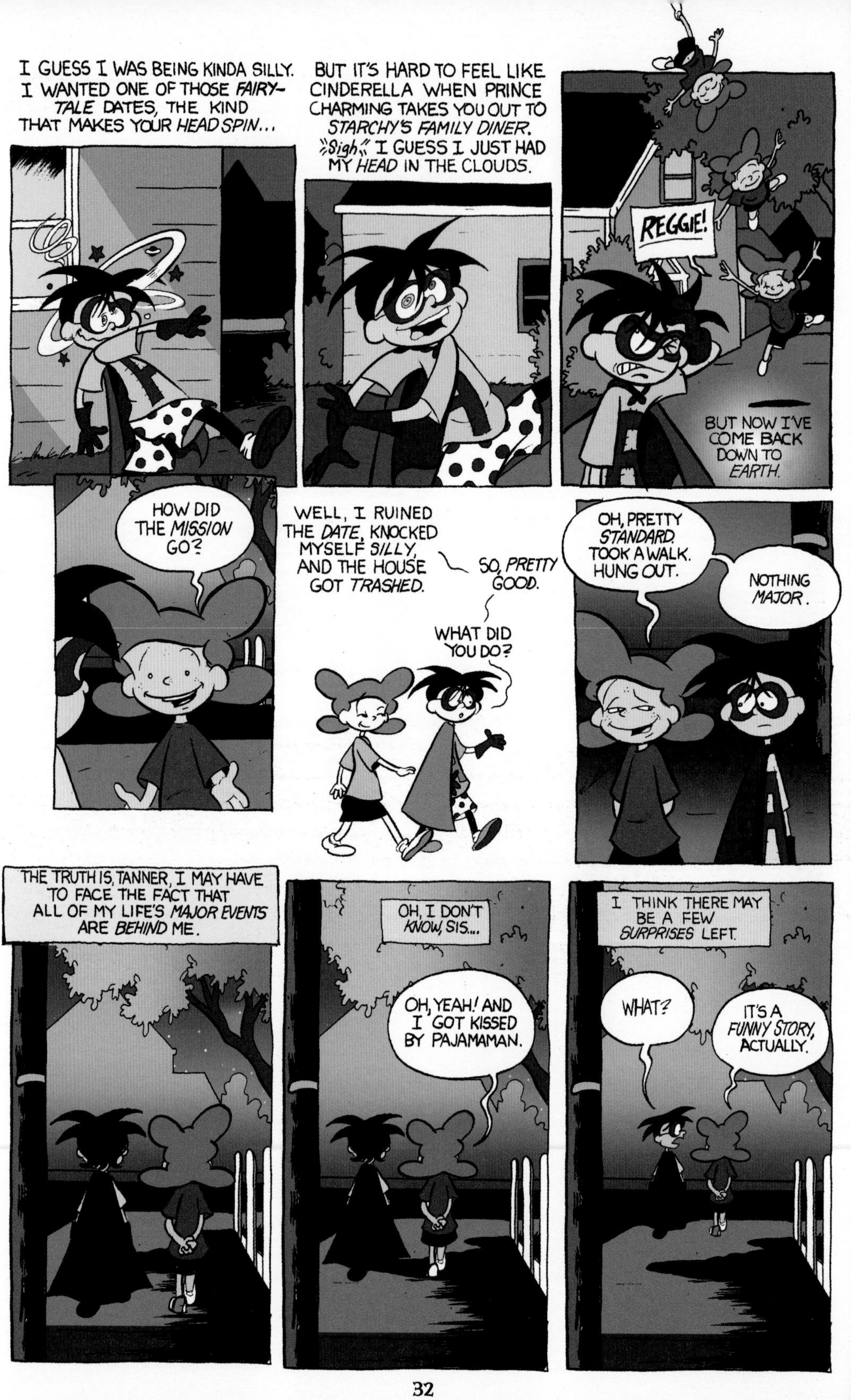
I GUESS I WAS BEING KINDA SILLY. I WANTED ONE OF THOSE *FAIRY-TALE* DATES, THE KIND THAT MAKES YOUR *HEAD SPIN*...
BUT IT'S HARD TO FEEL LIKE CINDERELLA WHEN PRINCE CHARMING TAKES YOU OUT TO *STARCHY'S FAMILY DINER*. *Sigh*. I GUESS I JUST HAD MY *HEAD* IN THE CLOUDS.
REGGIE!
BUT NOW I'VE COME BACK DOWN TO *EARTH*.
HOW DID THE *MISSION* GO?
WELL, I RUINED THE *DATE*, KNOCKED MYSELF *SILLY*, AND THE HOUSE GOT *TRASHED*.
SO, *PRETTY GOOD*.
WHAT DID YOU DO?
OH, PRETTY *STANDARD*. TOOK A WALK. HUNG OUT.
NOTHING *MAJOR*.
THE TRUTH IS, TANNER, I MAY HAVE TO FACE THE FACT THAT ALL OF MY LIFE'S *MAJOR EVENTS* ARE *BEHIND* ME.
OH, I DON'T *KNOW*, SIS...
OH, YEAH! AND I GOT KISSED BY PAJAMAMAN.
I THINK THERE MAY BE A FEW *SURPRISES* LEFT.
WHAT?
IT'S A *FUNNY STORY*, ACTUALLY.

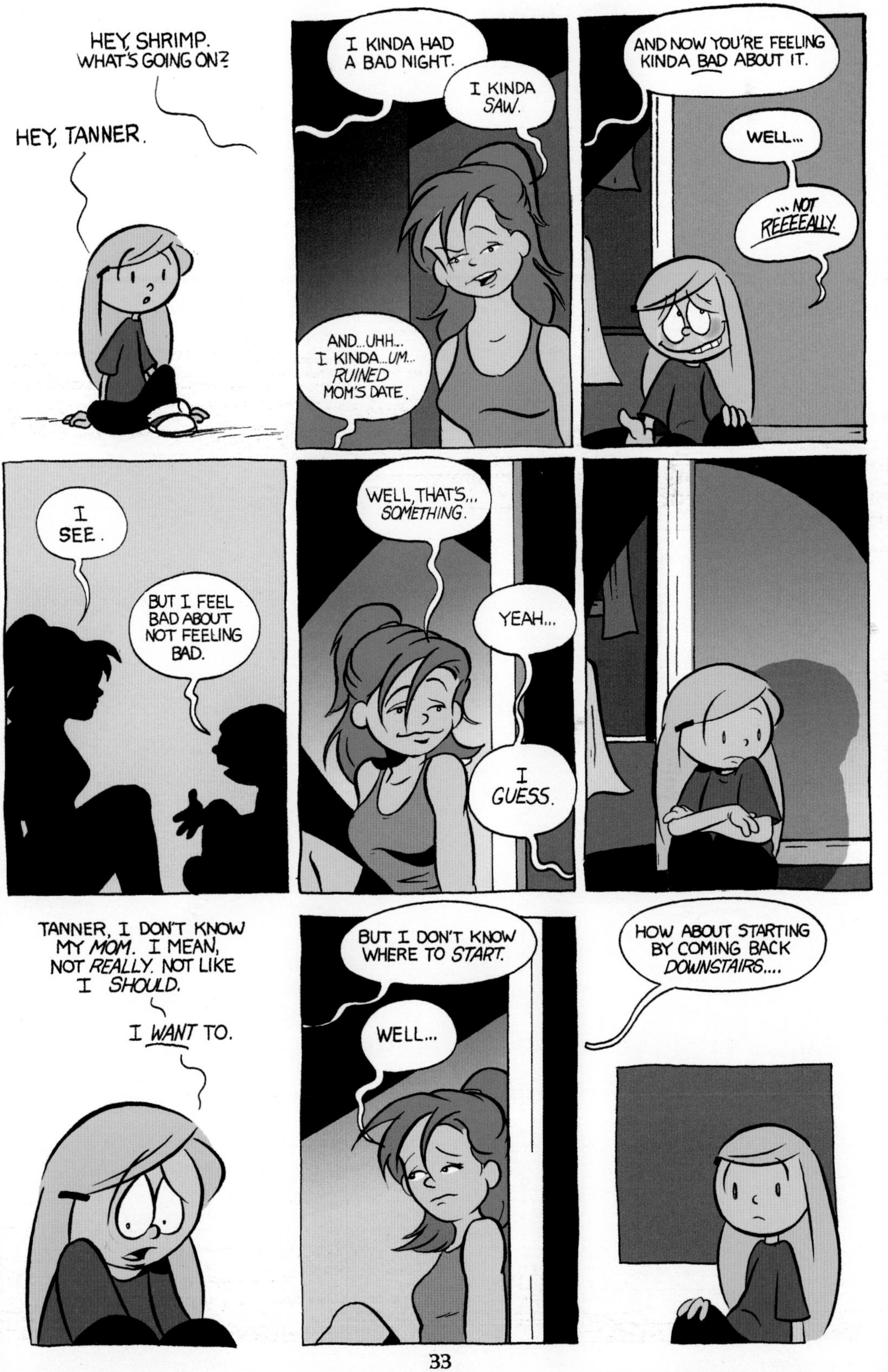
HEY, SHRIMP. WHAT'S GOING ON?
HEY, TANNER.
I KINDA HAD A BAD NIGHT.
I KINDA SAW.
AND...UHH... I KINDA...UM... RUINED MOM'S DATE.
AND NOW YOU'RE FEELING KINDA BAD ABOUT IT.
WELL...
...NOT REEEEALLY.
I SEE.
BUT I FEEL BAD ABOUT NOT FEELING BAD.
WELL, THAT'S... SOMETHING.
YEAH...
I GUESS.
TANNER, I DON'T KNOW MY MOM. I MEAN, NOT REALLY. NOT LIKE I SHOULD.
I WANT TO.
BUT I DON'T KNOW WHERE TO START.
WELL...
HOW ABOUT STARTING BY COMING BACK DOWNSTAIRS....

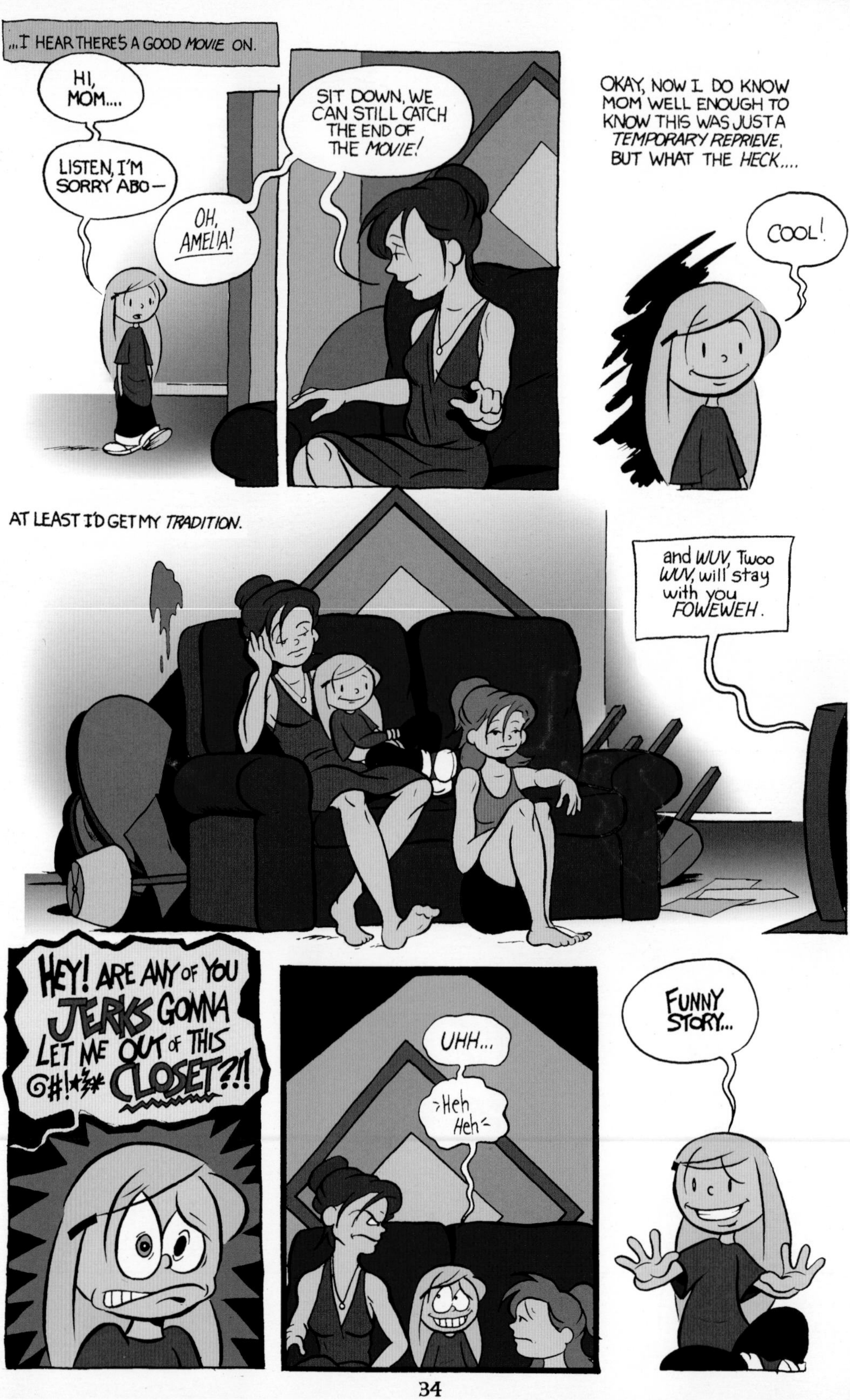
...I HEAR THERE'S A GOOD MOVIE ON.
HI, MOM....
LISTEN, I'M SORRY ABO—
OH, AMELIA!
SIT DOWN, WE CAN STILL CATCH THE END OF THE MOVIE!
OKAY, NOW I DO KNOW MOM WELL ENOUGH TO KNOW THIS WAS JUST A TEMPORARY REPRIEVE, BUT WHAT THE HECK....
COOL!
AT LEAST I'D GET MY TRADITION.
and WUV, Twoo WUV, will stay with you FOWEWEH.
HEY! ARE ANY OF YOU JERKS GONNA LET ME OUT OF THIS @#!*$* CLOSET?!!
UHH...
Heh Heh
FUNNY STORY...

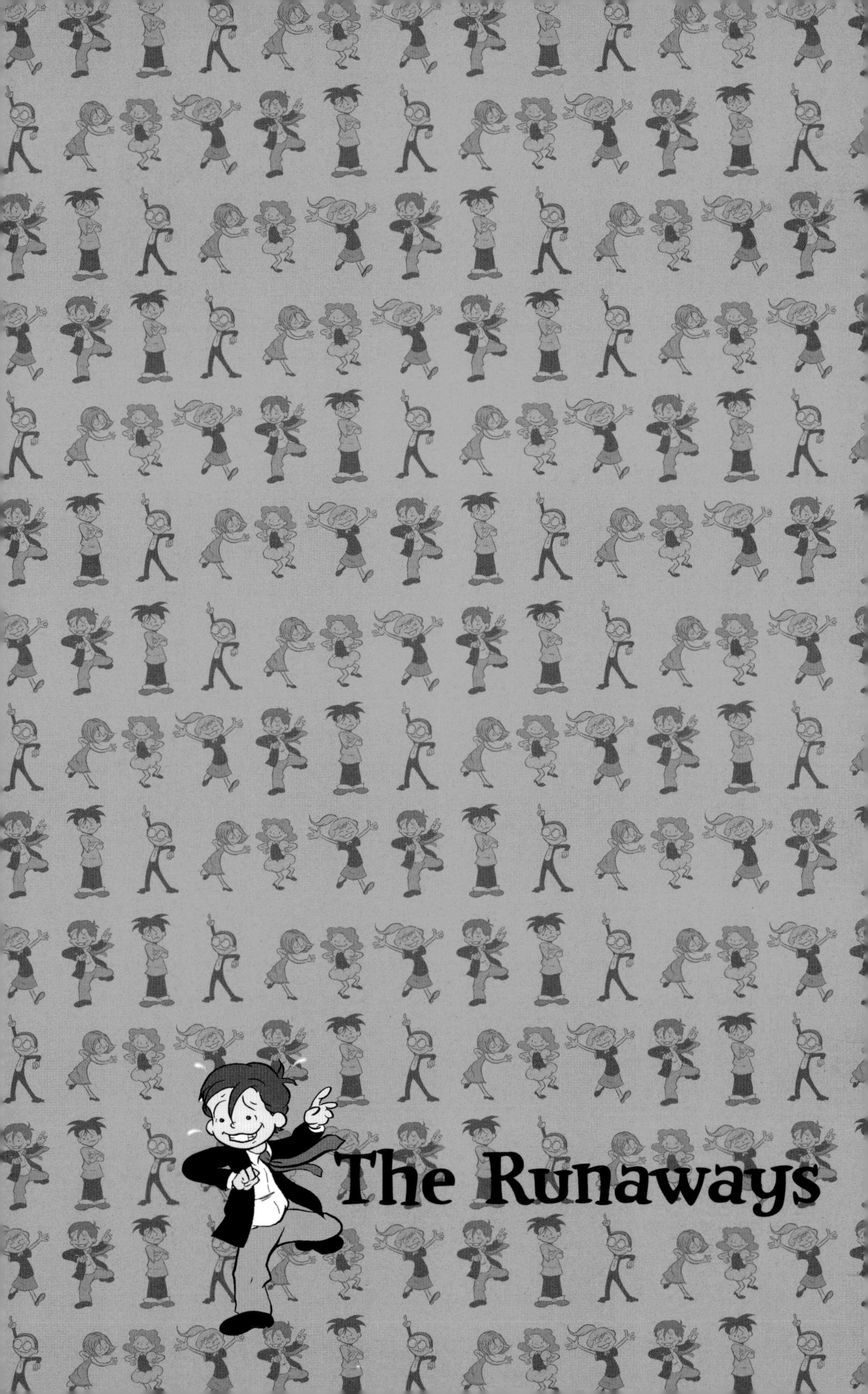

The Runaways

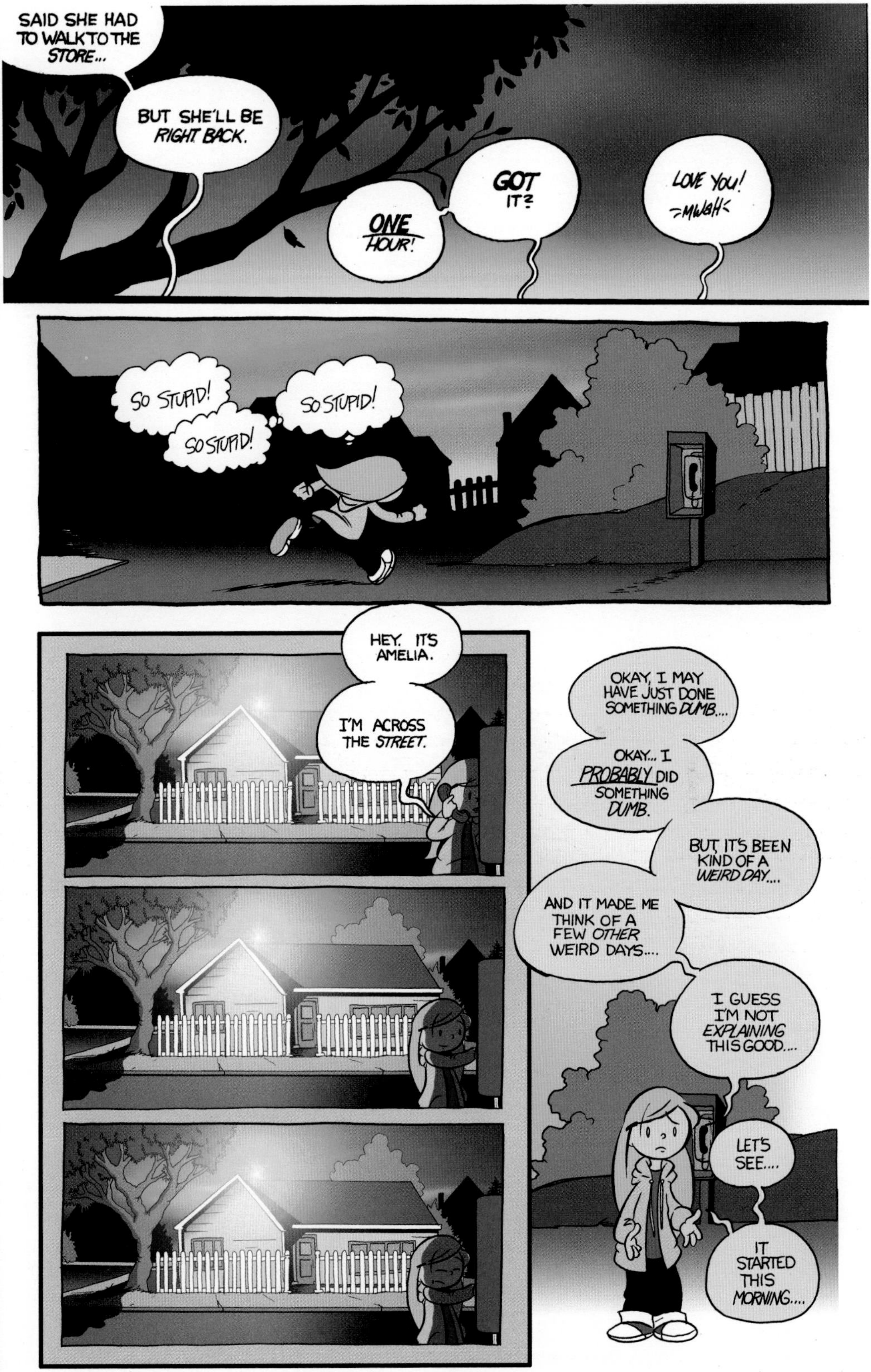
SAID SHE HAD TO WALK TO THE STORE...
BUT SHE'LL BE RIGHT BACK.
ONE HOUR!
GOT IT?
LOVE YOU! =MWAH=
SO STUPID!
SO STUPID!
SO STUPID!
HEY. IT'S AMELIA.
I'M ACROSS THE STREET.
OKAY, I MAY HAVE JUST DONE SOMETHING DUMB....
OKAY... I PROBABLY DID SOMETHING DUMB.
BUT, IT'S BEEN KIND OF A WEIRD DAY....
AND IT MADE ME THINK OF A FEW OTHER WEIRD DAYS....
I GUESS I'M NOT EXPLAINING THIS GOOD....
LET'S SEE....
IT STARTED THIS MORNING....

... THE FIRST DAY OF FIFTH GRADE.

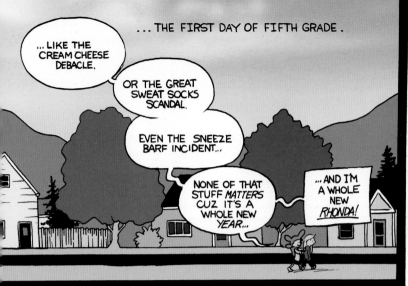

... LIKE THE CREAM CHEESE DEBACLE.

OR THE GREAT SWEAT SOCKS SCANDAL.

EVEN THE SNEEZE BARF INCIDENT...

NONE OF THAT STUFF *MATTERS* CUZ IT'S A WHOLE NEW *YEAR*...

... AND I'M A WHOLE NEW *RHONDA!*

OH, *YEAH?*

LEMME SEE....

Hmmmmm...

FRECKLES.

BONY *KNEES.*

LUMPY *HAIR.*

WOW! I CAN HARDLY *RECOGNIZE* YOU!

OH, YES...

VERRRY WITTY!

LAUGH IF YOU *WANT,* BUT THIS IS THE YEAR *EVERYTHING CHANGES* FOR *RHONDA BLEENIE!*

OKAY! IF YOU SAY SO!

I *SAY* SO.

AND. I. HAVE. *CUTE.* KNEES.

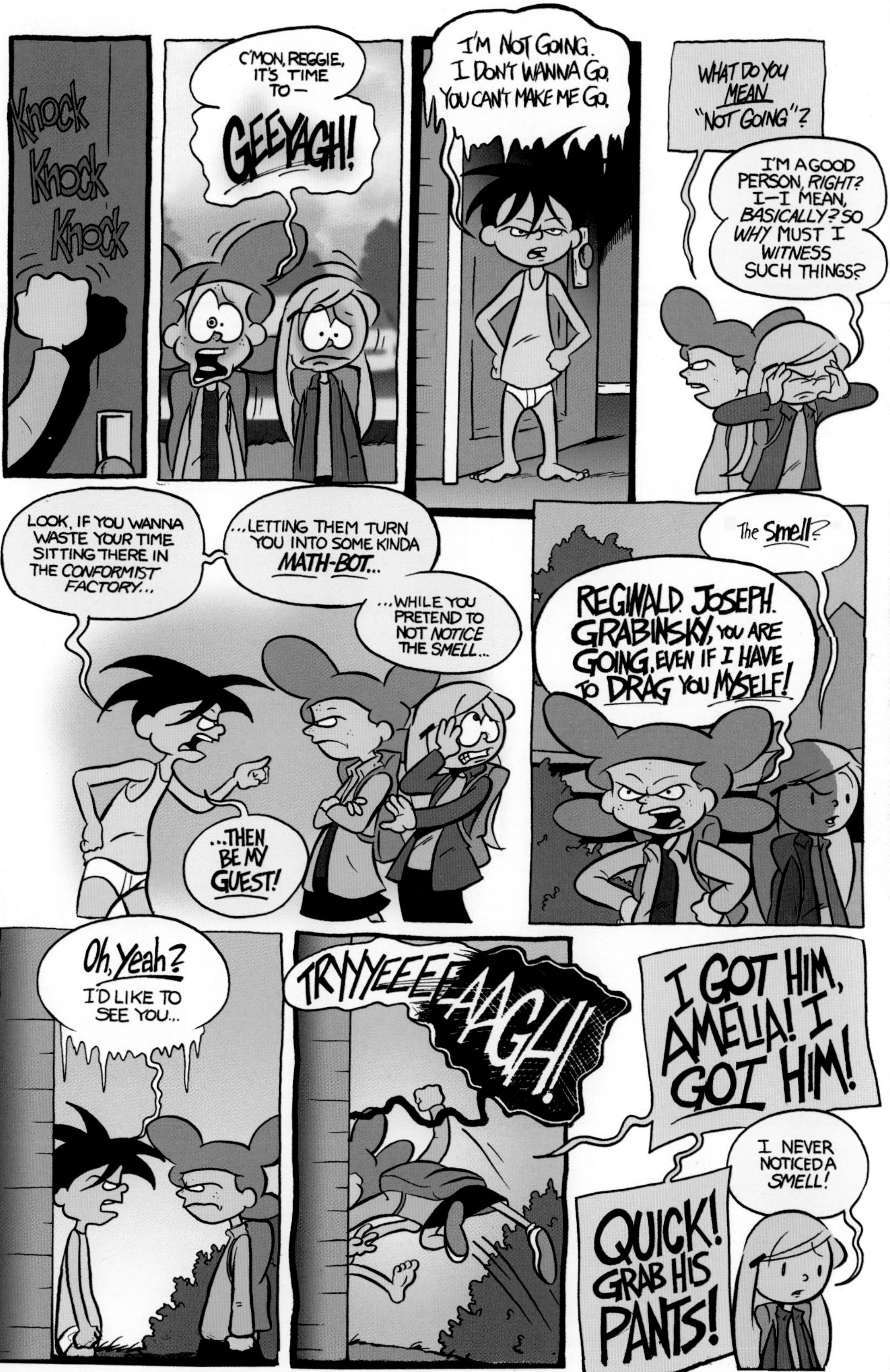
Knock Knock Knock
C'MON, REGGIE, IT'S TIME TO—
GEEYAGH!
I'M NOT GOING. I DON'T WANNA GO. YOU CAN'T MAKE ME GO.
WHAT DO YOU MEAN "NOT GOING"?
I'M A GOOD PERSON, RIGHT? I—I MEAN, BASICALLY? SO WHY MUST I WITNESS SUCH THINGS?
LOOK, IF YOU WANNA WASTE YOUR TIME SITTING THERE IN THE CONFORMIST FACTORY...
...LETTING THEM TURN YOU INTO SOME KINDA MATH-BOT...
...WHILE YOU PRETEND TO NOT NOTICE THE SMELL...
...THEN BE MY GUEST!
The Smell?
REGINALD JOSEPH GRABINSKY, YOU ARE GOING, EVEN IF I HAVE TO DRAG YOU MYSELF!
Oh, Yeah? I'D LIKE TO SEE YOU...
TRYYYEEEEAAGH!
I GOT HIM, AMELIA! I GOT HIM!
QUICK! GRAB HIS PANTS!
I NEVER NOTICED A SMELL!

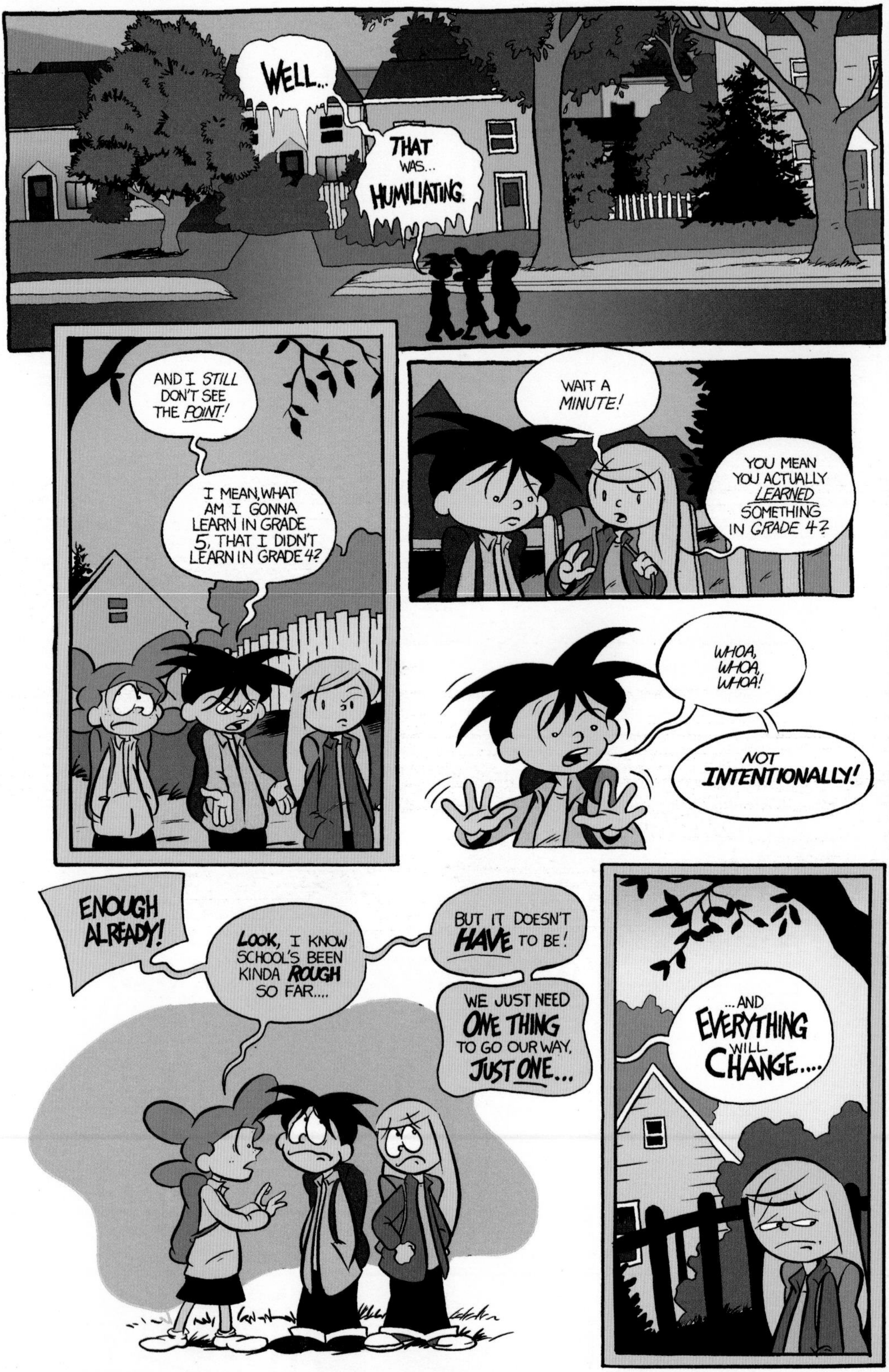
WELL...
THAT WAS... HUMILIATING.
AND I STILL DON'T SEE THE POINT!
I MEAN, WHAT AM I GONNA LEARN IN GRADE 5, THAT I DIDN'T LEARN IN GRADE 4?
WAIT A MINUTE!
YOU MEAN YOU ACTUALLY LEARNED SOMETHING IN GRADE 4?
WHOA, WHOA, WHOA!
NOT INTENTIONALLY!
ENOUGH ALREADY!
LOOK, I KNOW SCHOOL'S BEEN KINDA ROUGH SO FAR....
BUT IT DOESN'T HAVE TO BE!
WE JUST NEED ONE THING TO GO OUR WAY, JUST ONE...
...AND EVERYTHING WILL CHANGE....

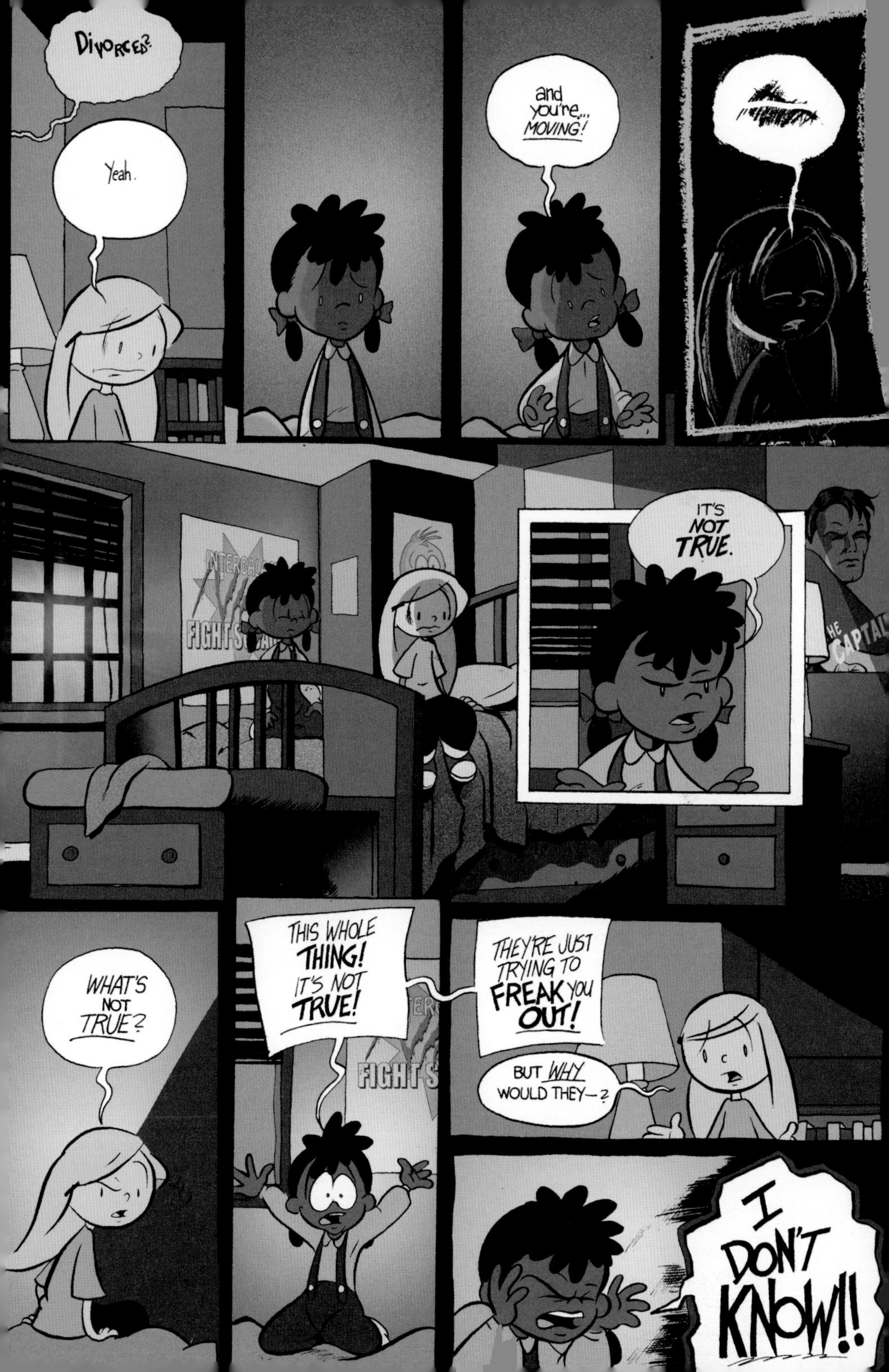
DIVORCED?
Yeah.
and you're... MOVING!
IT'S NOT TRUE.
INTERGALACTIC
FIGHT SQUAD
THE CAPTAIN
WHAT'S NOT TRUE?
THIS WHOLE THING! IT'S NOT TRUE!
THEY'RE JUST TRYING TO FREAK YOU OUT!
BUT WHY WOULD THEY—?
I DON'T KNOW!!

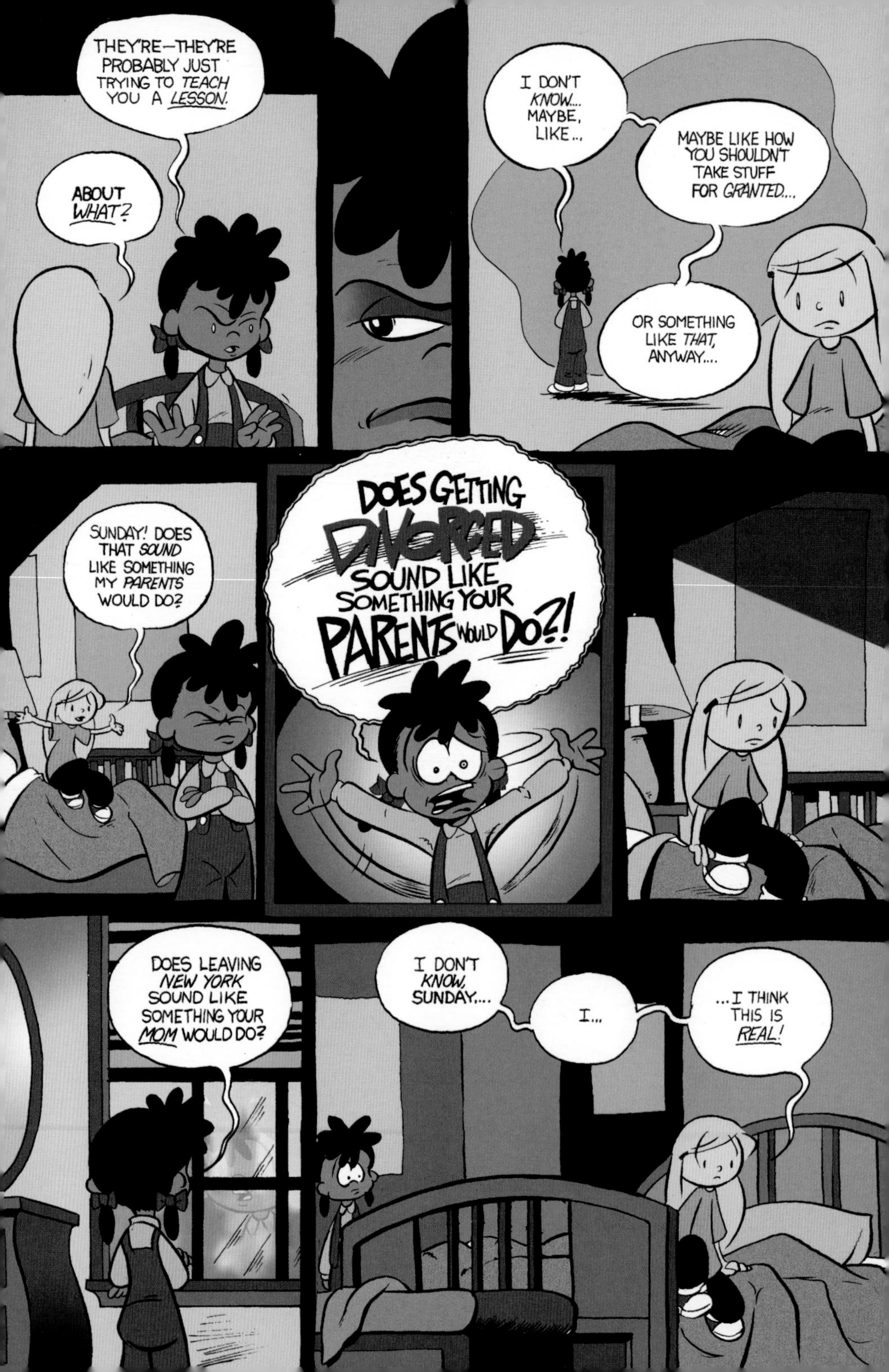
THEY'RE—THEY'RE PROBABLY JUST TRYING TO *TEACH* YOU A *LESSON*.
ABOUT *WHAT*?
I DON'T *KNOW*.... MAYBE, LIKE...,
MAYBE LIKE HOW YOU SHOULDN'T TAKE STUFF FOR *GRANTED*....
OR SOMETHING LIKE *THAT*, ANYWAY....
SUNDAY! DOES THAT *SOUND* LIKE SOMETHING MY *PARENTS* WOULD DO?
DOES GETTING DIVORCED SOUND LIKE SOMETHING YOUR PARENTS WOULD DO?!
DOES LEAVING *NEW YORK* SOUND LIKE SOMETHING YOUR *MOM* WOULD DO?
I DON'T *KNOW*, SUNDAY....
I...
...I THINK THIS IS *REAL*!

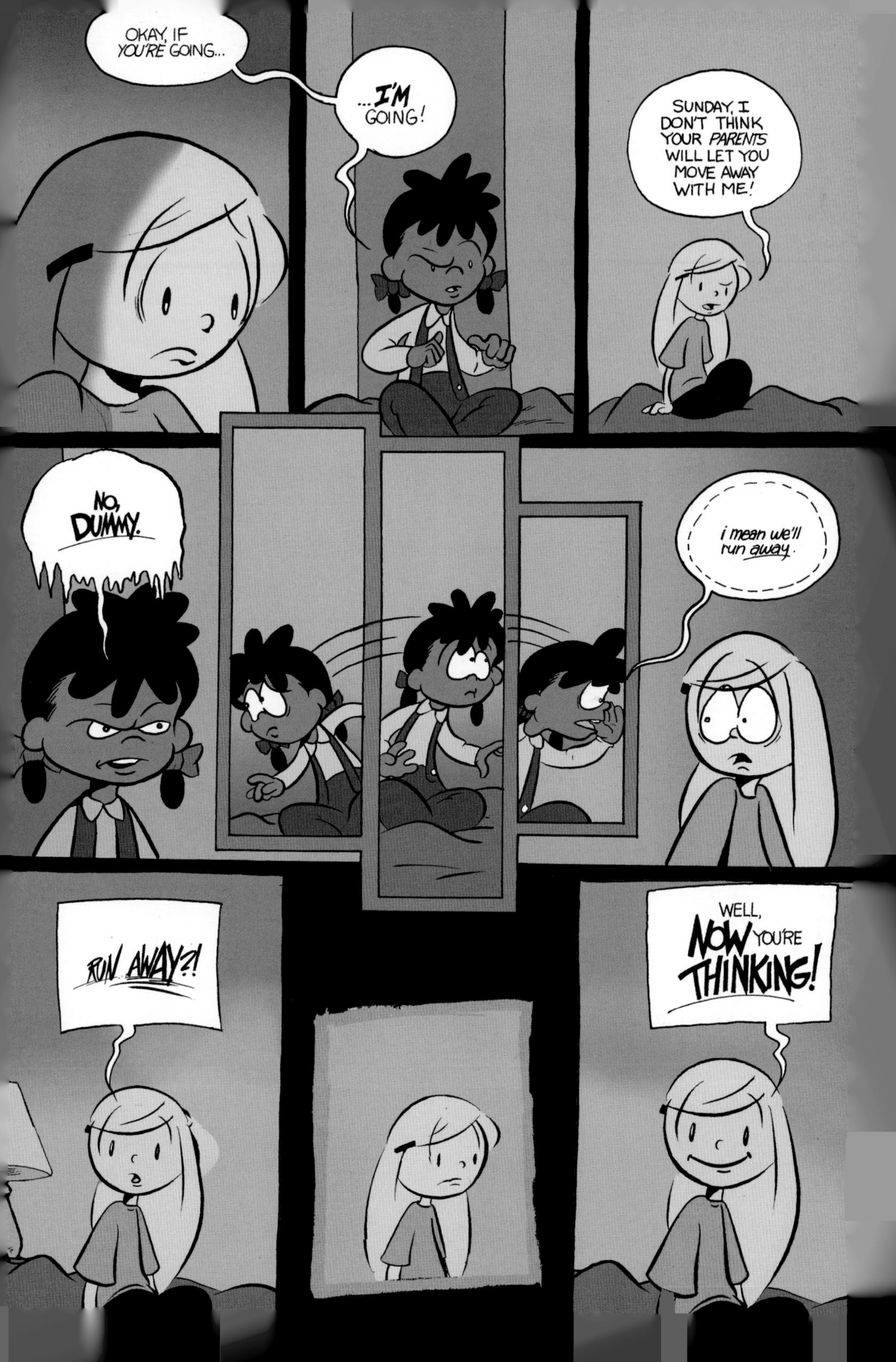

OKAY, IF YOU'RE GOING...
...I'M GOING!
SUNDAY, I DON'T THINK YOUR PARENTS WILL LET YOU MOVE AWAY WITH ME!
NO, DUMMY.
i mean we'll run away.
RUN AWAY?!
WELL, NOW YOU'RE THINKING!

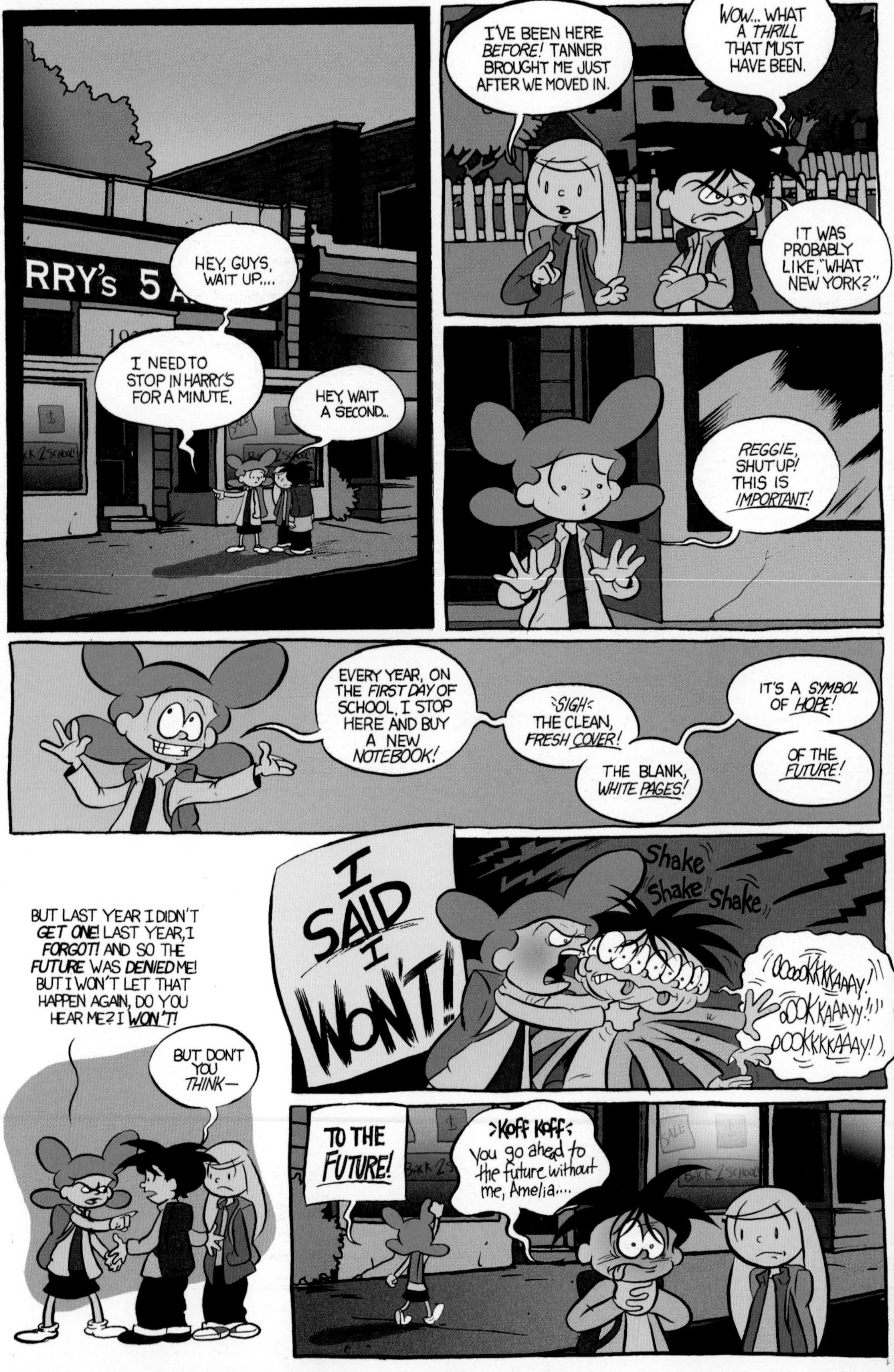

HEY, GUYS, WAIT UP....
I NEED TO STOP IN HARRY'S FOR A MINUTE.
HEY, WAIT A SECOND..
RRY's 5
I'VE BEEN HERE BEFORE! TANNER BROUGHT ME JUST AFTER WE MOVED IN.
WOW... WHAT A THRILL THAT MUST HAVE BEEN.
IT WAS PROBABLY LIKE, "WHAT NEW YORK?"
REGGIE, SHUT UP! THIS IS IMPORTANT!
EVERY YEAR, ON THE FIRST DAY OF SCHOOL, I STOP HERE AND BUY A NEW NOTEBOOK!
SIGH THE CLEAN, FRESH COVER!
THE BLANK, WHITE PAGES!
IT'S A SYMBOL OF HOPE!
OF THE FUTURE!
BUT LAST YEAR I DIDN'T GET ONE! LAST YEAR, I FORGOT! AND SO THE FUTURE WAS DENIED ME! BUT I WON'T LET THAT HAPPEN AGAIN, DO YOU HEAR ME? I WON'T!
BUT DON'T YOU THINK—
I SAID I WON'T!
Shake Shake Shake
OOOOOKKKKAAAY! OOOKKAAAYY! OOOKKKKAAAY!
TO THE FUTURE!
Koff Koff
You go ahead to the future without me, Amelia....

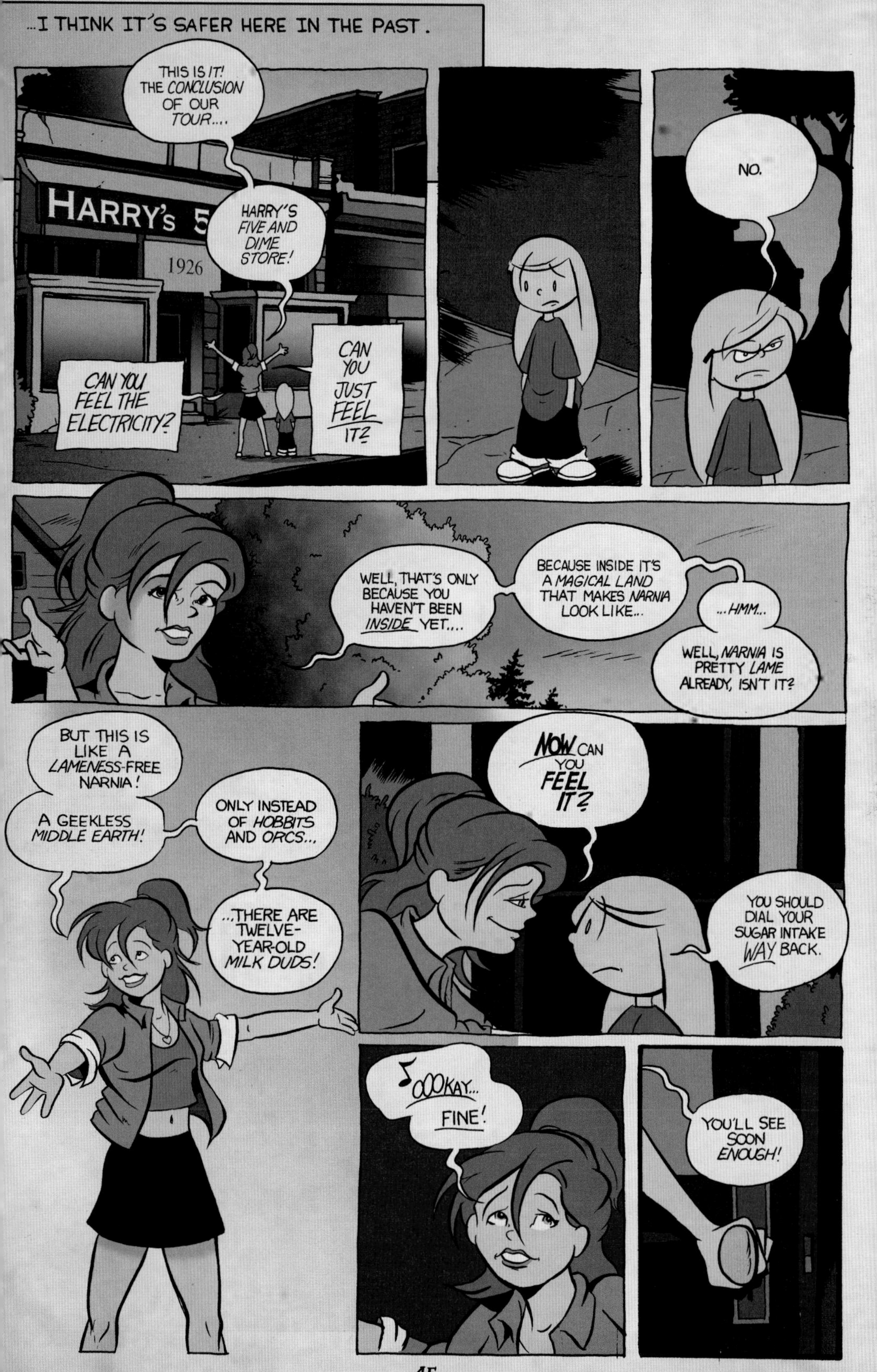
...I THINK IT'S SAFER HERE IN THE PAST.
THIS IS IT! THE CONCLUSION OF OUR TOUR....
HARRY'S 5
1926
HARRY'S FIVE AND DIME STORE!
CAN YOU FEEL THE ELECTRICITY?
CAN YOU JUST FEEL IT?
NO.
WELL, THAT'S ONLY BECAUSE YOU HAVEN'T BEEN INSIDE YET....
BECAUSE INSIDE IT'S A MAGICAL LAND THAT MAKES NARNIA LOOK LIKE...
...HMM...
WELL, NARNIA IS PRETTY LAME ALREADY, ISN'T IT?
BUT THIS IS LIKE A LAMENESS-FREE NARNIA!
A GEEKLESS MIDDLE EARTH!
ONLY INSTEAD OF HOBBITS AND ORCS...
...THERE ARE TWELVE-YEAR-OLD MILK DUDS!
NOW CAN YOU FEEL IT?
YOU SHOULD DIAL YOUR SUGAR INTAKE WAY BACK.
OOOKAY... FINE!
YOU'LL SEE SOON ENOUGH!

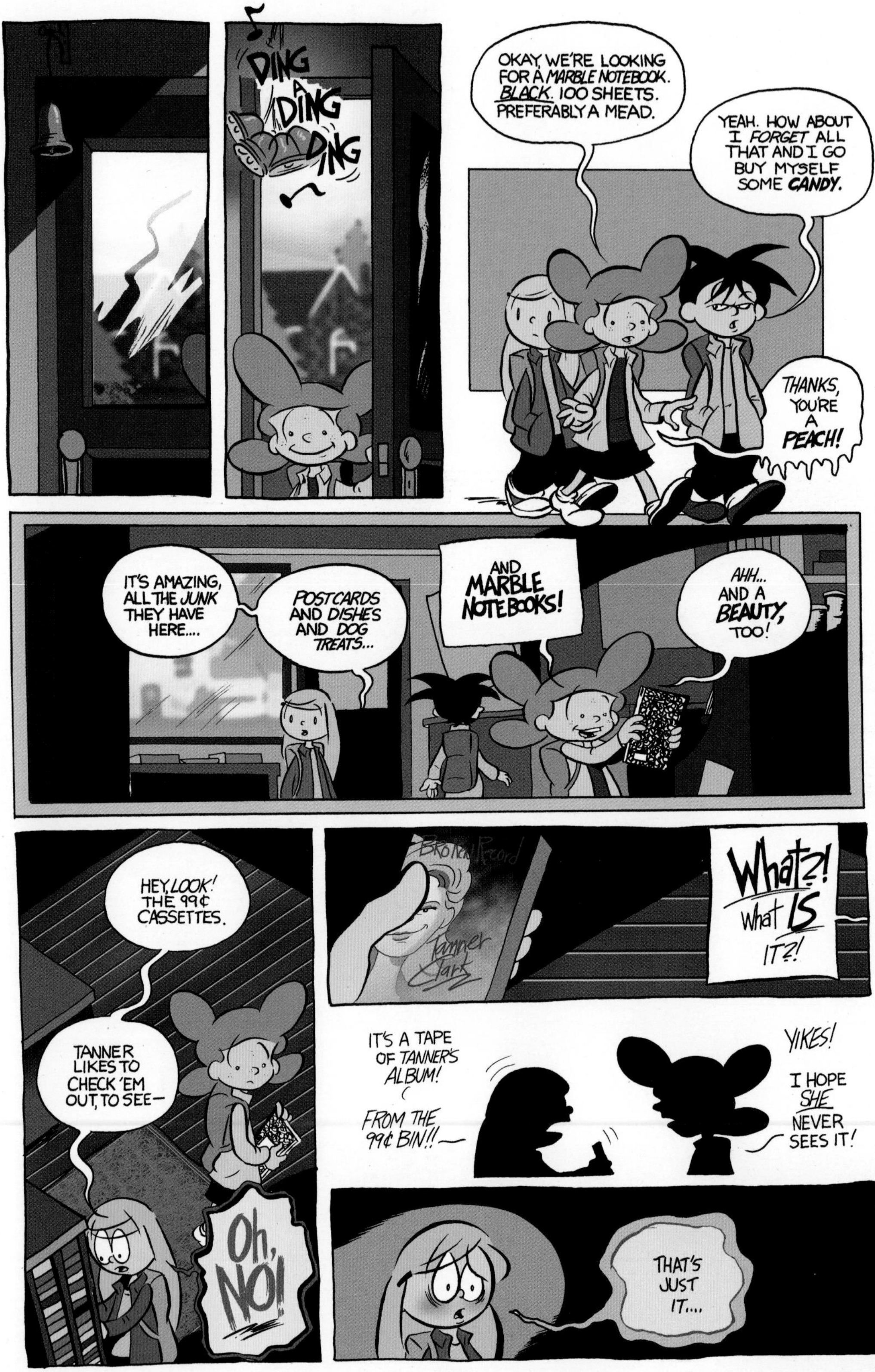

DING A DING DING
OKAY, WE'RE LOOKING FOR A MARBLE NOTEBOOK. BLACK. 100 SHEETS. PREFERABLY A MEAD.
YEAH. HOW ABOUT I FORGET ALL THAT AND I GO BUY MYSELF SOME CANDY.
THANKS, YOU'RE A PEACH!
IT'S AMAZING, ALL THE JUNK THEY HAVE HERE....
POSTCARDS AND DISHES AND DOG TREATS...
AND MARBLE NOTEBOOKS!
AHH... AND A BEAUTY, TOO!
HEY, LOOK! THE 99¢ CASSETTES.
TANNER LIKES TO CHECK 'EM OUT, TO SEE—
Oh, NO!
Broken Record
Tanner Clark
What?! What IS IT?!
IT'S A TAPE OF TANNER'S ALBUM!
FROM THE 99¢ BIN!!
YIKES!
I HOPE SHE NEVER SEES IT!
THAT'S JUST IT....

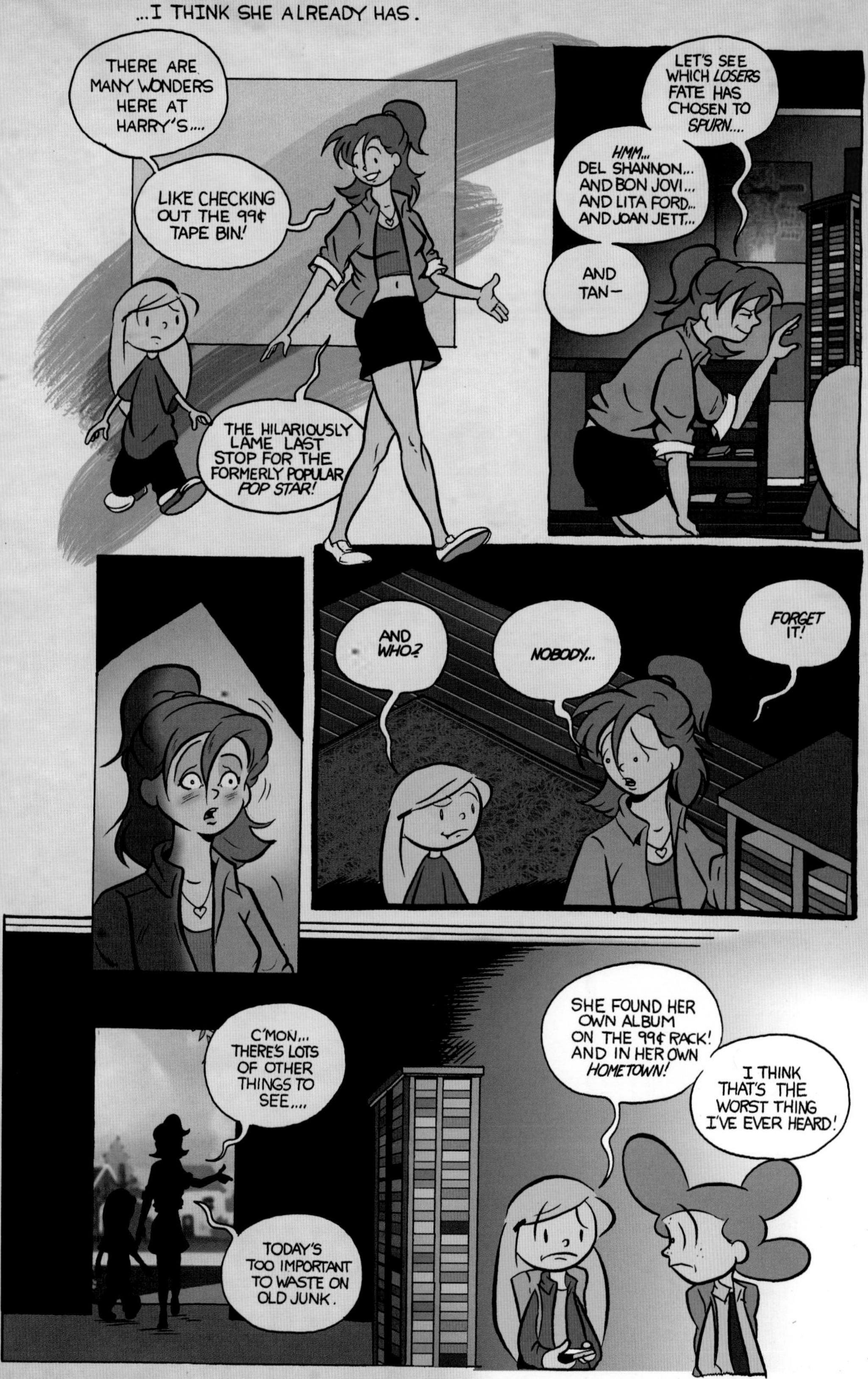
...I THINK SHE ALREADY HAS.
THERE ARE MANY WONDERS HERE AT HARRY'S....
LIKE CHECKING OUT THE 99¢ TAPE BIN!
THE HILARIOUSLY LAME LAST STOP FOR THE FORMERLY POPULAR POP STAR!
LET'S SEE WHICH LOSERS FATE HAS CHOSEN TO SPURN....
HMM... DEL SHANNON... AND BON JOVI... AND LITA FORD... AND JOAN JETT...
AND TAN—
AND WHO?
NOBODY...
FORGET IT!
C'MON... THERE'S LOTS OF OTHER THINGS TO SEE....
TODAY'S TOO IMPORTANT TO WASTE ON OLD JUNK.
SHE FOUND HER OWN ALBUM ON THE 99¢ RACK! AND IN HER OWN HOMETOWN!
I THINK THAT'S THE WORST THING I'VE EVER HEARD!

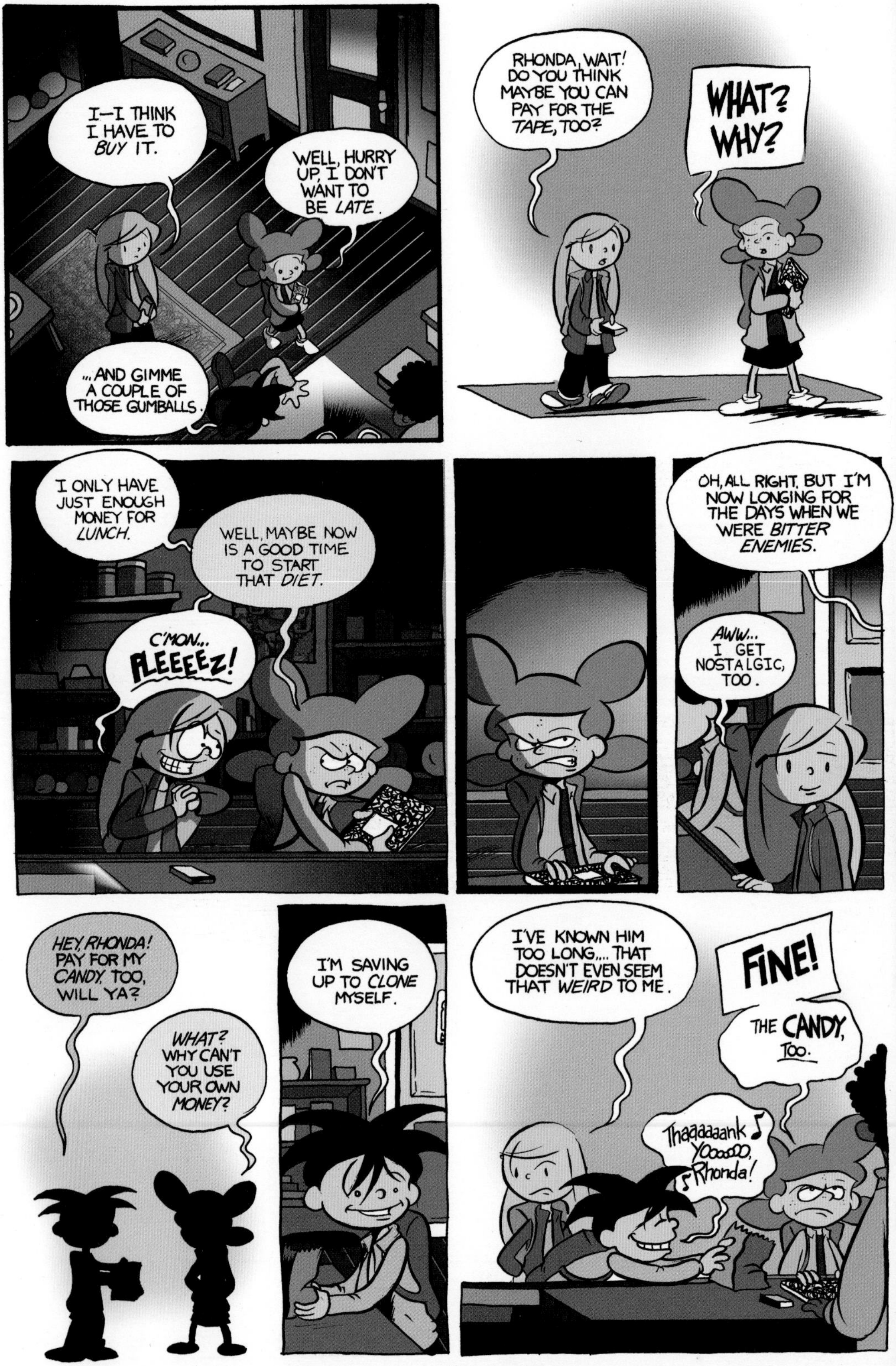

I—I THINK I HAVE TO *BUY* IT.
WELL, HURRY UP, I DON'T WANT TO BE *LATE*.
...AND GIMME A COUPLE OF THOSE GUMBALLS.
RHONDA, WAIT! DO YOU THINK MAYBE YOU CAN PAY FOR THE *TAPE*, TOO?
WHAT? WHY?
I ONLY HAVE JUST ENOUGH MONEY FOR *LUNCH*.
WELL, MAYBE NOW IS A GOOD TIME TO START THAT *DIET*.
C'MON... PLEEEEZ!
OH, ALL RIGHT, BUT I'M NOW LONGING FOR THE DAYS WHEN WE WERE *BITTER ENEMIES*.
AWW... I GET NOSTALGIC, TOO.
HEY, RHONDA! PAY FOR MY *CANDY*, TOO, WILL YA?
WHAT? WHY CAN'T YOU USE YOUR OWN *MONEY*?
I'M SAVING UP TO *CLONE* MYSELF.
I'VE KNOWN HIM TOO LONG.... THAT DOESN'T EVEN SEEM THAT *WEIRD* TO ME.
FINE!
THE **CANDY**, TOO.
Thaaaaaank Yooooooo, Rhonda!

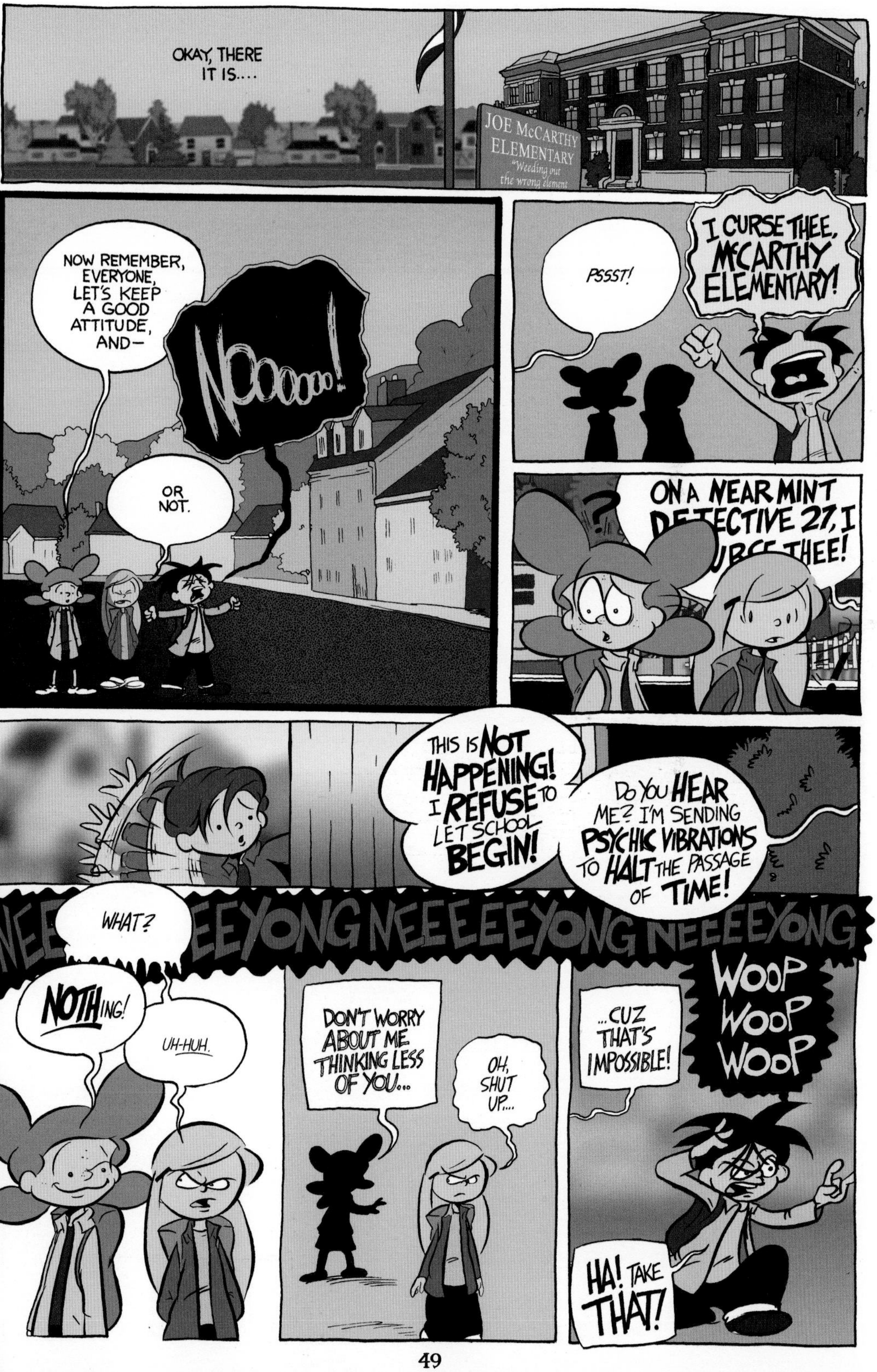
OKAY, THERE IT IS....
JOE McCARTHY ELEMENTARY
"Weeding out the wrong element"
NOW REMEMBER, EVERYONE, LET'S KEEP A GOOD ATTITUDE, AND—
NOOOOOO!
OR NOT.
PSSST!
I CURSE THEE, McCARTHY ELEMENTARY!
ON A NEAR MINT DETECTIVE 27, I CURSE THEE!
THIS IS NOT HAPPENING! I REFUSE TO LET SCHOOL BEGIN!
DO YOU HEAR ME? I'M SENDING PSYCHIC VIBRATIONS TO HALT THE PASSAGE OF TIME!
NEEEEEYONG NEEEEEYONG NEEEEEYONG
WHAT?
NOTHING!
UH-HUH.
DON'T WORRY ABOUT ME THINKING LESS OF YOU...
OH, SHUT UP...
...CUZ THAT'S IMPOSSIBLE!
WOOP WOOP WOOP
HA! TAKE THAT!

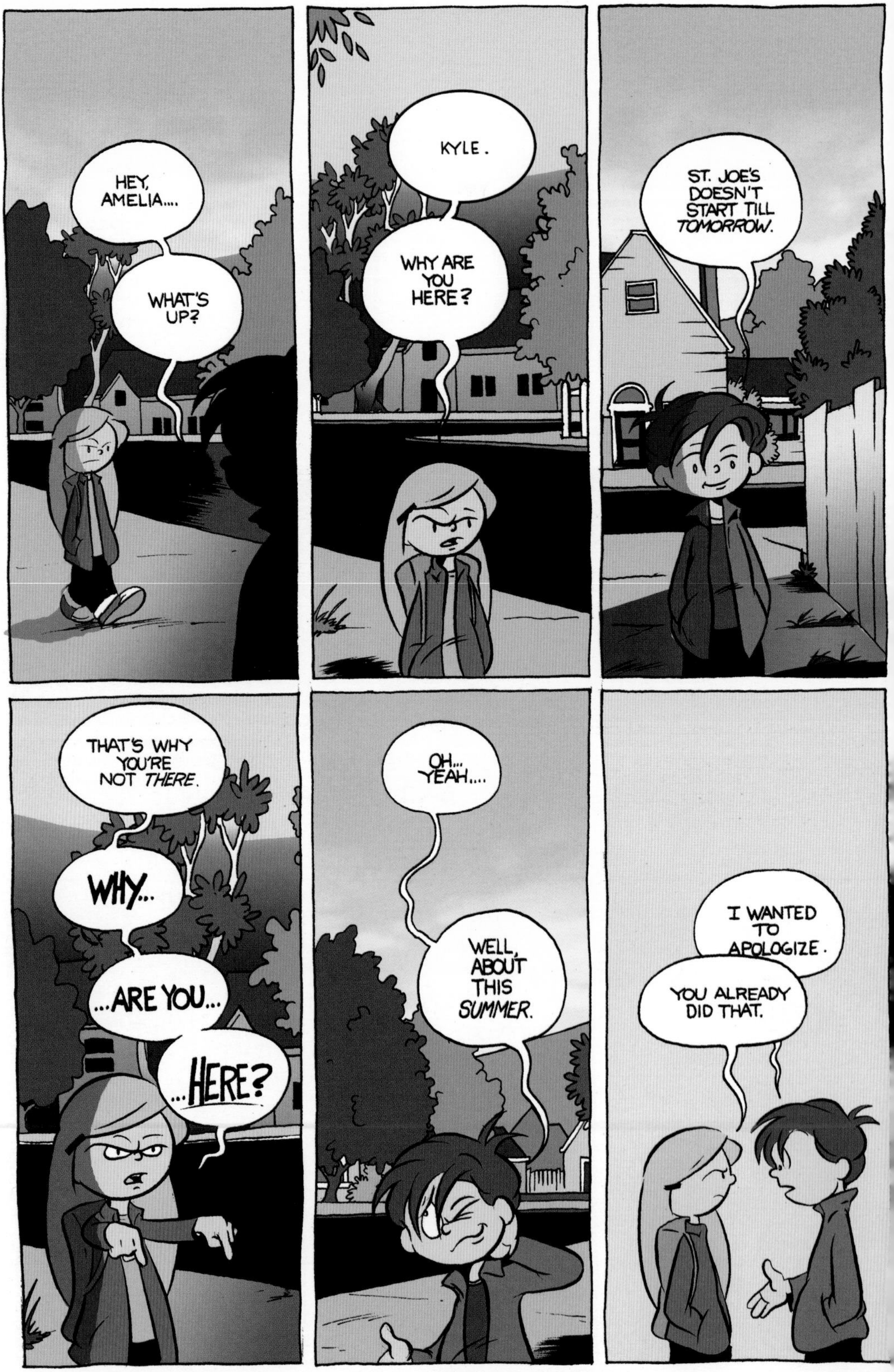
HEY, AMELIA....
WHAT'S UP?
KYLE.
WHY ARE YOU HERE?
ST. JOE'S DOESN'T START TILL *TOMORROW*.
THAT'S WHY YOU'RE NOT *THERE*.
WHY...
...ARE YOU...
...HERE?
OH... YEAH....
WELL, ABOUT THIS *SUMMER*.
I WANTED TO APOLOGIZE.
YOU ALREADY DID THAT.

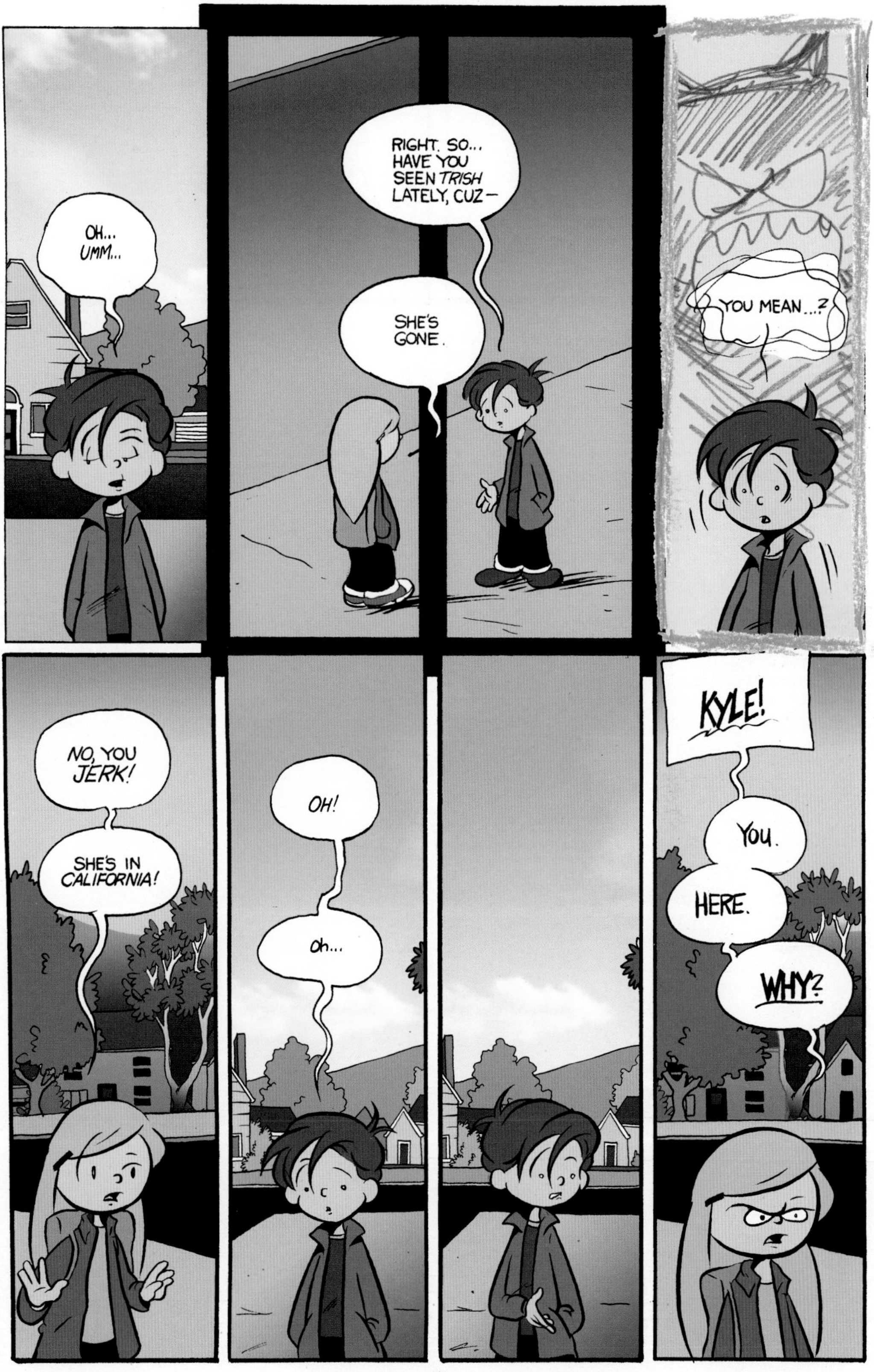
OH... UMM...
RIGHT. SO... HAVE YOU SEEN TRISH LATELY, CUZ—
SHE'S GONE.
YOU MEAN...?
NO, YOU JERK!
SHE'S IN CALIFORNIA!
OH!
Oh...
KYLE!
You.
HERE.
WHY?

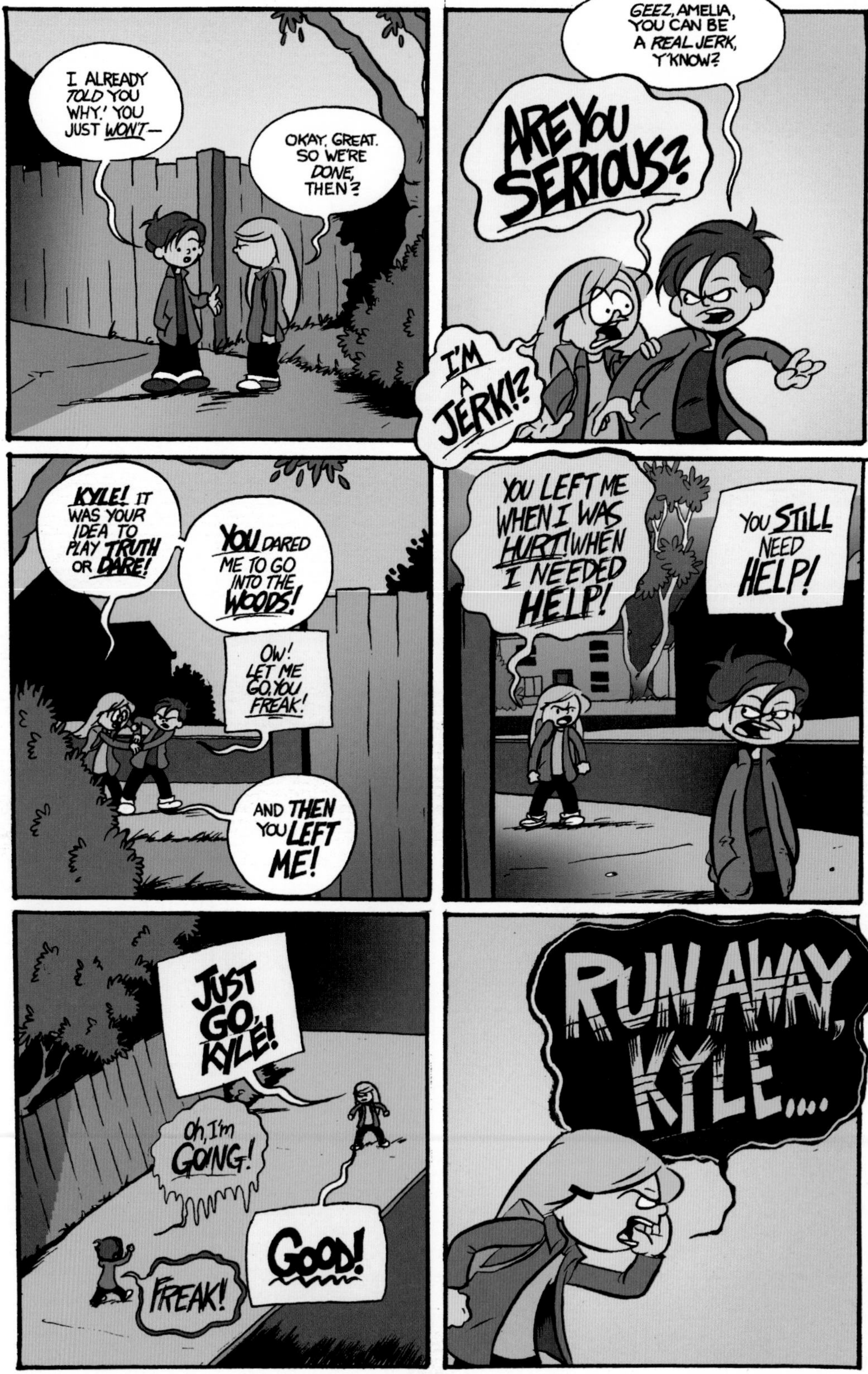
I ALREADY TOLD YOU WHY! YOU JUST WON'T—
OKAY, GREAT. SO WE'RE DONE, THEN?
GEEZ, AMELIA, YOU CAN BE A REAL JERK, Y'KNOW?
ARE YOU SERIOUS?
I'M A JERK!?
KYLE! IT WAS YOUR IDEA TO PLAY TRUTH OR DARE!
YOU DARED ME TO GO INTO THE WOODS!
OW! LET ME GO, YOU FREAK!
AND THEN YOU LEFT ME!
YOU LEFT ME WHEN I WAS HURT! WHEN I NEEDED HELP!
YOU STILL NEED HELP!
JUST GO, KYLE!
Oh, I'm GOING!
GOOD!
FREAK!
RUN AWAY, KYLE...

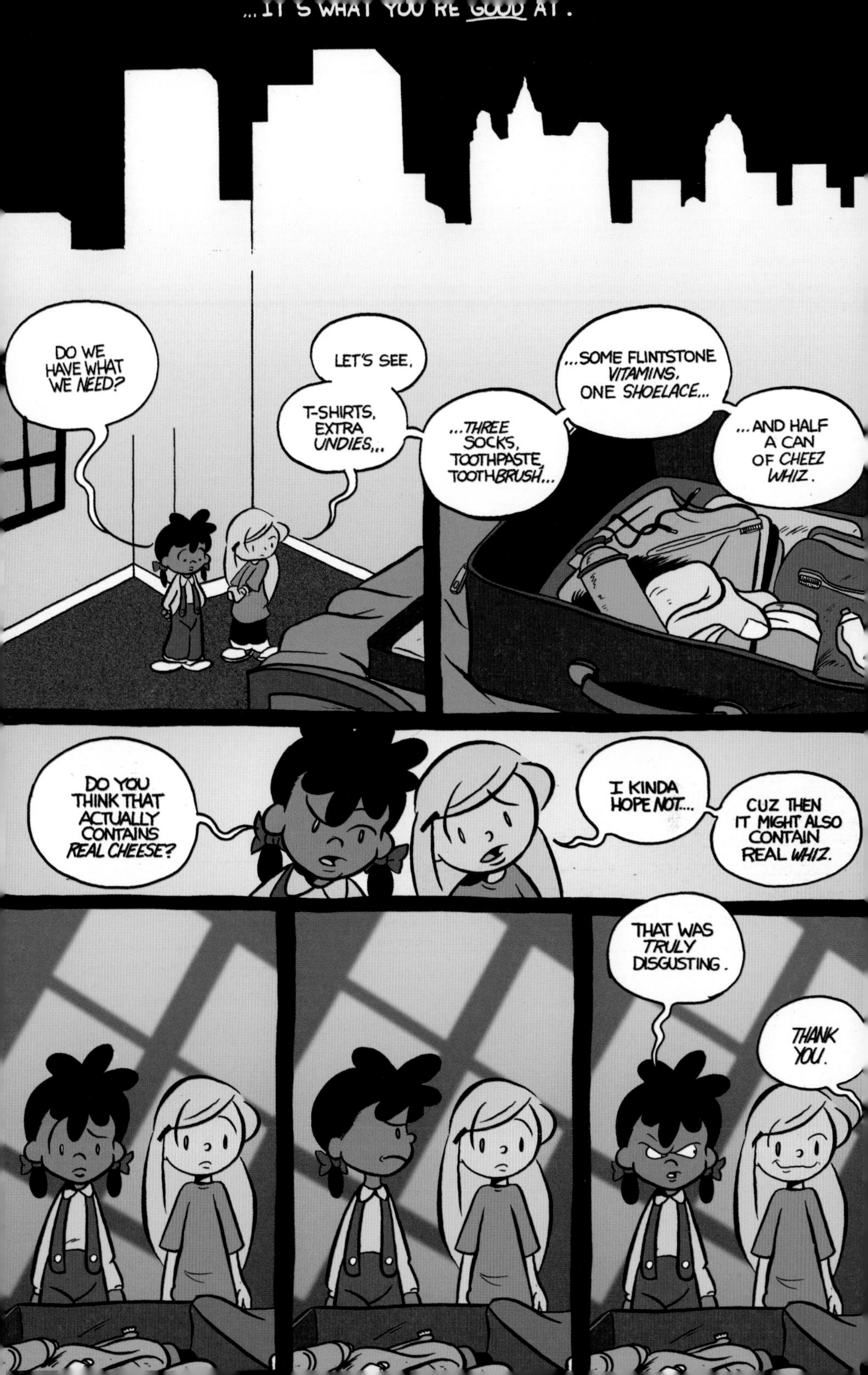
...IT'S WHAT YOU'RE GOOD AT.
DO WE HAVE WHAT WE NEED?
LET'S SEE.
T-SHIRTS, EXTRA UNDIES,...
...THREE SOCKS, TOOTHPASTE, TOOTHBRUSH...
...SOME FLINTSTONE VITAMINS, ONE SHOELACE...
...AND HALF A CAN OF CHEEZ WHIZ.
DO YOU THINK THAT ACTUALLY CONTAINS REAL CHEESE?
I KINDA HOPE NOT....
CUZ THEN IT MIGHT ALSO CONTAIN REAL WHIZ.
THAT WAS TRULY DISGUSTING.
THANK YOU.

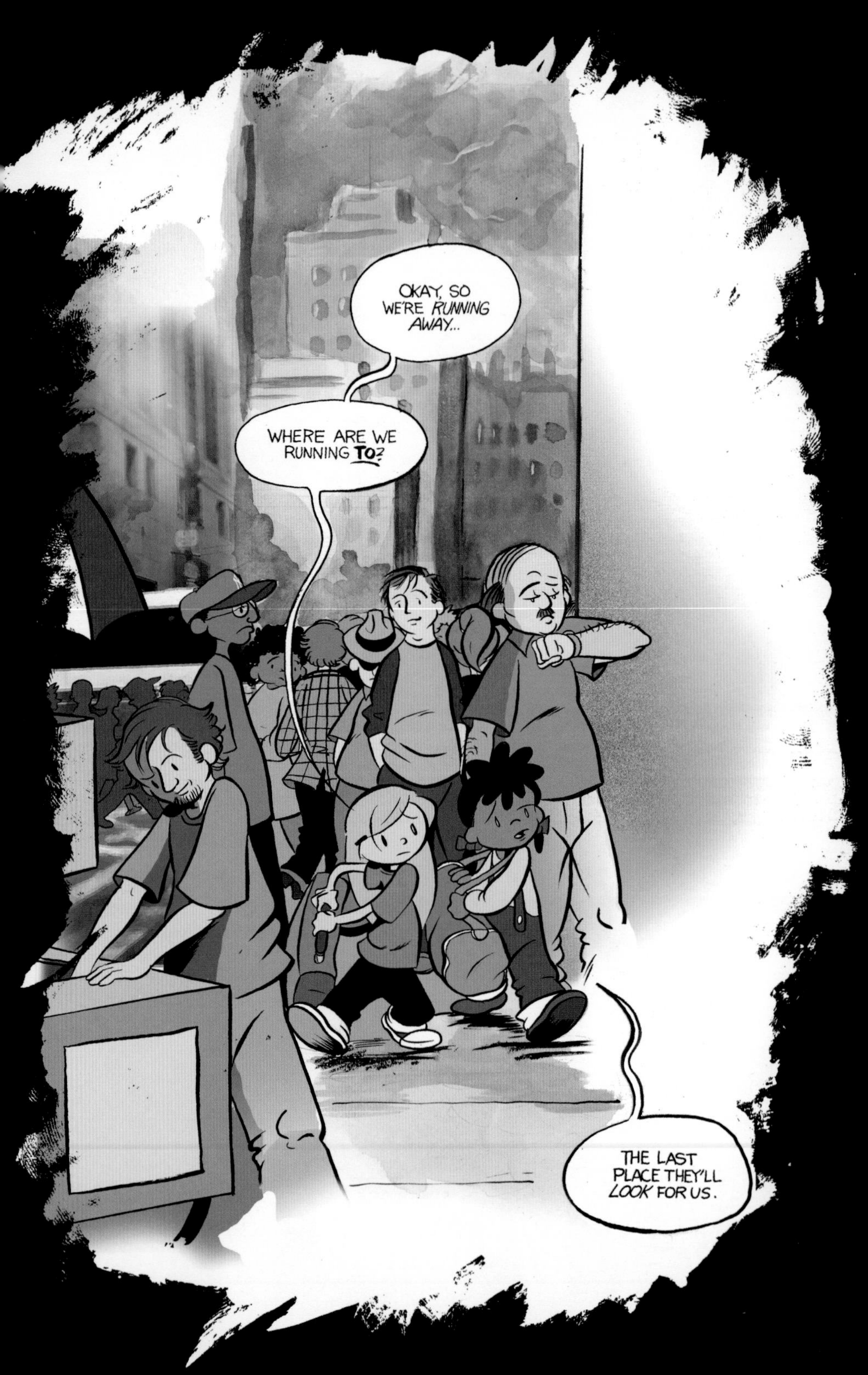
OKAY, SO WE'RE RUNNING AWAY...
WHERE ARE WE RUNNING TO?
THE LAST PLACE THEY'LL LOOK FOR US.

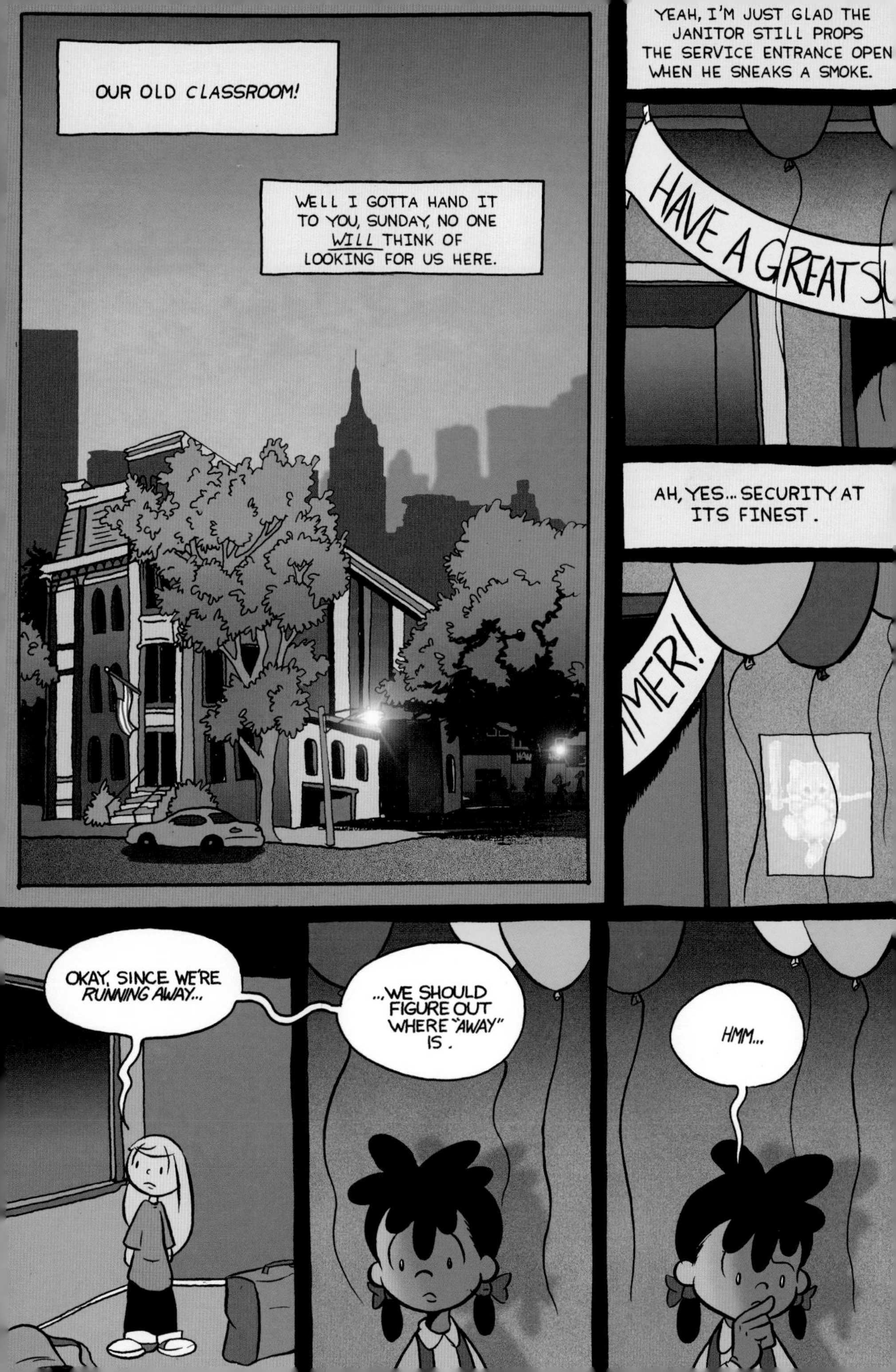
OUR OLD CLASSROOM!
WELL I GOTTA HAND IT TO YOU, SUNDAY, NO ONE WILL THINK OF LOOKING FOR US HERE.
YEAH, I'M JUST GLAD THE JANITOR STILL PROPS THE SERVICE ENTRANCE OPEN WHEN HE SNEAKS A SMOKE.
HAVE A GREAT SU
AH, YES... SECURITY AT ITS FINEST.
MER!
OKAY, SINCE WE'RE RUNNING AWAY...
...WE SHOULD FIGURE OUT WHERE "AWAY" IS.
HMM...

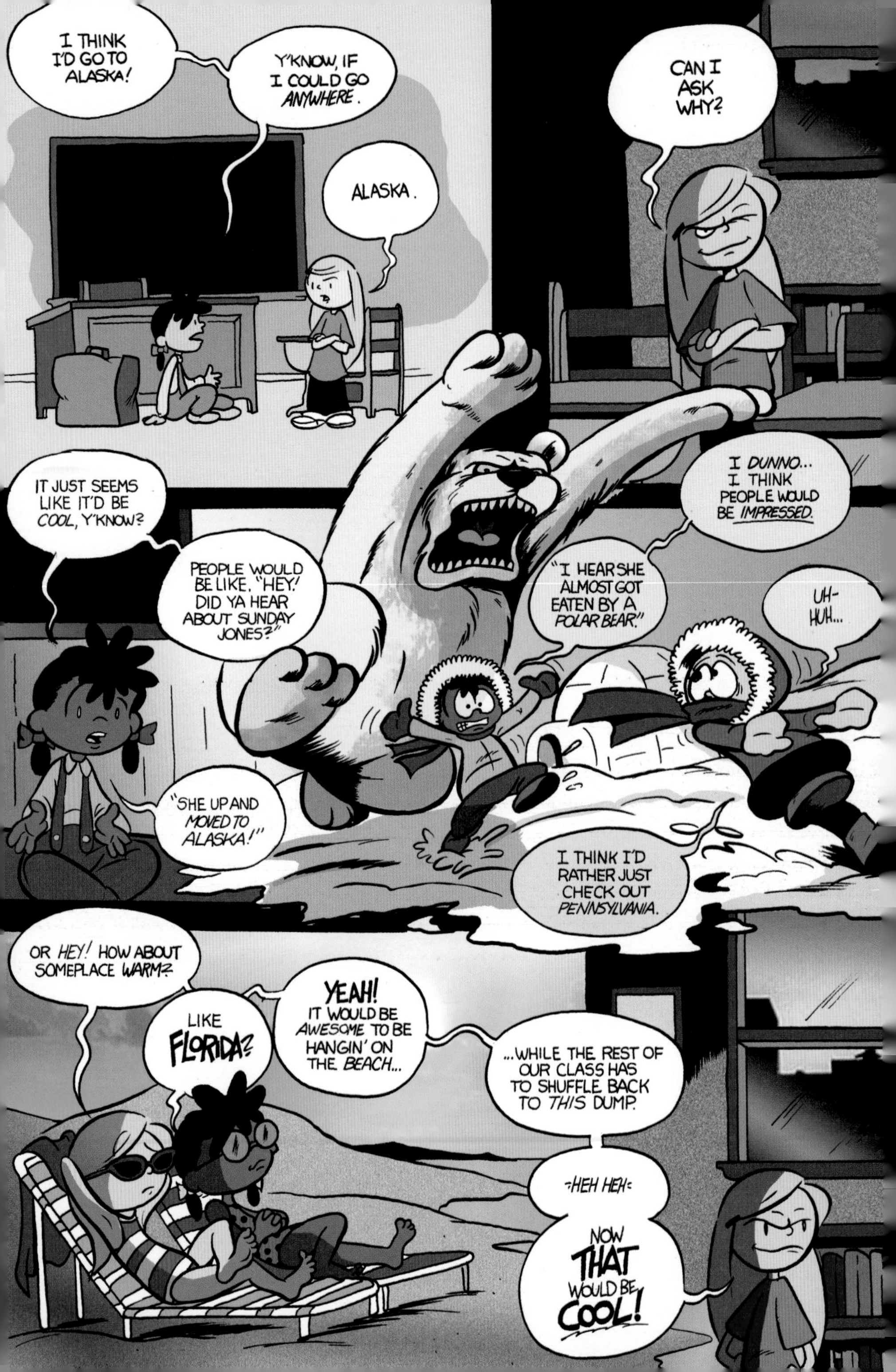
I THINK I'D GO TO ALASKA!
Y'KNOW, IF I COULD GO *ANYWHERE*.
ALASKA.
CAN I ASK WHY?
IT JUST SEEMS LIKE IT'D BE *COOL*, Y'KNOW?
PEOPLE WOULD BE LIKE, "HEY! DID YA HEAR ABOUT SUNDAY JONES?"
"SHE UP AND *MOVED TO ALASKA!*"
"I HEAR SHE ALMOST GOT EATEN BY A *POLAR BEAR*."
UH-HUH...
I *DUNNO*... I THINK PEOPLE WOULD BE *IMPRESSED*.
I THINK I'D RATHER JUST CHECK OUT *PENNSYLVANIA*.
OR *HEY!* HOW ABOUT SOMEPLACE *WARM*?
LIKE FLORIDA?
YEAH! IT WOULD BE *AWESOME* TO BE HANGIN' ON THE *BEACH*...
...WHILE THE REST OF OUR CLASS HAS TO SHUFFLE BACK TO *THIS* DUMP.
HEH HEH
NOW THAT WOULD BE COOL!

WE'D NEVER HAVE TO SEE THOSE *JERKS* AGAIN.

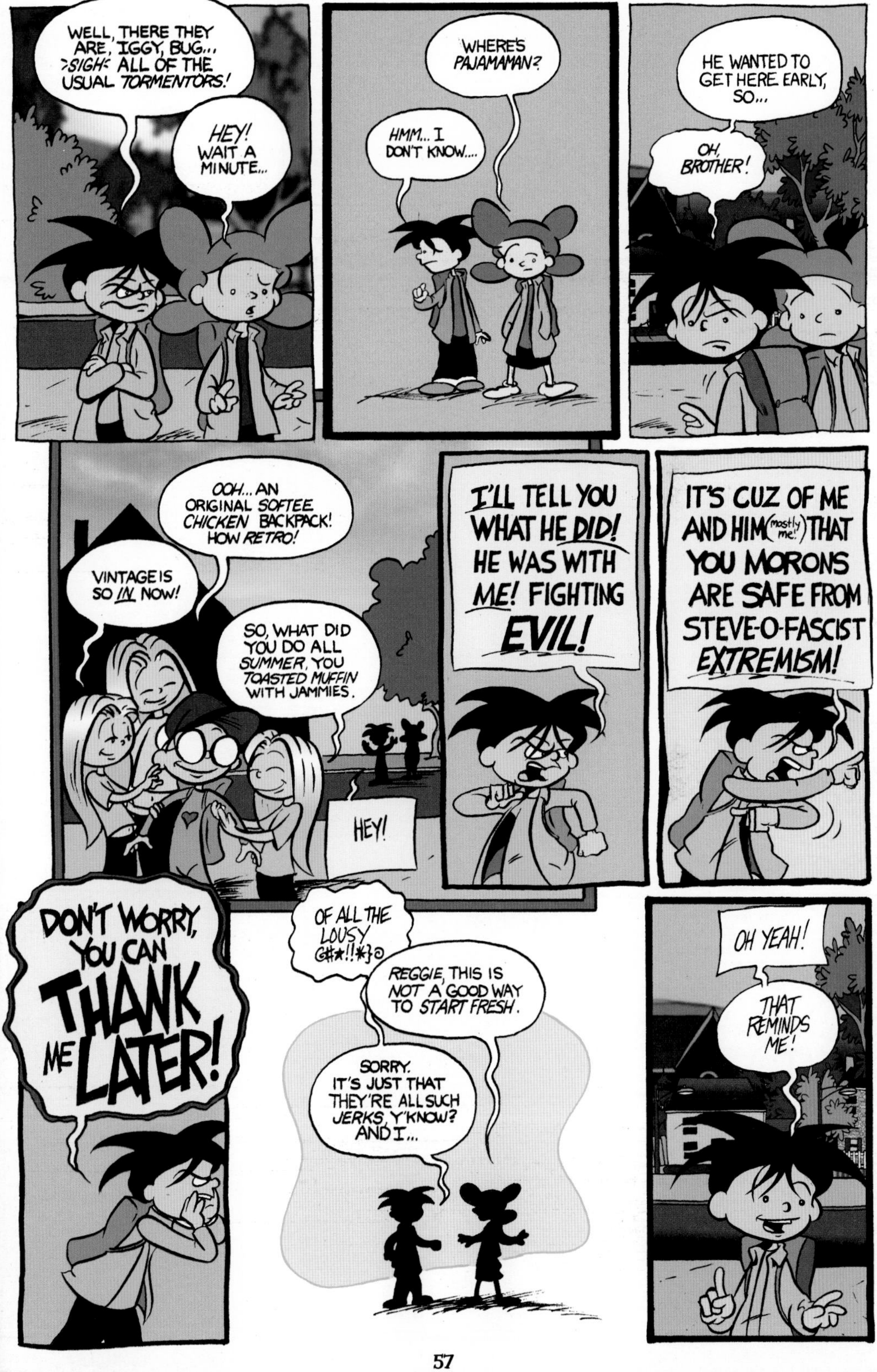

WELL, THERE THEY ARE, IGGY, BUG... >SIGH< ALL OF THE USUAL TORMENTORS!
HEY! WAIT A MINUTE...
WHERE'S PAJAMAMAN?
HMM... I DON'T KNOW....
HE WANTED TO GET HERE EARLY, SO...
OH, BROTHER!
OOH... AN ORIGINAL SOFTEE CHICKEN BACKPACK! HOW RETRO!
VINTAGE IS SO IN NOW!
SO, WHAT DID YOU DO ALL SUMMER, YOU TOASTED MUFFIN WITH JAMMIES.
HEY!
I'LL TELL YOU WHAT HE DID! HE WAS WITH ME! FIGHTING EVIL!
IT'S CUZ OF ME AND HIM (mostly me!) THAT YOU MORONS ARE SAFE FROM STEVE-O-FASCIST EXTREMISM!
DON'T WORRY, YOU CAN THANK ME LATER!
OF ALL THE LOUSY G#★!!✱}☺
REGGIE, THIS IS NOT A GOOD WAY TO START FRESH.
SORRY. IT'S JUST THAT THEY'RE ALL SUCH JERKS, Y'KNOW? AND I...
OH YEAH!
THAT REMINDS ME!

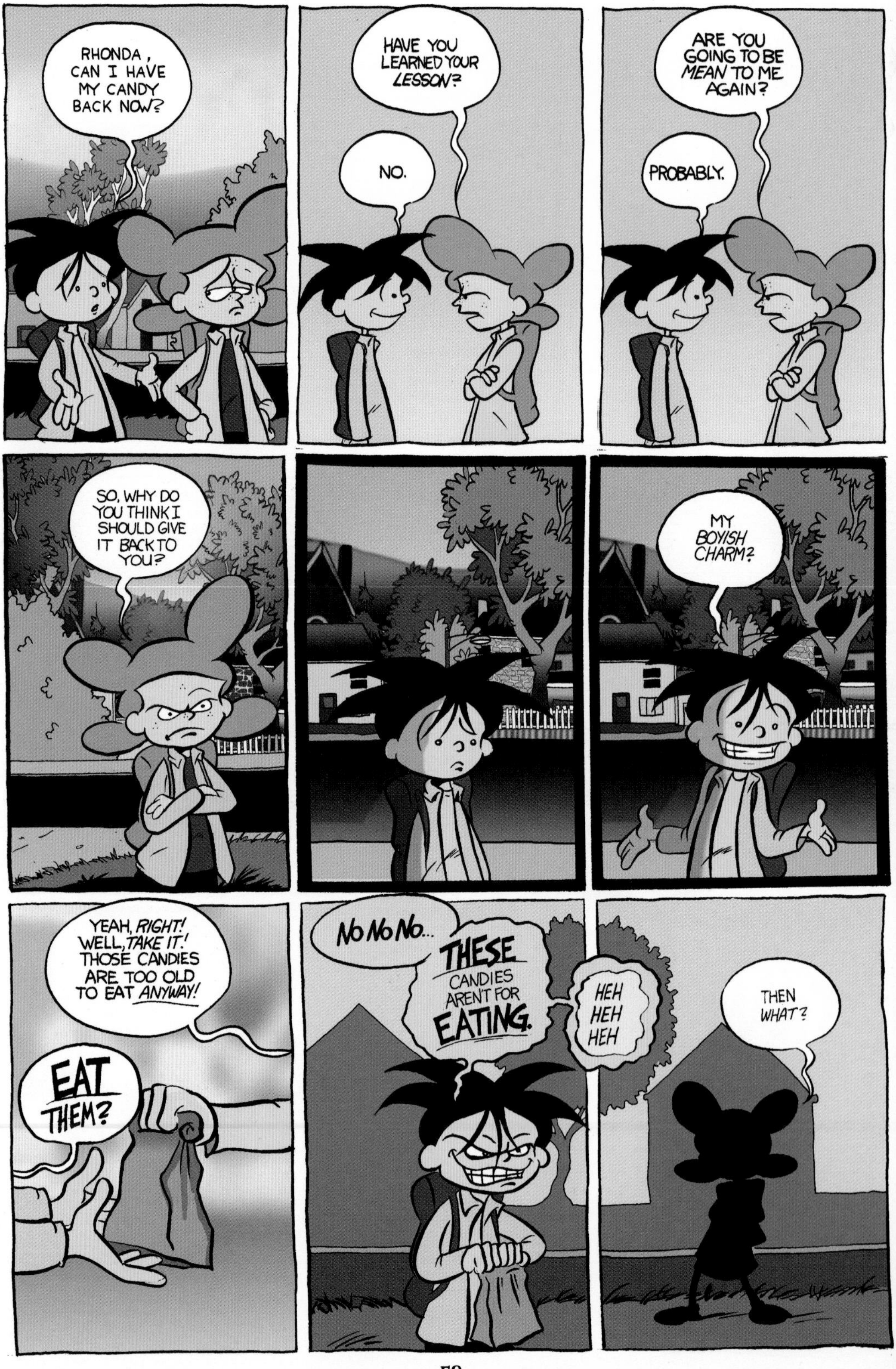
RHONDA, CAN I HAVE MY CANDY BACK NOW?
HAVE YOU LEARNED YOUR LESSON?
NO.
ARE YOU GOING TO BE MEAN TO ME AGAIN?
PROBABLY.
SO, WHY DO YOU THINK I SHOULD GIVE IT BACK TO YOU?
MY BOYISH CHARM?
YEAH, RIGHT! WELL, TAKE IT! THOSE CANDIES ARE TOO OLD TO EAT ANYWAY!
EAT THEM?
No No No...
THESE CANDIES AREN'T FOR EATING.
HEH HEH HEH
THEN WHAT?

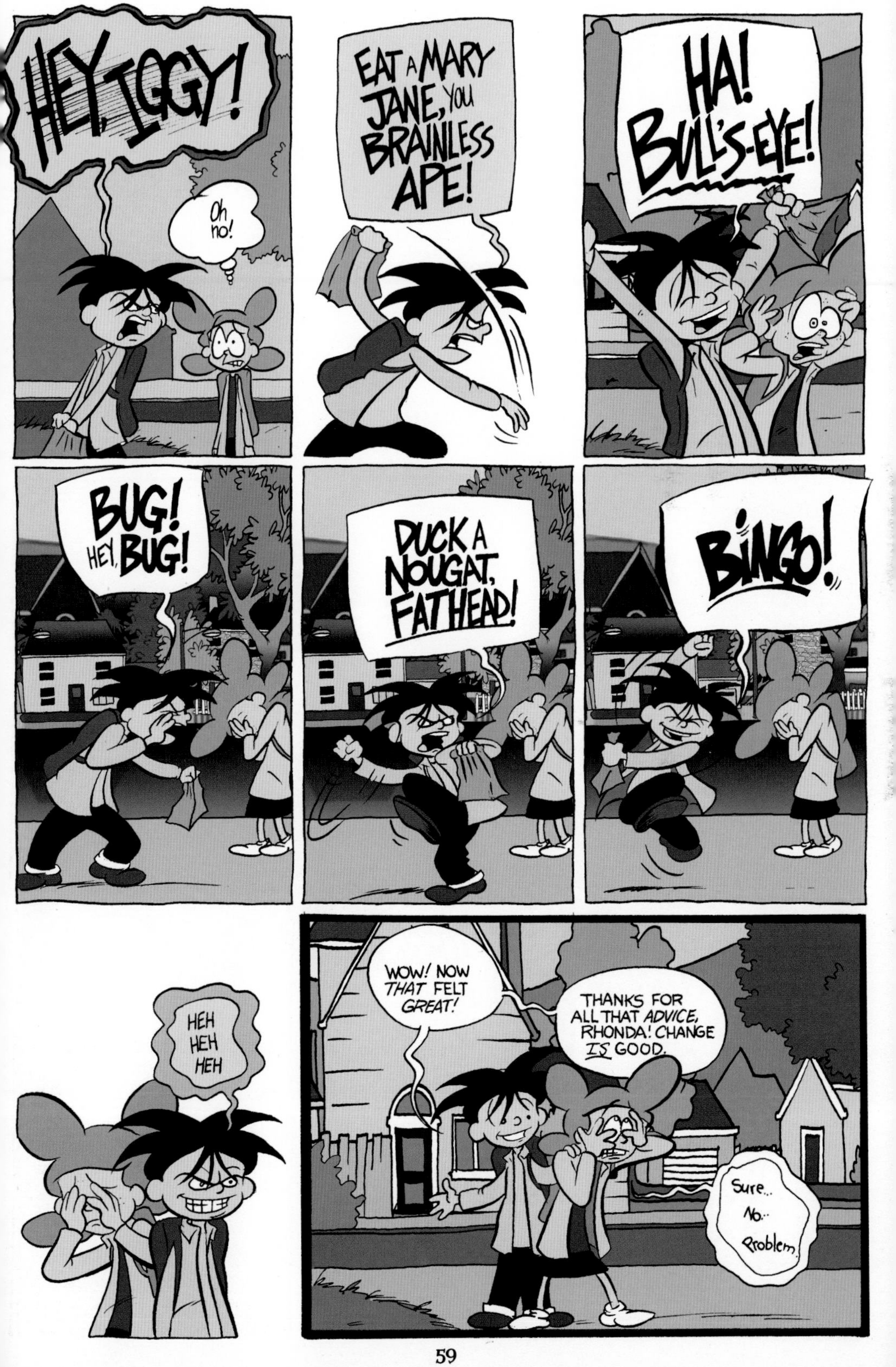

HEY, IGGY!
Oh no!
EAT A MARY JANE, YOU BRAINLESS APE!
HA! BULL'S-EYE!
BUG! HEY, BUG!
DUCK A NOUGAT, FATHEAD!
BINGO!
HEH HEH HEH
WOW! NOW THAT FELT GREAT!
THANKS FOR ALL THAT ADVICE, RHONDA! CHANGE IS GOOD.
Sure.. No.. Problem.

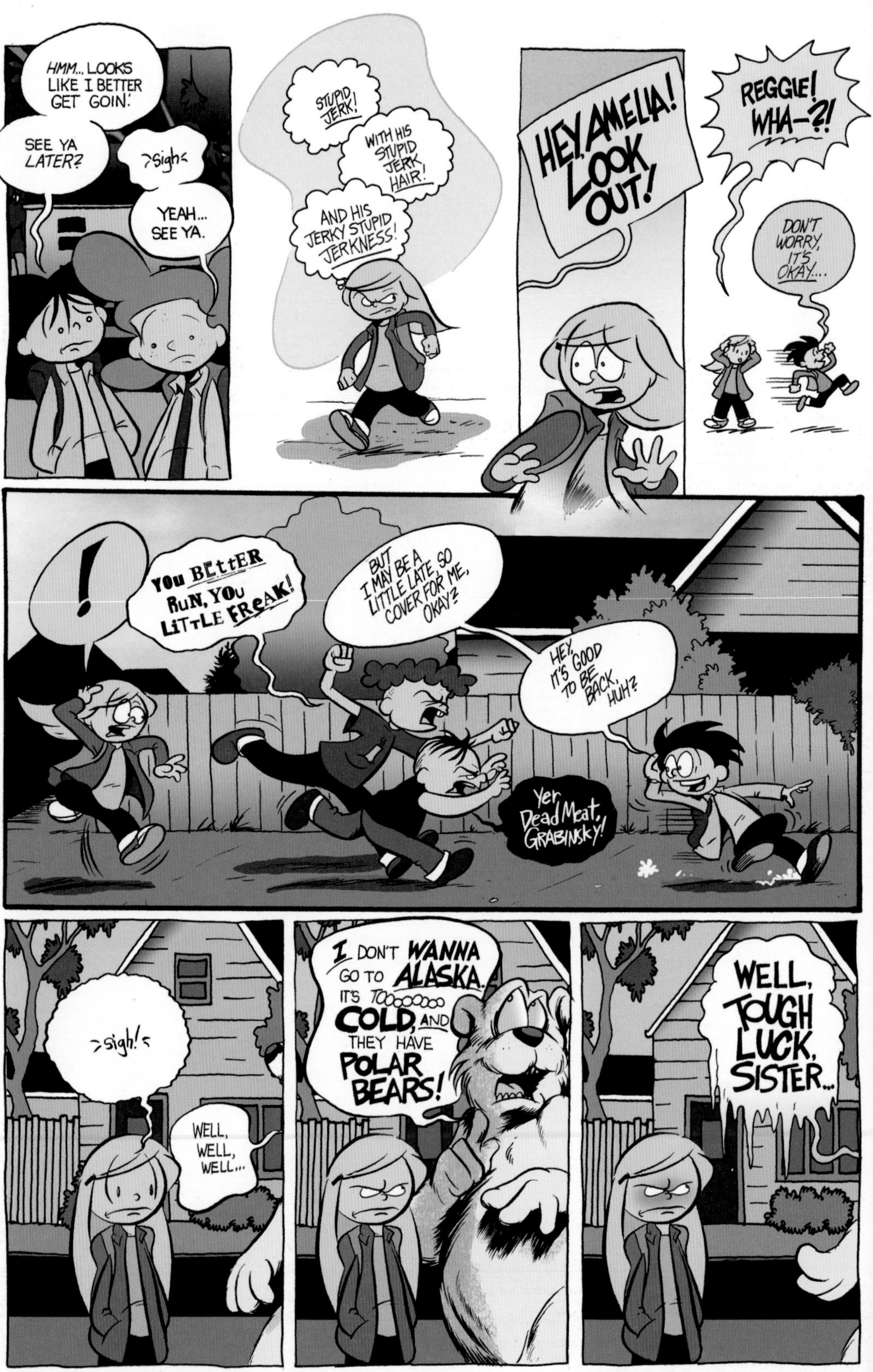
HMM... LOOKS LIKE I BETTER GET GOIN'.
SEE YA LATER?
>sigh<
YEAH... SEE YA.
STUPID JERK!
WITH HIS STUPID JERK HAIR!
AND HIS JERKY STUPID JERKNESS!
HEY, AMELIA! LOOK OUT!
REGGIE! WHA-?!
DON'T WORRY, IT'S OKAY....
!
YOU BETTER RUN, YOU LITTLE FREAK!
BUT I MAY BE A LITTLE LATE, SO COVER FOR ME, OKAY?
HEY, IT'S GOOD TO BE BACK, HUH?
Yer Dead Meat, GRABINSKY!
>sigh!<
WELL, WELL, WELL...
I DON'T WANNA GO TO ALASKA. IT'S TOOOOOOOO COLD, AND THEY HAVE POLAR BEARS!
WELL, TOUGH LUCK, SISTER...

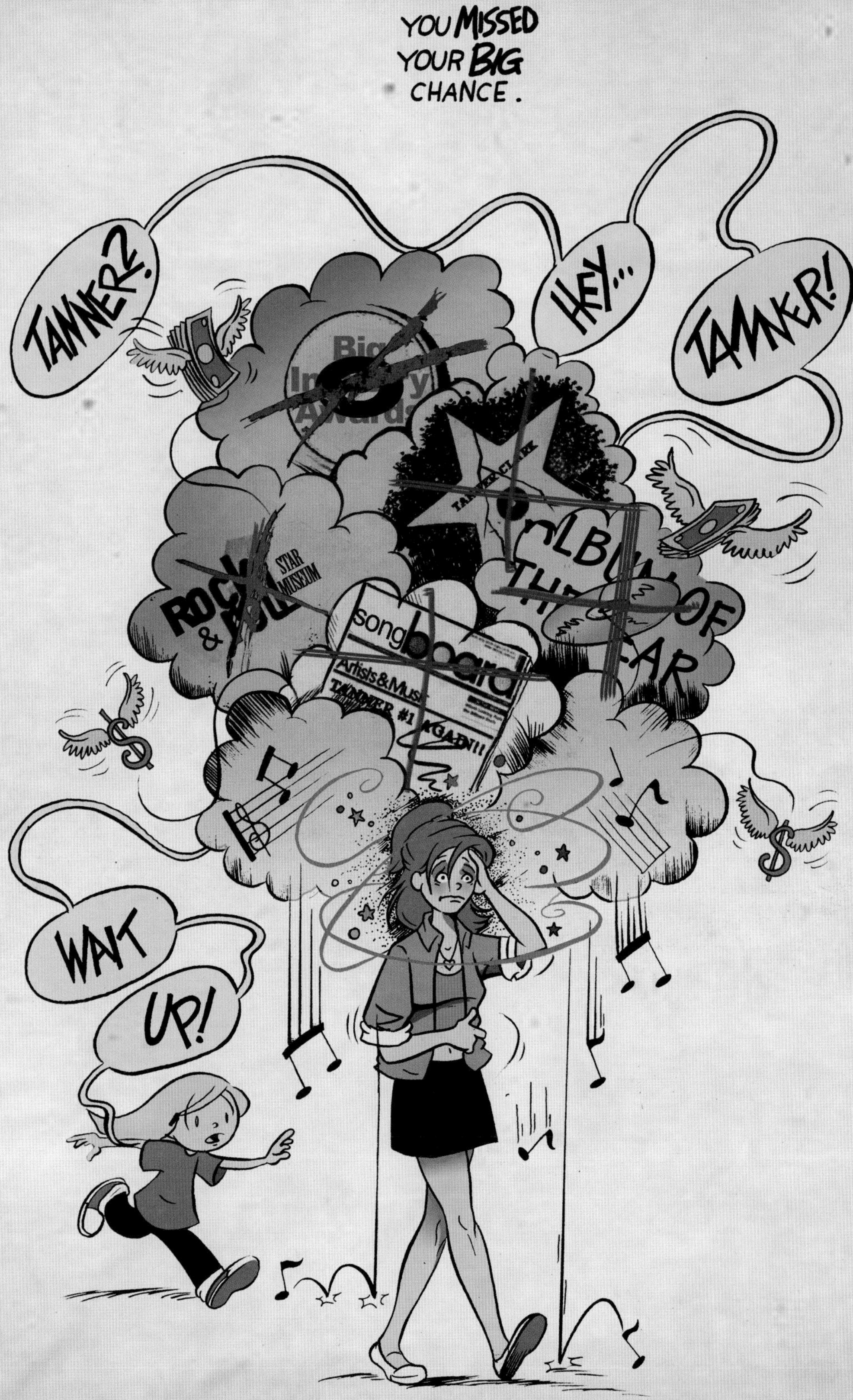
YOU MISSED YOUR BIG CHANCE.
TANNER?
HEY...
TANNER!
WAIT UP!

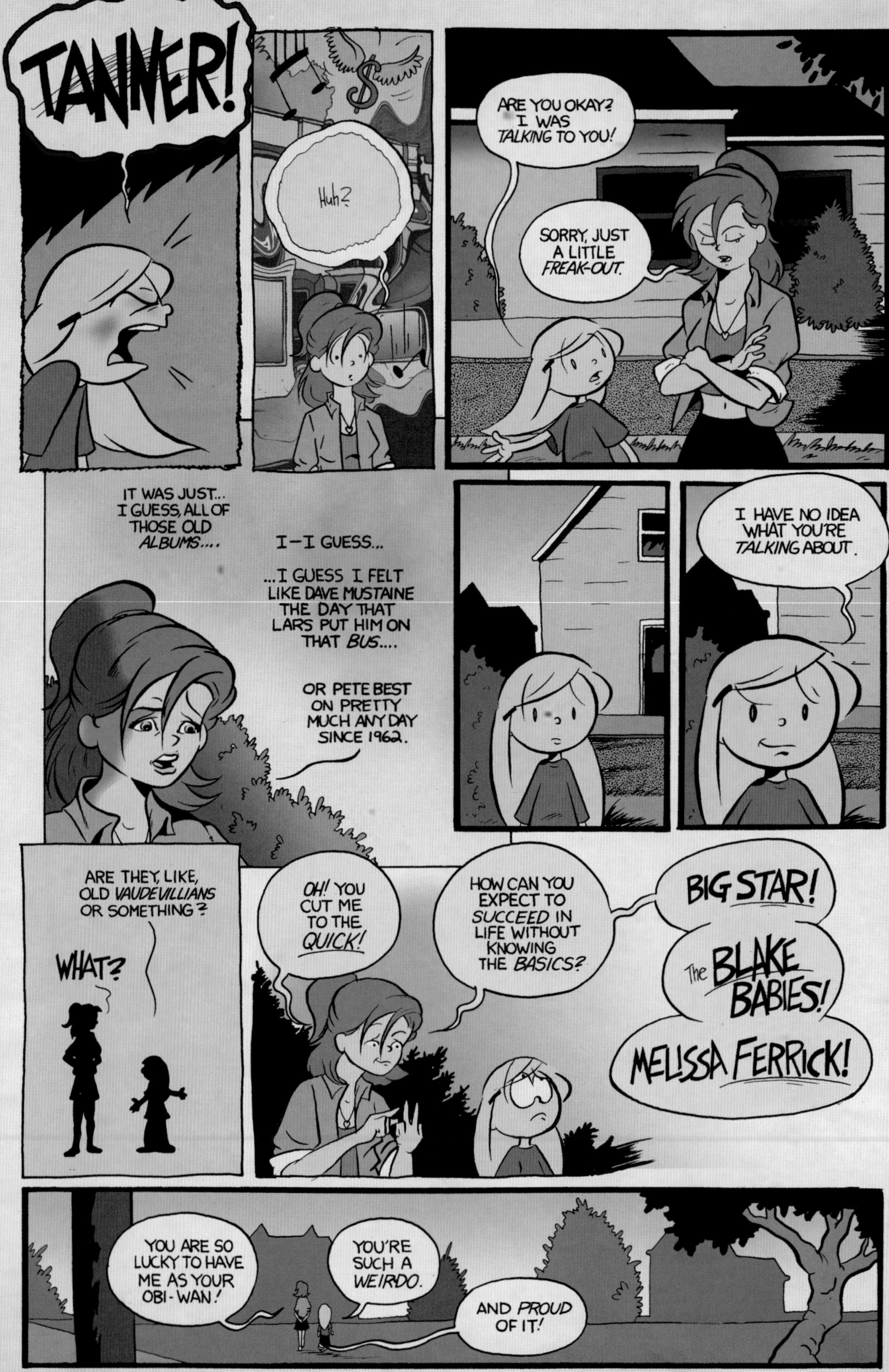
TANNER!
Huh?
ARE YOU OKAY? I WAS TALKING TO YOU!
SORRY, JUST A LITTLE FREAK-OUT.
IT WAS JUST... I GUESS, ALL OF THOSE OLD ALBUMS....
I—I GUESS...
...I GUESS I FELT LIKE DAVE MUSTAINE THE DAY THAT LARS PUT HIM ON THAT BUS....
OR PETE BEST ON PRETTY MUCH ANY DAY SINCE 1962.
I HAVE NO IDEA WHAT YOU'RE TALKING ABOUT.
ARE THEY, LIKE, OLD VAUDEVILLIANS OR SOMETHING?
WHAT?
OH! YOU CUT ME TO THE QUICK!
HOW CAN YOU EXPECT TO SUCCEED IN LIFE WITHOUT KNOWING THE BASICS?
BIG STAR!
The BLAKE BABIES!
MELISSA FERRICK!
YOU ARE SO LUCKY TO HAVE ME AS YOUR OBI-WAN!
YOU'RE SUCH A WEIRDO.
AND PROUD OF IT!

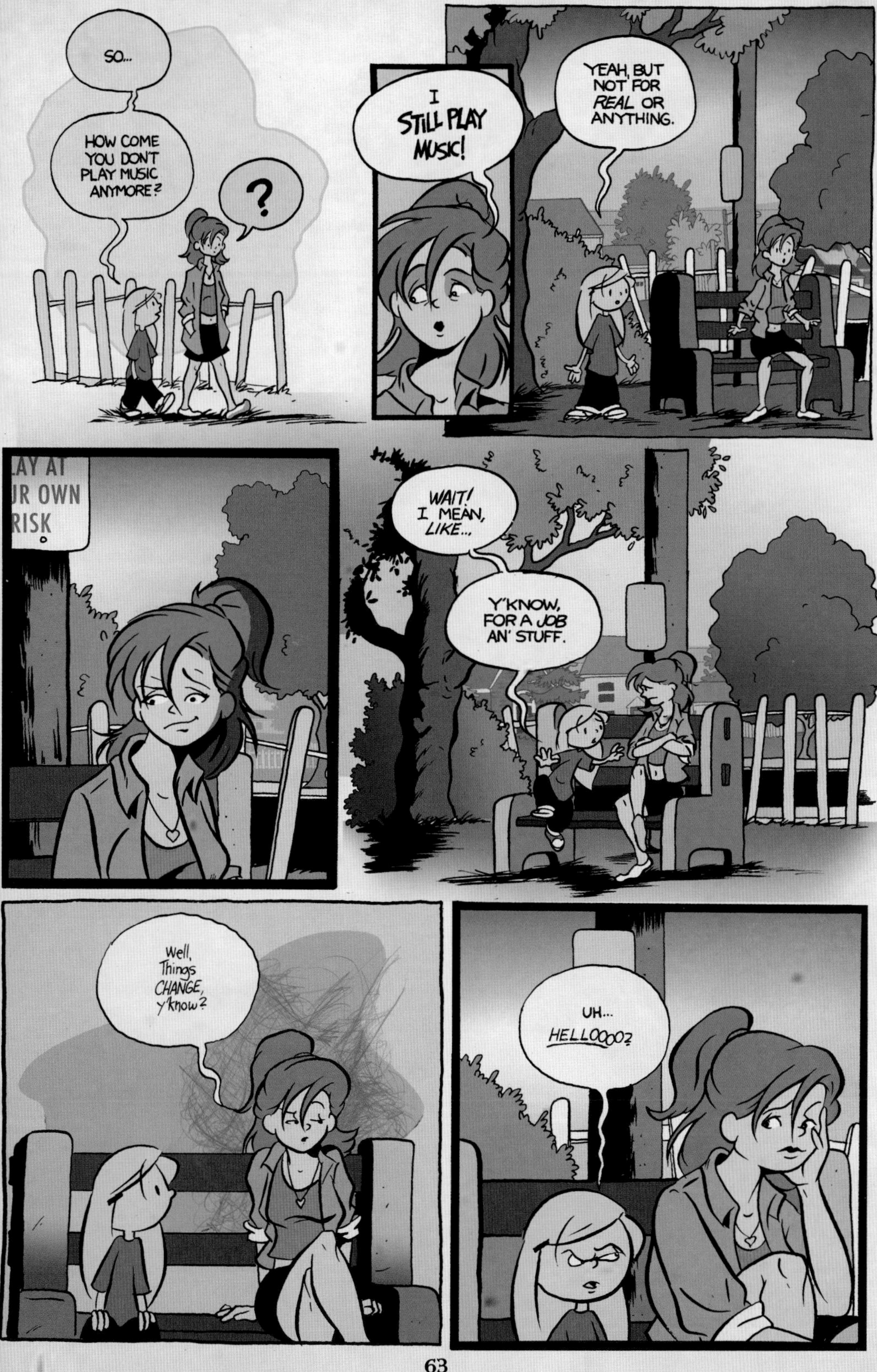
SO...
HOW COME YOU DON'T PLAY MUSIC ANYMORE?
?
I STILL PLAY MUSIC!
YEAH, BUT NOT FOR REAL OR ANYTHING.
LAY AT UR OWN RISK
WAIT! I MEAN, LIKE...
Y'KNOW, FOR A JOB AN' STUFF.
Well, Things CHANGE, y'know?
UH... HELLOOOO?

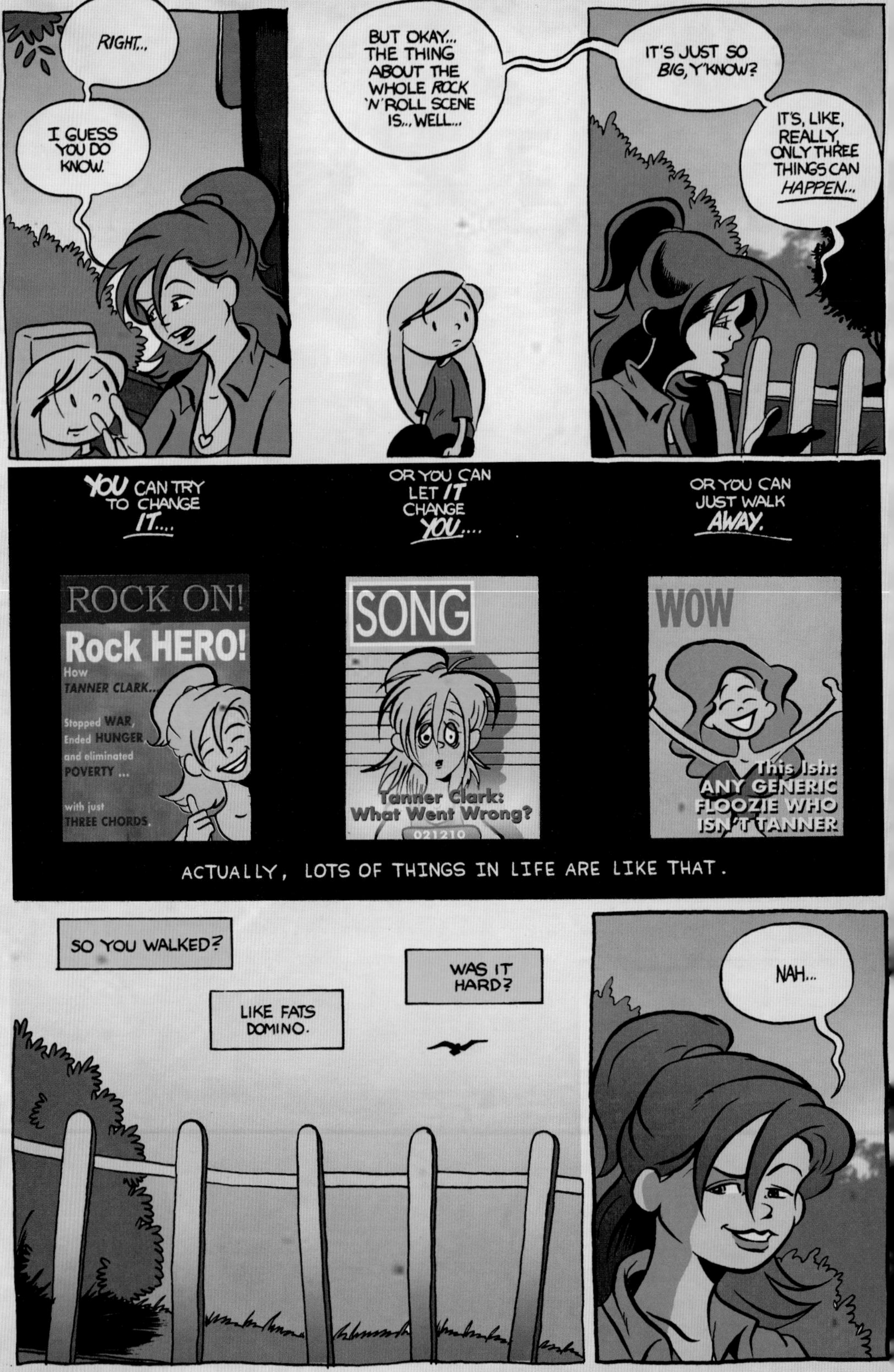
RIGHT...
I GUESS YOU DO KNOW.
BUT OKAY... THE THING ABOUT THE WHOLE ROCK 'N' ROLL SCENE IS... WELL...
IT'S JUST SO BIG, Y'KNOW?
IT'S, LIKE, REALLY, ONLY THREE THINGS CAN HAPPEN...
YOU CAN TRY TO CHANGE IT....
ROCK ON!
Rock HERO!
How TANNER CLARK...
Stopped WAR, Ended HUNGER, and eliminated POVERTY ...
with just THREE CHORDS.
OR YOU CAN LET IT CHANGE YOU....
SONG
Tanner Clark: What Went Wrong?
021210
OR YOU CAN JUST WALK AWAY.
WOW
This Ish: ANY GENERIC FLOOZIE WHO ISN'T TANNER
ACTUALLY, LOTS OF THINGS IN LIFE ARE LIKE THAT.
SO YOU WALKED?
LIKE FATS DOMINO.
WAS IT HARD?
NAH...

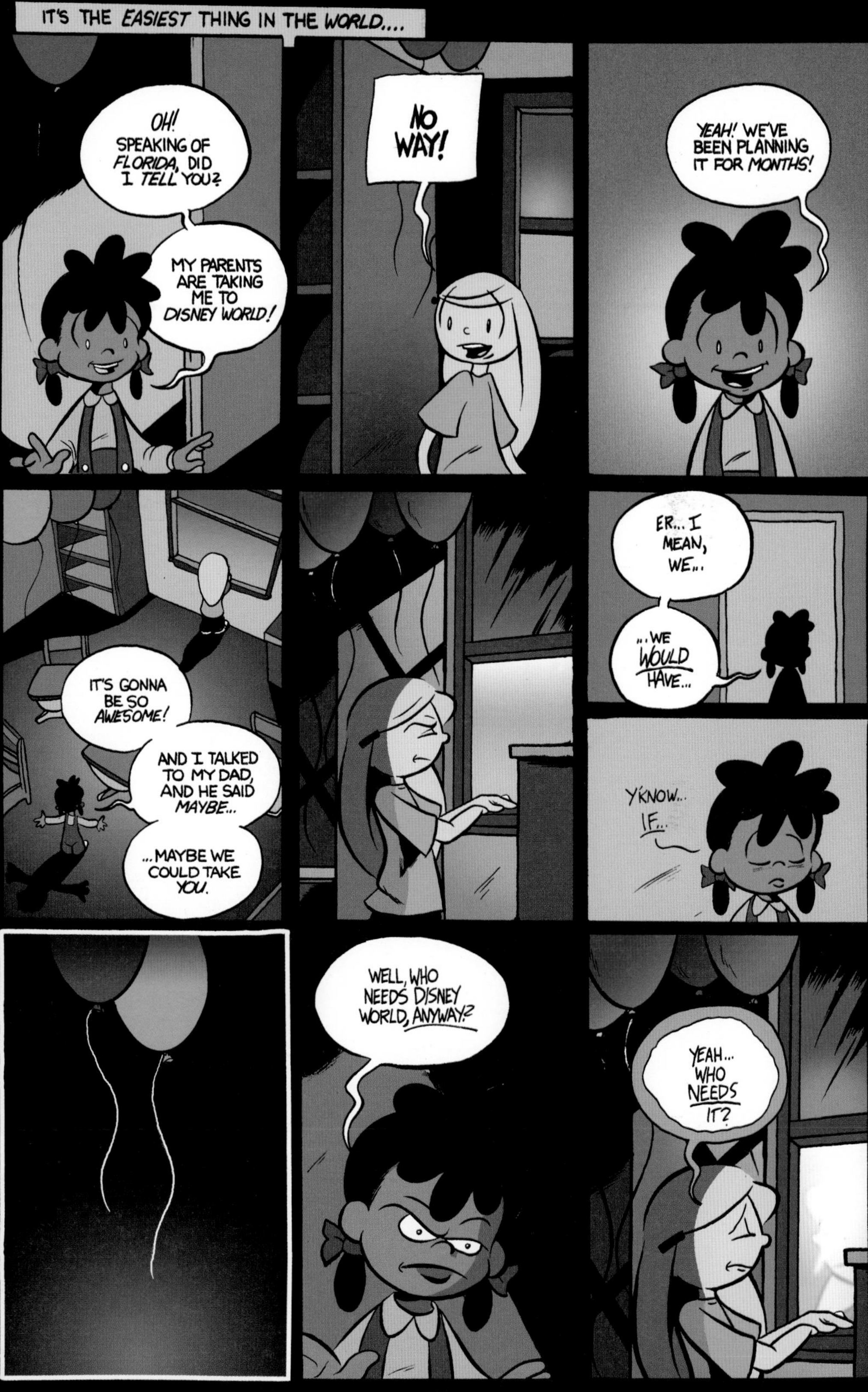
IT'S THE EASIEST THING IN THE WORLD....
OH! SPEAKING OF FLORIDA, DID I TELL YOU?
MY PARENTS ARE TAKING ME TO DISNEY WORLD!
NO WAY!
YEAH! WE'VE BEEN PLANNING IT FOR MONTHS!
IT'S GONNA BE SO AWESOME!
AND I TALKED TO MY DAD, AND HE SAID MAYBE...
...MAYBE WE COULD TAKE YOU.
ER... I MEAN, WE...
...WE WOULD HAVE...
Y'KNOW... IF...
WELL, WHO NEEDS DISNEY WORLD, ANYWAY?
YEAH... WHO NEEDS IT?

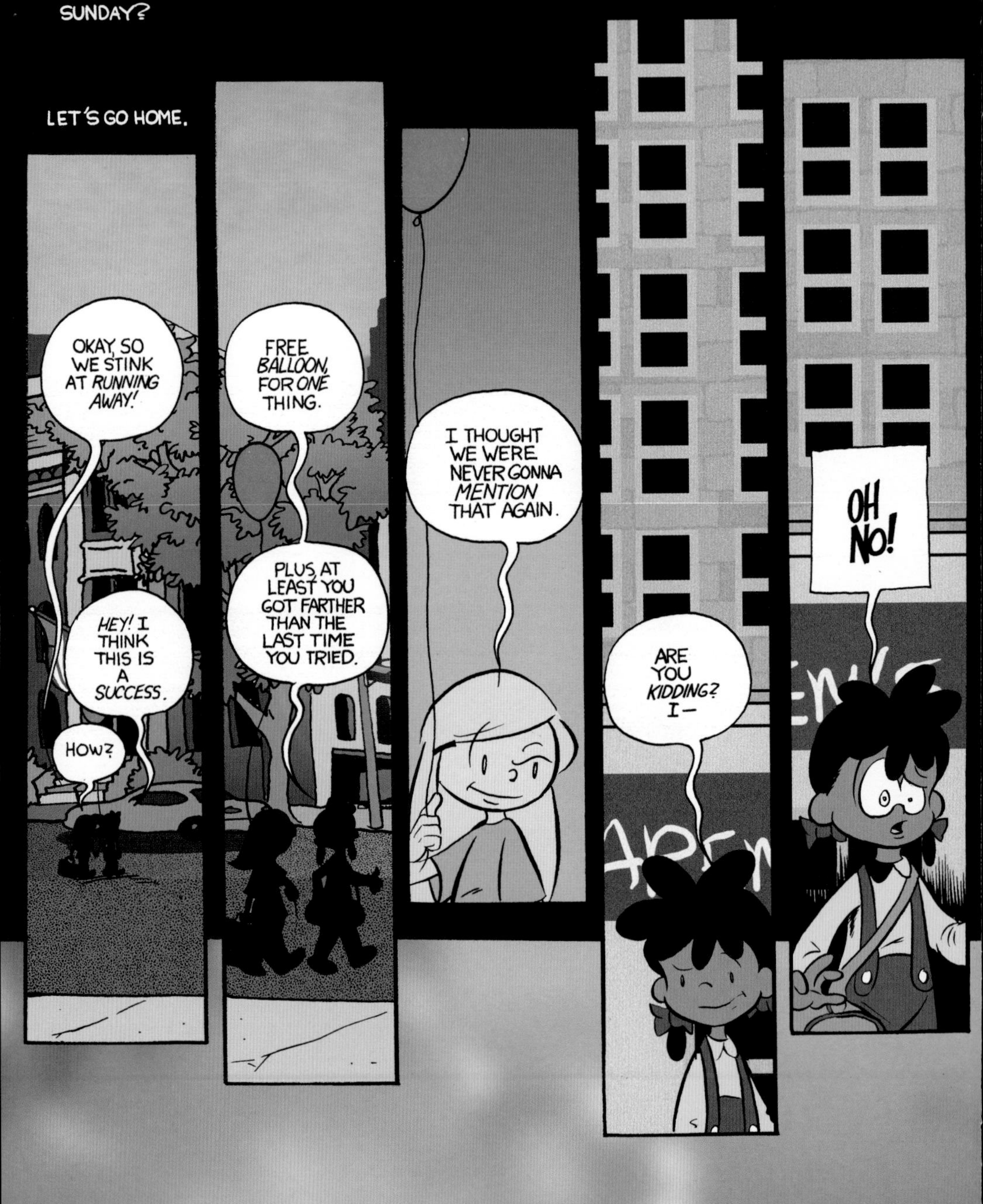
SUNDAY?
LET'S GO HOME.
OKAY, SO WE STINK AT RUNNING AWAY!
HEY! I THINK THIS IS A SUCCESS.
HOW?
FREE BALLOON, FOR ONE THING.
PLUS, AT LEAST YOU GOT FARTHER THAN THE LAST TIME YOU TRIED.
I THOUGHT WE WERE NEVER GONNA MENTION THAT AGAIN.
ARE YOU KIDDING? I—
OH NO!

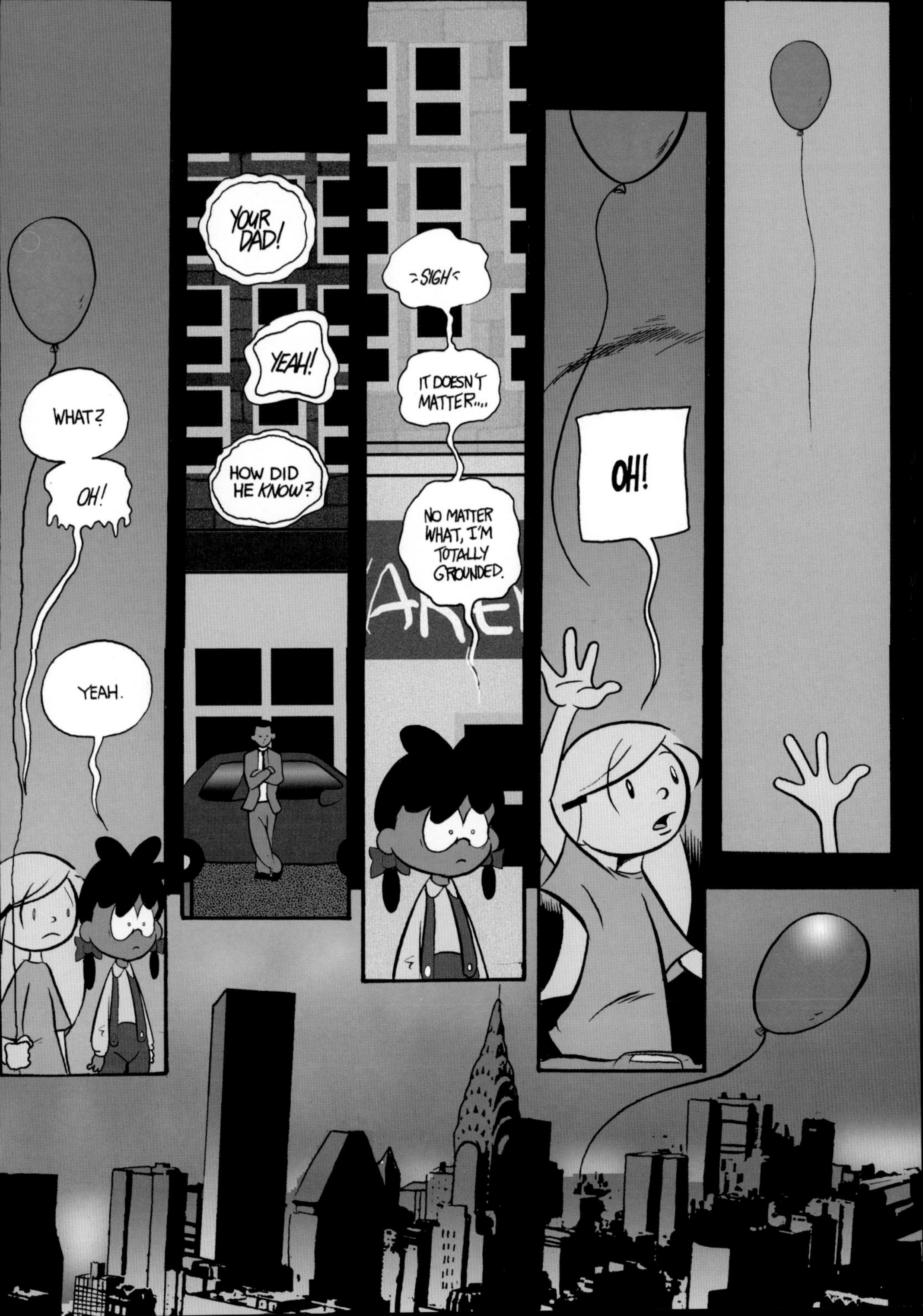
WHAT?
OH!
YEAH.
YOUR DAD!
YEAH!
HOW DID HE KNOW?
SIGH
IT DOESN'T MATTER....
NO MATTER WHAT, I'M TOTALLY GROUNDED.
OH!

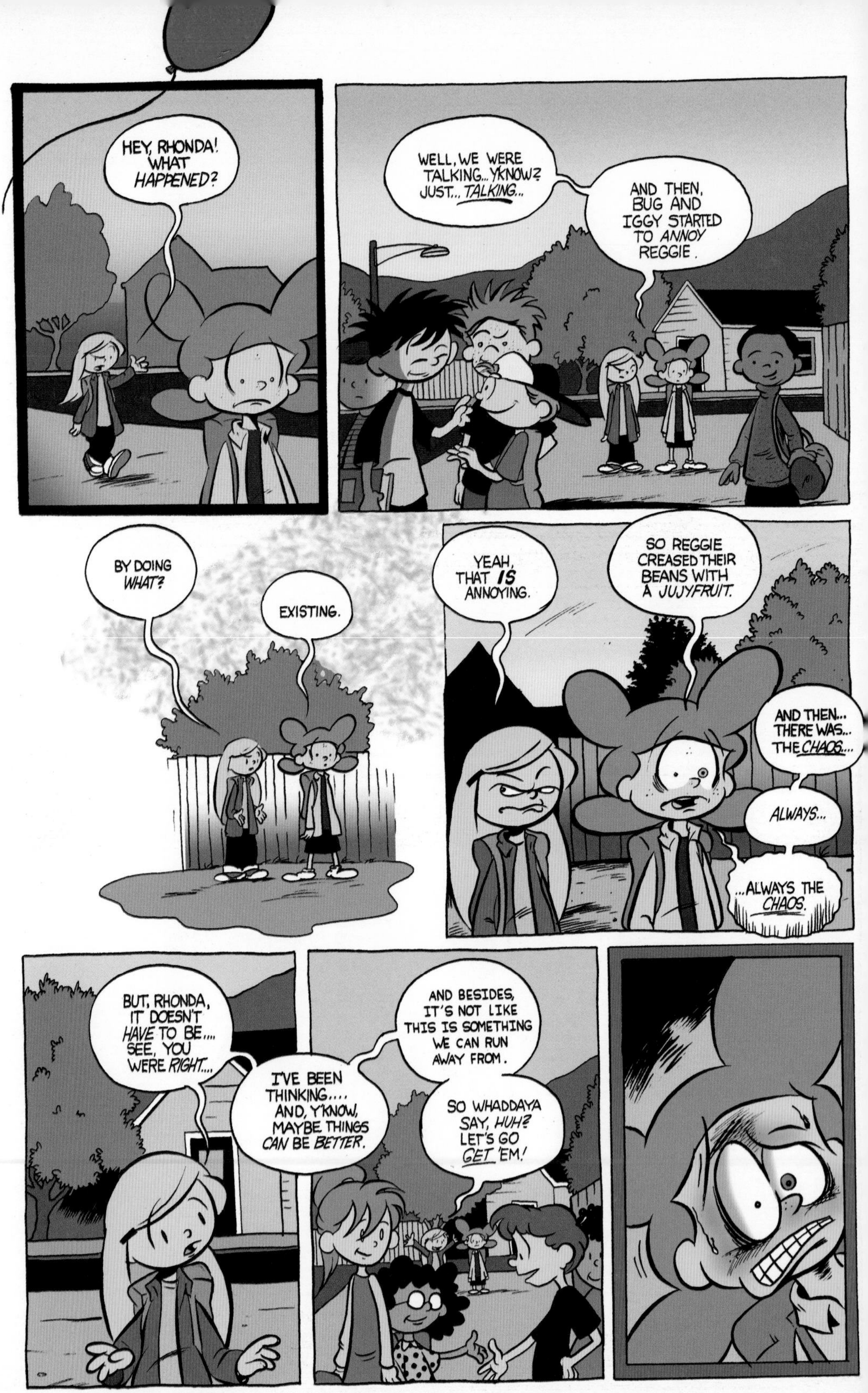
HEY, RHONDA! WHAT HAPPENED?
WELL, WE WERE TALKING... Y'KNOW? JUST... TALKING...
AND THEN, BUG AND IGGY STARTED TO ANNOY REGGIE.
BY DOING WHAT?
EXISTING.
YEAH, THAT IS ANNOYING.
SO REGGIE CREASED THEIR BEANS WITH A JUJYFRUIT.
AND THEN... THERE WAS... THE CHAOS....
ALWAYS...
...ALWAYS THE CHAOS.
BUT, RHONDA, IT DOESN'T HAVE TO BE.... SEE, YOU WERE RIGHT....
I'VE BEEN THINKING.... AND, Y'KNOW, MAYBE THINGS CAN BE BETTER.
AND BESIDES, IT'S NOT LIKE THIS IS SOMETHING WE CAN RUN AWAY FROM.
SO WHADDAYA SAY, HUH? LET'S GO GET 'EM!

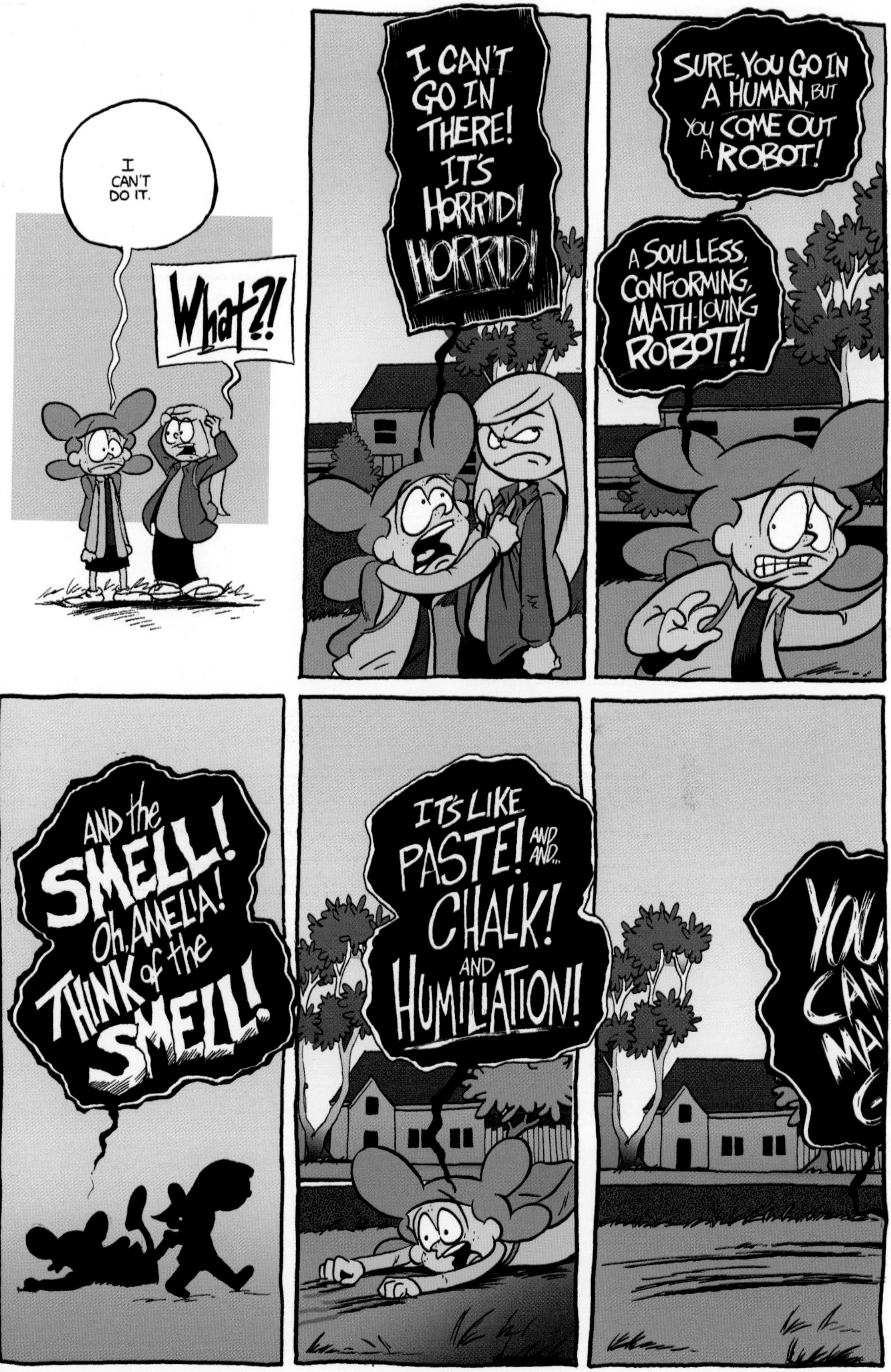
I CAN'T DO IT.
What?!
I CAN'T GO IN THERE! IT'S HORRID! HORRID!
SURE, YOU GO IN A HUMAN, BUT YOU COME OUT A ROBOT!
A SOULLESS, CONFORMING, MATH-LOVING ROBOT!!
AND the SMELL! Oh, AMELIA! THINK of the SMELL!
IT'S LIKE PASTE! AND AND... CHALK! AND HUMILIATION!

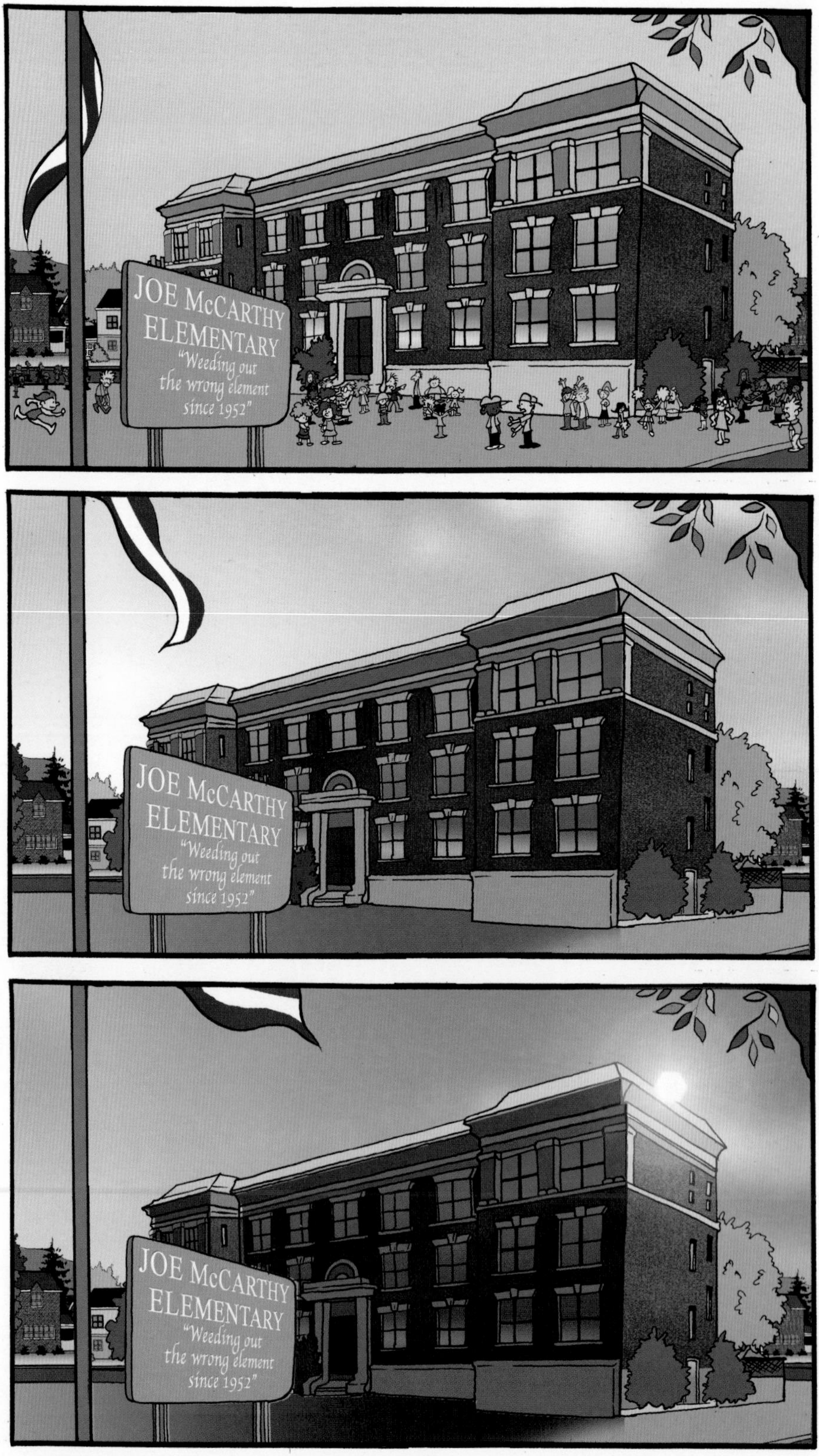
JOE McCARTHY
ELEMENTARY
"Weeding out
the wrong element
since 1952"
JOE McCARTHY
ELEMENTARY
"Weeding out
the wrong element
since 1952"
JOE McCARTHY
ELEMENTARY
"Weeding out
the wrong element
since 1952"

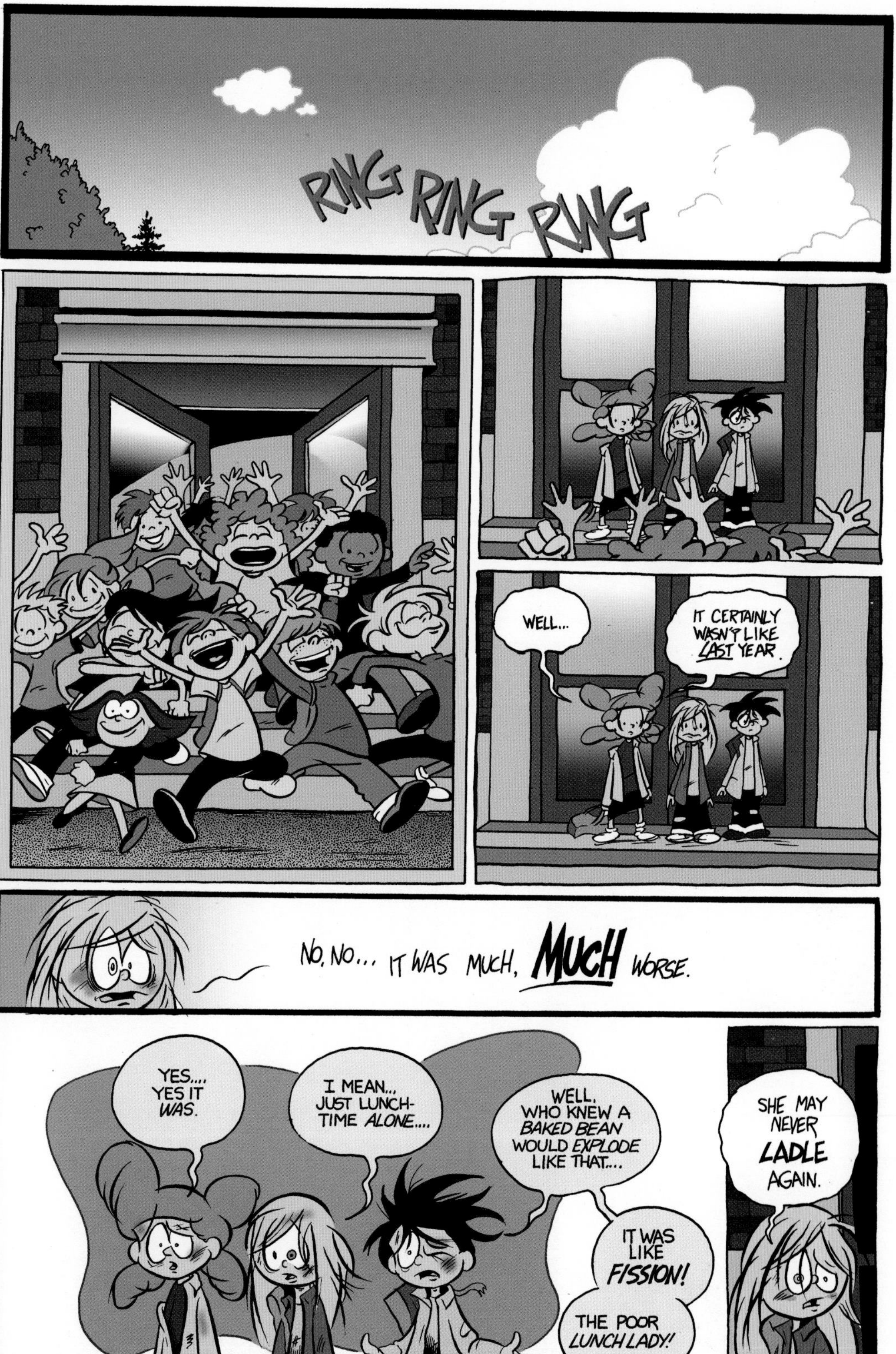

RING RING RING
WELL...
IT CERTAINLY WASN'T LIKE LAST YEAR.
NO, NO... IT WAS MUCH, MUCH WORSE.
YES..., YES IT WAS.
I MEAN.., JUST LUNCH-TIME ALONE....
WELL. WHO KNEW A BAKED BEAN WOULD EXPLODE LIKE THAT....
IT WAS LIKE FISSION!
THE POOR LUNCH LADY!
SHE MAY NEVER LADLE AGAIN.

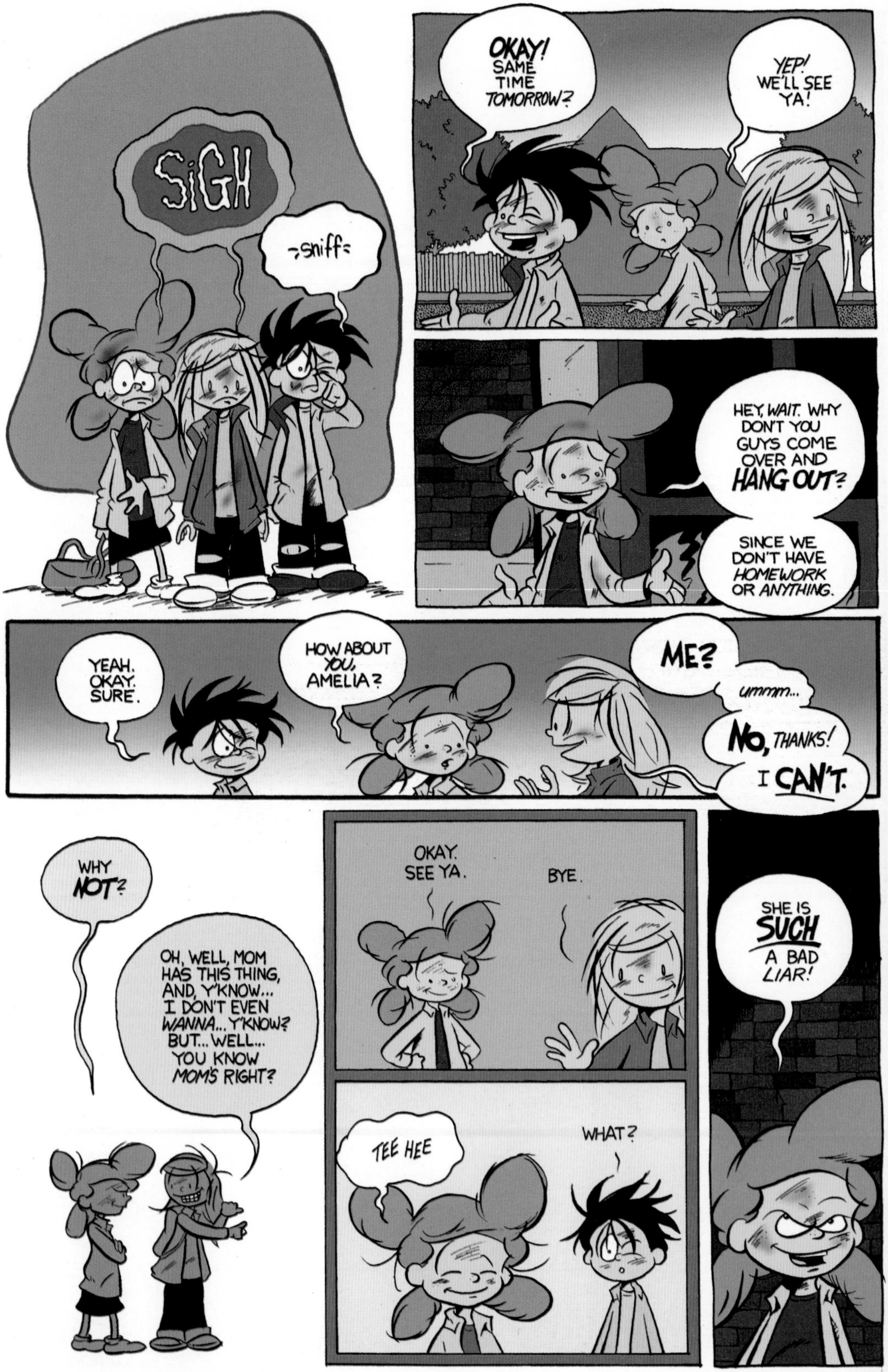
SiGH
~sniff~
OKAY! SAME TIME TOMORROW?
YEP! WE'LL SEE YA!
HEY, WAIT. WHY DON'T YOU GUYS COME OVER AND HANG OUT?
SINCE WE DON'T HAVE HOMEWORK OR ANYTHING.
YEAH. OKAY. SURE.
HOW ABOUT YOU, AMELIA?
ME?
ummm...
NO, THANKS!
I CAN'T.
WHY NOT?
OH, WELL, MOM HAS THIS THING, AND, Y'KNOW... I DON'T EVEN WANNA... Y'KNOW? BUT... WELL... YOU KNOW MOM'S RIGHT?
OKAY. SEE YA.
BYE.
TEE HEE
WHAT?
SHE IS SUCH A BAD LIAR!

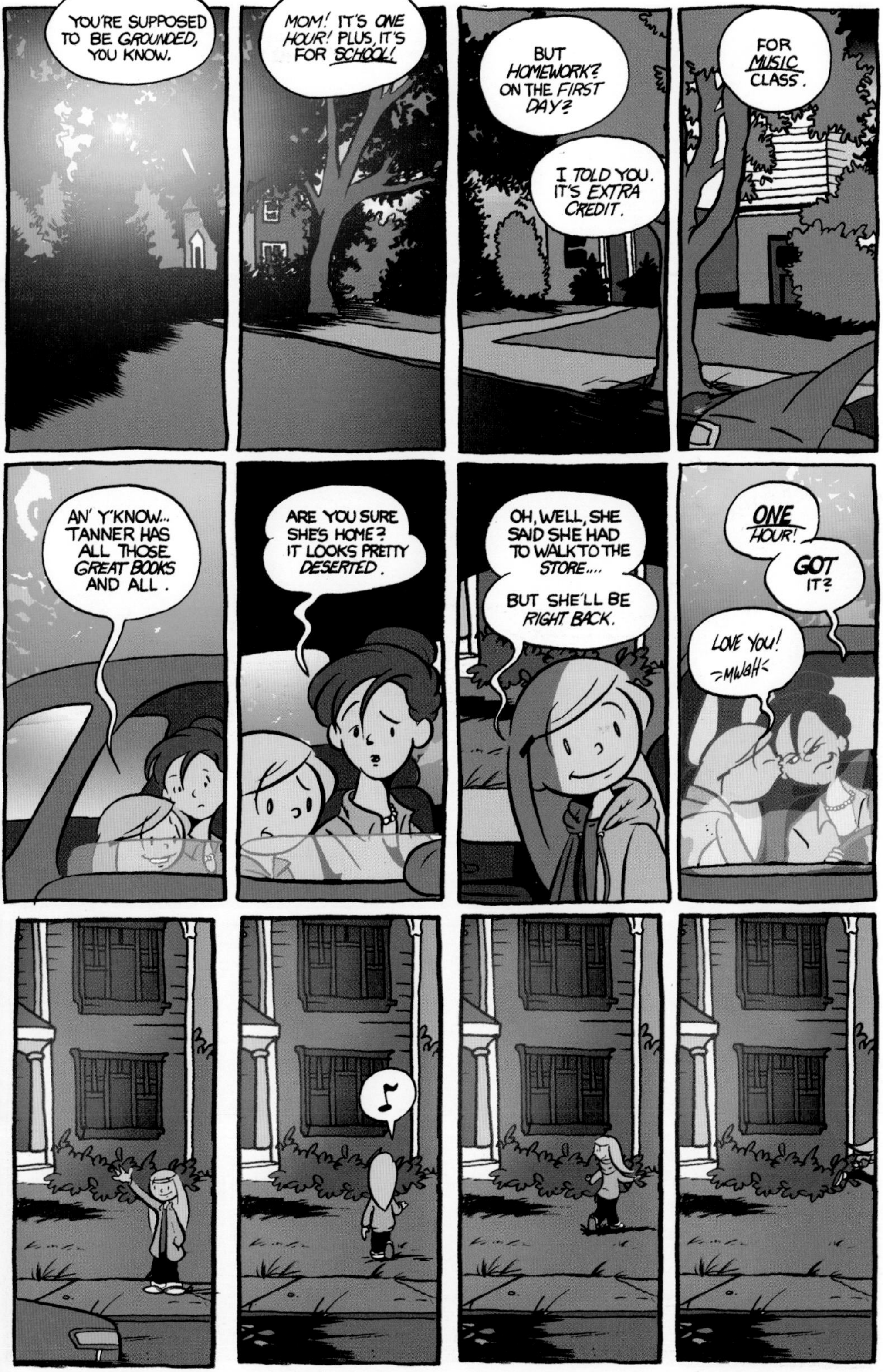
YOU'RE SUPPOSED TO BE GROUNDED, YOU KNOW.
MOM! IT'S ONE HOUR! PLUS, IT'S FOR SCHOOL!
BUT HOMEWORK? ON THE FIRST DAY?
I TOLD YOU. IT'S EXTRA CREDIT.
FOR MUSIC CLASS.
AN' Y'KNOW... TANNER HAS ALL THOSE GREAT BOOKS AND ALL.
ARE YOU SURE SHE'S HOME? IT LOOKS PRETTY DESERTED.
OH, WELL, SHE SAID SHE HAD TO WALK TO THE STORE....
BUT SHE'LL BE RIGHT BACK.
ONE HOUR!
GOT IT?
LOVE YOU! -MWAH-

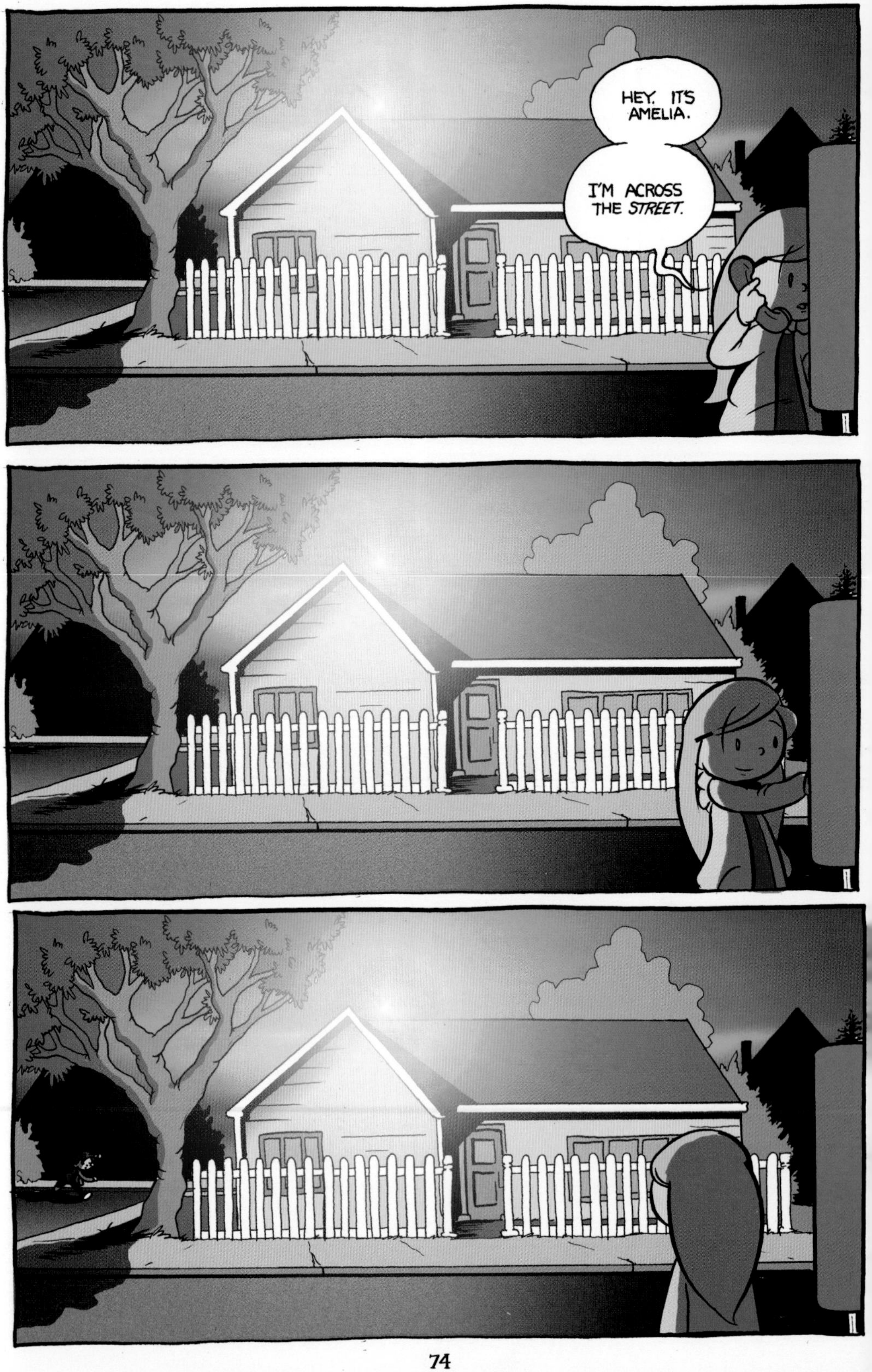
HEY. IT'S AMELIA.
I'M ACROSS THE *STREET*.

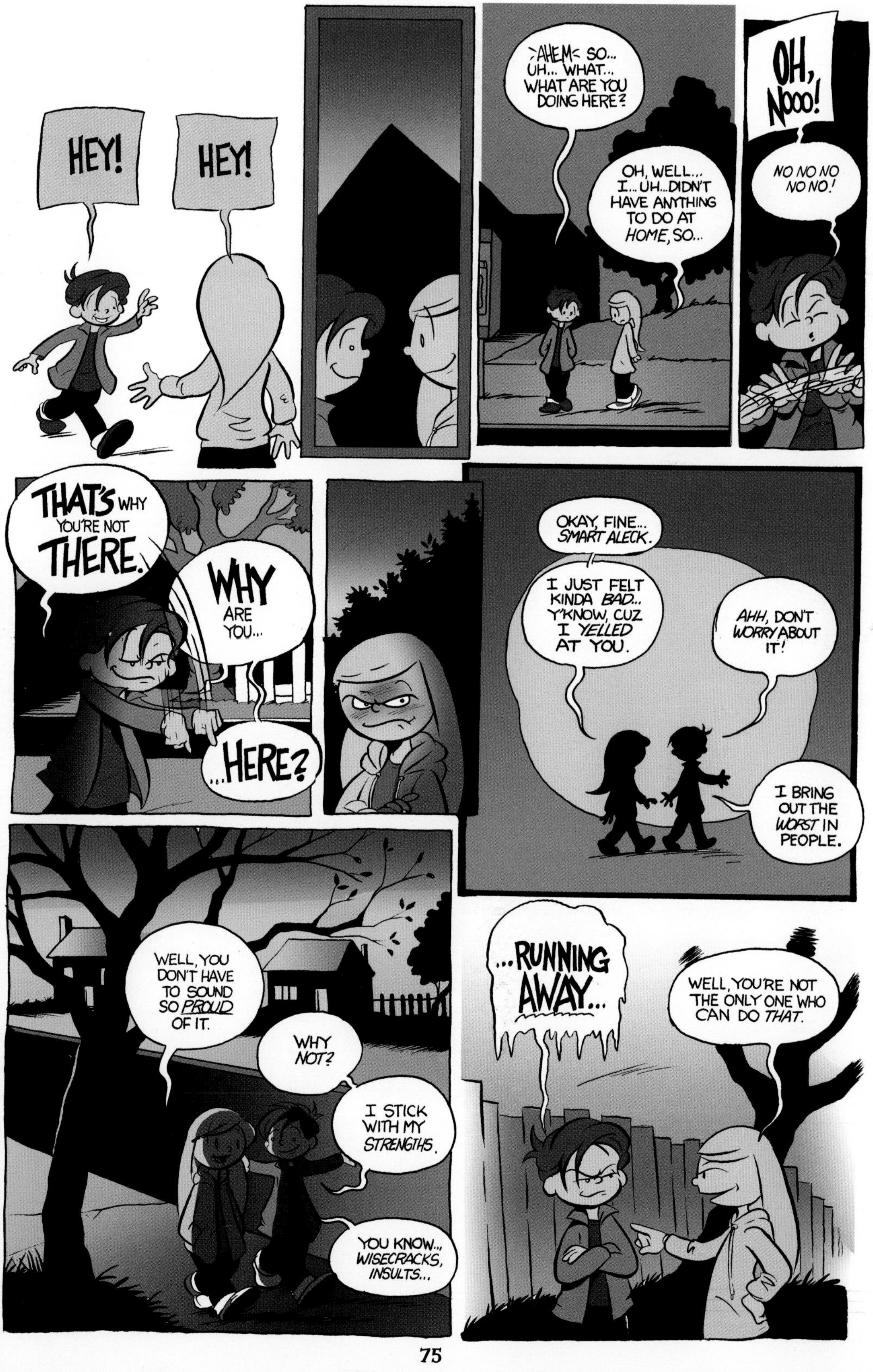
HEY!
HEY!
>AHEM< SO... UH... WHAT... WHAT ARE YOU DOING HERE?
OH, WELL... I... UH... DIDN'T HAVE ANYTHING TO DO AT HOME, SO...
OH, NOOO!
NO NO NO NO NO!
THAT'S WHY YOU'RE NOT THERE.
WHY ARE YOU...
...HERE?
OKAY, FINE... SMART ALECK.
I JUST FELT KINDA BAD... Y'KNOW, CUZ I YELLED AT YOU.
AHH, DON'T WORRY ABOUT IT!
I BRING OUT THE WORST IN PEOPLE.
WELL, YOU DON'T HAVE TO SOUND SO PROUD OF IT.
WHY NOT?
I STICK WITH MY STRENGTHS.
YOU KNOW... WISECRACKS, INSULTS...
...RUNNING AWAY...
WELL, YOU'RE NOT THE ONLY ONE WHO CAN DO THAT.

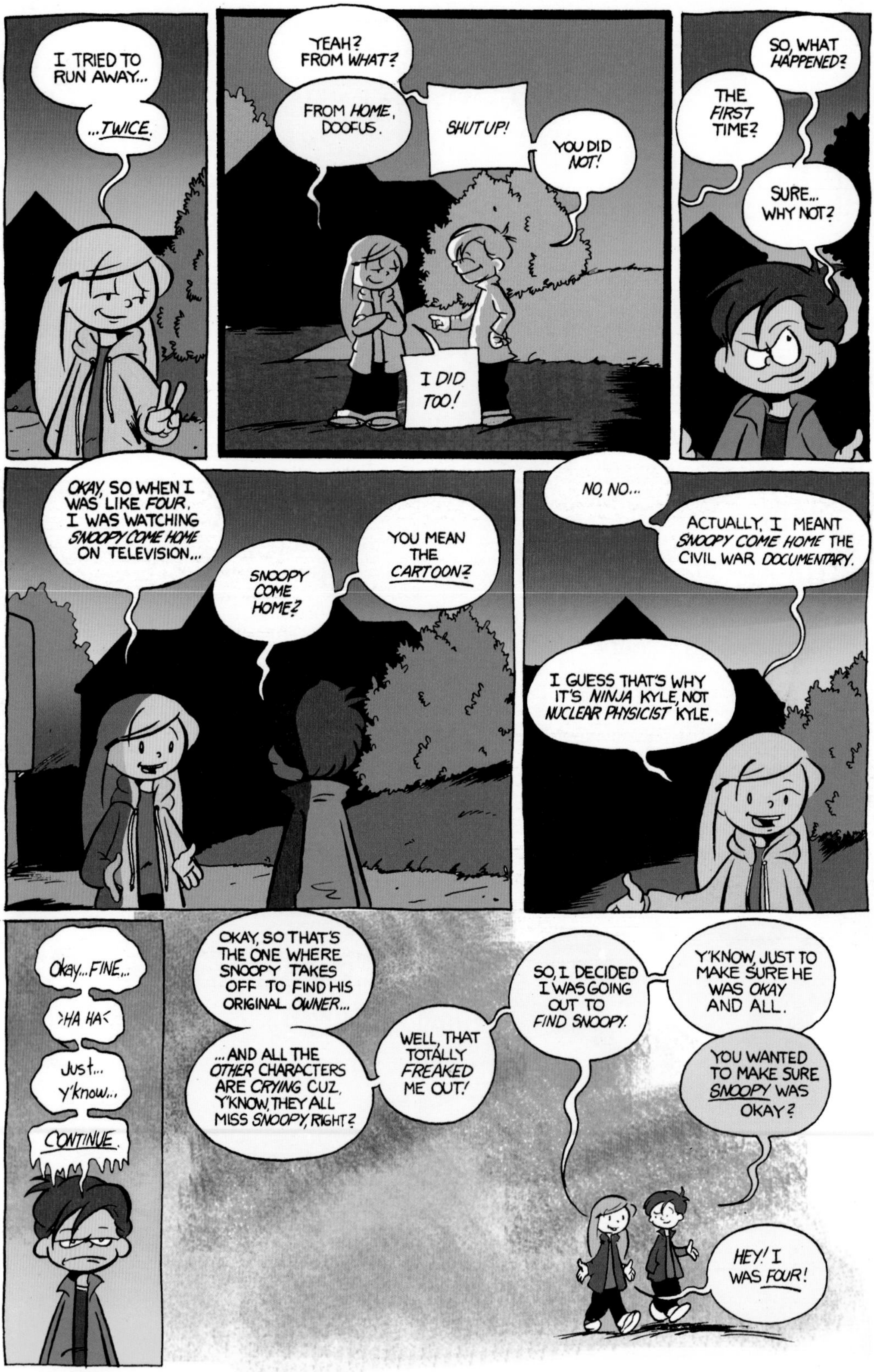
I TRIED TO RUN AWAY...
...TWICE.
YEAH? FROM WHAT?
FROM HOME, DOOFUS.
SHUT UP!
YOU DID NOT!
I DID TOO!
SO, WHAT HAPPENED?
THE FIRST TIME?
SURE... WHY NOT?
OKAY, SO WHEN I WAS LIKE FOUR, I WAS WATCHING SNOOPY COME HOME ON TELEVISION...
SNOOPY COME HOME?
YOU MEAN THE CARTOON?
NO, NO...
ACTUALLY, I MEANT SNOOPY COME HOME THE CIVIL WAR DOCUMENTARY.
I GUESS THAT'S WHY IT'S NINJA KYLE, NOT NUCLEAR PHYSICIST KYLE.
Okay... FINE...
>HA HA<
Just... y'know...
CONTINUE.
OKAY, SO THAT'S THE ONE WHERE SNOOPY TAKES OFF TO FIND HIS ORIGINAL OWNER...
...AND ALL THE OTHER CHARACTERS ARE CRYING CUZ, Y'KNOW, THEY ALL MISS SNOOPY, RIGHT?
WELL, THAT TOTALLY FREAKED ME OUT!
SO, I DECIDED I WAS GOING OUT TO FIND SNOOPY.
Y'KNOW, JUST TO MAKE SURE HE WAS OKAY AND ALL.
YOU WANTED TO MAKE SURE SNOOPY WAS OKAY?
HEY! I WAS FOUR!

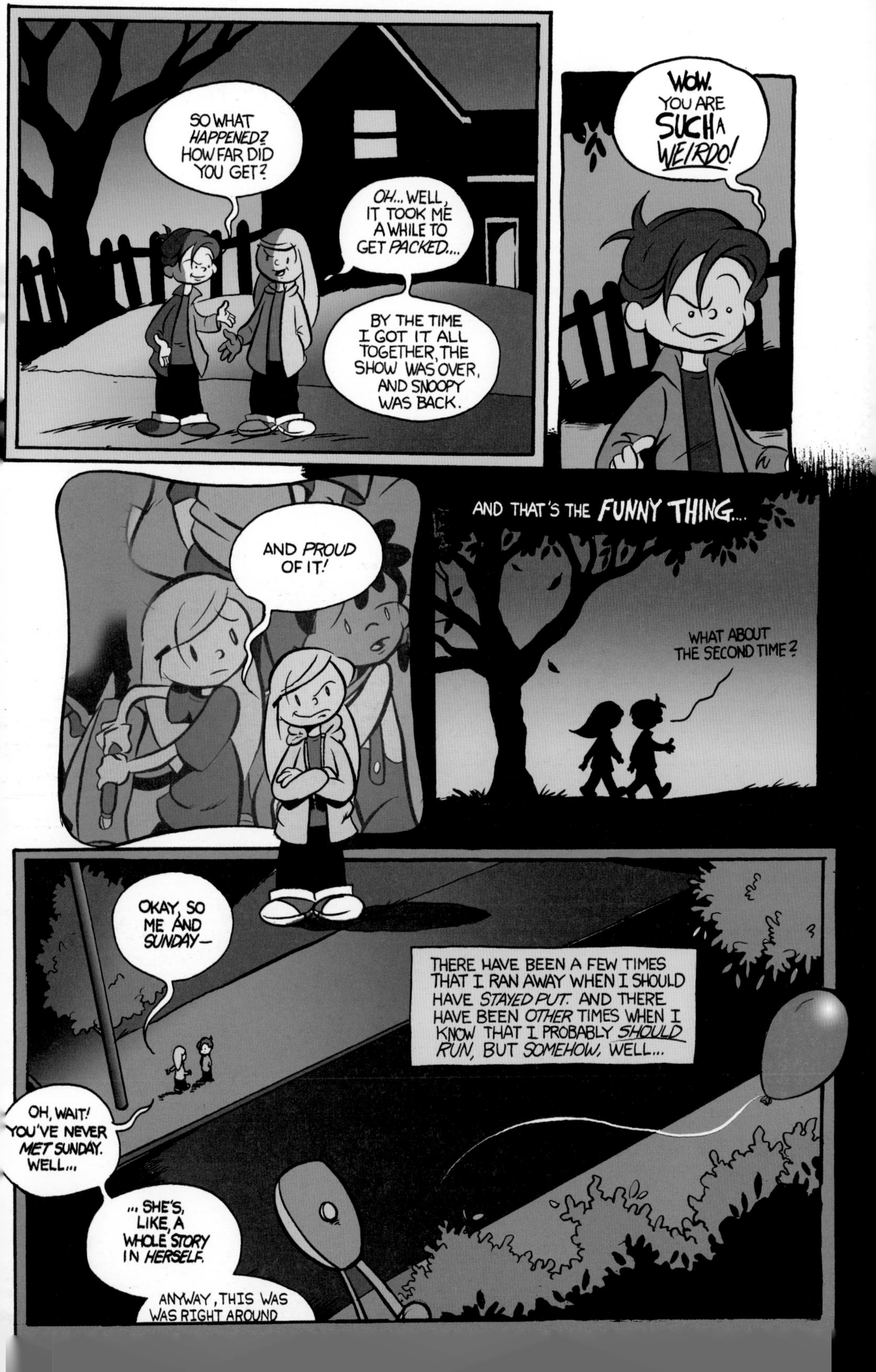
SO WHAT HAPPENED? HOW FAR DID YOU GET?
OH... WELL, IT TOOK ME A WHILE TO GET PACKED...
BY THE TIME I GOT IT ALL TOGETHER, THE SHOW WAS OVER, AND SNOOPY WAS BACK.
WOW. YOU ARE SUCH A WEIRDO!
AND PROUD OF IT!
AND THAT'S THE FUNNY THING...
WHAT ABOUT THE SECOND TIME?
OKAY, SO ME AND SUNDAY—
THERE HAVE BEEN A FEW TIMES THAT I RAN AWAY WHEN I SHOULD HAVE STAYED PUT. AND THERE HAVE BEEN OTHER TIMES WHEN I KNOW THAT I PROBABLY SHOULD RUN, BUT SOMEHOW, WELL...
OH, WAIT! YOU'VE NEVER MET SUNDAY. WELL...
... SHE'S, LIKE, A WHOLE STORY IN HERSELF.
ANYWAY, THIS WAS WAS RIGHT AROUND

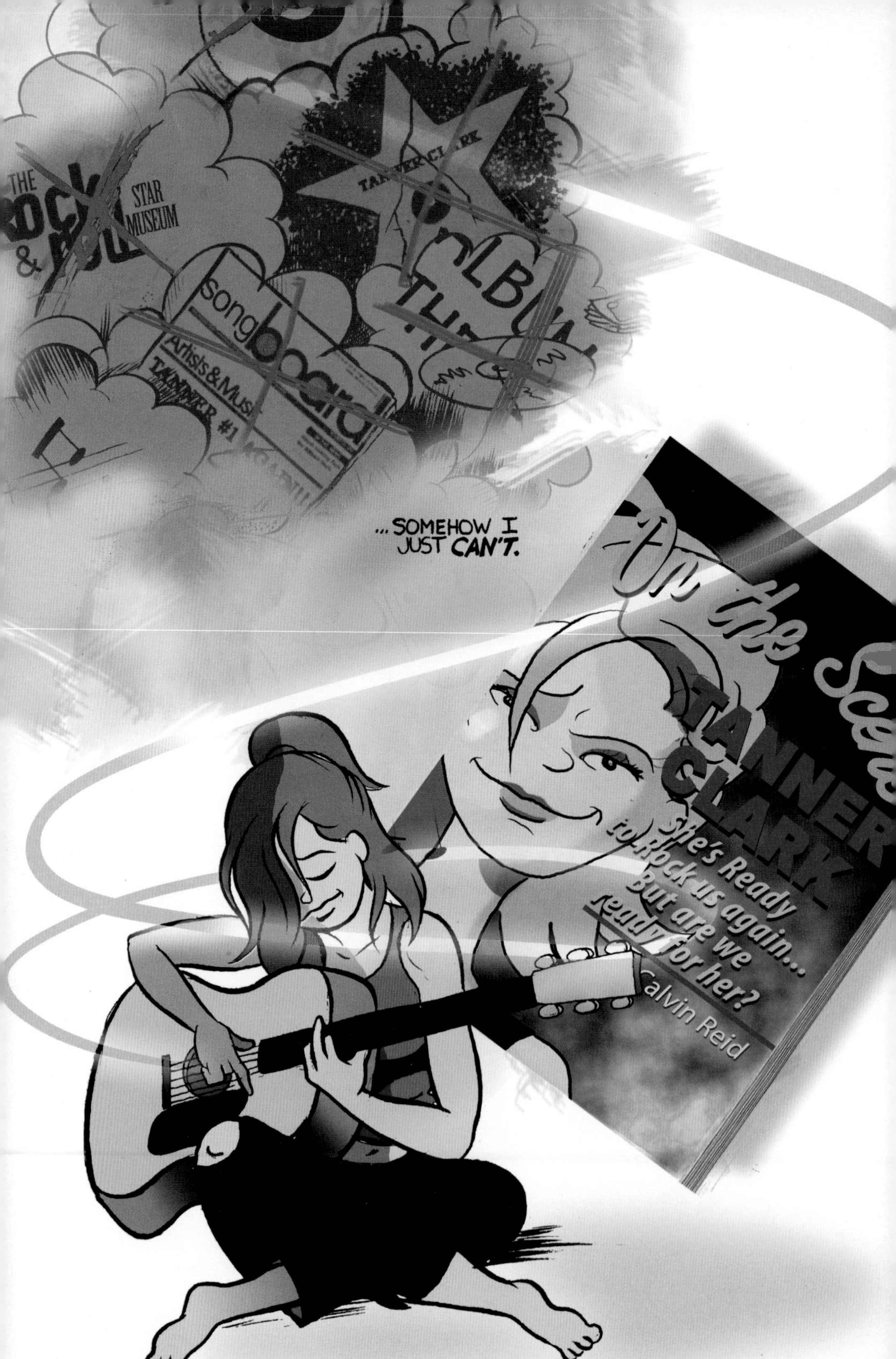
THE
STAR
MUSEUM
TANNER CLARK
song
TANNER #1
...SOMEHOW I JUST CAN'T.
TANNER CLARK
She's Ready to Rock us again... But are we ready for her?
Calvin Reid

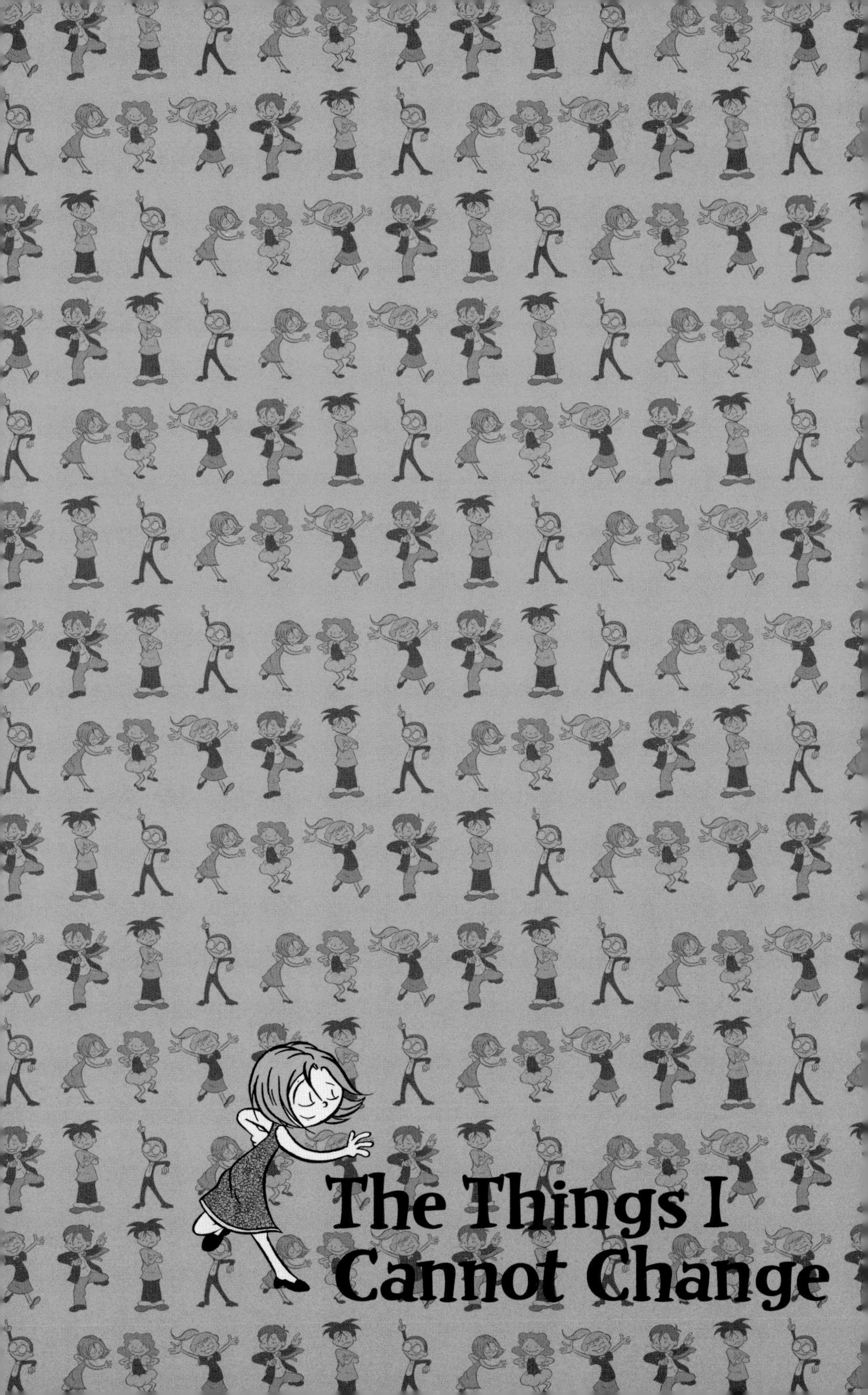
The Things I
Cannot Change

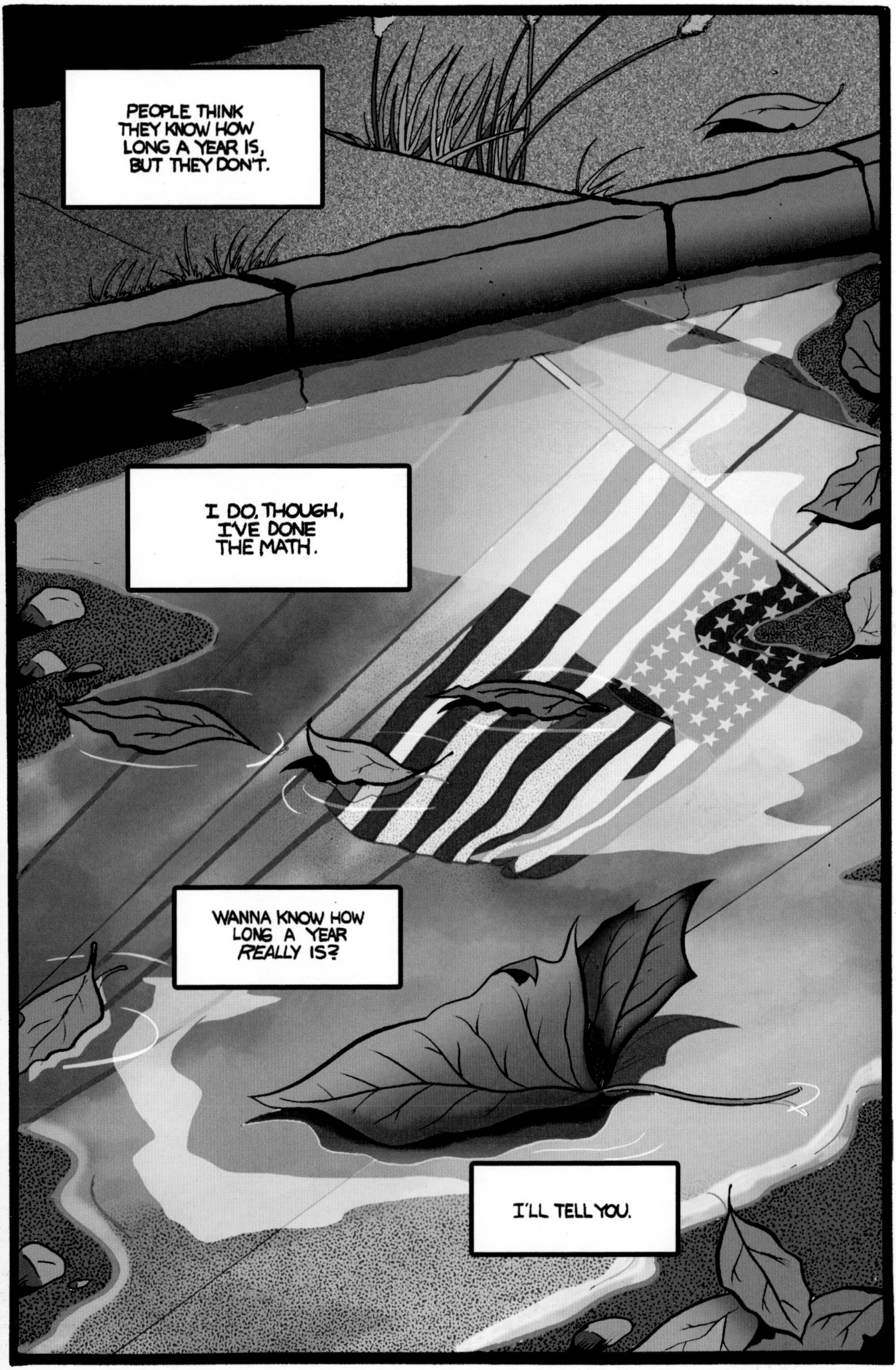
PEOPLE THINK THEY KNOW HOW LONG A YEAR IS, BUT THEY DON'T.
I DO, THOUGH. I'VE DONE THE MATH.
WANNA KNOW HOW LONG A YEAR *REALLY* IS?
I'LL TELL YOU.

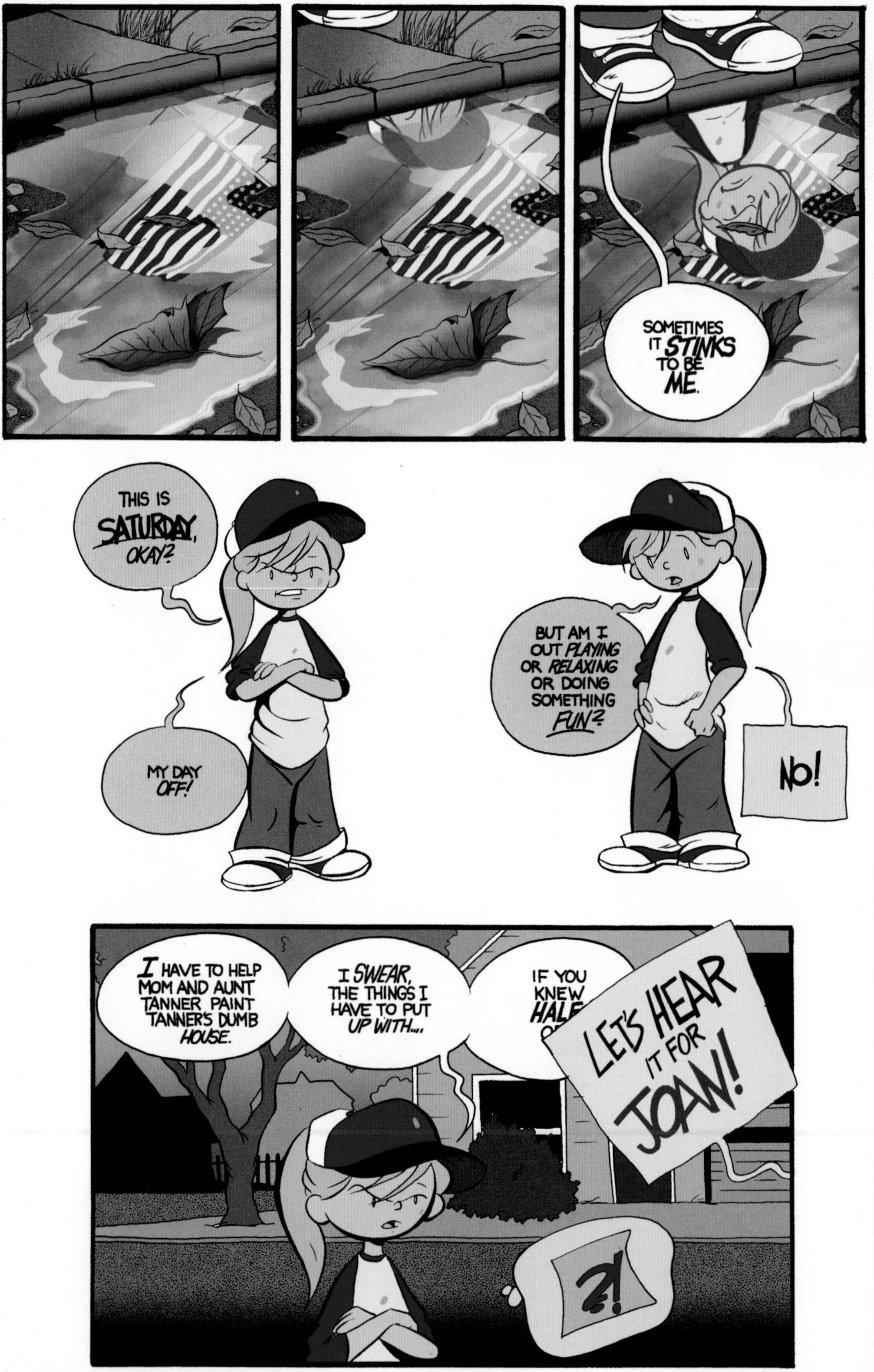
SOMETIMES IT STINKS TO BE ME.
THIS IS SATURDAY, OKAY?
MY DAY OFF!
BUT AM I OUT PLAYING OR RELAXING OR DOING SOMETHING FUN?
NO!
I HAVE TO HELP MOM AND AUNT TANNER PAINT TANNER'S DUMB HOUSE.
I SWEAR, THE THINGS I HAVE TO PUT UP WITH...
IF YOU KNEW HALF
LET'S HEAR IT FOR JOAN!
?!

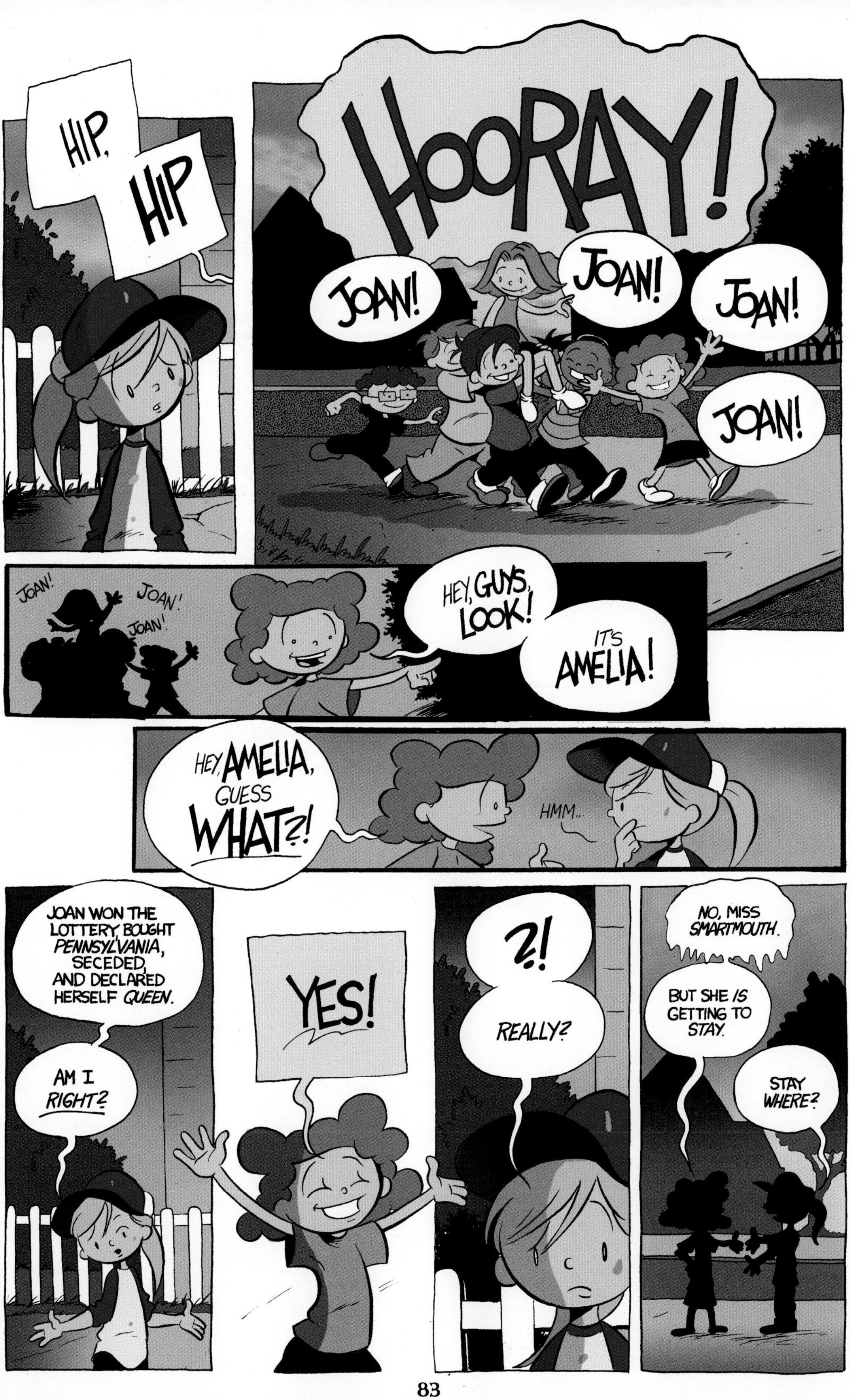
HIP,
HIP
HOORAY!
JOAN!
JOAN!
JOAN!
JOAN!
JOAN!
JOAN!
JOAN!
HEY, GUYS, LOOK!
IT'S AMELIA!
HEY, AMELIA, GUESS WHAT?!
HMM...
JOAN WON THE LOTTERY, BOUGHT PENNSYLVANIA, SECEDED, AND DECLARED HERSELF QUEEN.
AM I RIGHT?
YES!
?!
REALLY?
NO, MISS SMARTMOUTH.
BUT SHE IS GETTING TO STAY.
STAY WHERE?

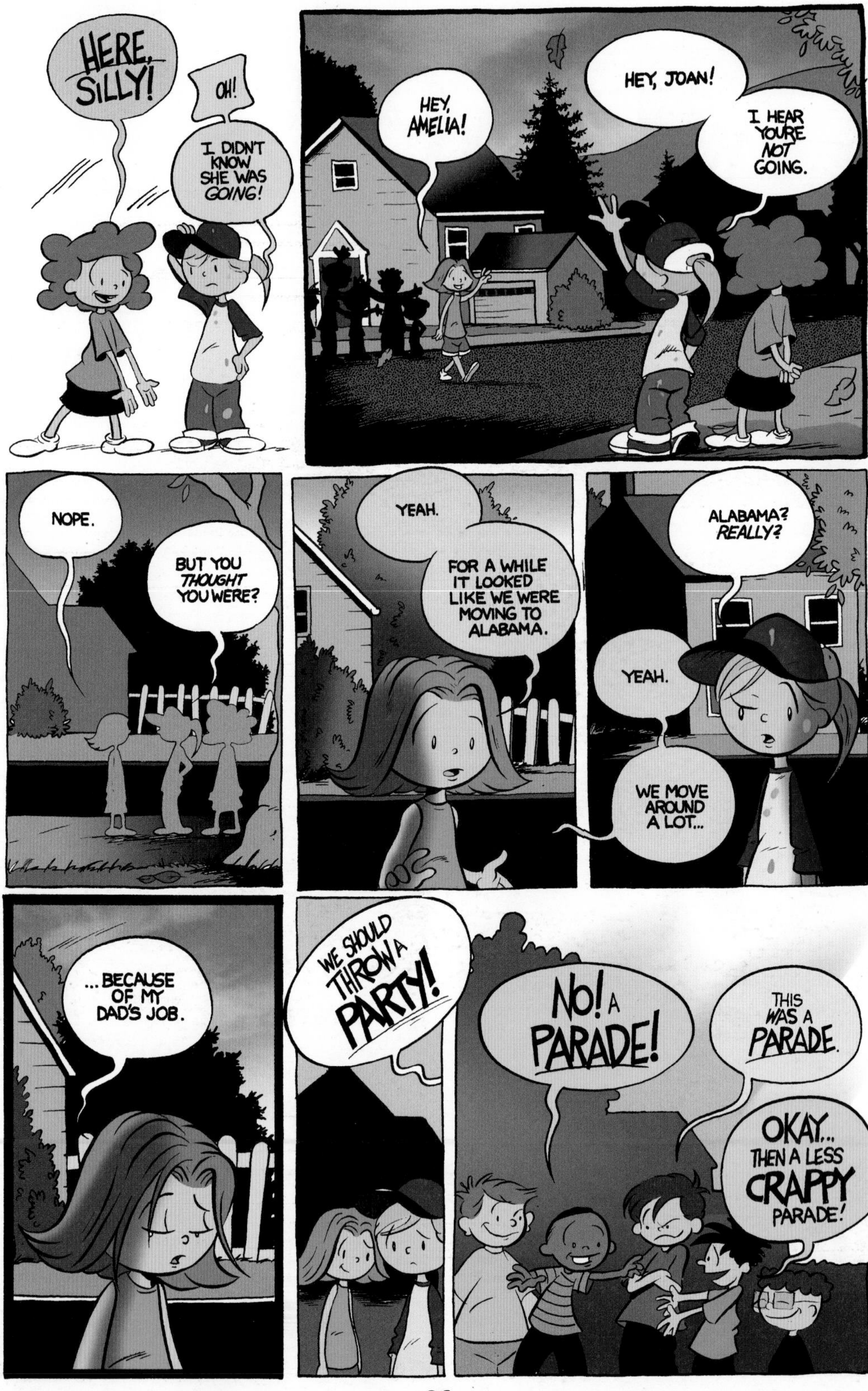
HERE, SILLY!
OH!
I DIDN'T KNOW SHE WAS GOING!
HEY, AMELIA!
HEY, JOAN!
I HEAR YOU'RE NOT GOING.
NOPE.
BUT YOU THOUGHT YOU WERE?
YEAH.
FOR A WHILE IT LOOKED LIKE WE WERE MOVING TO ALABAMA.
ALABAMA? REALLY?
YEAH.
WE MOVE AROUND A LOT...
... BECAUSE OF MY DAD'S JOB.
WE SHOULD THROW A PARTY!
NO! A PARADE!
THIS WAS A PARADE.
OKAY... THEN A LESS CRAPPY PARADE!

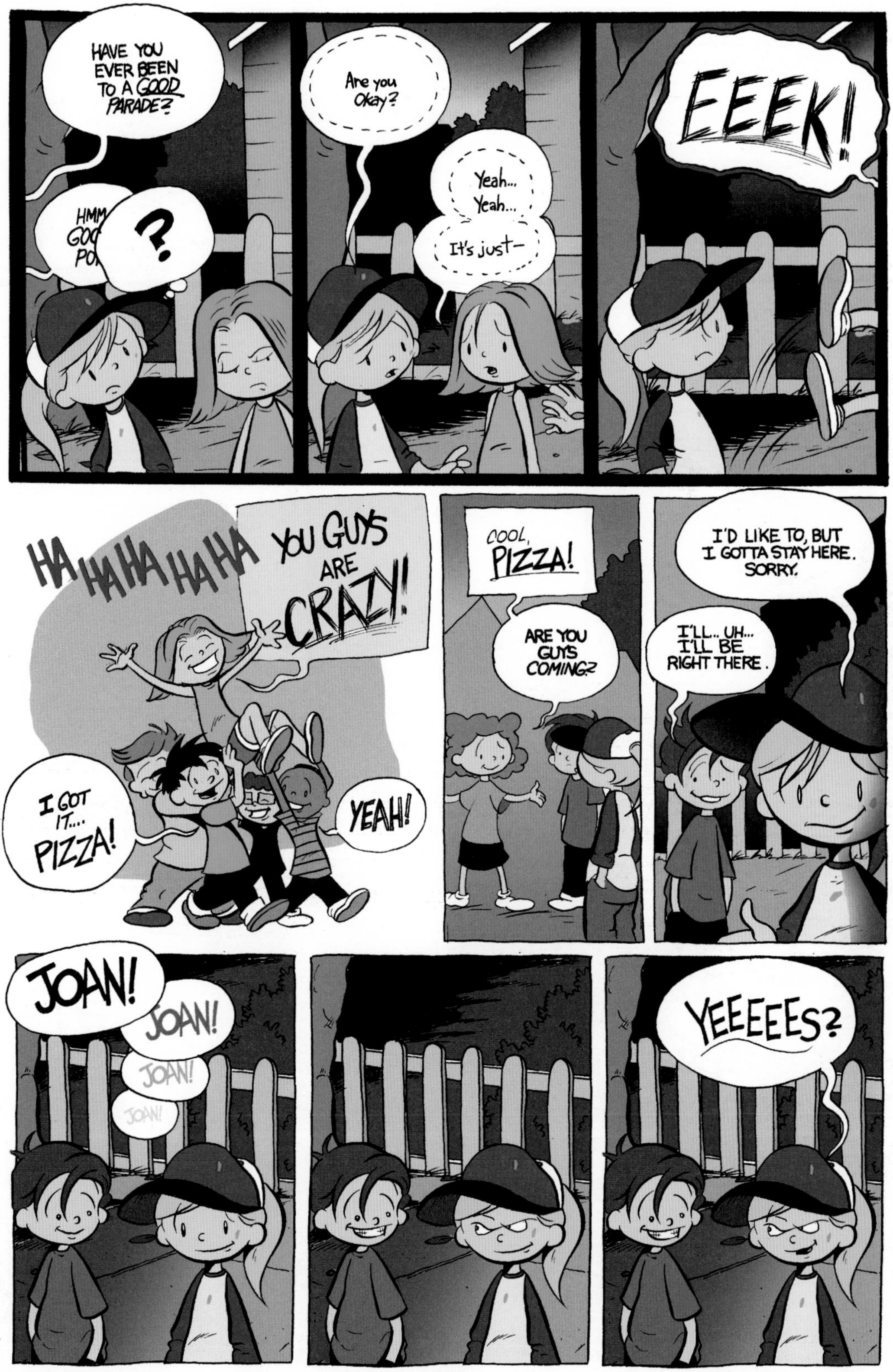
HAVE YOU EVER BEEN TO A GOOD PARADE?
?
Are you Okay?
Yeah... Yeah...
It's just—
EEEK!
HA HA HA HA HA HA
YOU GUYS ARE CRAZY!
I GOT IT.... PIZZA!
YEAH!
COOL, PIZZA!
ARE YOU GUYS COMING?
I'D LIKE TO, BUT I GOTTA STAY HERE. SORRY.
I'LL... UH... I'LL BE RIGHT THERE.
JOAN!
JOAN!
JOAN!
JOAN!
YEEEEES?

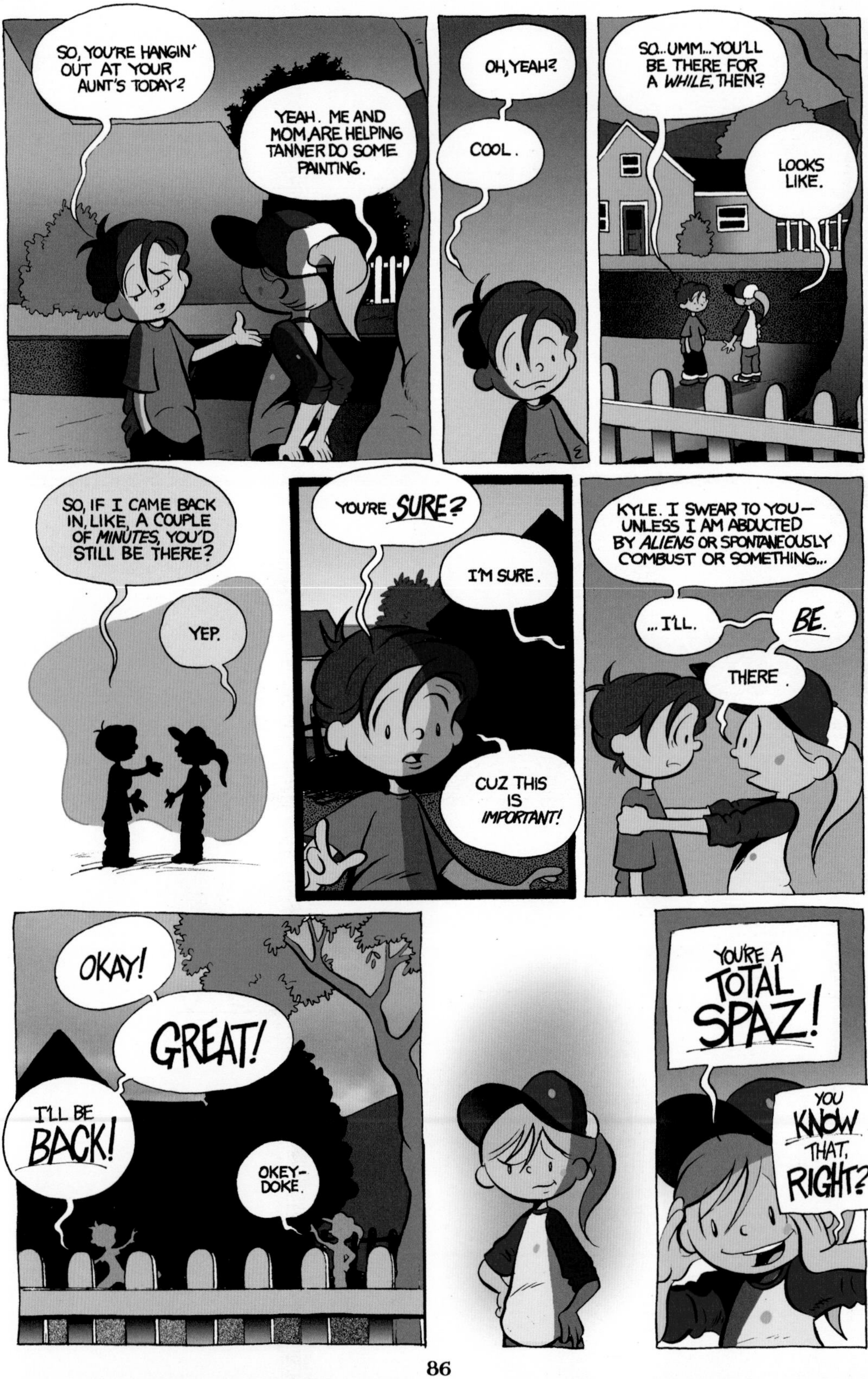
SO, YOU'RE HANGIN' OUT AT YOUR AUNT'S TODAY?
YEAH. ME AND MOM ARE HELPING TANNER DO SOME PAINTING.
OH, YEAH?
COOL.
SO...UMM...YOU'LL BE THERE FOR A *WHILE*, THEN?
LOOKS LIKE.
SO, IF I CAME BACK IN, LIKE, A COUPLE OF *MINUTES*, YOU'D STILL BE THERE?
YEP.
YOU'RE SURE?
I'M SURE.
CUZ THIS IS *IMPORTANT*!
KYLE. I SWEAR TO YOU— UNLESS I AM ABDUCTED BY *ALIENS* OR SPONTANEOUSLY COMBUST OR SOMETHING...
...I'LL.
BE.
THERE.
OKAY!
GREAT!
I'LL BE BACK!
OKEY-DOKE.
YOU'RE A TOTAL SPAZ!
YOU KNOW THAT, RIGHT?

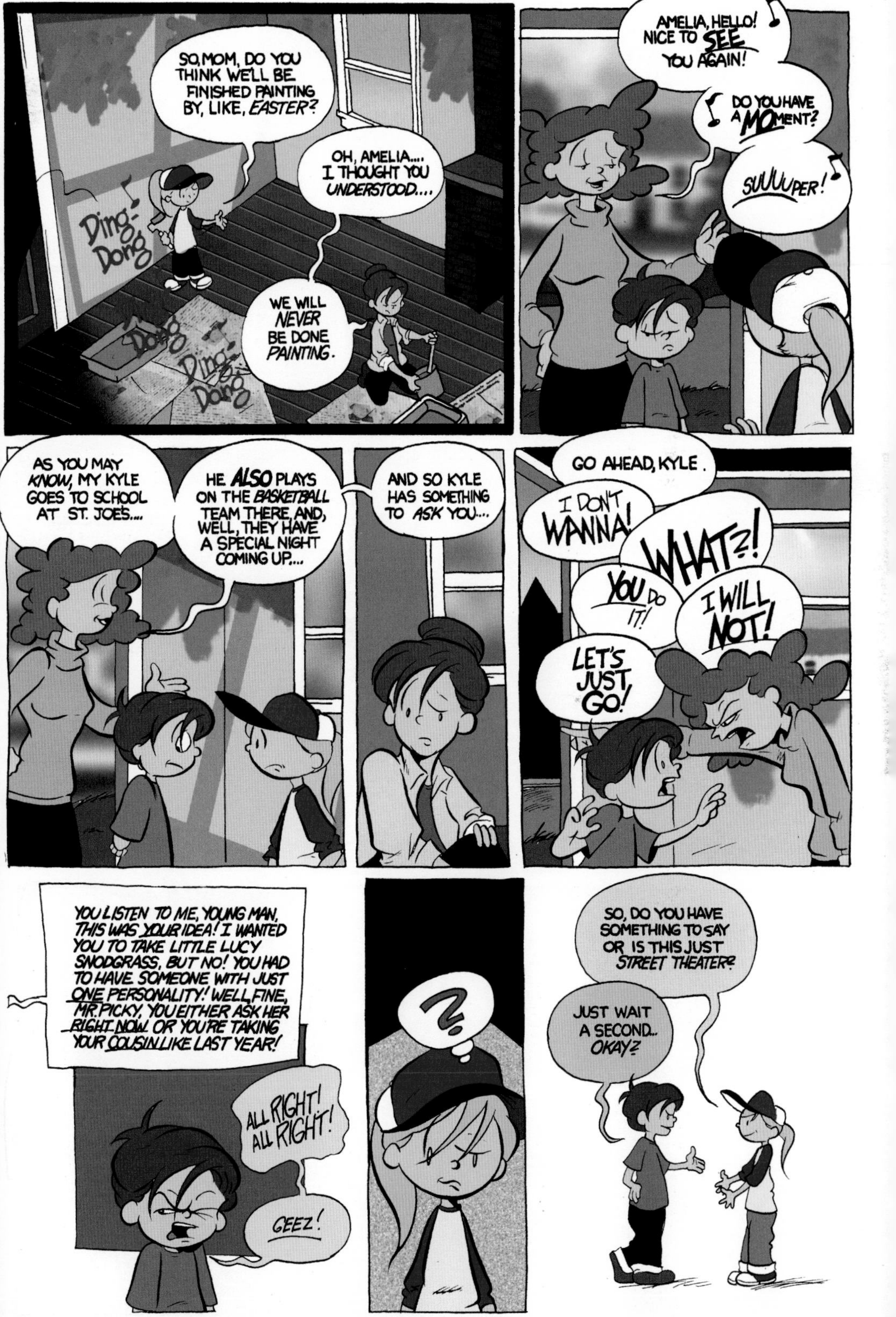
SO, MOM, DO YOU THINK WE'LL BE FINISHED PAINTING BY, LIKE, EASTER?
Ding-Dong
OH, AMELIA.... I THOUGHT YOU UNDERSTOOD....
WE WILL NEVER BE DONE PAINTING.
Ding-Dong
Ding-Dong
AMELIA, HELLO! NICE TO SEE YOU AGAIN!
DO YOU HAVE A MOMENT?
SUUUUPER!
AS YOU MAY KNOW, MY KYLE GOES TO SCHOOL AT ST. JOE'S....
HE ALSO PLAYS ON THE BASKETBALL TEAM THERE, AND, WELL, THEY HAVE A SPECIAL NIGHT COMING UP....
AND SO KYLE HAS SOMETHING TO ASK YOU....
GO AHEAD, KYLE.
I DON'T WANNA!
WHAT?!
YOU DO IT!
I WILL NOT!
LET'S JUST GO!
YOU LISTEN TO ME, YOUNG MAN, THIS WAS YOUR IDEA! I WANTED YOU TO TAKE LITTLE LUCY SNODGRASS, BUT NO! YOU HAD TO HAVE SOMEONE WITH JUST ONE PERSONALITY! WELL, FINE, MR. PICKY, YOU EITHER ASK HER RIGHT NOW OR YOU'RE TAKING YOUR COUSIN LIKE LAST YEAR!
ALL RIGHT! ALL RIGHT!
GEEZ!
?
SO, DO YOU HAVE SOMETHING TO SAY OR IS THIS JUST STREET THEATER?
JUST WAIT A SECOND... OKAY?

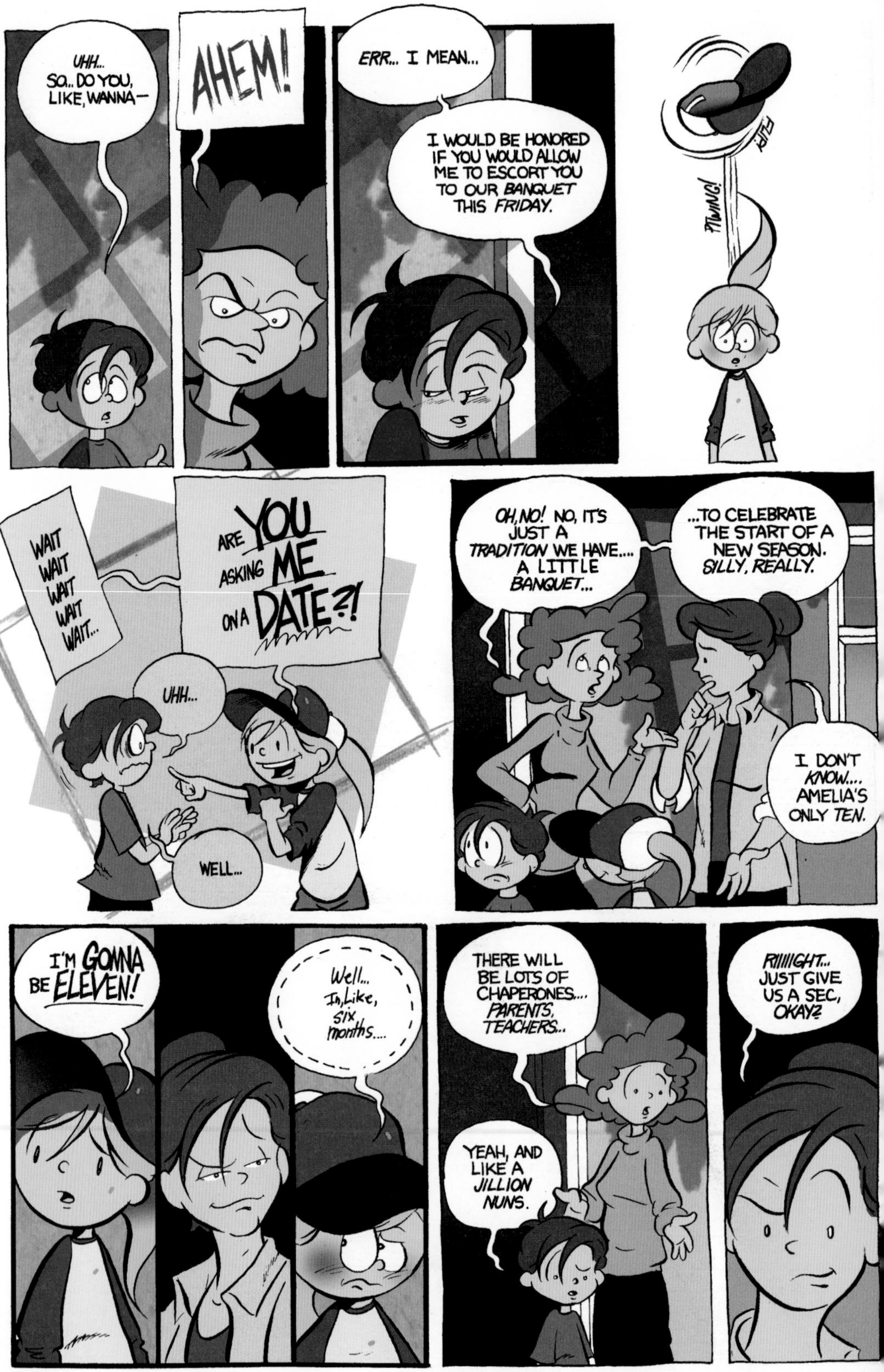

UHH... SO... DO YOU, LIKE, WANNA—
AHEM!
ERR... I MEAN...
I WOULD BE HONORED IF YOU WOULD ALLOW ME TO ESCORT YOU TO OUR BANQUET THIS FRIDAY.
FLIP
PTWING!
WAIT WAIT WAIT WAIT WAIT...
ARE YOU ASKING ME ON A DATE?!
UHH...
WELL...
OH, NO! NO, IT'S JUST A TRADITION WE HAVE.... A LITTLE BANQUET...
...TO CELEBRATE THE START OF A NEW SEASON. SILLY, REALLY.
I DON'T KNOW.... AMELIA'S ONLY TEN.
I'M GONNA BE ELEVEN!
Well... In, Like, six months....
THERE WILL BE LOTS OF CHAPERONES.... PARENTS, TEACHERS...
YEAH, AND LIKE A JILLION NUNS.
RIIIIGHT... JUST GIVE US A SEC, OKAY?

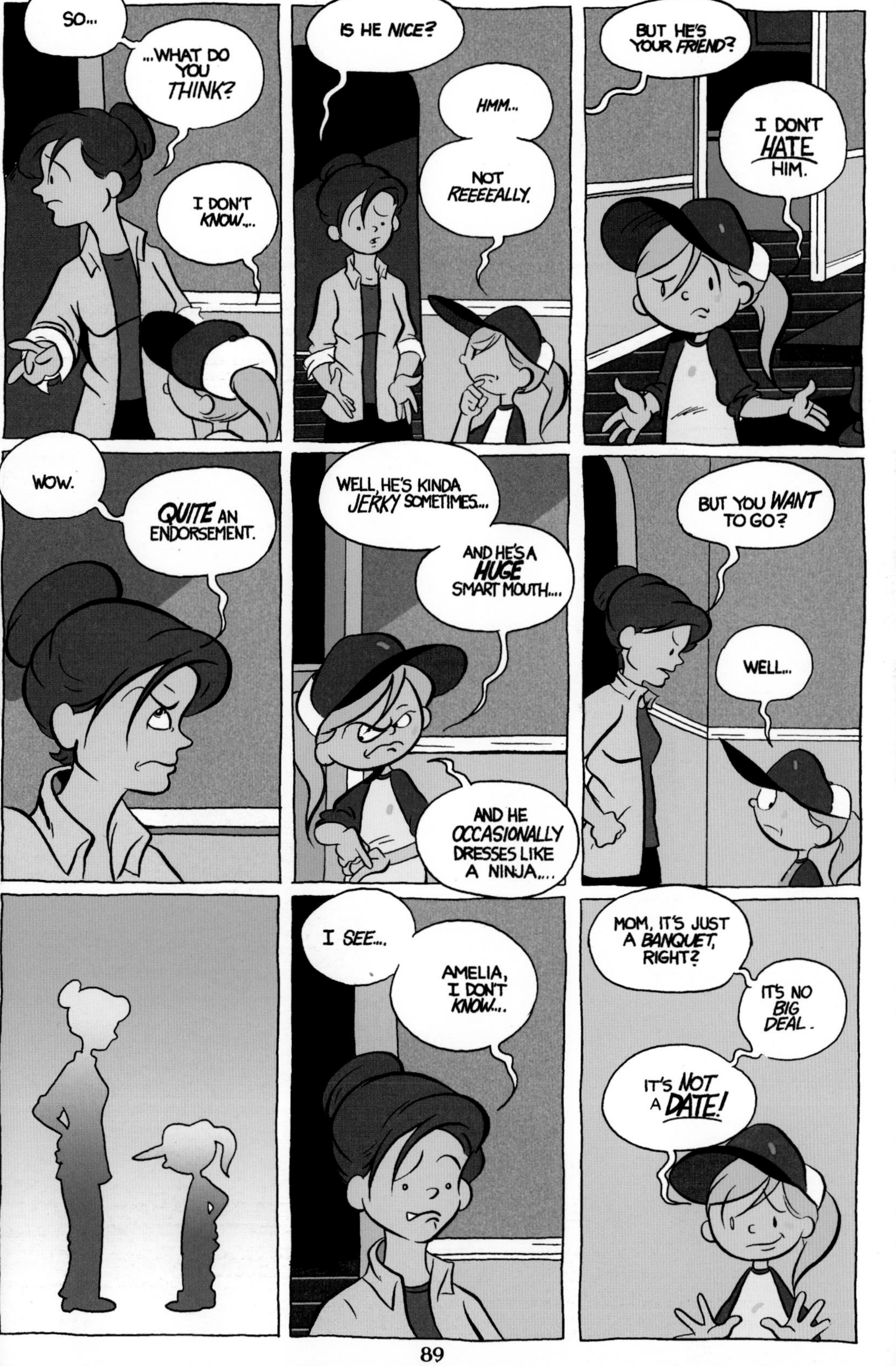
SO...
...WHAT DO YOU THINK?
I DON'T KNOW....
IS HE NICE?
HMM...
NOT REEEEALLY.
BUT HE'S YOUR FRIEND?
I DON'T HATE HIM.
WOW.
QUITE AN ENDORSEMENT.
WELL, HE'S KINDA JERKY SOMETIMES...
AND HE'S A HUGE SMART MOUTH....
AND HE OCCASIONALLY DRESSES LIKE A NINJA....
BUT YOU WANT TO GO?
WELL...
I SEE....
AMELIA, I DON'T KNOW....
MOM, IT'S JUST A BANQUET, RIGHT?
IT'S NO BIG DEAL.
IT'S NOT A DATE!

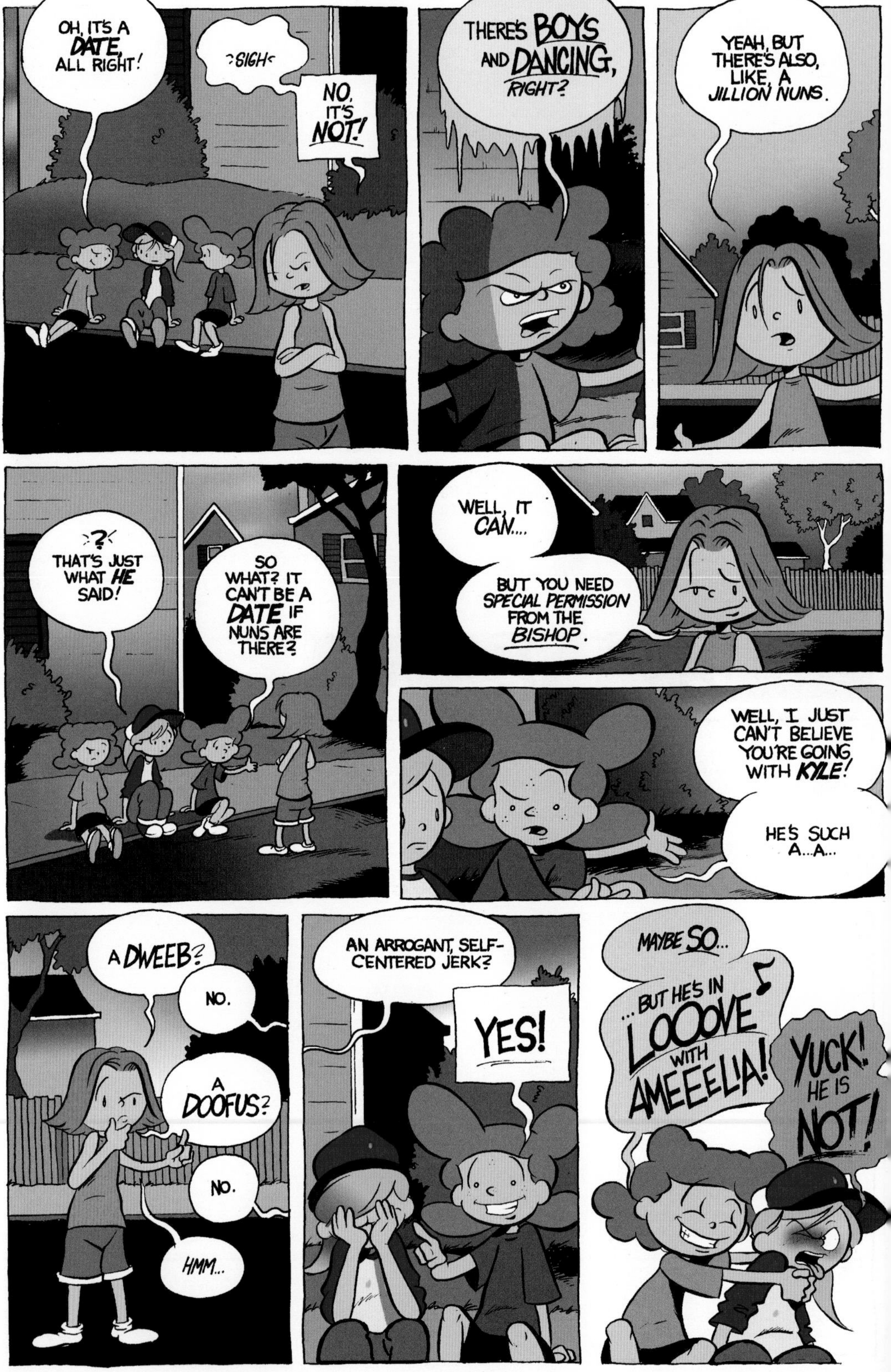
OH, IT'S A DATE, ALL RIGHT!
SIGH
NO, IT'S NOT!
THERE'S BOYS AND DANCING, RIGHT?
YEAH, BUT THERE'S ALSO, LIKE, A JILLION NUNS.
?
THAT'S JUST WHAT HE SAID!
SO WHAT? IT CAN'T BE A DATE IF NUNS ARE THERE?
WELL, IT CAN....
BUT YOU NEED SPECIAL PERMISSION FROM THE BISHOP.
WELL, I JUST CAN'T BELIEVE YOU'RE GOING WITH KYLE!
HE'S SUCH A...A...
A DWEEB?
NO.
A DOOFUS?
NO.
HMM...
AN ARROGANT, SELF-CENTERED JERK?
YES!
MAYBE SO...
...BUT HE'S IN LOOOVE WITH AMEEELIA!
YUCK! HE IS NOT!

PLUS... **SHUT UP!**

SHEESH!

SOMEONE MIGHT *HEAR!*

OH, *I* GET IT....

WANNA KEEP YOUR OPTIONS OPEN... PLAY THE *FIELD* A LITTLE...

HEY, JOAN, MIND IF I SLUG YOUR *FRIEND?*

SURE... WHATEVER...

UMM. I'LL BE RIGHT *BACK.*

I'M WORRIED ABOUT HER.

SHE'S BEEN ACTING *WEIRD* LATELY.

SHE *HAS?*

YEAH. I MEAN, SHE'S ALWAYS *KINDA* WEIRD, BUT THIS IS *DIFFERENT....*

IT'S *SAD* WEIRD.

I SAW HER THE OTHER DAY, AND I *THINK* SHE WAS *CRYING.*

I RAN UP AND SAID, "JOAN! JOAN! ARE YOU OKAY?"

BUT SHE JUST SWORE AT ME AND PUNCHED ME IN THE *ARM.*

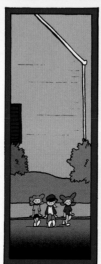

SO...

...IT REALLY *IS* A DATE?

OH, DON'T *WORRY* ABOUT IT...,

JOAN IS ON THE TEAM, SO SHE'LL BE THERE.

AND SAM IS *ESCORTING* ME!

WE'LL GET YOU *THROUGH* IT.

I GUESS IT MAY NOT SURPRISE YOU TO HEAR THAT THAT DIDN'T REALLY *ENCOURAGE* ME.

I WAS PRETTY SURE I'D SCORE A NEW DRESS FOR THIS, BUT THAT WAS A NO GO.

SO I JUST DUG OUT THE OLD *CLASS PHOTO* OUTFIT.

STILL, I THINK I LOOKED *PRETTY CUTE!*

SO THEN IT WAS TIME TO SIT AND WAIT FOR THE DOORBELL TO GO...

♪ DING-DONG

I COULDN'T *WAIT* TO SEE WHAT HE'D SAY....

Birktshnook?

G'Flabbin!

OKAAAAY...

A LITTLE *WEIRD*...

...BUT I TOOK IT AS A *COMPLIMENT*....

SO THEN ALL WE HAD TO DO WAS GET TO KYLE'S MOM'S CAR, WHICH WASN'T SO EASY SINCE WE HAD TO GET PAST KYLE'S MOM AND HER CAMERA AND <u>MY</u> MOM AND HER *RADIATING FORCEFIELD* OF *NERVOUSNESS.*

WHICH I *RETURNED*...

NICE *TIE,* NERD BOY!

This is a *NIGHTMARE!*

Welcome to my *LIFE!*

Click Click Click click

Click click Click Click Click Click Click Click

WE FINALLY MADE IT, AND WERE ON OUR WAY. I GUESS WE WERE KINDA NERVOUS, CUZ WE WERE REALLY *QUIET*...OR AT LEAST *TWO* OF US WERE...

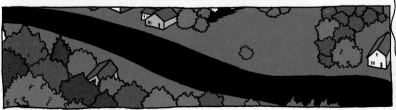

MY LOOOOVE DOES IT GOOOOOOD

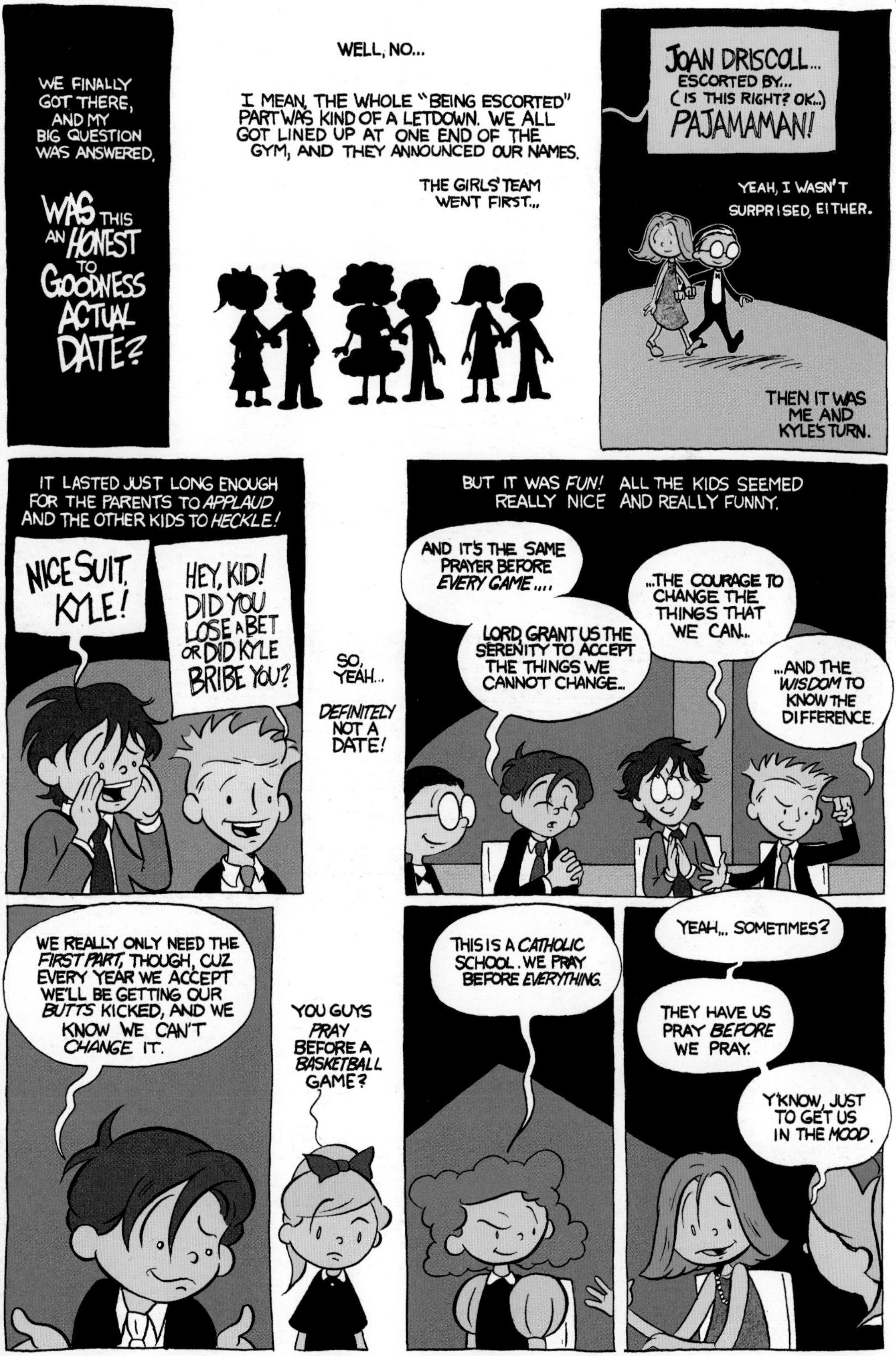
WE FINALLY GOT THERE, AND MY BIG QUESTION WAS ANSWERED.
WAS THIS AN HONEST TO GOODNESS ACTUAL DATE?
WELL, NO...
I MEAN, THE WHOLE "BEING ESCORTED" PART WAS KIND OF A LETDOWN. WE ALL GOT LINED UP AT ONE END OF THE GYM, AND THEY ANNOUNCED OUR NAMES.
THE GIRLS' TEAM WENT FIRST...
JOAN DRISCOLL... ESCORTED BY... (IS THIS RIGHT? OK..) PAJAMAMAN!
YEAH, I WASN'T SURPRISED, EITHER.
THEN IT WAS ME AND KYLE'S TURN.
IT LASTED JUST LONG ENOUGH FOR THE PARENTS TO APPLAUD AND THE OTHER KIDS TO HECKLE!
NICE SUIT, KYLE!
HEY, KID! DID YOU LOSE A BET OR DID KYLE BRIBE YOU?
SO, YEAH... DEFINITELY NOT A DATE!
BUT IT WAS FUN! ALL THE KIDS SEEMED REALLY NICE AND REALLY FUNNY.
AND IT'S THE SAME PRAYER BEFORE EVERY GAME....
LORD, GRANT US THE SERENITY TO ACCEPT THE THINGS WE CANNOT CHANGE..
...THE COURAGE TO CHANGE THE THINGS THAT WE CAN..
...AND THE WISDOM TO KNOW THE DIFFERENCE.
WE REALLY ONLY NEED THE FIRST PART, THOUGH, CUZ EVERY YEAR WE ACCEPT WE'LL BE GETTING OUR BUTTS KICKED, AND WE KNOW WE CAN'T CHANGE IT.
YOU GUYS PRAY BEFORE A BASKETBALL GAME?
THIS IS A CATHOLIC SCHOOL. WE PRAY BEFORE EVERYTHING.
YEAH... SOMETIMES?
THEY HAVE US PRAY BEFORE WE PRAY.
Y'KNOW, JUST TO GET US IN THE MOOD.

SO, YEAH... IT WAS *DEFINITELY FUN!*

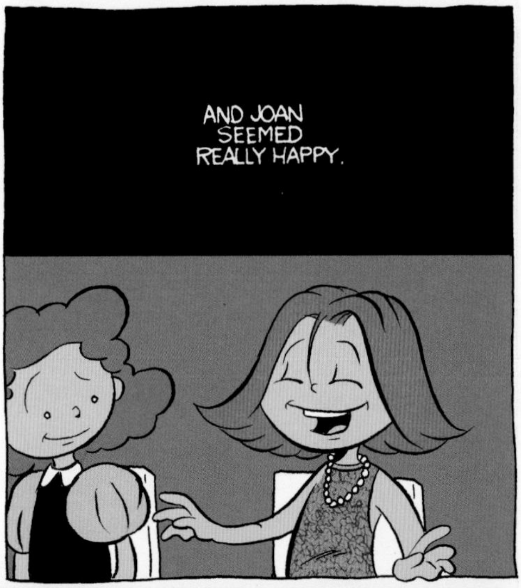
AND JOAN SEEMED REALLY HAPPY.

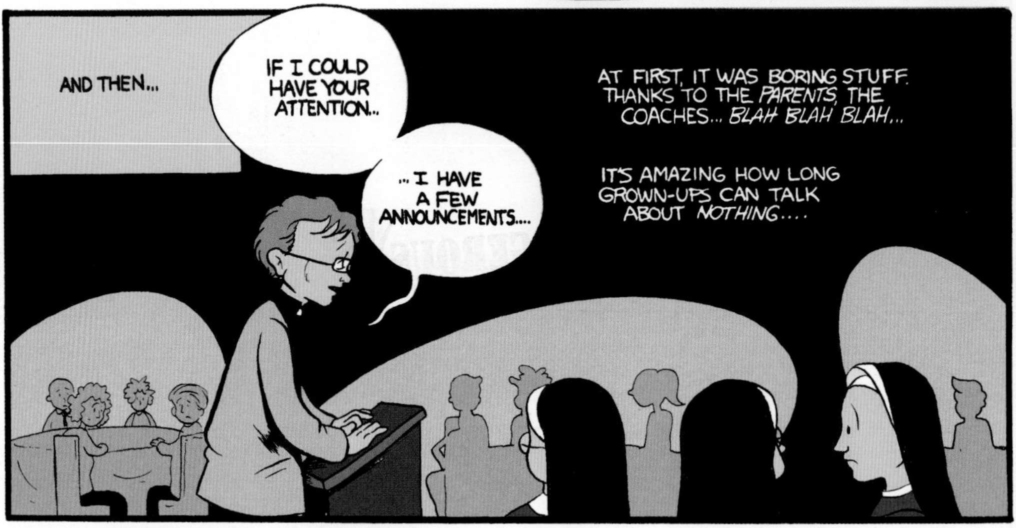
AND THEN...
IF I COULD HAVE YOUR ATTENTION...
...I HAVE A FEW ANNOUNCEMENTS....
AT FIRST, IT WAS BORING STUFF. THANKS TO THE *PARENTS*, THE COACHES... *BLAH BLAH BLAH*...
IT'S AMAZING HOW LONG GROWN-UPS CAN TALK ABOUT *NOTHING*....

BUT THEN HE ASKED SOMEONE NAMED CAPTAIN DRISCOLL TO STAND.

IT WAS JOAN'S DAD.

HE WAS WEARING AN ARMY UNIFORM... A REAL FANCY ONE.

HE LOOKED IMPRESSIVE.

LIKE AN ACTION FIGURE.

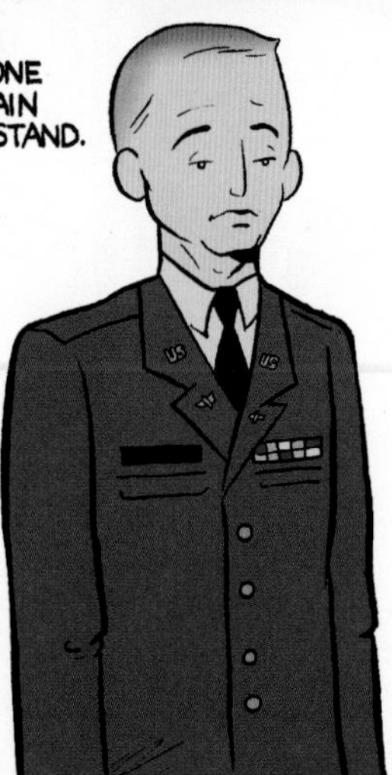

NO, THAT'S STUPID, NOT AN ACTION FIGURE... LIKE...

I DON'T KNOW... JUST IMPRESSIVE.

ANYWAY, THE PRIEST STARTED TALKING ABOUT ALL MISTER... ERR... <u>*CAPTAIN*</u> DRISCOLL HAD DONE FOR THE SCHOOL...

AND HOW HARD IT WAS GOING TO BE...

... HOW *HARD*...

...TO HAVE TO SAY GOOD-BYE.

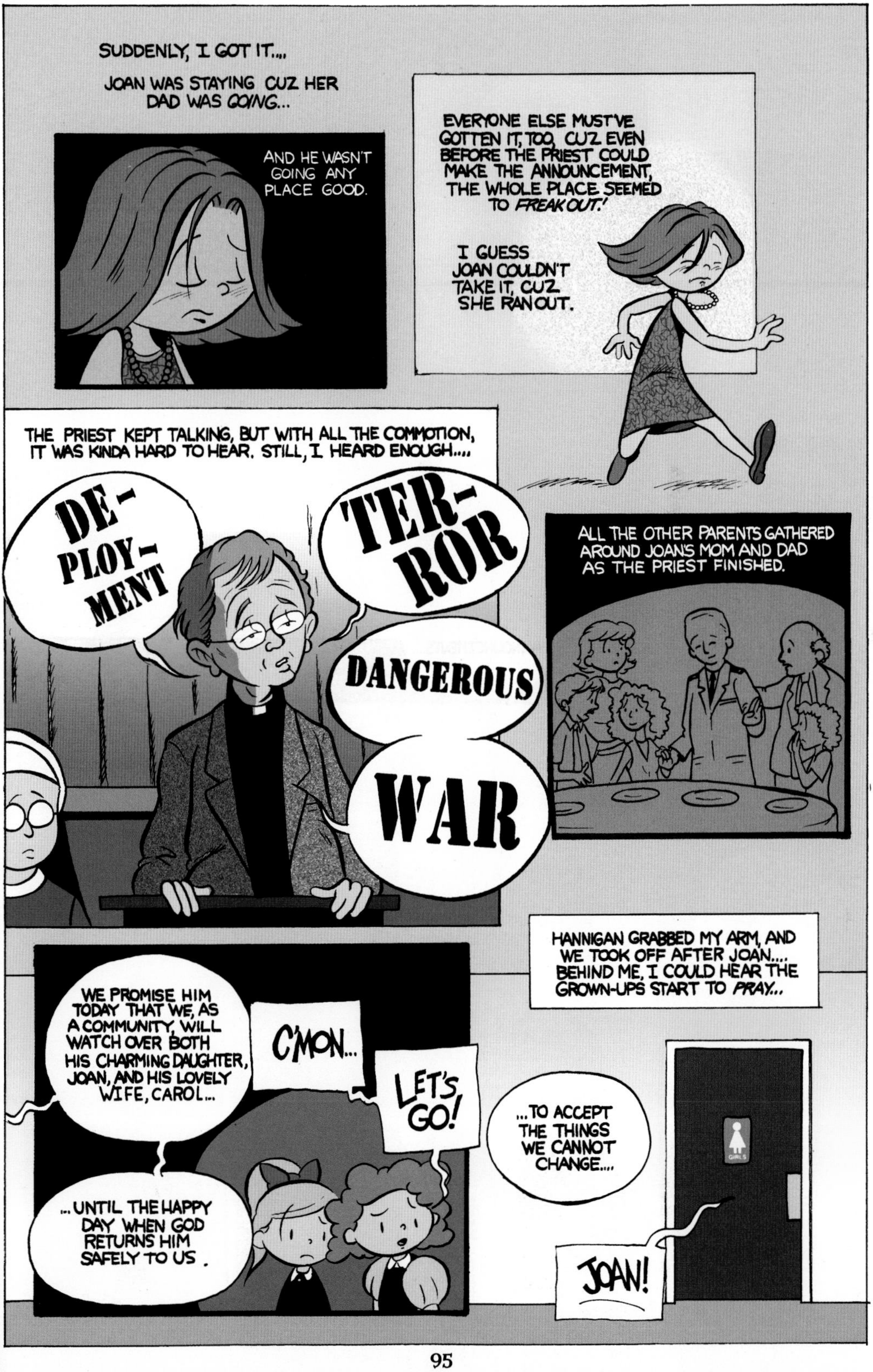
SUDDENLY, I GOT IT....
JOAN WAS STAYING CUZ HER DAD WAS *GOING*...
AND HE WASN'T GOING ANY PLACE GOOD.
EVERYONE ELSE MUST'VE GOTTEN IT, TOO, CUZ EVEN BEFORE THE PRIEST COULD MAKE THE ANNOUNCEMENT, THE WHOLE PLACE SEEMED TO *FREAK OUT!*
I GUESS JOAN COULDN'T TAKE IT, CUZ SHE RAN OUT.
THE PRIEST KEPT TALKING, BUT WITH ALL THE COMMOTION, IT WAS KINDA HARD TO HEAR. STILL, I HEARD ENOUGH....
DE-PLOY-MENT
TER-ROR
DANGEROUS
WAR
ALL THE OTHER PARENTS GATHERED AROUND JOAN'S MOM AND DAD AS THE PRIEST FINISHED.
WE PROMISE HIM TODAY THAT WE, AS A COMMUNITY, WILL WATCH OVER BOTH HIS CHARMING DAUGHTER, JOAN, AND HIS LOVELY WIFE, CAROL...
...UNTIL THE HAPPY DAY WHEN GOD RETURNS HIM SAFELY TO US.
C'MON...
LET'S GO!
HANNIGAN GRABBED MY ARM, AND WE TOOK OFF AFTER JOAN.... BEHIND ME, I COULD HEAR THE GROWN-UPS START TO *PRAY*...
...TO ACCEPT THE THINGS WE CANNOT CHANGE....
GIRLS
JOAN!

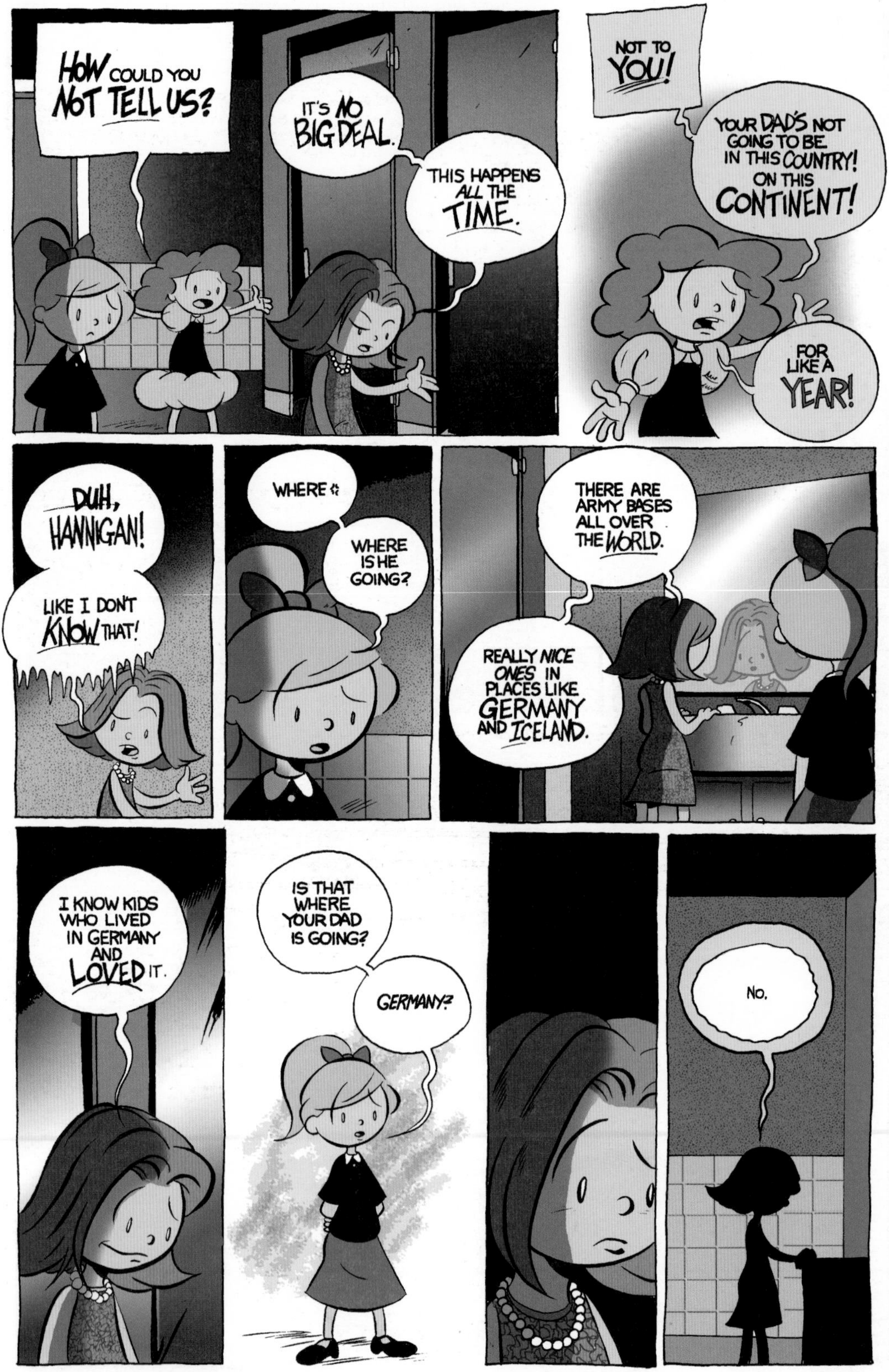
HOW COULD YOU NOT TELL US?
IT'S NO BIG DEAL.
THIS HAPPENS ALL THE TIME.
NOT TO YOU!
YOUR DAD'S NOT GOING TO BE IN THIS COUNTRY! ON THIS CONTINENT!
FOR LIKE A YEAR!
DUH, HANNIGAN!
LIKE I DON'T KNOW THAT!
WHERE?
WHERE IS HE GOING?
THERE ARE ARMY BASES ALL OVER THE WORLD.
REALLY NICE ONES IN PLACES LIKE GERMANY AND ICELAND.
I KNOW KIDS WHO LIVED IN GERMANY AND LOVED IT.
IS THAT WHERE YOUR DAD IS GOING?
GERMANY?
NO.

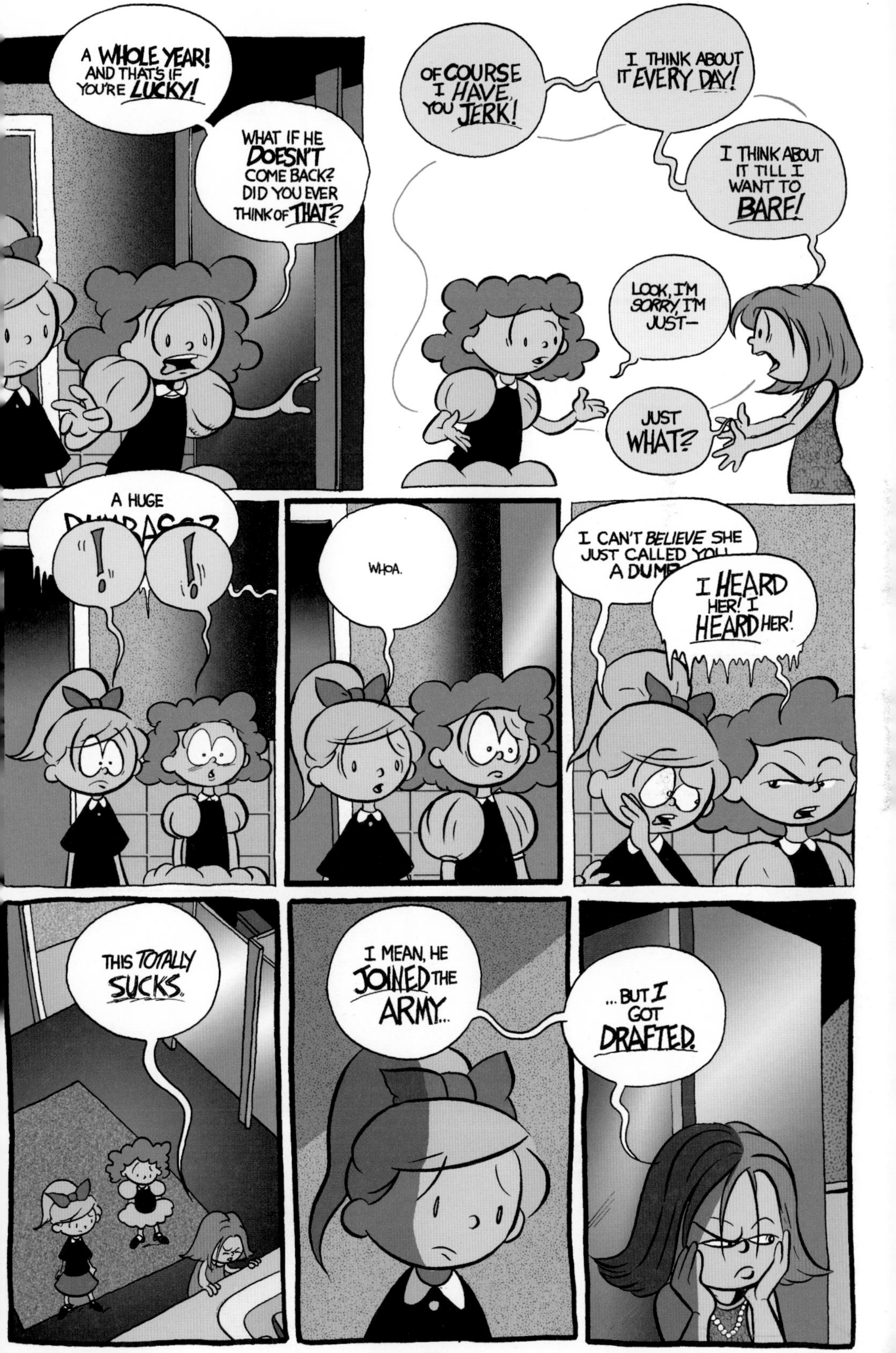
A WHOLE YEAR! AND THAT'S IF YOU'RE LUCKY!
WHAT IF HE DOESN'T COME BACK? DID YOU EVER THINK OF THAT?
OF COURSE I HAVE, YOU JERK!
I THINK ABOUT IT EVERY DAY!
I THINK ABOUT IT TILL I WANT TO BARF!
LOOK, I'M SORRY, I'M JUST—
JUST WHAT?
A HUGE
!
!
WHOA.
I CAN'T BELIEVE SHE JUST CALLED
I HEARD HER! I HEARD HER!
THIS TOTALLY SUCKS.
I MEAN, HE JOINED THE ARMY...
...BUT I GOT DRAFTED.

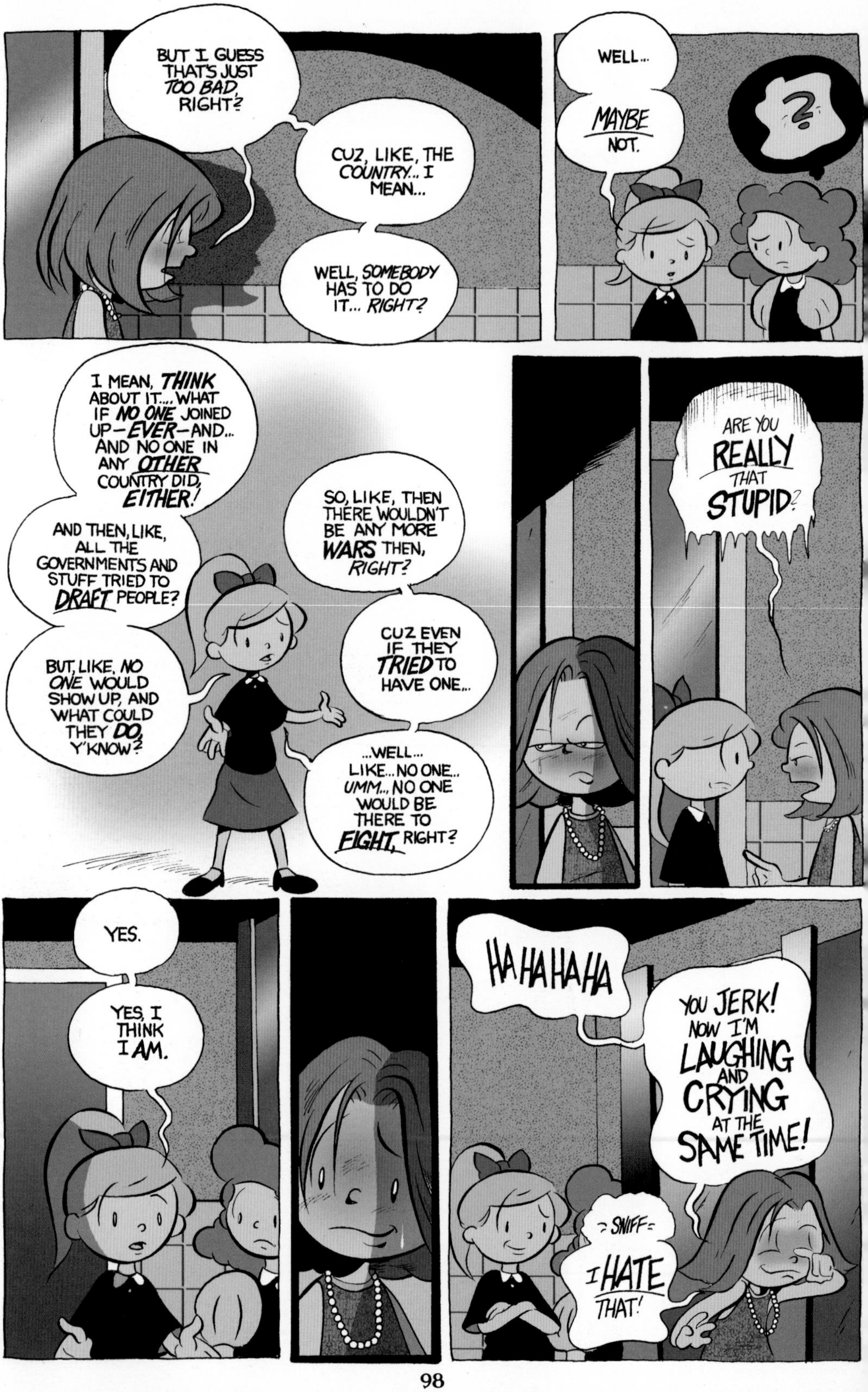
BUT I GUESS THAT'S JUST TOO BAD, RIGHT?
CUZ, LIKE, THE COUNTRY... I MEAN...
WELL, SOMEBODY HAS TO DO IT... RIGHT?
WELL...
MAYBE NOT.
?
I MEAN, THINK ABOUT IT.... WHAT IF NO ONE JOINED UP—EVER—AND... AND NO ONE IN ANY OTHER COUNTRY DID, EITHER!
AND THEN, LIKE, ALL THE GOVERNMENTS AND STUFF TRIED TO DRAFT PEOPLE?
BUT, LIKE, NO ONE WOULD SHOW UP, AND WHAT COULD THEY DO, Y'KNOW?
SO, LIKE, THEN THERE WOULDN'T BE ANY MORE WARS THEN, RIGHT?
CUZ EVEN IF THEY TRIED TO HAVE ONE...
...WELL... LIKE... NO ONE... UMM... NO ONE WOULD BE THERE TO FIGHT, RIGHT?
ARE YOU REALLY THAT STUPID?
YES.
YES, I THINK I AM.
HA HA HA HA HA
YOU JERK! NOW I'M LAUGHING AND CRYING AT THE SAME TIME!
SNIFF
I HATE THAT!

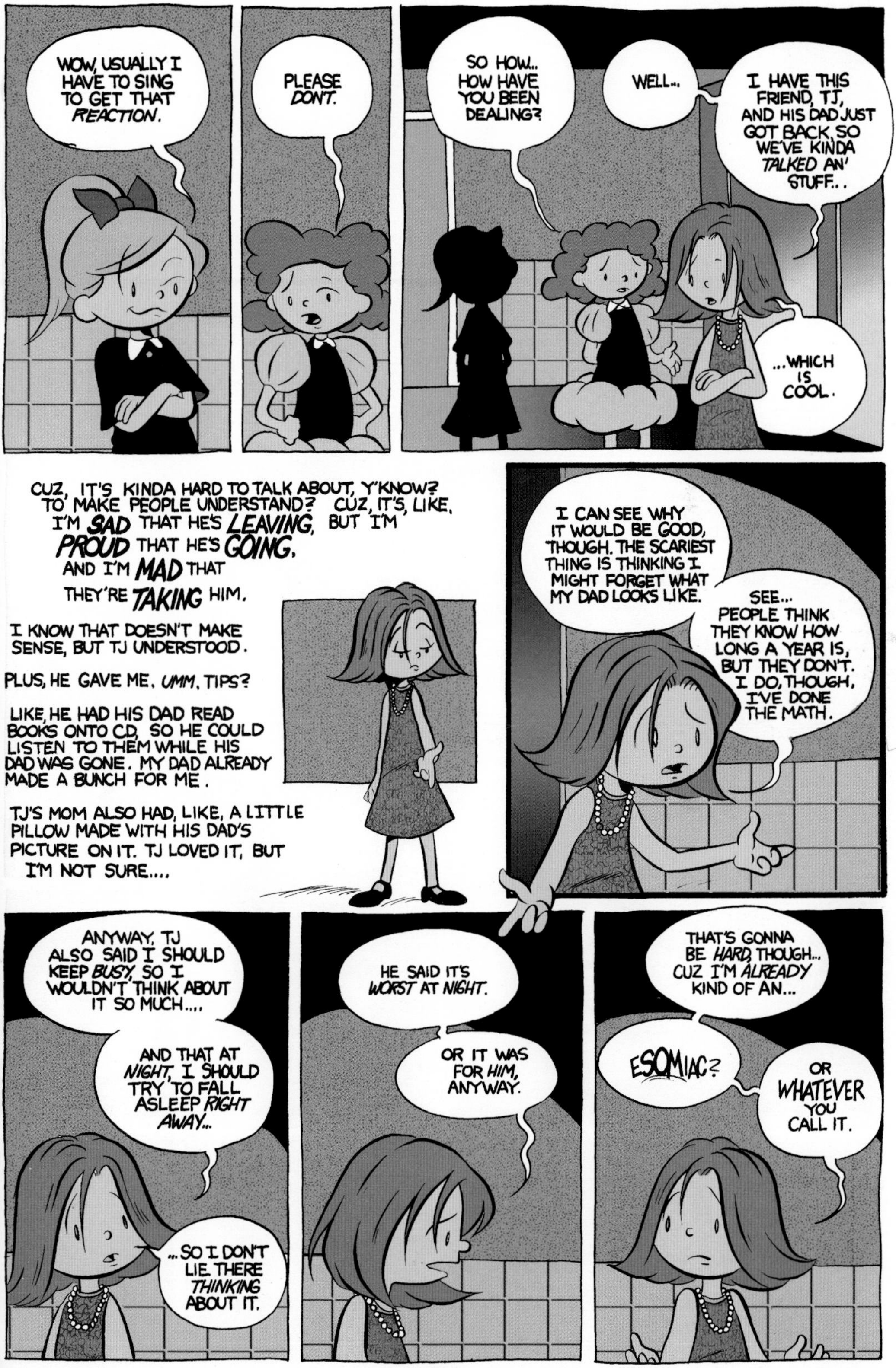
WOW, USUALLY I HAVE TO SING TO GET THAT *REACTION*.
PLEASE *DON'T*.
SO HOW... HOW HAVE YOU BEEN DEALING?
WELL...
I HAVE THIS FRIEND, TJ, AND HIS DAD JUST GOT BACK, SO WE'VE KINDA *TALKED* AN' STUFF...
...WHICH IS COOL.
CUZ, IT'S KINDA HARD TO TALK ABOUT, Y'KNOW? TO MAKE PEOPLE UNDERSTAND? CUZ, IT'S, LIKE, I'M **SAD** THAT HE'S **LEAVING**, BUT I'M **PROUD** THAT HE'S **GOING**, AND I'M **MAD** THAT THEY'RE **TAKING** HIM.
I KNOW THAT DOESN'T MAKE SENSE, BUT TJ UNDERSTOOD.
PLUS, HE GAVE ME, *UMM*, TIPS?
LIKE, HE HAD HIS DAD READ BOOKS ONTO CD, SO HE COULD LISTEN TO THEM WHILE HIS DAD WAS GONE. MY DAD ALREADY MADE A BUNCH FOR ME.
TJ'S MOM ALSO HAD, LIKE, A LITTLE PILLOW MADE WITH HIS DAD'S PICTURE ON IT. TJ LOVED IT, BUT I'M NOT SURE....
I CAN SEE WHY IT WOULD BE GOOD, THOUGH. THE SCARIEST THING IS THINKING I MIGHT FORGET WHAT MY DAD LOOKS LIKE.
SEE... PEOPLE THINK THEY KNOW HOW LONG A YEAR IS, BUT THEY DON'T. I DO, THOUGH. I'VE DONE THE MATH.
ANYWAY, TJ ALSO SAID I SHOULD KEEP *BUSY*, SO I WOULDN'T THINK ABOUT IT SO MUCH....
AND THAT AT *NIGHT*, I SHOULD TRY TO FALL ASLEEP *RIGHT AWAY*...
...SO I DON'T LIE THERE *THINKING* ABOUT IT.
HE SAID IT'S *WORST* AT *NIGHT*.
OR IT WAS FOR *HIM*, ANYWAY.
THAT'S GONNA BE *HARD*, THOUGH... CUZ I'M *ALREADY* KIND OF AN...
ESOMIAC?
OR **WHATEVER** YOU CALL IT.

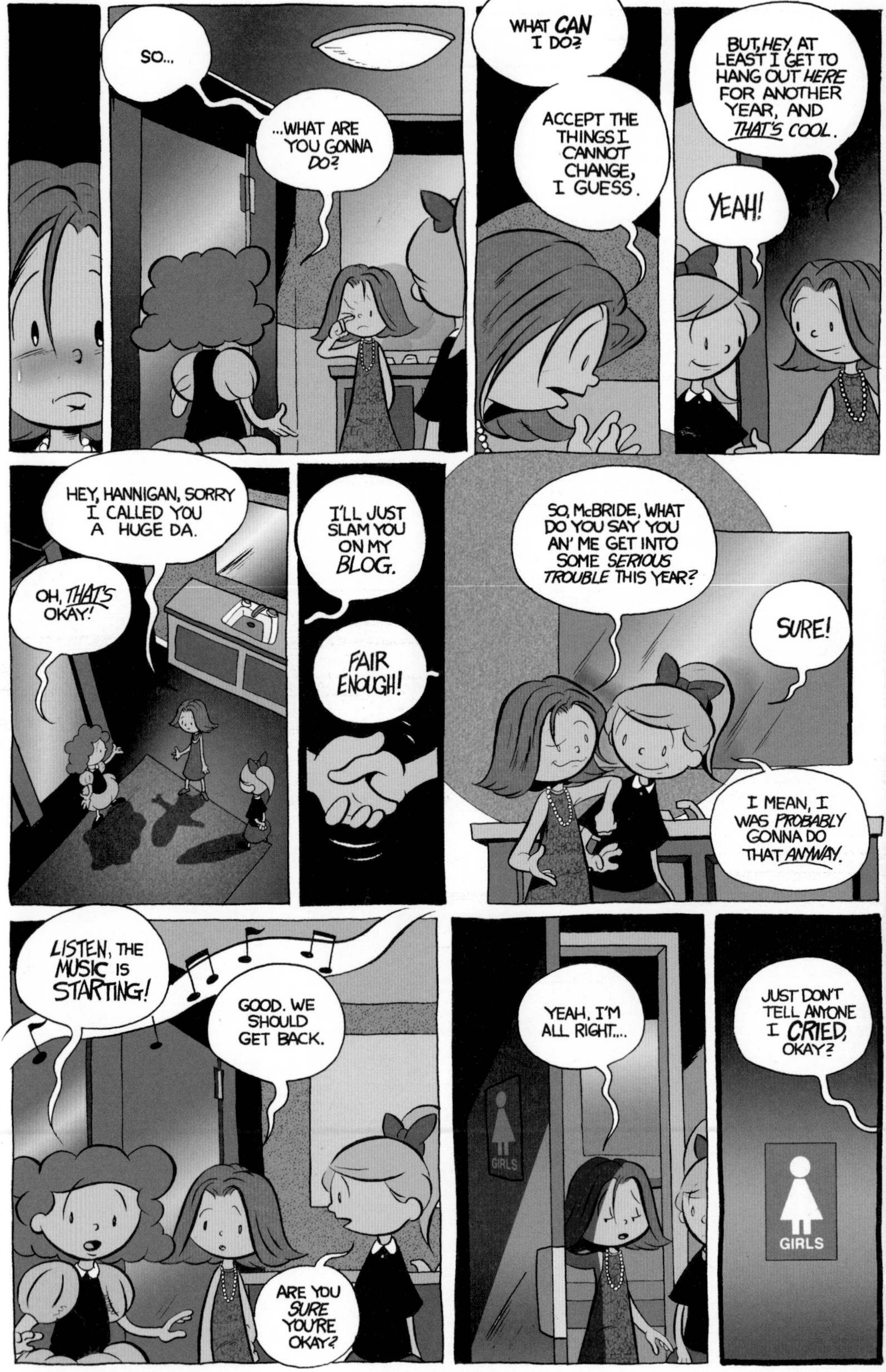
SO...
...WHAT ARE YOU GONNA DO?
WHAT CAN I DO?
ACCEPT THE THINGS I CANNOT CHANGE, I GUESS.
BUT, HEY, AT LEAST I GET TO HANG OUT HERE FOR ANOTHER YEAR, AND THAT'S COOL.
YEAH!
HEY, HANNIGAN, SORRY I CALLED YOU A HUGE DA.
OH, THAT'S OKAY!
I'LL JUST SLAM YOU ON MY BLOG.
FAIR ENOUGH!
SO, McBRIDE, WHAT DO YOU SAY YOU AN' ME GET INTO SOME SERIOUS TROUBLE THIS YEAR?
SURE!
I MEAN, I WAS PROBABLY GONNA DO THAT ANYWAY.
LISTEN, THE MUSIC IS STARTING!
GOOD. WE SHOULD GET BACK.
ARE YOU SURE YOU'RE OKAY?
GIRLS
YEAH, I'M ALL RIGHT....
JUST DON'T TELL ANYONE I CRIED, OKAY?
GIRLS

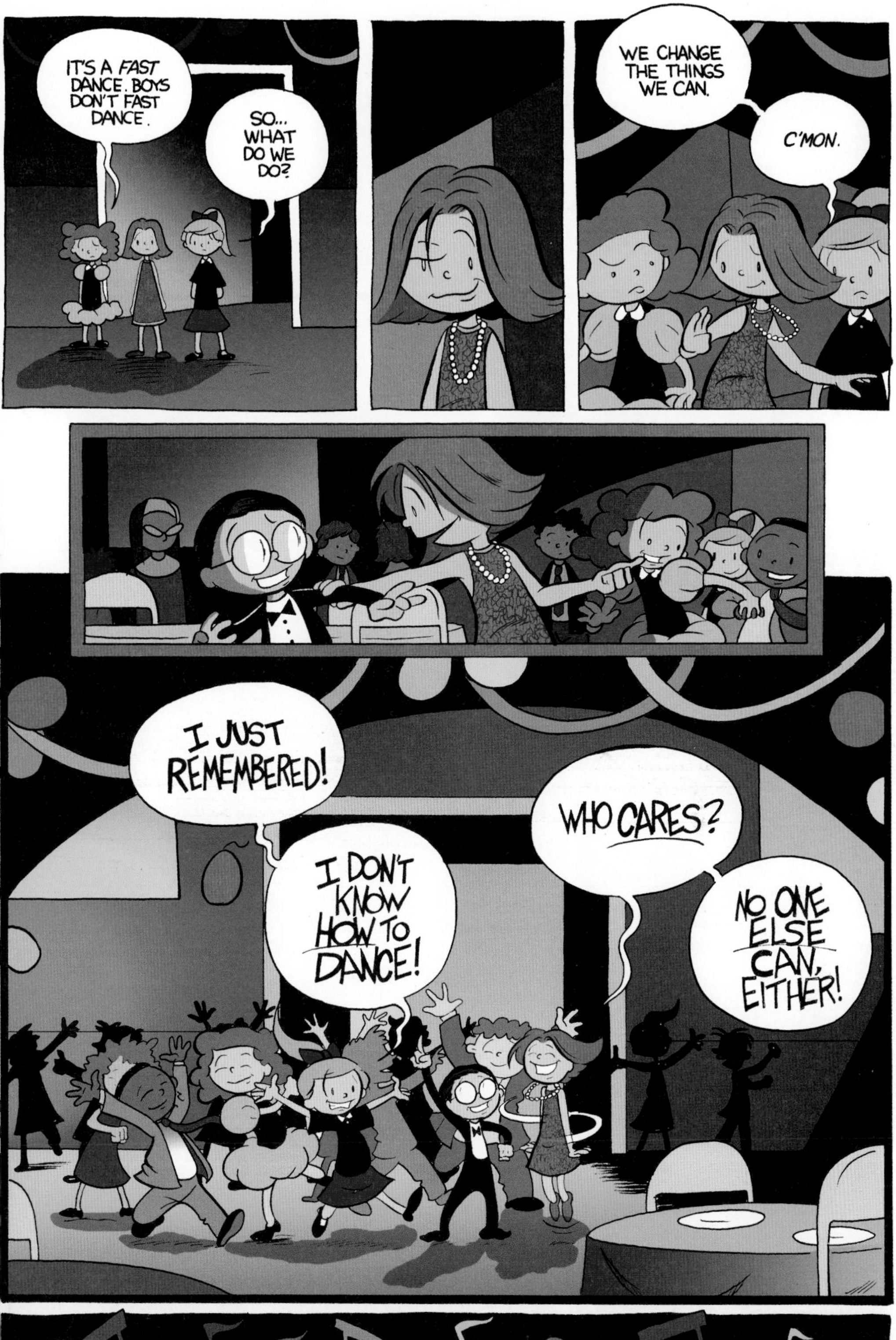
IT'S A *FAST* DANCE. BOYS DON'T FAST DANCE.
SO... WHAT DO WE DO?
WE CHANGE THE THINGS WE CAN.
C'MON.
I JUST REMEMBERED!
I DON'T KNOW HOW TO DANCE!
WHO CARES?
NO ONE ELSE CAN, EITHER!

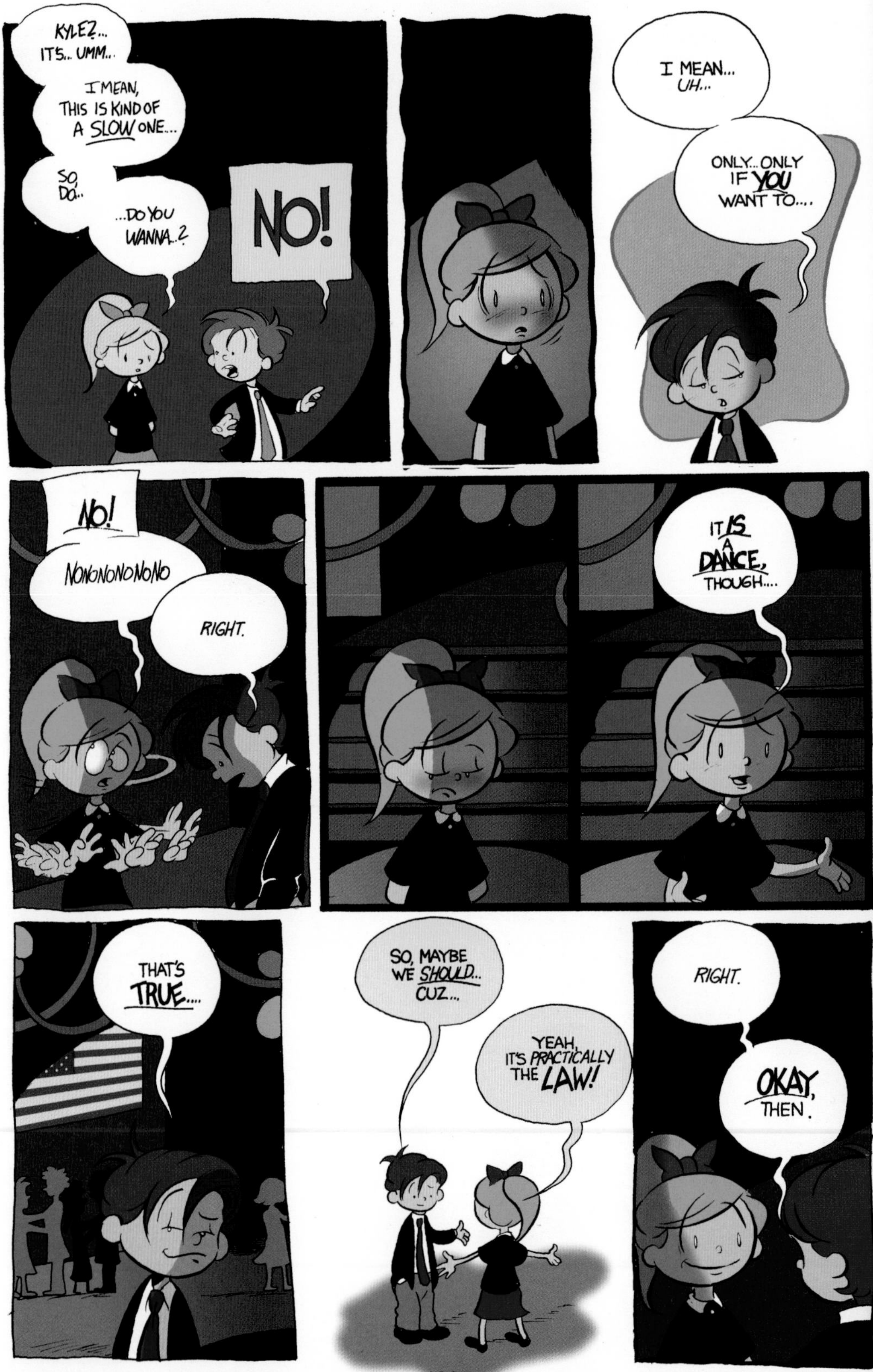
KYLE?... IT'S... UMM...
I MEAN, THIS IS KIND OF A SLOW ONE...
SO, DO...
...DO YOU WANNA...?
NO!
I MEAN... UH...
ONLY... ONLY IF YOU WANT TO....
NO!
NONONONONONO
RIGHT.
IT IS A DANCE, THOUGH....
THAT'S TRUE....
SO, MAYBE WE SHOULD... CUZ...
YEAH, IT'S PRACTICALLY THE LAW!
RIGHT.
OKAY, THEN.

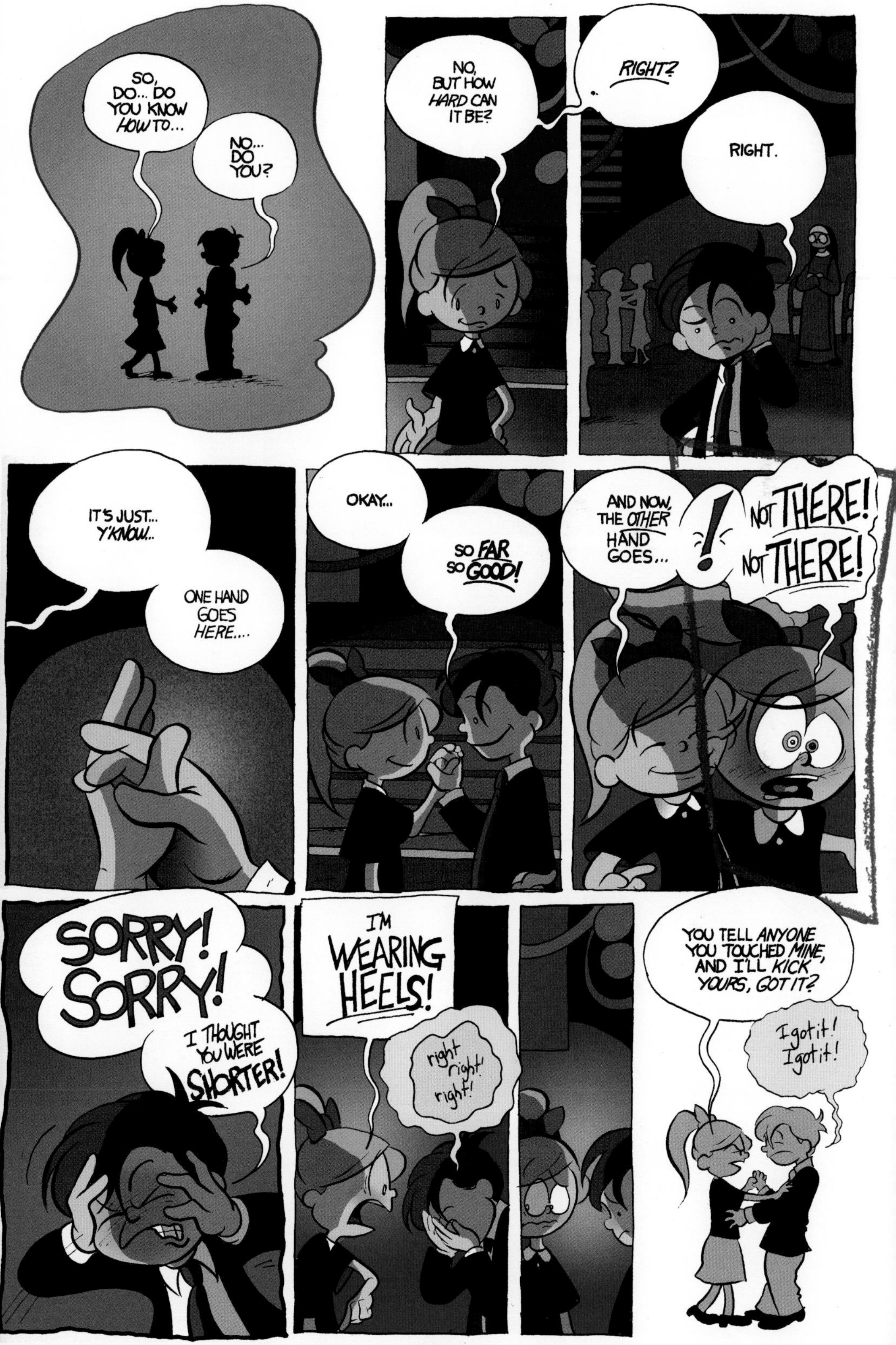
SO, DO... DO YOU KNOW HOW TO...
NO... DO YOU?
NO, BUT HOW HARD CAN IT BE?
RIGHT?
RIGHT.
IT'S JUST... Y'KNOW...
ONE HAND GOES HERE....
OKAY...
SO FAR SO GOOD!
AND NOW, THE OTHER HAND GOES...
!
NOT THERE! NOT THERE!
SORRY! SORRY!
I THOUGHT YOU WERE SHORTER!
I'M WEARING HEELS!
right right! right!
YOU TELL ANYONE YOU TOUCHED MINE, AND I'LL KICK YOURS, GOT IT?
I got it! I got it!

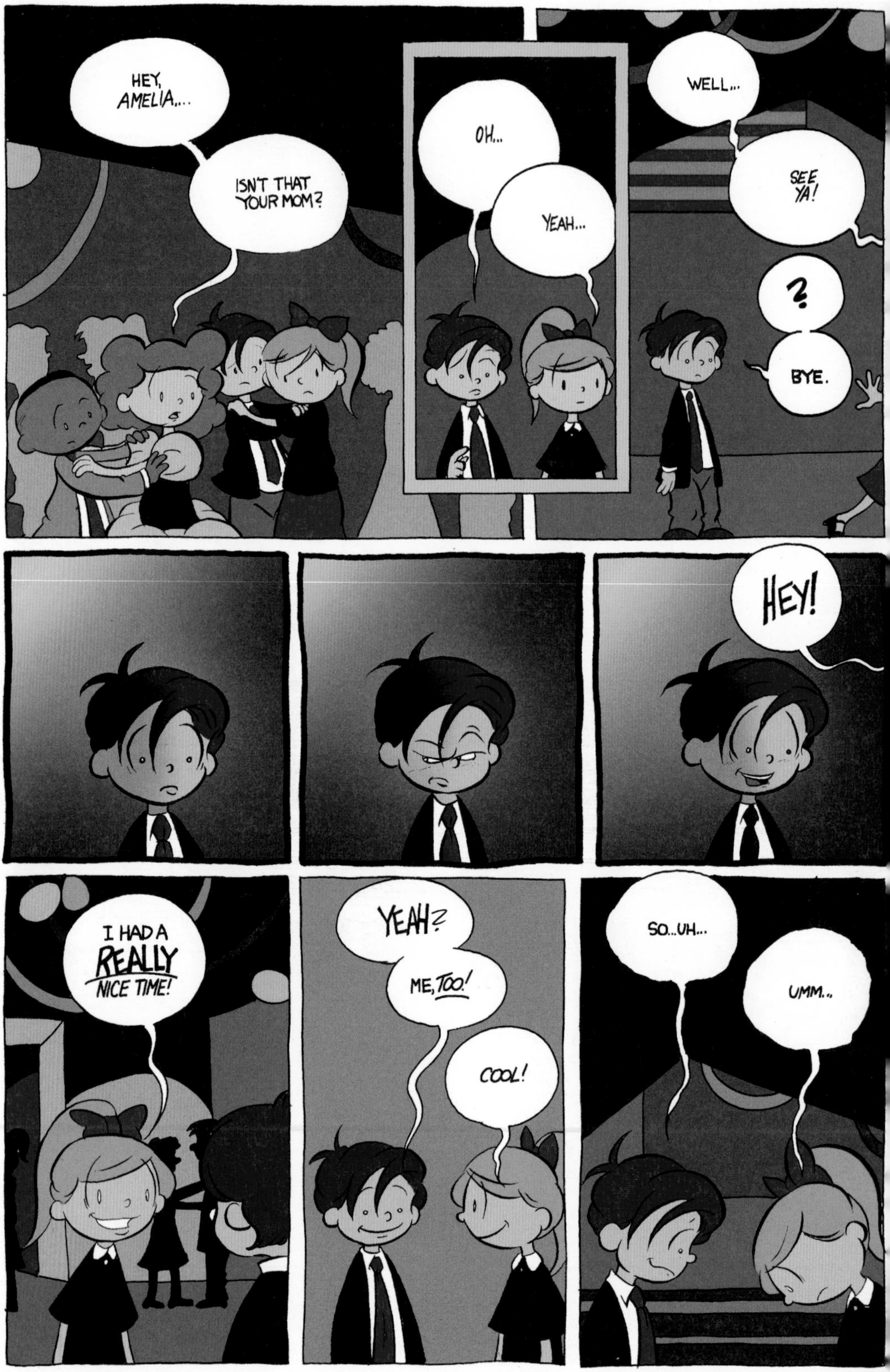
HEY, AMELIA,...
ISN'T THAT YOUR MOM?
OH...
YEAH...
WELL...
SEE YA!
?
BYE.
HEY!
I HAD A REALLY NICE TIME!
YEAH?
ME, TOO!
COOL!
SO...UH...
UMM...

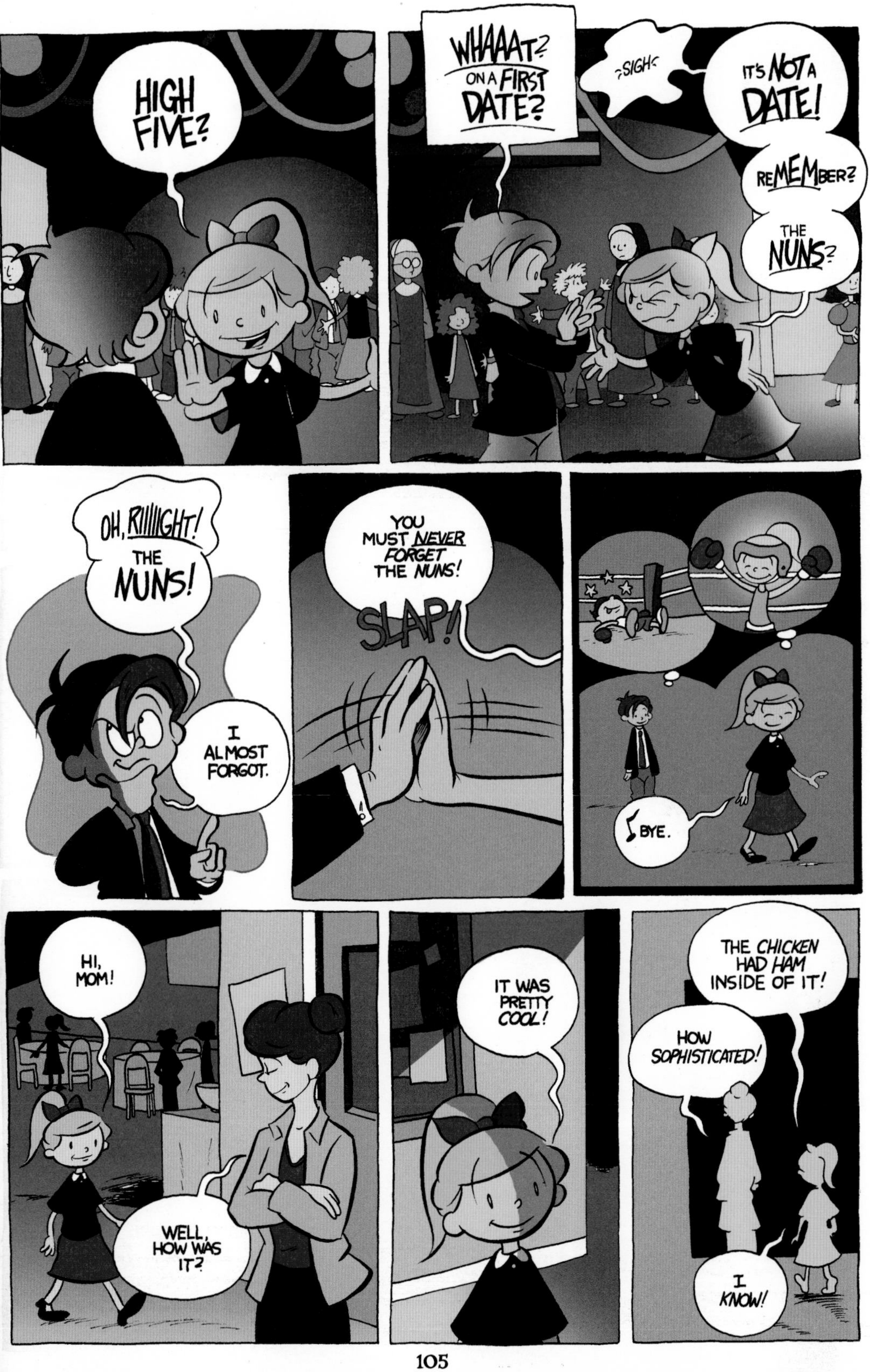
HIGH FIVE?
WHAAAT? ON A FIRST DATE?
¿SIGH¿
IT'S NOT A DATE!
REMEMBER?
THE NUNS?
OH, RIIIIGHT! THE NUNS!
I ALMOST FORGOT.
YOU MUST NEVER FORGET THE NUNS!
SLAP!
BYE.
HI, MOM!
WELL, HOW WAS IT?
IT WAS PRETTY COOL!
THE CHICKEN HAD HAM INSIDE OF IT!
HOW SOPHISTICATED!
I KNOW!

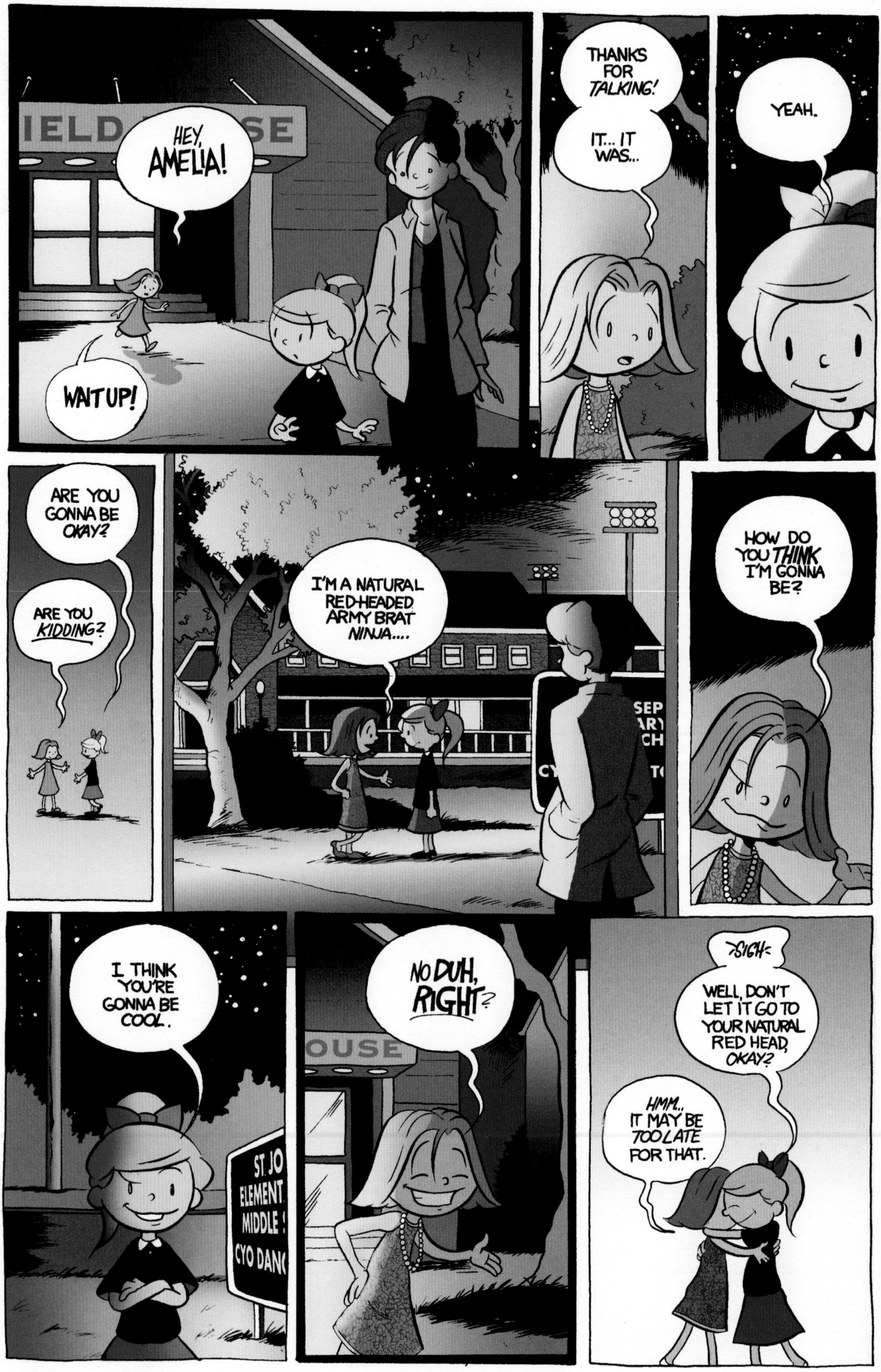
IELD SE
HEY, AMELIA!
WAIT UP!
THANKS FOR TALKING!
IT... IT WAS...
YEAH.
ARE YOU GONNA BE OKAY?
ARE YOU KIDDING?
I'M A NATURAL RED-HEADED ARMY BRAT NINJA....
HOW DO YOU THINK I'M GONNA BE?
I THINK YOU'RE GONNA BE COOL.
ST. JO ELEMENT MIDDLE CYO DANC
NO DUH, RIGHT?
OUSE
-SIGH-
WELL, DON'T LET IT GO TO YOUR NATURAL RED HEAD, OKAY?
HMM... IT MAY BE TOO LATE FOR THAT.

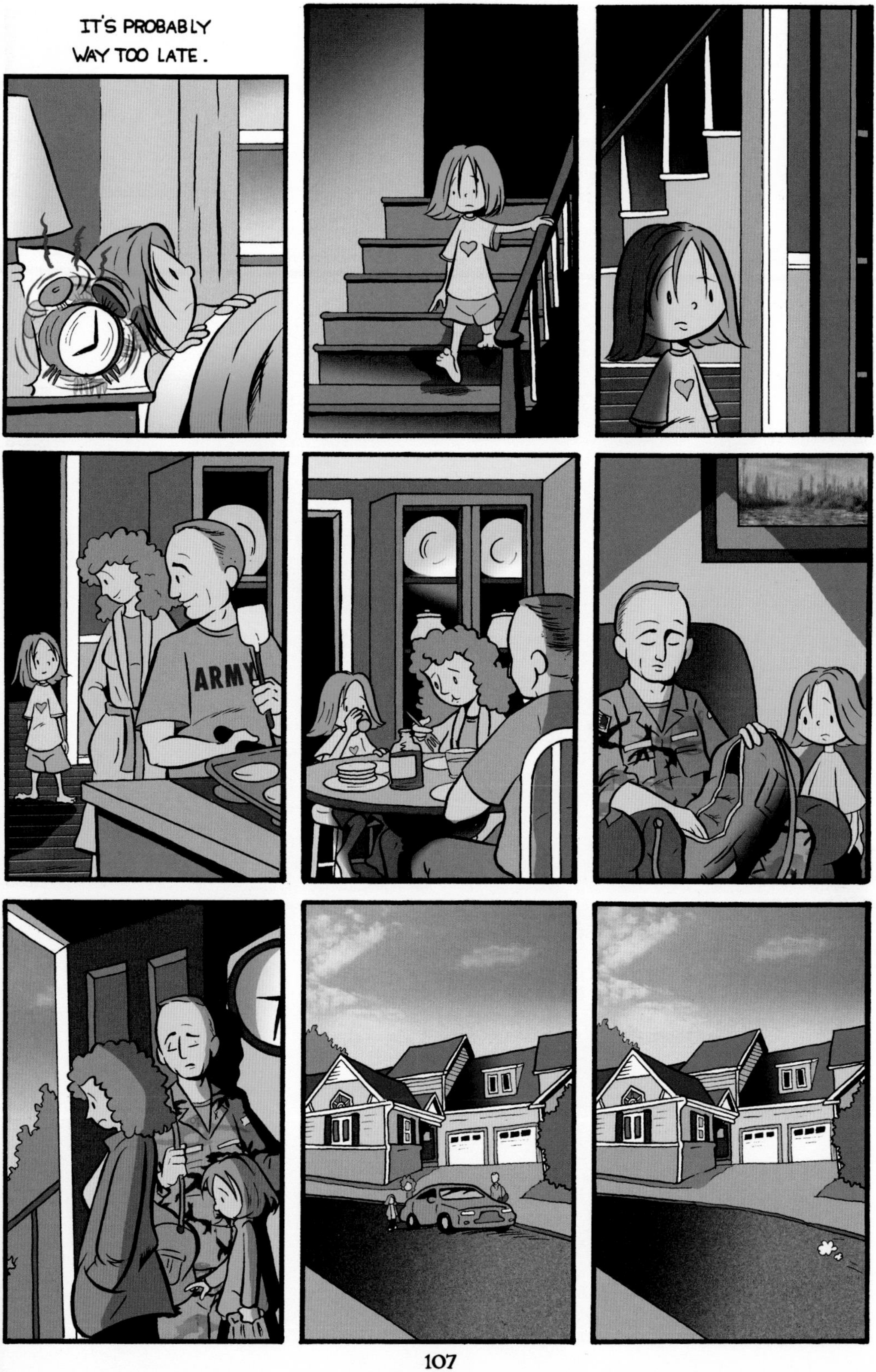
IT'S PROBABLY
WAY TOO LATE.
ARMY

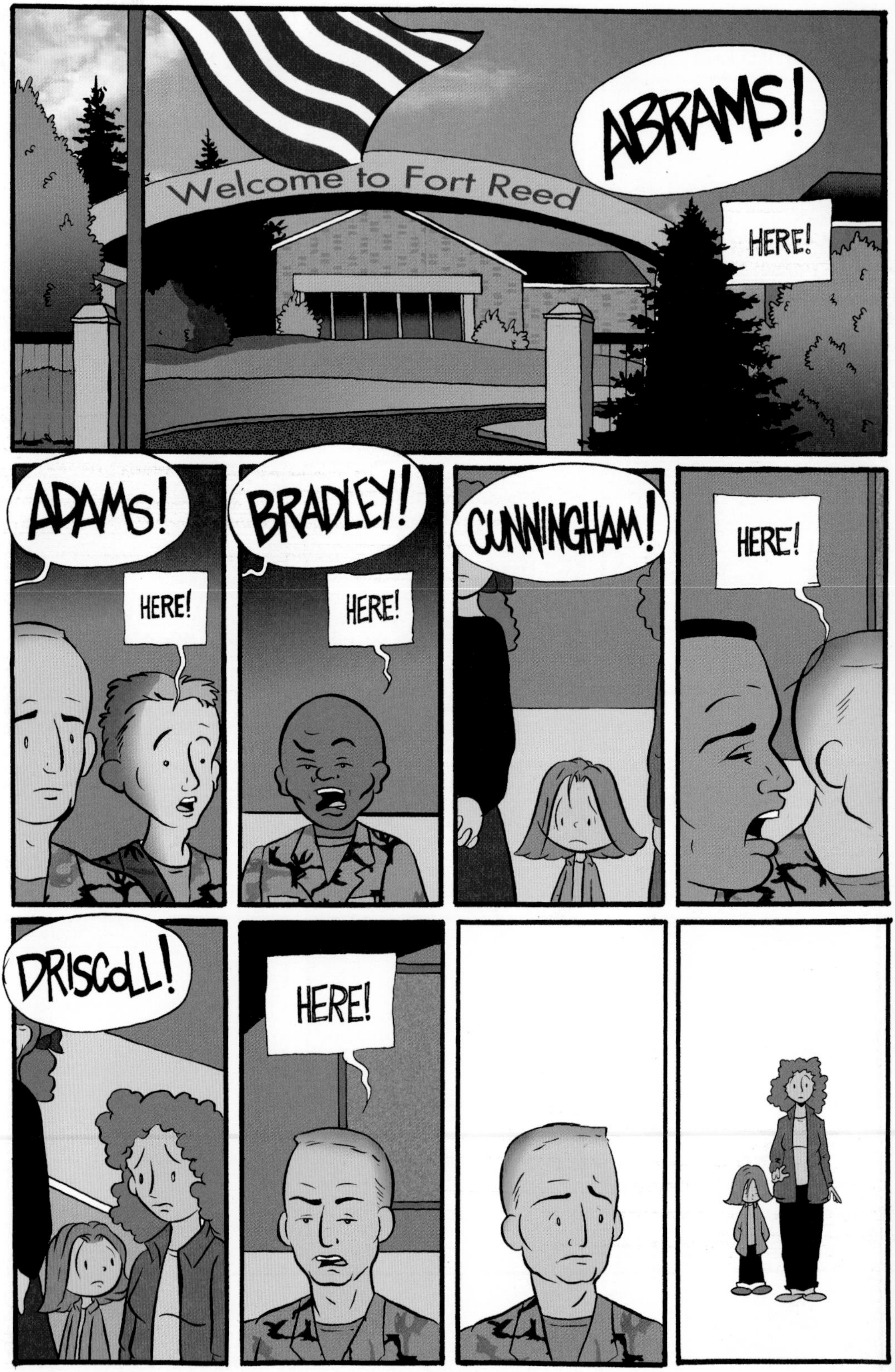
Welcome to Fort Reed
ABRAMS!
HERE!
ADAMS!
HERE!
BRADLEY!
HERE!
CUNNINGHAM!
HERE!
DRISCOLL!
HERE!

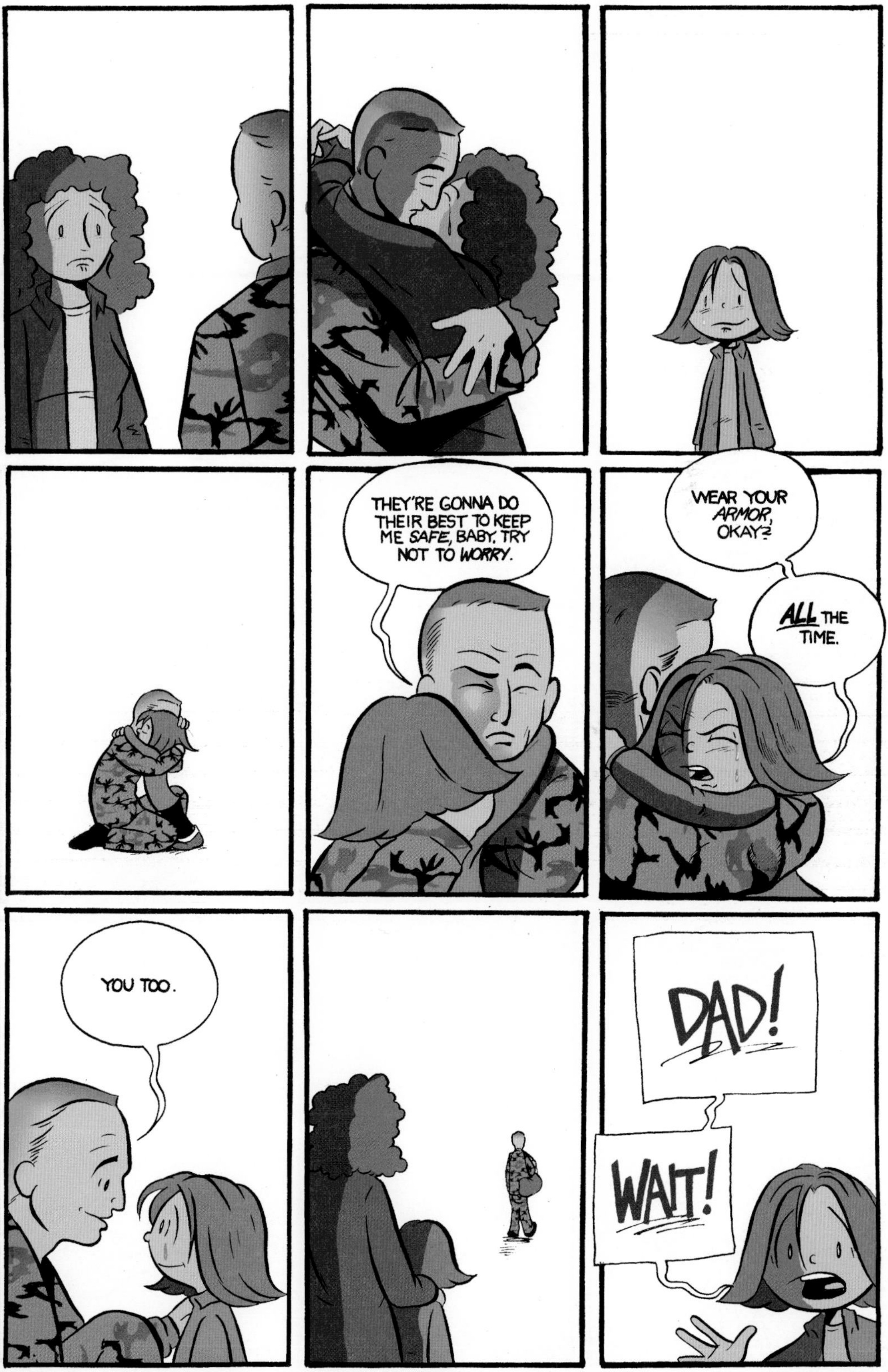
THEY'RE GONNA DO THEIR BEST TO KEEP ME SAFE, BABY. TRY NOT TO WORRY.
WEAR YOUR ARMOR, OKAY?
ALL THE TIME.
YOU TOO.
DAD!
WAIT!

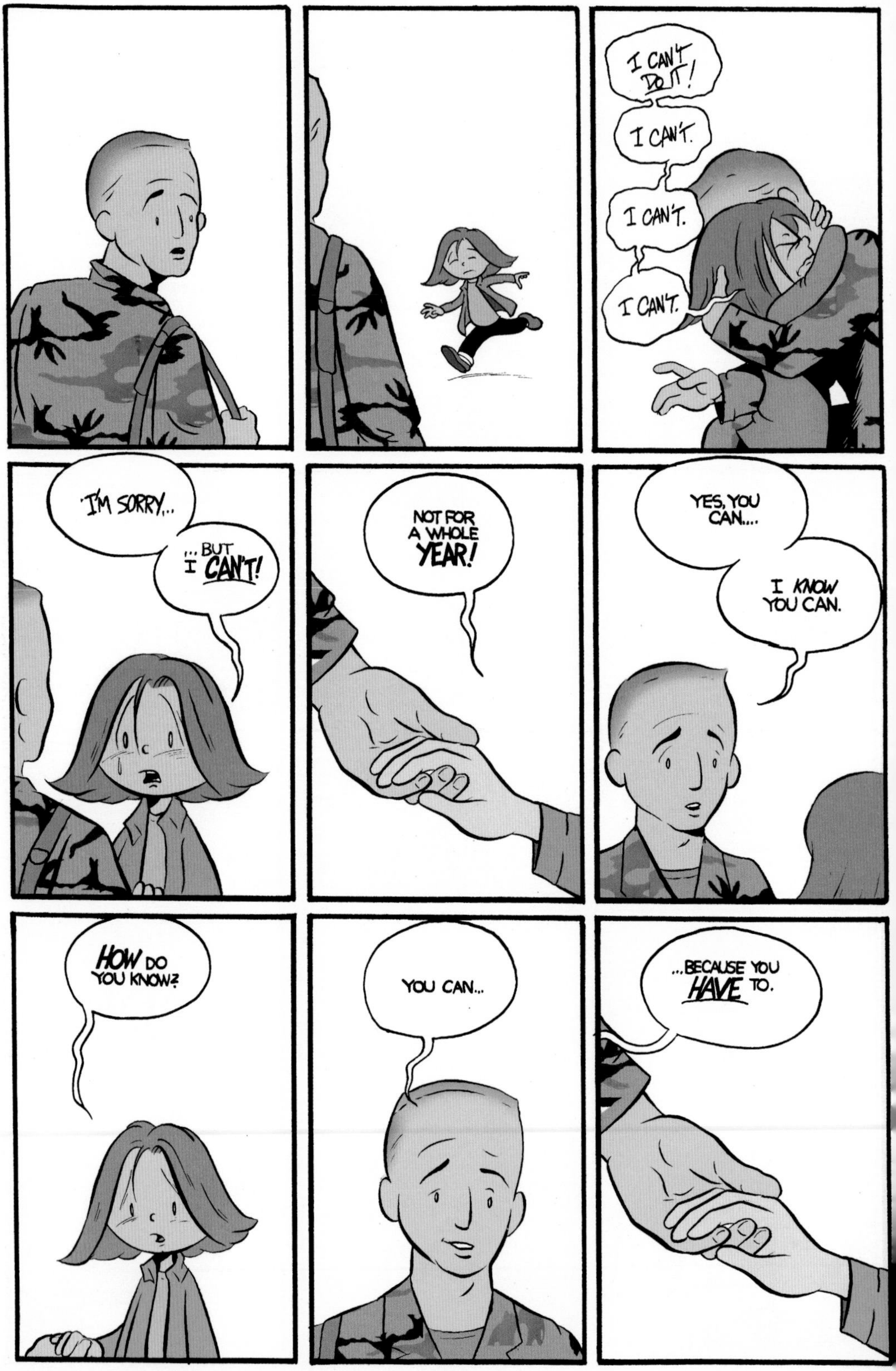
I CAN'T DO IT!
I CAN'T.
I CAN'T.
I CAN'T.
I'M SORRY...
...BUT I CAN'T!
NOT FOR A WHOLE YEAR!
YES, YOU CAN...
I KNOW YOU CAN.
HOW DO YOU KNOW?
YOU CAN...
...BECAUSE YOU HAVE TO.

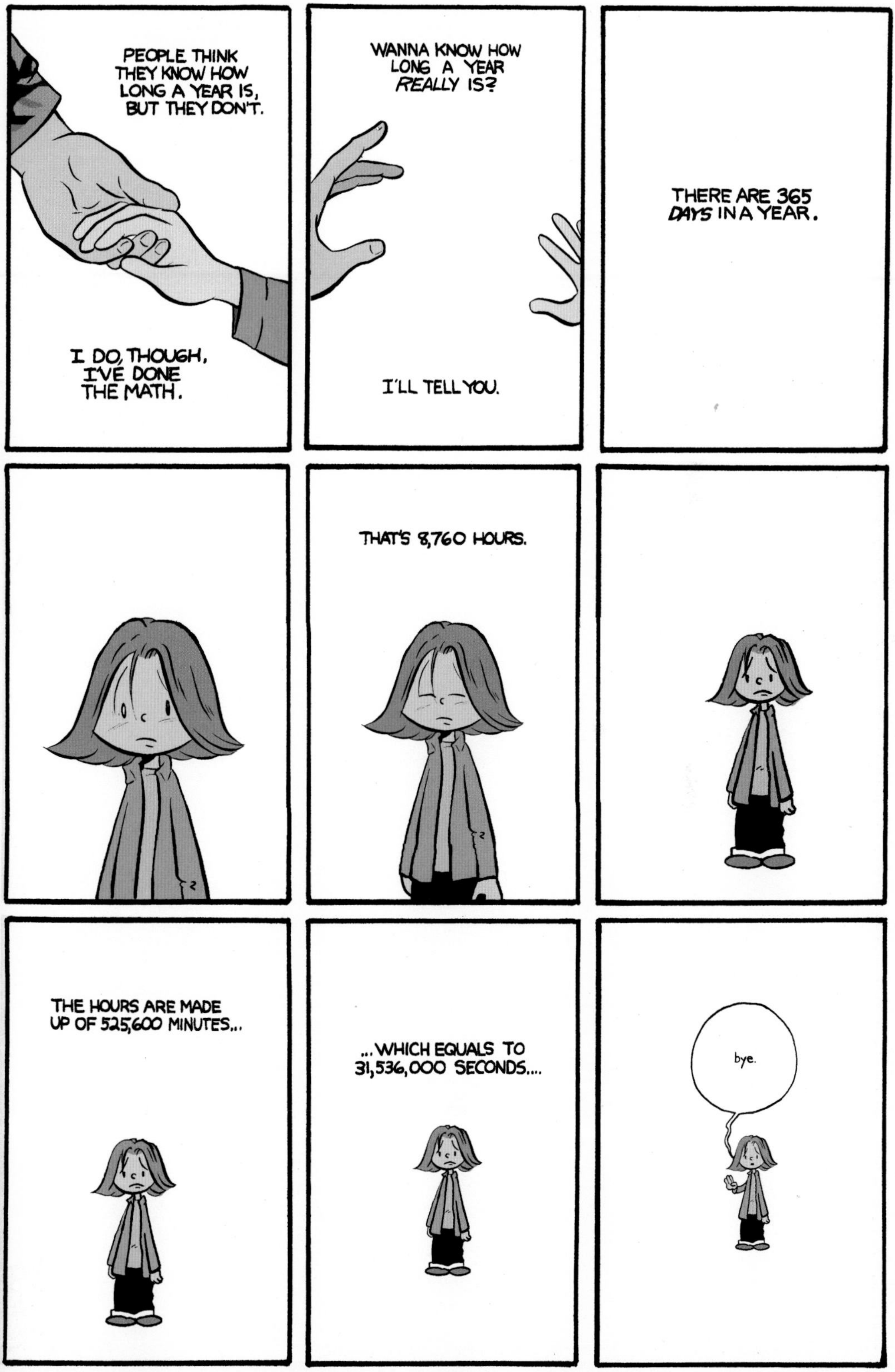
PEOPLE THINK THEY KNOW HOW LONG A YEAR IS, BUT THEY DON'T.
I DO, THOUGH, I'VE DONE THE MATH.
WANNA KNOW HOW LONG A YEAR *REALLY* IS?
I'LL TELL YOU.
THERE ARE 365 *DAYS* IN A YEAR.
THAT'S 8,760 HOURS.
THE HOURS ARE MADE UP OF 525,600 MINUTES...
...WHICH EQUALS TO 31,536,000 SECONDS....
bye.

ONE-ONE THOUSAND...

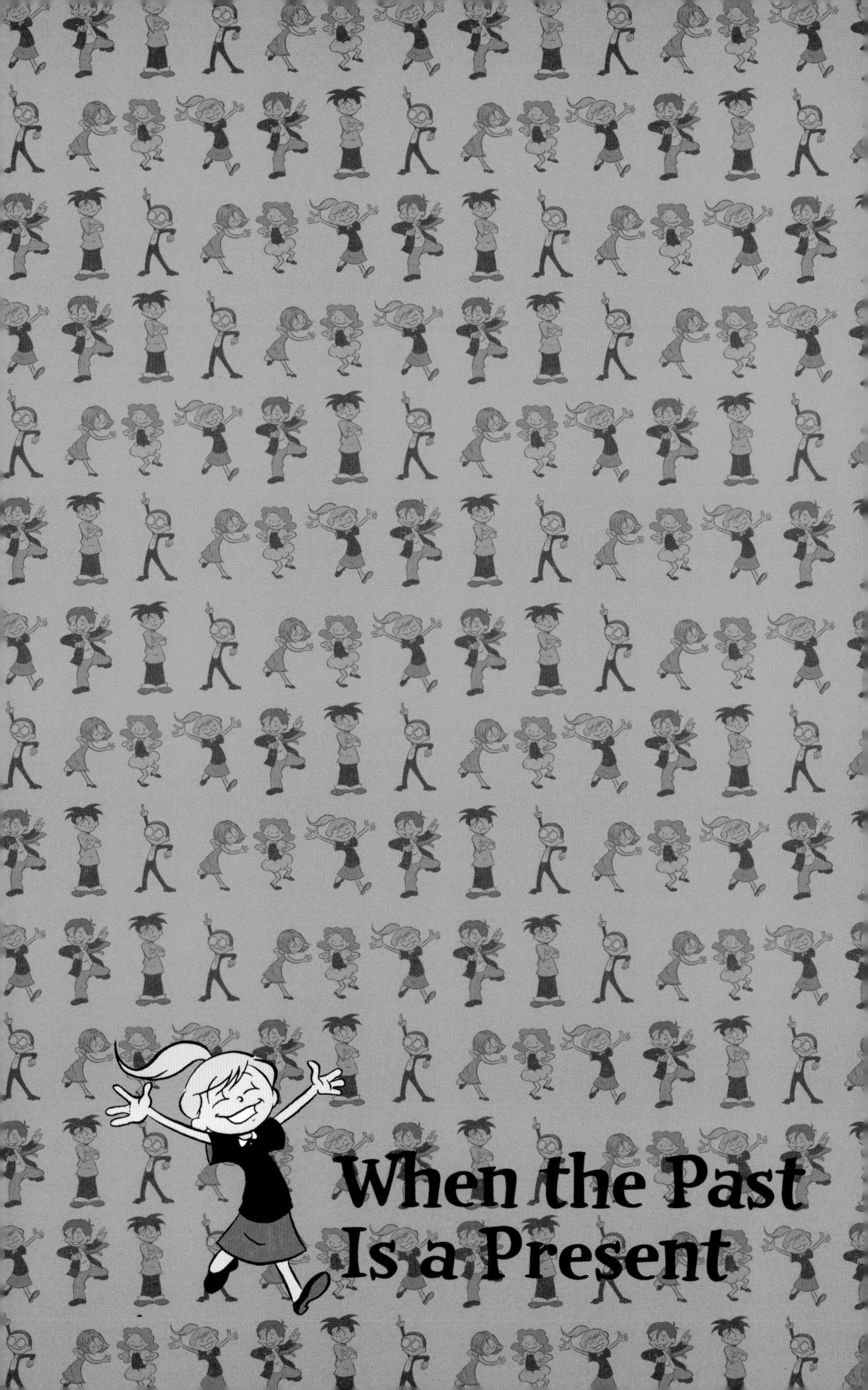

When the Past Is a Present

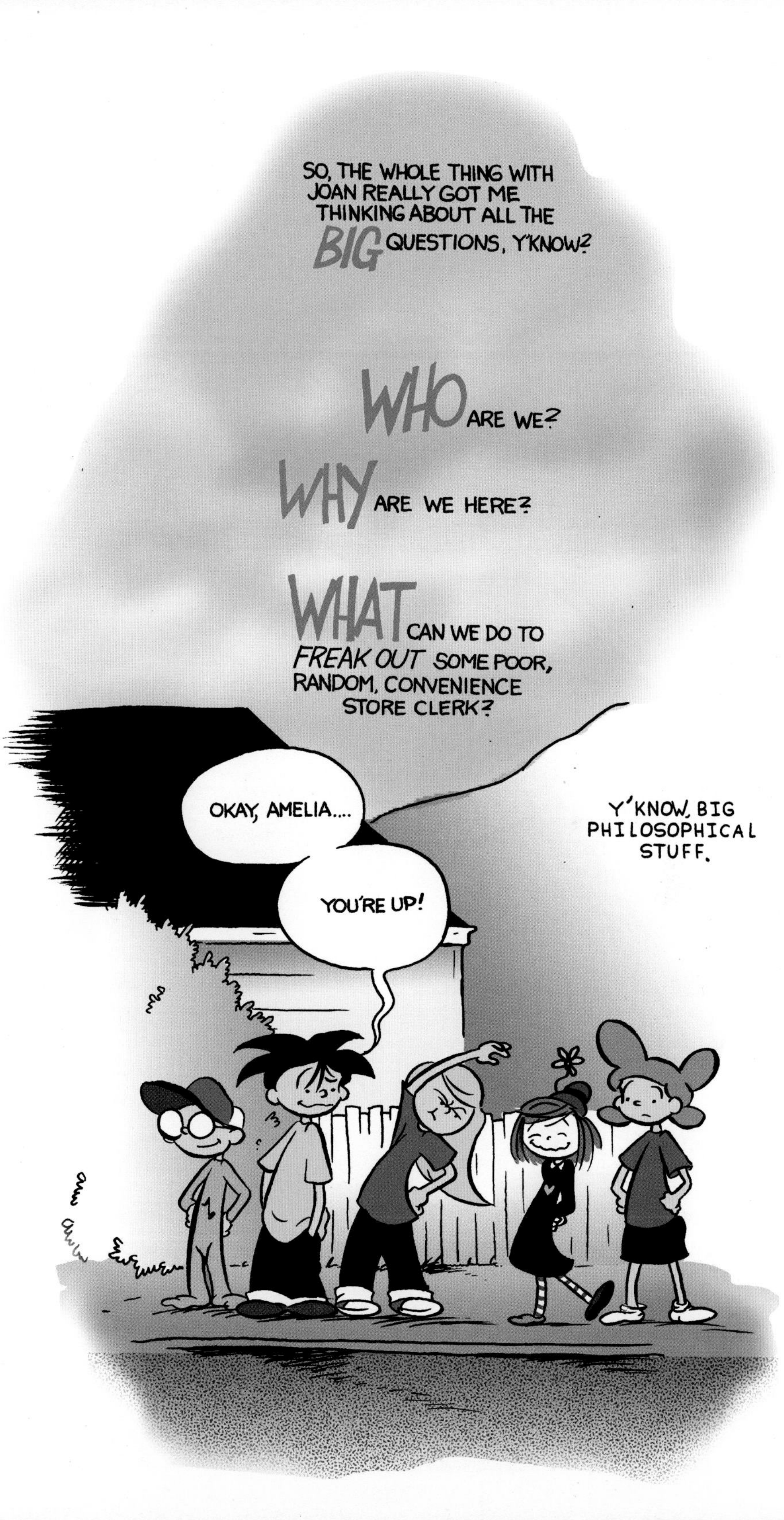
SO, THE WHOLE THING WITH JOAN REALLY GOT ME THINKING ABOUT ALL THE BIG QUESTIONS, Y'KNOW?
WHO ARE WE?
WHY ARE WE HERE?
WHAT CAN WE DO TO FREAK OUT SOME POOR, RANDOM, CONVENIENCE STORE CLERK?
Y'KNOW, BIG PHILOSOPHICAL STUFF.
OKAY, AMELIA....
YOU'RE UP!

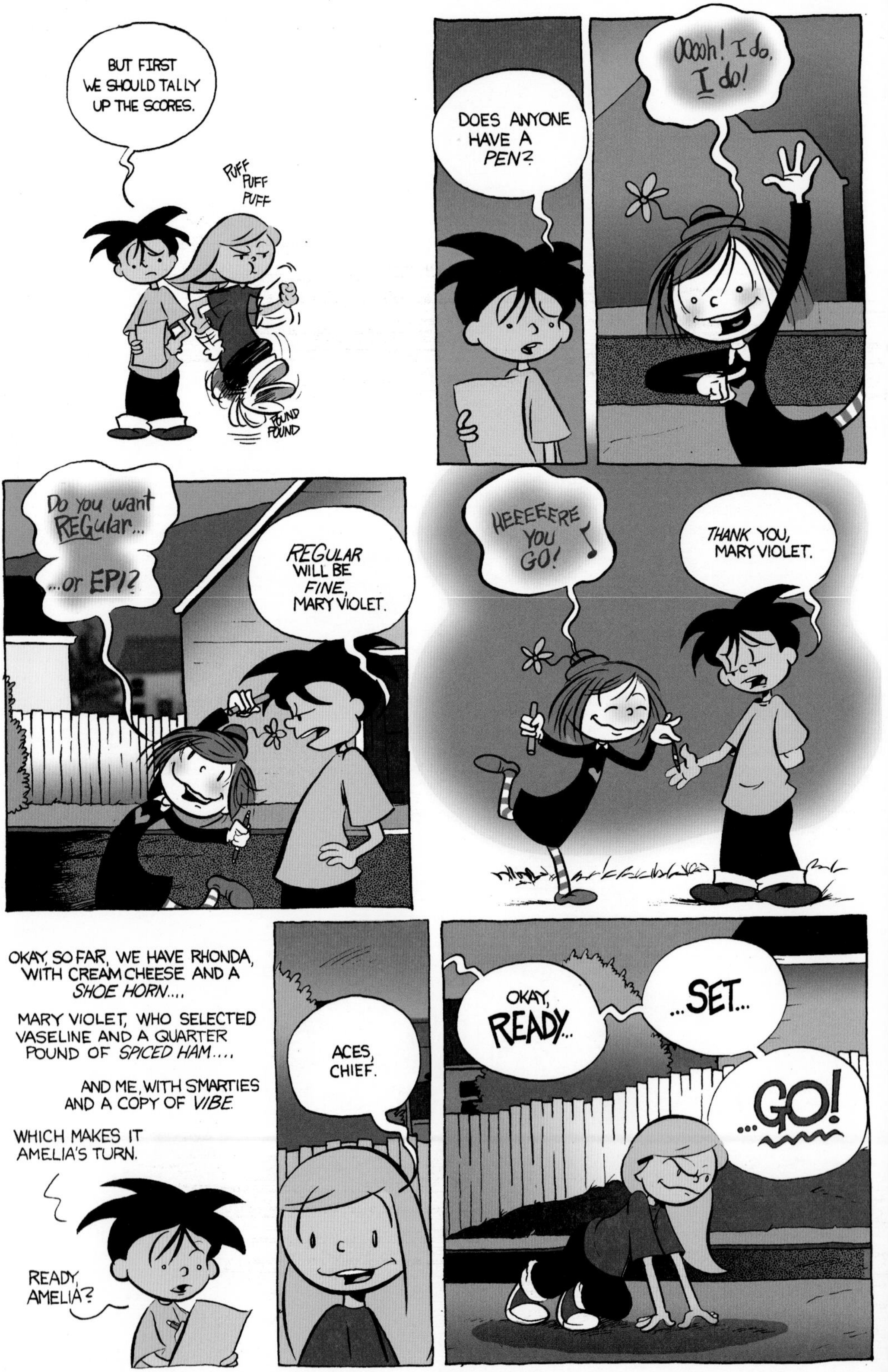
BUT FIRST WE SHOULD TALLY UP THE SCORES.
PUFF PUFF PUFF
POUND POUND
DOES ANYONE HAVE A PEN?
Ooooh! I do, I do!
Do you want REGular... ...or EPI?
REGULAR WILL BE FINE, MARY VIOLET.
HEEEEERE YOU GO!
THANK YOU, MARY VIOLET.
OKAY, SO FAR, WE HAVE RHONDA, WITH CREAM CHEESE AND A SHOE HORN....
MARY VIOLET, WHO SELECTED VASELINE AND A QUARTER POUND OF SPICED HAM....
AND ME, WITH SMARTIES AND A COPY OF VIBE.
WHICH MAKES IT AMELIA'S TURN.
READY, AMELIA?
ACES, CHIEF.
OKAY, READY...
...SET...
...GO!

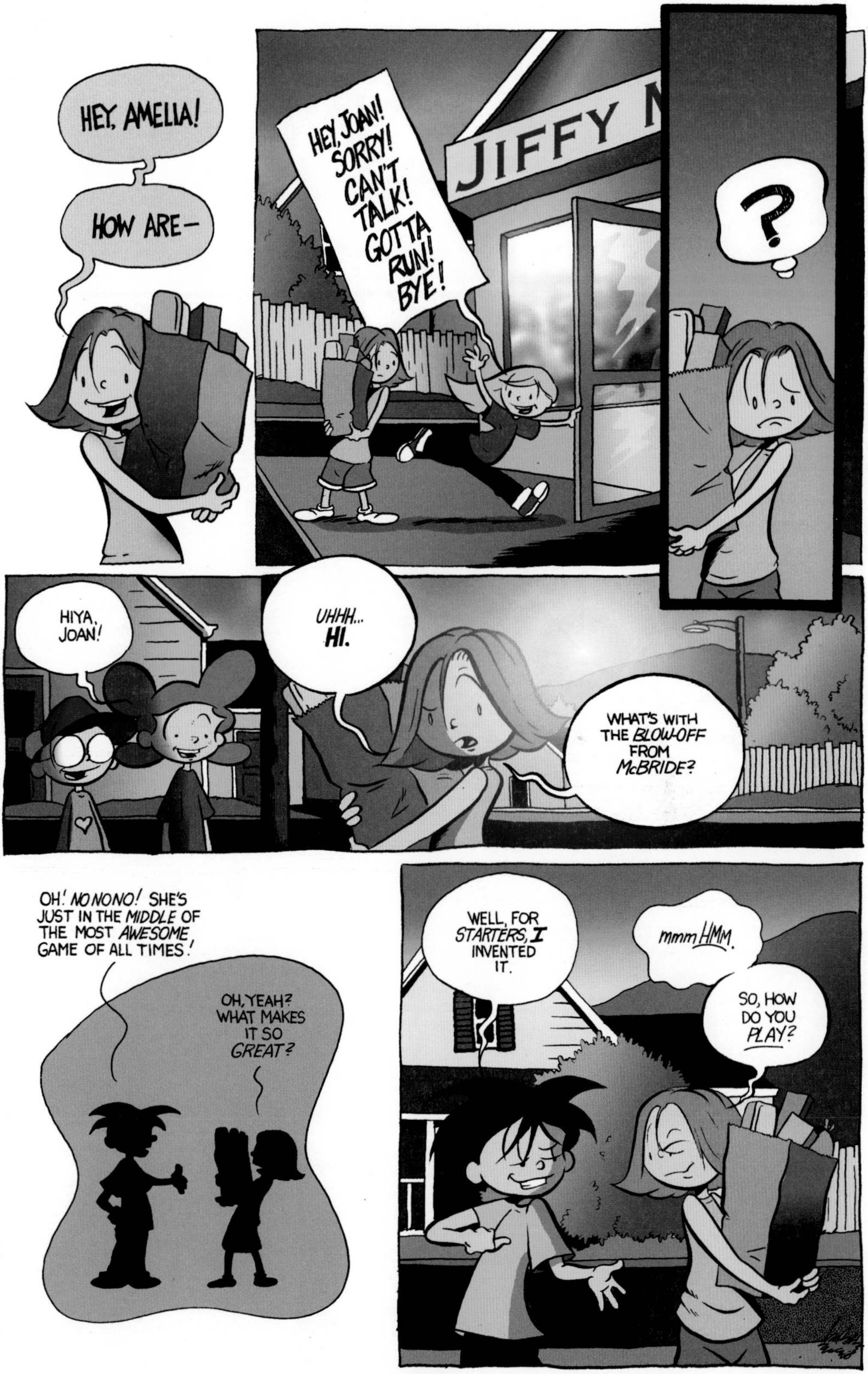

HEY, AMELIA!
HOW ARE—
HEY, JOAN! SORRY! CAN'T TALK! GOTTA RUN! BYE!
JIFFY M
?
HIYA, JOAN!
UHHH... HI.
WHAT'S WITH THE BLOW-OFF FROM McBRIDE?
OH! NO NO NO! SHE'S JUST IN THE MIDDLE OF THE MOST AWESOME GAME OF ALL TIMES!
OH, YEAH? WHAT MAKES IT SO GREAT?
WELL, FOR STARTERS, I INVENTED IT.
mmm HMM.
SO, HOW DO YOU PLAY?

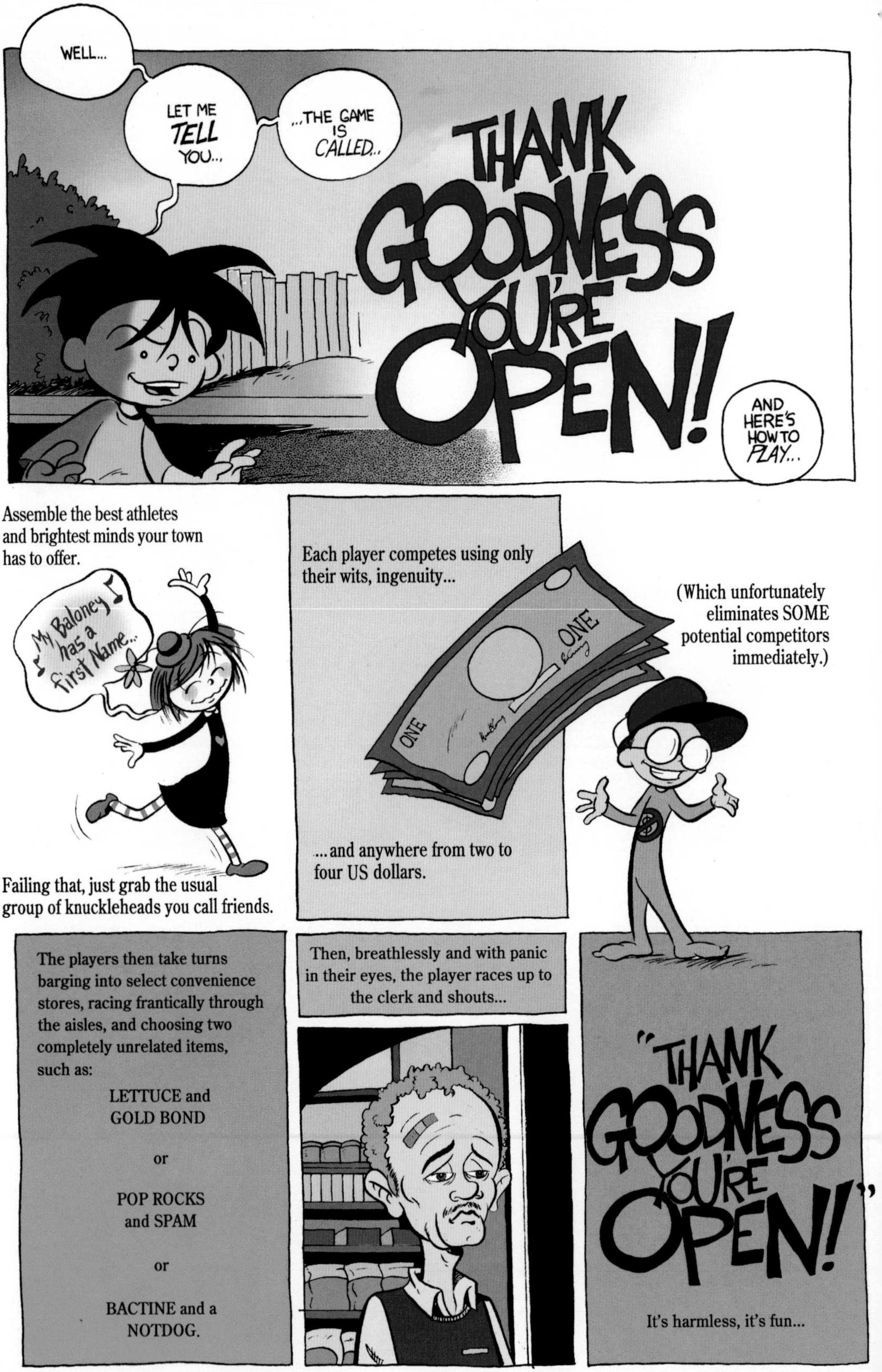
WELL...
LET ME TELL YOU...
...THE GAME IS CALLED...
THANK GOODNESS YOU'RE OPEN!
AND HERE'S HOW TO PLAY...
Assemble the best athletes and brightest minds your town has to offer.
My Baloney has a first Name...
Failing that, just grab the usual group of knuckleheads you call friends.
Each player competes using only their wits, ingenuity...
ONE
ONE
...and anywhere from two to four US dollars.
(Which unfortunately eliminates SOME potential competitors immediately.)
The players then take turns barging into select convenience stores, racing frantically through the aisles, and choosing two completely unrelated items, such as:
LETTUCE and GOLD BOND
or
POP ROCKS and SPAM
or
BACTINE and a NOTDOG.
Then, breathlessly and with panic in their eyes, the player races up to the clerk and shouts...
"THANK GOODNESS YOU'RE OPEN!"
It's harmless, it's fun...

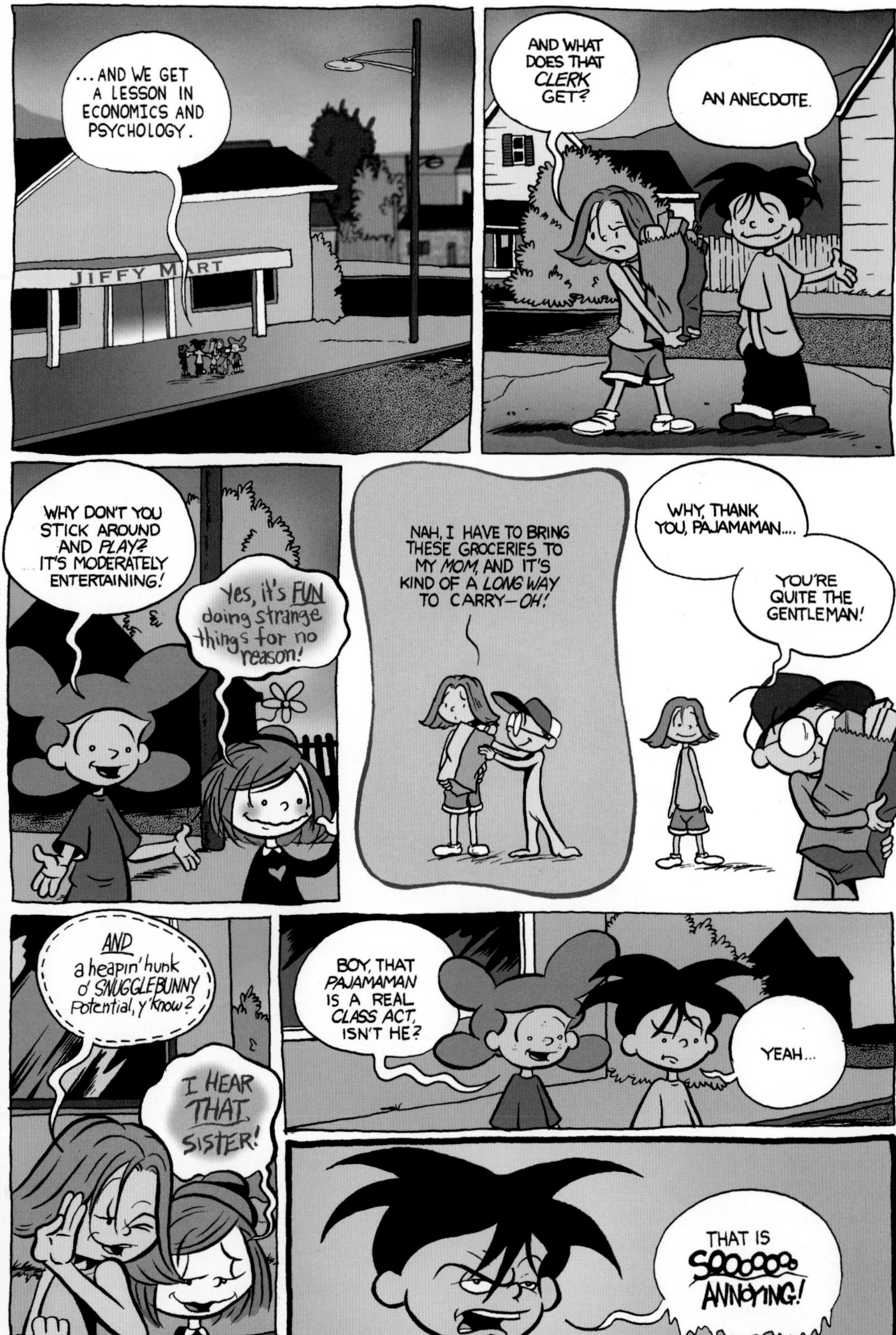

...AND WE GET A LESSON IN ECONOMICS AND PSYCHOLOGY.
JIFFY MART
AND WHAT DOES THAT CLERK GET?
AN ANECDOTE.
WHY DON'T YOU STICK AROUND AND PLAY? IT'S MODERATELY ENTERTAINING!
Yes, it's FUN doing strange things for no reason!
NAH, I HAVE TO BRING THESE GROCERIES TO MY MOM, AND IT'S KIND OF A LONG WAY TO CARRY—OH!
WHY, THANK YOU, PAJAMAMAN....
YOU'RE QUITE THE GENTLEMAN!
AND a heapin' hunk o' SNUGGLEBUNNY Potential, y'know?
I HEAR THAT, SISTER!
BOY, THAT PAJAMAMAN IS A REAL CLASS ACT, ISN'T HE?
YEAH...
THAT IS SOOOOOO ANNOYING!

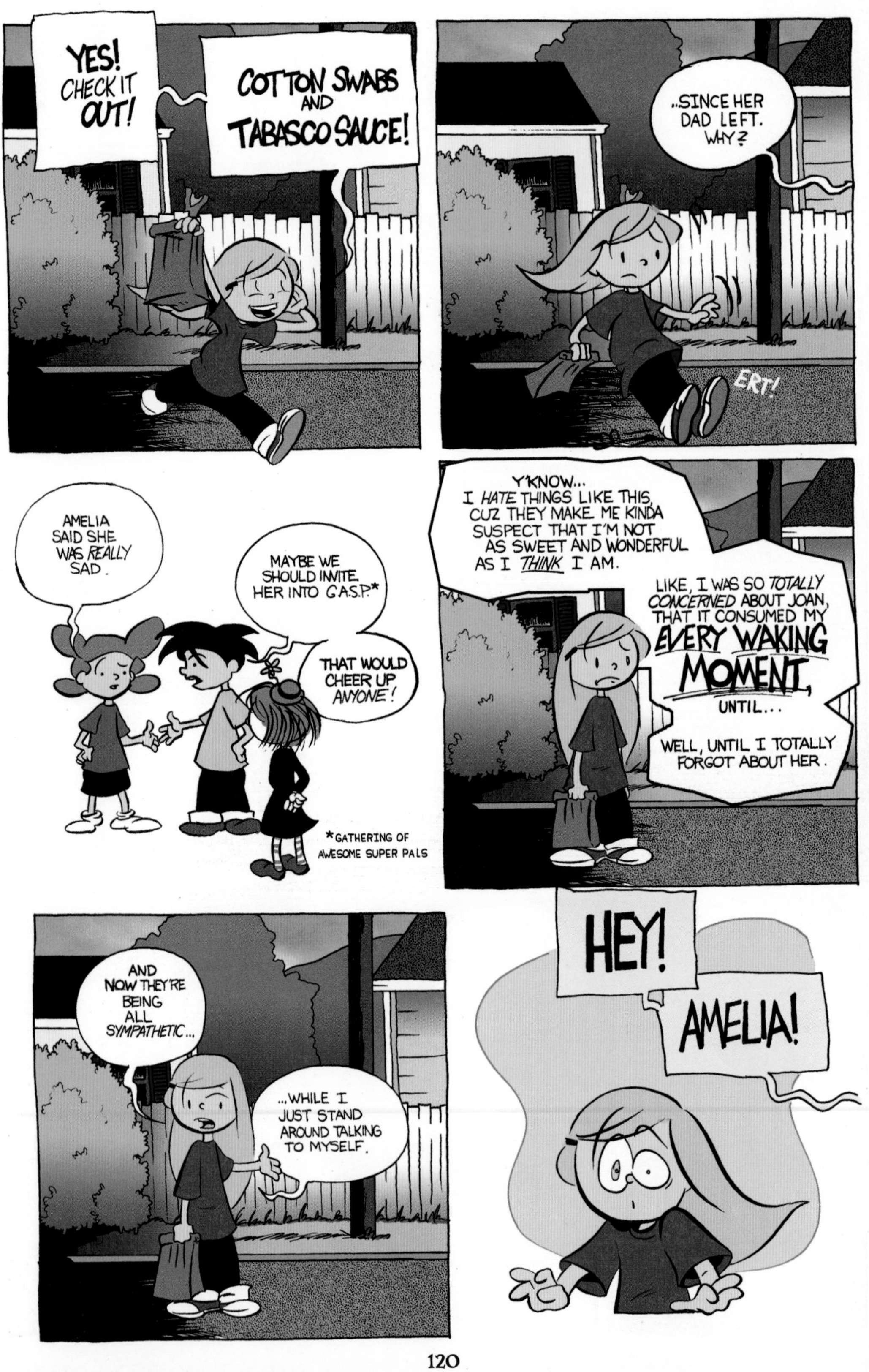
YES! CHECK IT OUT!
COTTON SWABS AND TABASCO SAUCE!
..SINCE HER DAD LEFT. WHY?
ERT!
AMELIA SAID SHE WAS REALLY SAD.
MAYBE WE SHOULD INVITE HER INTO G.A.S.P.*
THAT WOULD CHEER UP ANYONE!
*GATHERING OF AWESOME SUPER PALS
Y'KNOW... I HATE THINGS LIKE THIS, CUZ THEY MAKE ME KINDA SUSPECT THAT I'M NOT AS SWEET AND WONDERFUL AS I THINK I AM.
LIKE, I WAS SO TOTALLY CONCERNED ABOUT JOAN, THAT IT CONSUMED MY EVERY WAKING MOMENT, UNTIL...
WELL, UNTIL I TOTALLY FORGOT ABOUT HER.
AND NOW THEY'RE BEING ALL SYMPATHETIC...
...WHILE I JUST STAND AROUND TALKING TO MYSELF.
HEY!
AMELIA!

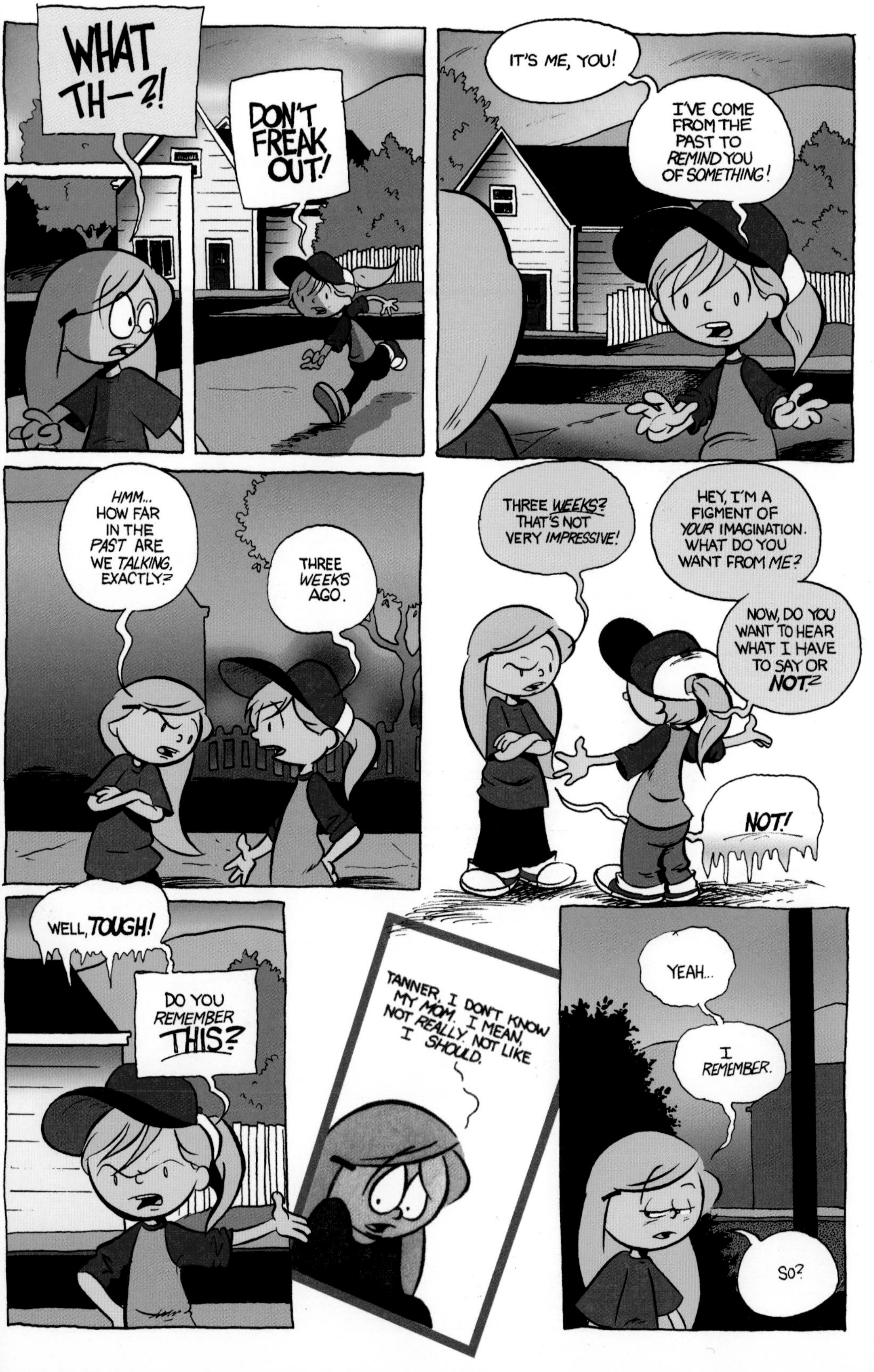
WHAT TH—?!
DON'T FREAK OUT!
IT'S ME, YOU!
I'VE COME FROM THE PAST TO REMIND YOU OF SOMETHING!
HMM... HOW FAR IN THE PAST ARE WE TALKING, EXACTLY?
THREE WEEKS AGO.
THREE WEEKS? THAT'S NOT VERY IMPRESSIVE!
HEY, I'M A FIGMENT OF YOUR IMAGINATION. WHAT DO YOU WANT FROM ME?
NOW, DO YOU WANT TO HEAR WHAT I HAVE TO SAY OR NOT?
NOT!
WELL, TOUGH!
DO YOU REMEMBER THIS?
TANNER, I DON'T KNOW MY MOM. I MEAN, NOT REALLY. NOT LIKE I SHOULD.
YEAH...
I REMEMBER.
SO?

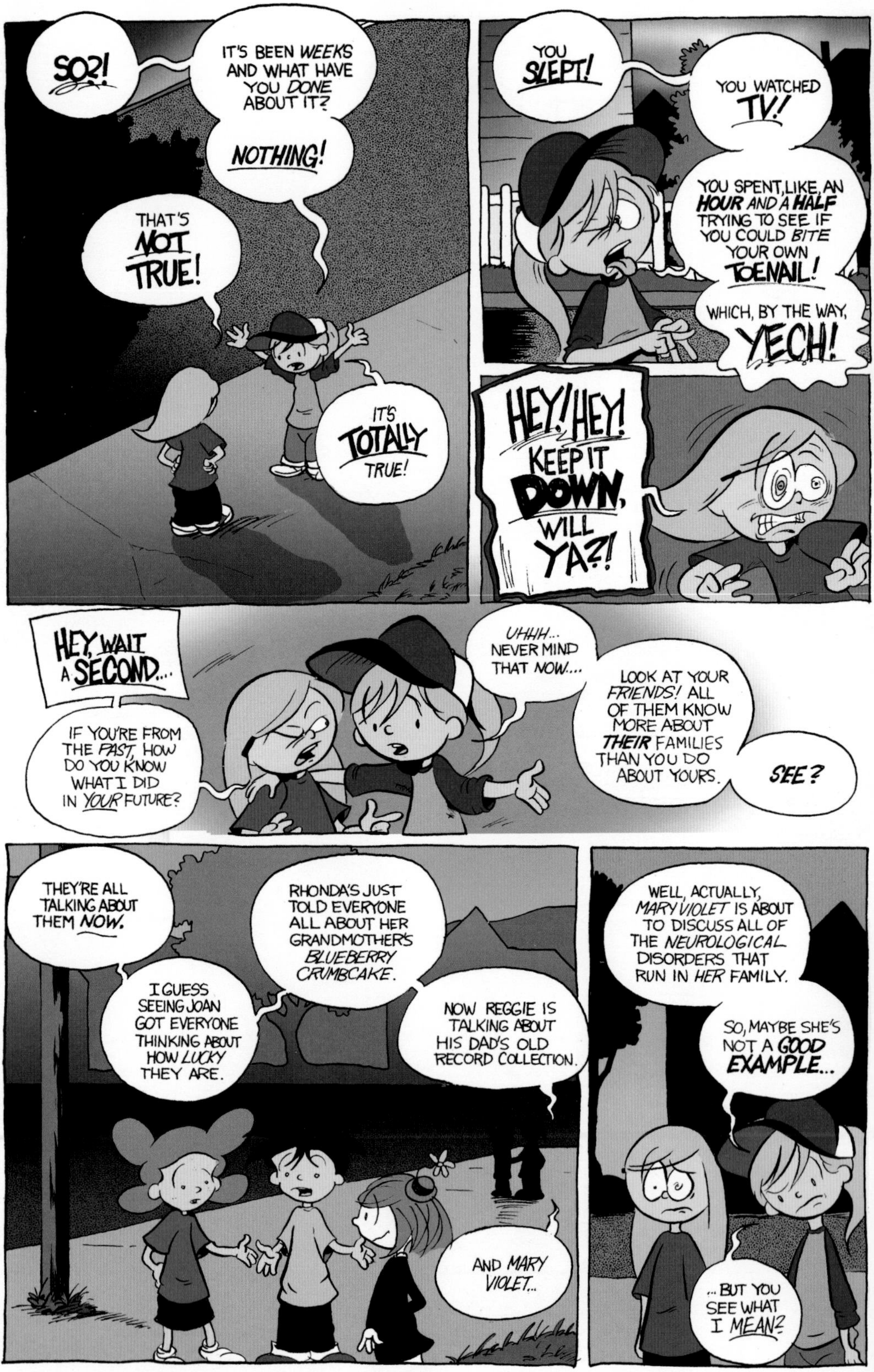
SO?!
IT'S BEEN WEEKS AND WHAT HAVE YOU DONE ABOUT IT?
NOTHING!
THAT'S NOT TRUE!
IT'S TOTALLY TRUE!
YOU SLEPT!
YOU WATCHED TV!
YOU SPENT, LIKE, AN HOUR AND A HALF TRYING TO SEE IF YOU COULD BITE YOUR OWN TOENAIL!
WHICH, BY THE WAY, YECH!
HEY! HEY! KEEP IT DOWN, WILL YA?!
HEY, WAIT A SECOND....
IF YOU'RE FROM THE PAST, HOW DO YOU KNOW WHAT I DID IN YOUR FUTURE?
UHHH... NEVER MIND THAT NOW....
LOOK AT YOUR FRIENDS! ALL OF THEM KNOW MORE ABOUT THEIR FAMILIES THAN YOU DO ABOUT YOURS.
SEE?
THEY'RE ALL TALKING ABOUT THEM NOW.
I GUESS SEEING JOAN GOT EVERYONE THINKING ABOUT HOW LUCKY THEY ARE.
RHONDA'S JUST TOLD EVERYONE ALL ABOUT HER GRANDMOTHER'S BLUEBERRY CRUMBCAKE.
NOW REGGIE IS TALKING ABOUT HIS DAD'S OLD RECORD COLLECTION.
AND MARY VIOLET...
WELL, ACTUALLY, MARY VIOLET IS ABOUT TO DISCUSS ALL OF THE NEUROLOGICAL DISORDERS THAT RUN IN HER FAMILY.
SO, MAYBE SHE'S NOT A GOOD EXAMPLE...
...BUT YOU SEE WHAT I MEAN?

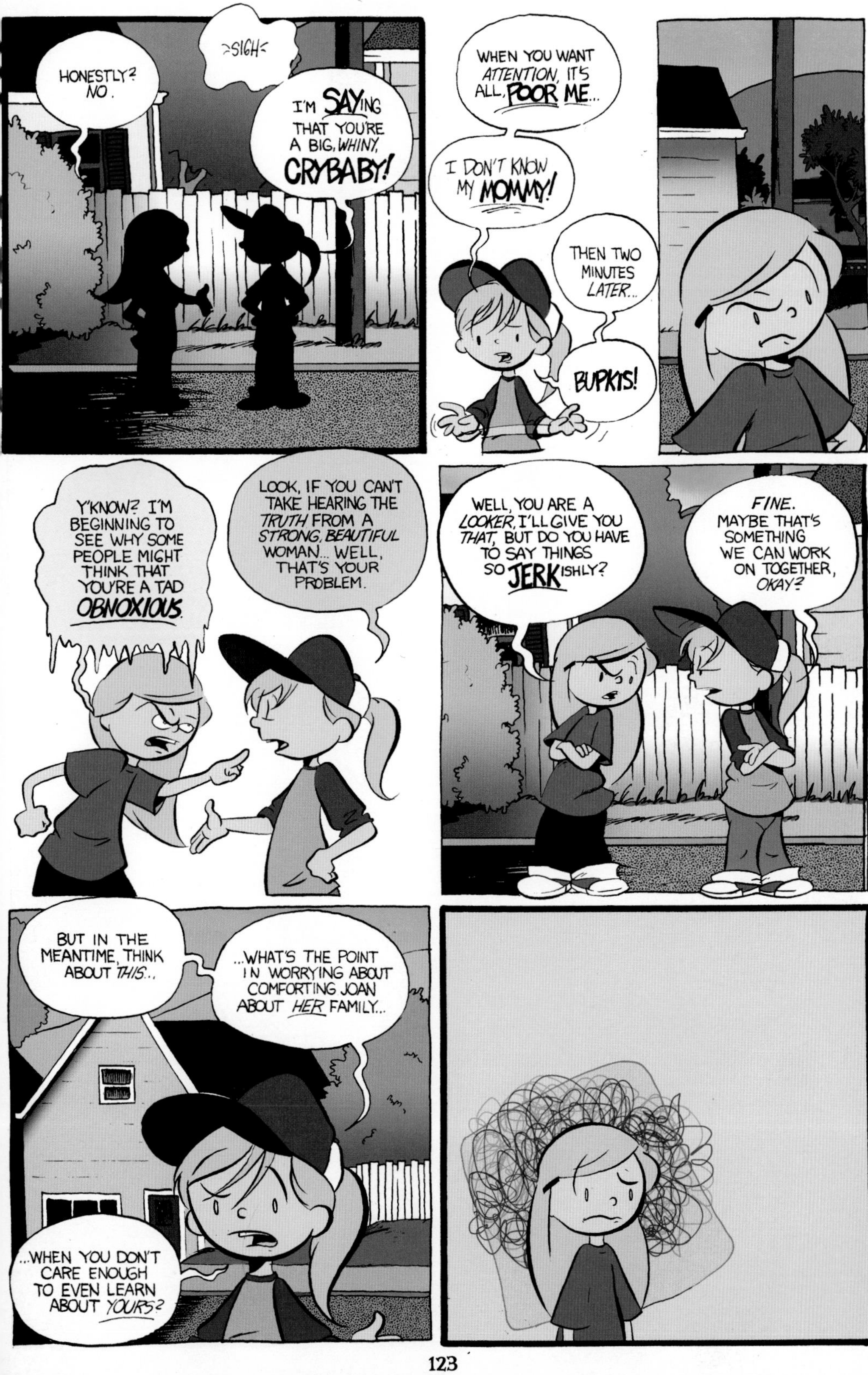
HONESTLY? NO.
>SIGH<
I'M SAYING THAT YOU'RE A BIG, WHINY, CRYBABY!
WHEN YOU WANT ATTENTION, IT'S ALL, POOR ME...
I DON'T KNOW MY MOMMY!
THEN TWO MINUTES LATER...
BUPKIS!
Y'KNOW? I'M BEGINNING TO SEE WHY SOME PEOPLE MIGHT THINK THAT YOU'RE A TAD OBNOXIOUS.
LOOK, IF YOU CAN'T TAKE HEARING THE TRUTH FROM A STRONG, BEAUTIFUL WOMAN... WELL, THAT'S YOUR PROBLEM.
WELL, YOU ARE A LOOKER, I'LL GIVE YOU THAT, BUT DO YOU HAVE TO SAY THINGS SO JERKISHLY?
FINE. MAYBE THAT'S SOMETHING WE CAN WORK ON TOGETHER, OKAY?
BUT IN THE MEANTIME, THINK ABOUT THIS...
...WHAT'S THE POINT IN WORRYING ABOUT COMFORTING JOAN ABOUT HER FAMILY...
...WHEN YOU DON'T CARE ENOUGH TO EVEN LEARN ABOUT YOURS?

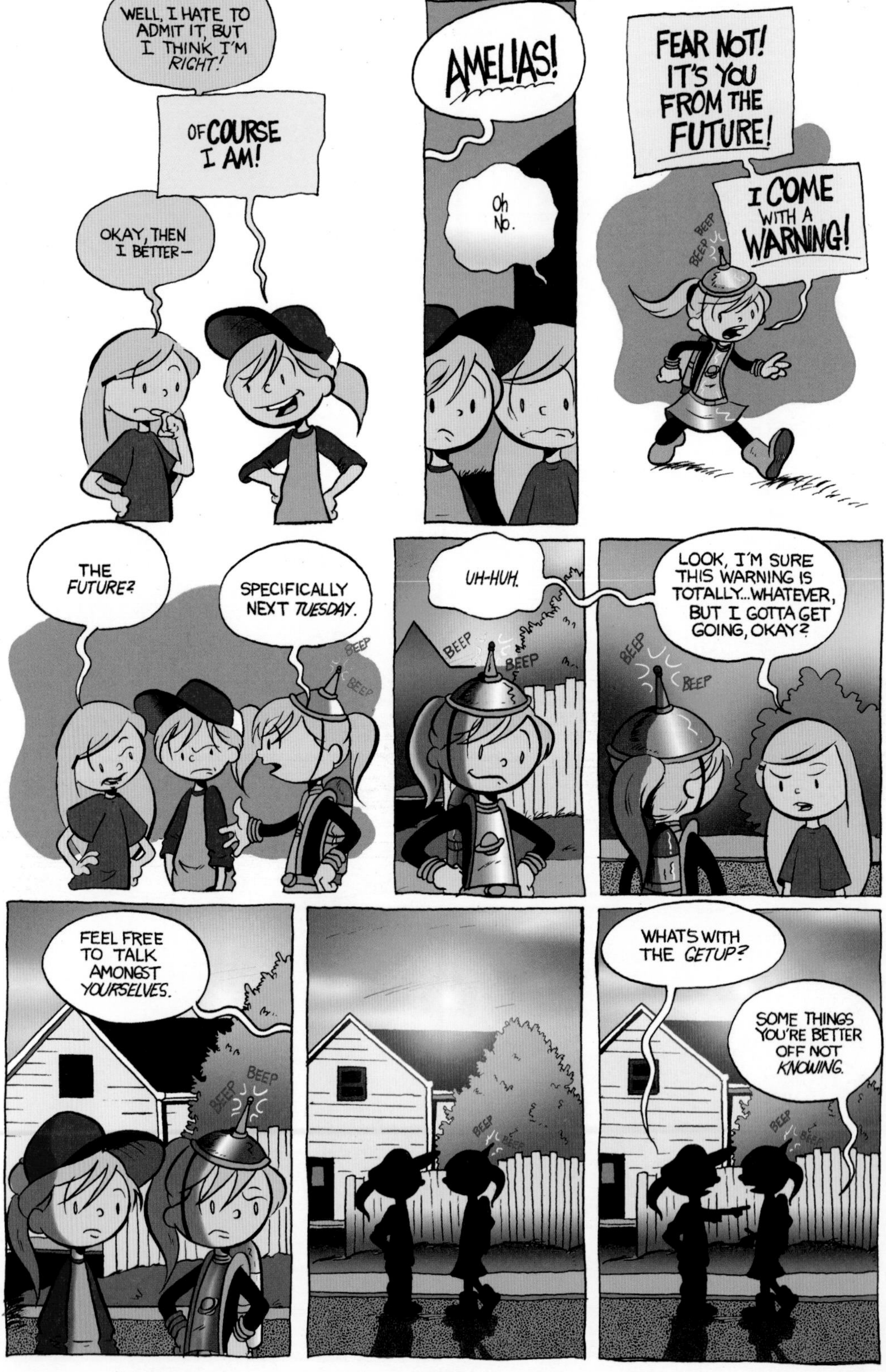
WELL, I HATE TO ADMIT IT, BUT I THINK I'M RIGHT!
OF COURSE I AM!
OKAY, THEN I BETTER—
AMELIAS!
Oh No.
FEAR NOT! IT'S YOU FROM THE FUTURE!
I COME WITH A WARNING!
BEEP BEEP
THE FUTURE?
SPECIFICALLY NEXT TUESDAY.
BEEP BEEP
UH-HUH.
BEEP BEEP
LOOK, I'M SURE THIS WARNING IS TOTALLY...WHATEVER, BUT I GOTTA GET GOING, OKAY?
BEEP BEEP
FEEL FREE TO TALK AMONGST YOURSELVES.
BEEP BEEP
BEEP BEEP
WHAT'S WITH THE GETUP?
SOME THINGS YOU'RE BETTER OFF NOT KNOWING.

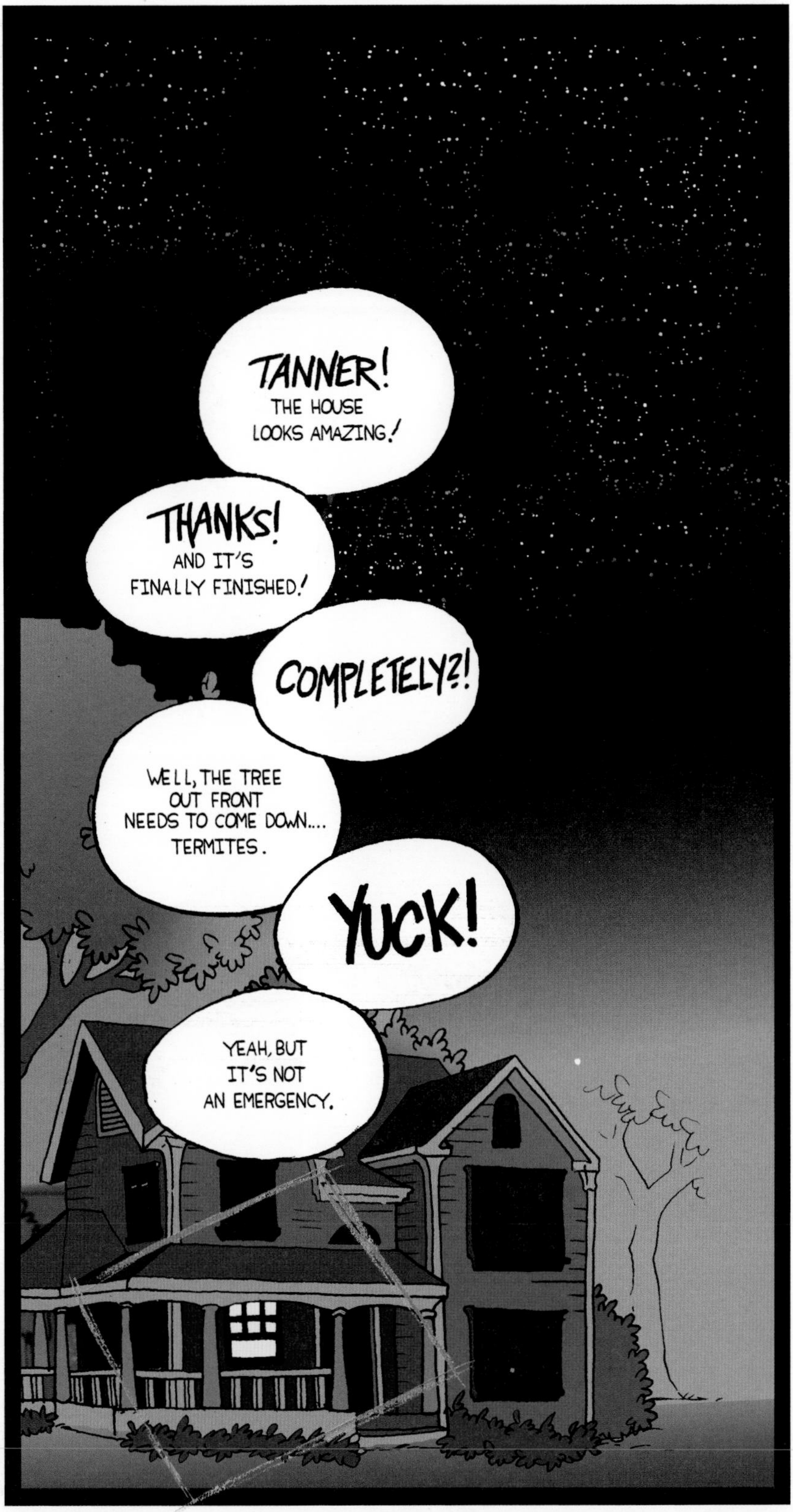
TANNER! THE HOUSE LOOKS AMAZING!
THANKS! AND IT'S FINALLY FINISHED!
COMPLETELY?!
WELL, THE TREE OUT FRONT NEEDS TO COME DOWN.... TERMITES.
YUCK!
YEAH, BUT IT'S NOT AN EMERGENCY.

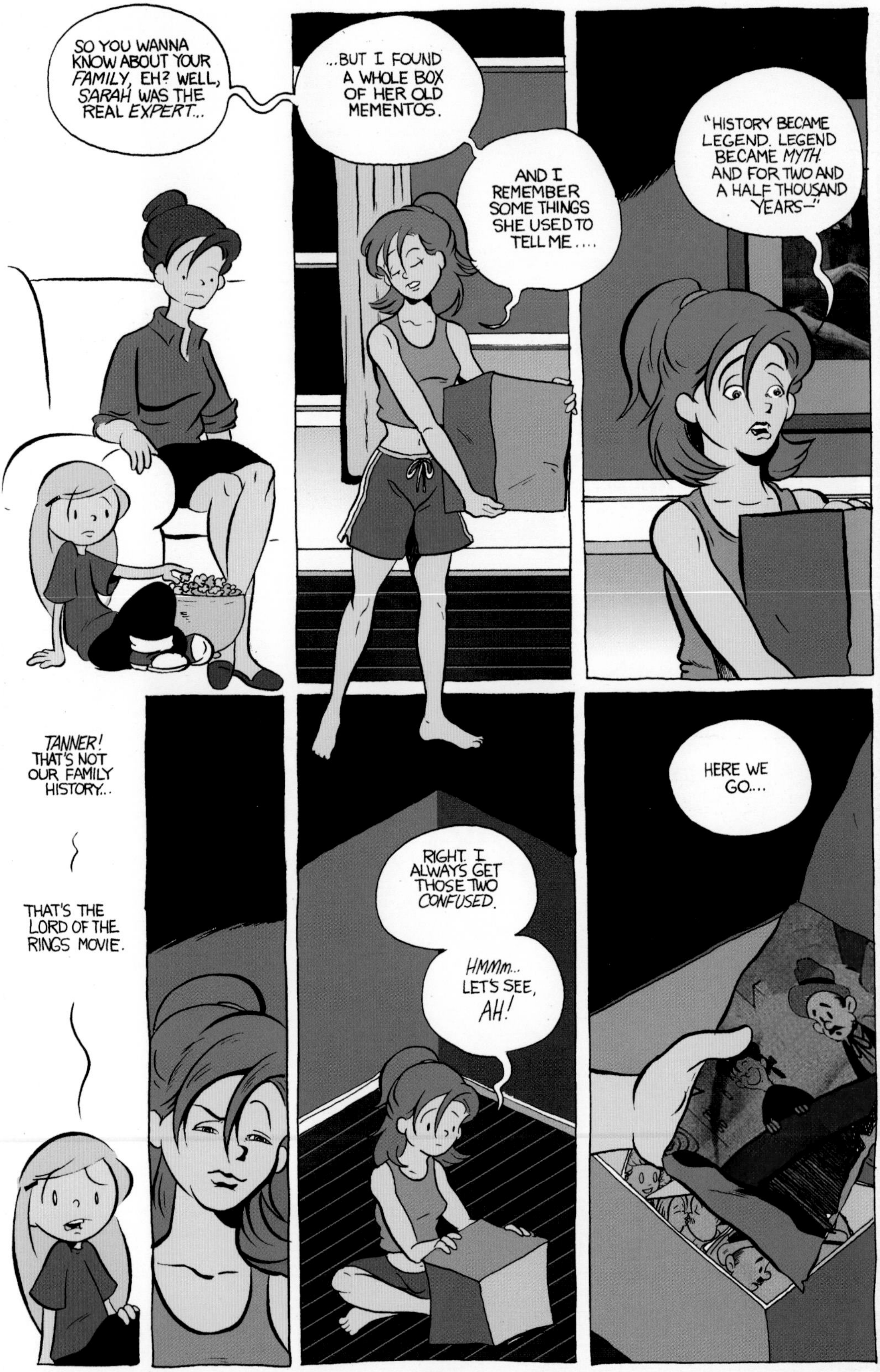
SO YOU WANNA KNOW ABOUT YOUR FAMILY, EH? WELL, SARAH WAS THE REAL EXPERT...
...BUT I FOUND A WHOLE BOX OF HER OLD MEMENTOS.
AND I REMEMBER SOME THINGS SHE USED TO TELL ME....
"HISTORY BECAME LEGEND. LEGEND BECAME MYTH. AND FOR TWO AND A HALF THOUSAND YEARS—"
TANNER! THAT'S NOT OUR FAMILY HISTORY...
THAT'S THE LORD OF THE RINGS MOVIE.
RIGHT. I ALWAYS GET THOSE TWO CONFUSED.
HMMm... LET'S SEE, AH!
HERE WE GO....

ARTHUR T. FLETCHER ARRIVES IN USA

Joined by new bride Louise.

We don't know much about the Clark side of the family, and if you want to know about the Irish McBrides, you'll have to ask your dad.

But we know a lot about your grandmother's family, the Fletchers.

Arthur T. Fletcher grew up in England, the youngest child of George and Delores Fletcher. Now there were only two things Arthur wanted in the whole world: to marry his childhood sweetheart, Louise, and to move to America.

Unfortunately his entire family hated both Louise and the US, and made Arthur swear an oath that he would stay put and stay single (or at least marry someone more suitable).

So Arthur did what he believed was most sensible. He waited until everyone else in his family croaked and then did what he wanted.

So, as one century faded into the next, Arthur and Louise arrived in America.

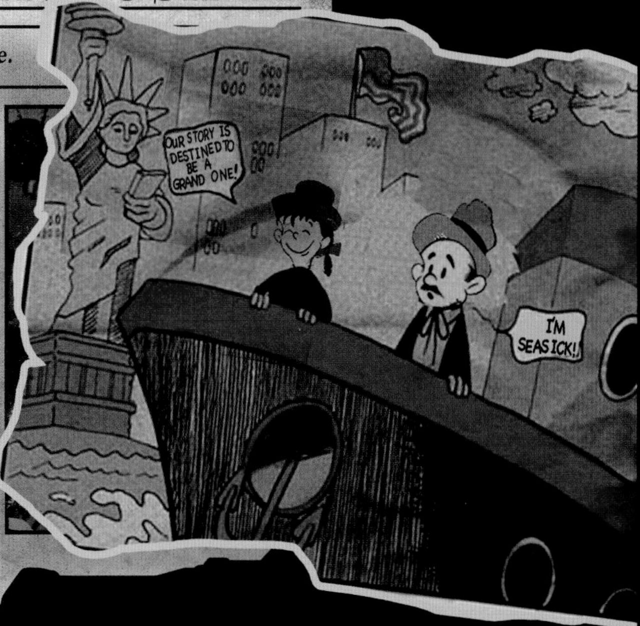
OUR STORY IS DESTINED TO BE A GRAND ONE!
I'M SEASICK!

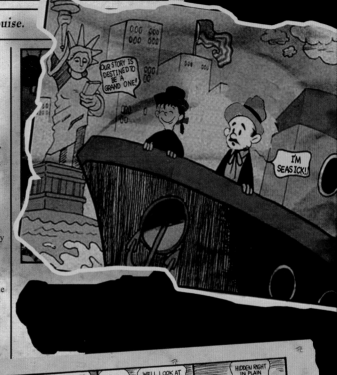

FLETCHER'S FOLLIES

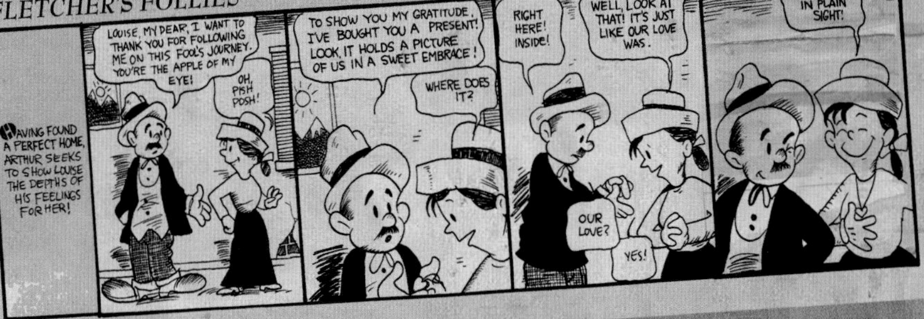
HAVING FOUND A PERFECT HOME, ARTHUR SEEKS TO SHOW LOUISE THE DEPTHS OF HIS FEELINGS FOR HER!
LOUISE, MY DEAR, I WANT TO THANK YOU FOR FOLLOWING ME ON THIS FOOL'S JOURNEY. YOU'RE THE APPLE OF MY EYE!
OH, PISH POSH!
TO SHOW YOU MY GRATITUDE, I'VE BOUGHT YOU A PRESENT! LOOK, IT HOLDS A PICTURE OF US IN A SWEET EMBRACE!
WHERE DOES IT?
RIGHT HERE! INSIDE!
WELL, LOOK AT THAT! IT'S JUST LIKE OUR LOVE WAS.
OUR LOVE?
YES!
HIDDEN RIGHT IN PLAIN SIGHT!

FLETCHER BUYS WIFE GIFT

Neighbors thrown into jealous rage.

Eventually the couple found themselves in Indiana, where a distant cousin of Louise owned a farm. Arthur was so happy to be in the land of his dreams and so grateful for the patience and devotion Louise had showed him that he bought her a present—a simple, delicate, and beautif locket.

Louise kept the locket for the next thirty years until, on the day of her only son John's wedding, she passed it on to his bride, Edna.

Now, Arthur had long since acquired his own farm, so John and Edna stayed on helping. By now, John and Edna had three children of their own: Jerome, Sarah, and Grace.

But try as he might, John just wasn't a farmer. So on the day of his tenth wedding anniversary, John Fletcher opened the Family Valley General Store. No one but Edna believed it would succeed. Even John himself doubted it.

But somehow, against unbelievable odds, it did. It thrived through depression and war.

It even outlived John himself. It's still there today.

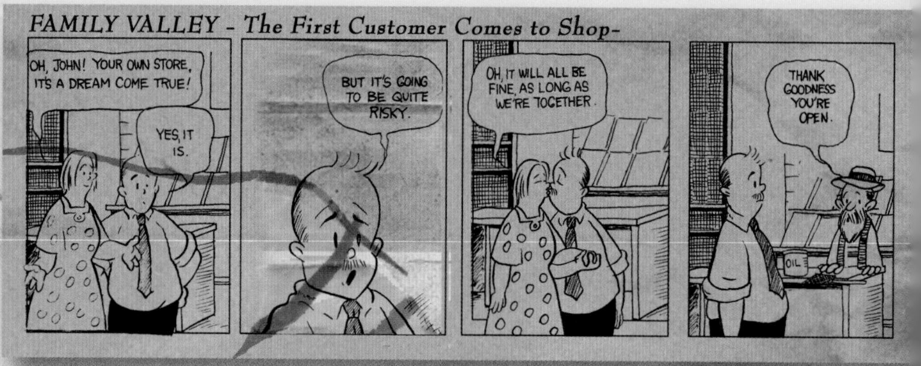
FAMILY VALLEY - The First Customer Comes to Shop-
OH, JOHN! YOUR OWN STORE, IT'S A DREAM COME TRUE!
YES, IT IS.
BUT IT'S GOING TO BE QUITE RISKY.
OH, IT WILL ALL BE FINE, AS LONG AS WE'RE TOGETHER.
THANK GOODNESS YOU'RE OPEN.
OIL

Unfortunately, during all the chaos and commotion of building the store, Edna lost the locket. Even though she searched and searched, it never turned up.

One day, years after it was lost, Sarah found the locket in a field behind the store. She had no idea of the object's significance. It was weeks before she discovered that the little heart charm opened and she found a picture of her parents' wedding inside.

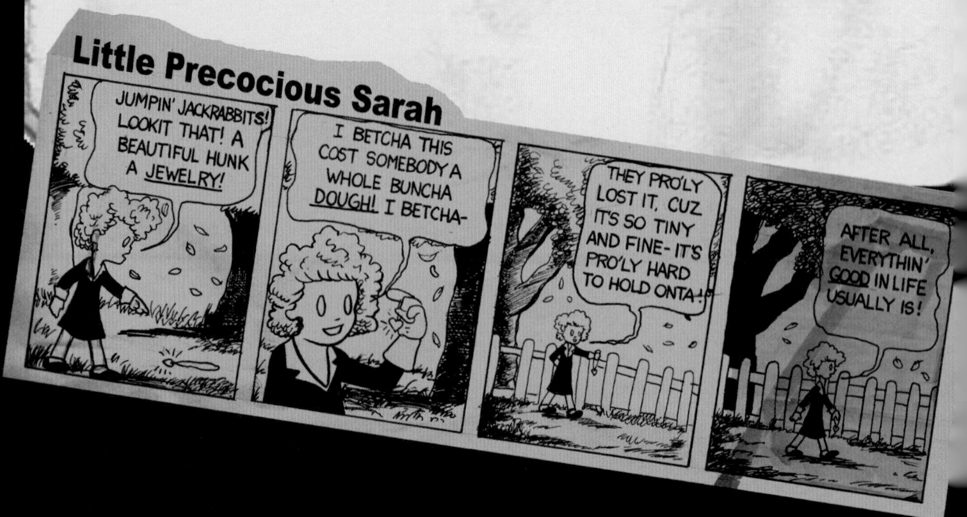
Little Precocious Sarah
JUMPIN' JACKRABBITS! LOOKIT THAT! A BEAUTIFUL HUNK A JEWELRY!
I BETCHA THIS COST SOMEBODY A WHOLE BUNCHA DOUGH! I BETCHA-
THEY PRO'LY LOST IT, CUZ IT'S SO TINY AND FINE- IT'S PRO'LY HARD TO HOLD ONTA!
AFTER ALL, EVERYTHIN' GOOD IN LIFE USUALLY IS!

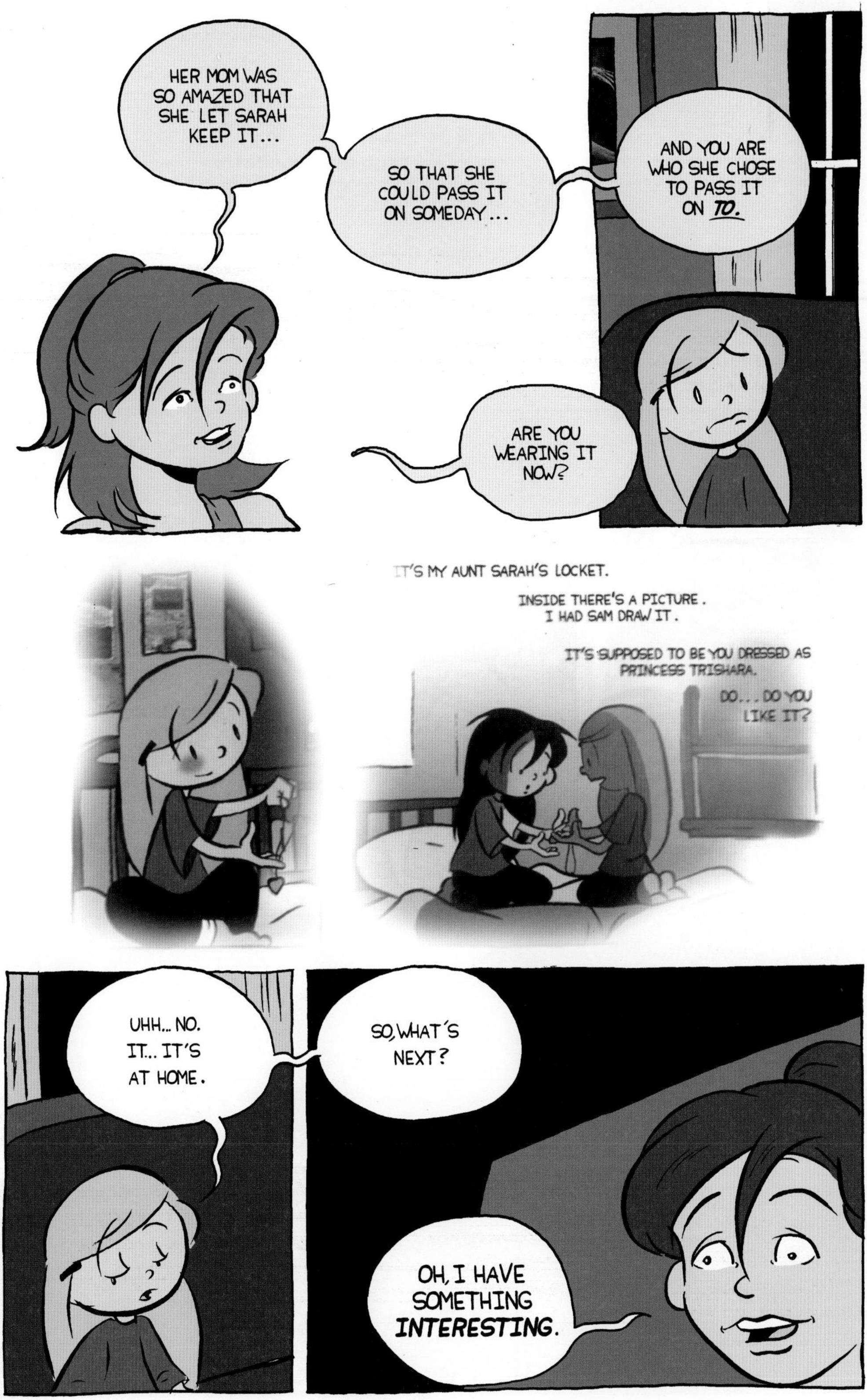
HER MOM WAS SO AMAZED THAT SHE LET SARAH KEEP IT...
SO THAT SHE COULD PASS IT ON SOMEDAY...
AND YOU ARE WHO SHE CHOSE TO PASS IT ON *TO.*
ARE YOU WEARING IT NOW?
IT'S MY AUNT SARAH'S LOCKET.
INSIDE THERE'S A PICTURE. I HAD SAM DRAW IT.
IT'S SUPPOSED TO BE YOU DRESSED AS PRINCESS TRISHARA.
DO... DO YOU LIKE IT?
UHH... NO. IT... IT'S AT HOME.
SO, WHAT'S NEXT?
OH, I HAVE SOMETHING **INTERESTING**.

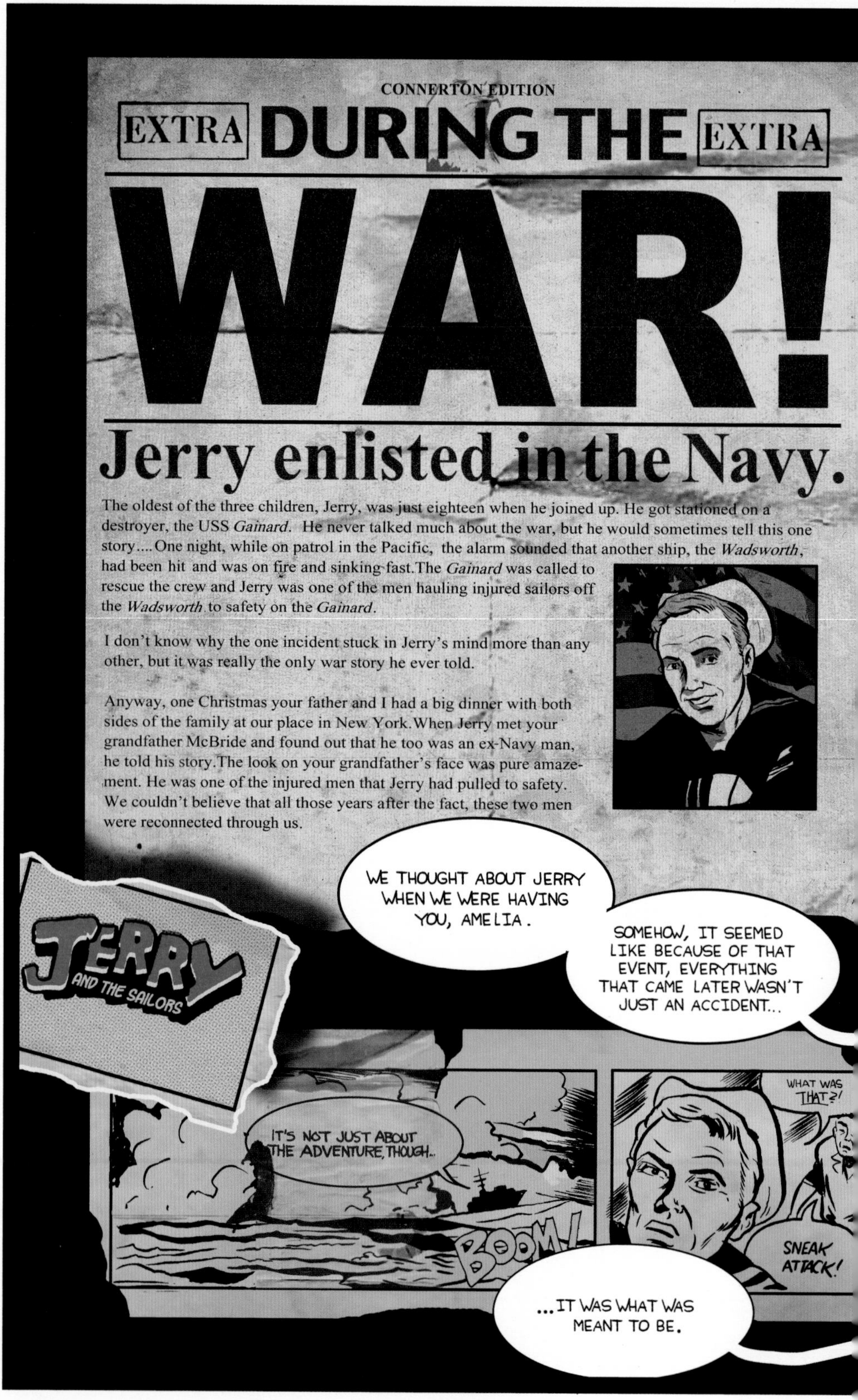

CONNERTON EDITION

EXTRA **DURING THE** EXTRA

WAR!

Jerry enlisted in the Navy.

The oldest of the three children, Jerry, was just eighteen when he joined up. He got stationed on a destroyer, the USS *Gainard*. He never talked much about the war, but he would sometimes tell this one story.... One night, while on patrol in the Pacific, the alarm sounded that another ship, the *Wadsworth*, had been hit and was on fire and sinking fast. The *Gainard* was called to rescue the crew and Jerry was one of the men hauling injured sailors off the *Wadsworth* to safety on the *Gainard*.

I don't know why the one incident stuck in Jerry's mind more than any other, but it was really the only war story he ever told.

Anyway, one Christmas your father and I had a big dinner with both sides of the family at our place in New York. When Jerry met your grandfather McBride and found out that he too was an ex-Navy man, he told his story. The look on your grandfather's face was pure amazement. He was one of the injured men that Jerry had pulled to safety. We couldn't believe that all those years after the fact, these two men were reconnected through us.

WE THOUGHT ABOUT JERRY WHEN WE WERE HAVING YOU, AMELIA.
SOMEHOW, IT SEEMED LIKE BECAUSE OF THAT EVENT, EVERYTHING THAT CAME LATER WASN'T JUST AN ACCIDENT...
JERRY AND THE SAILORS
IT'S NOT JUST ABOUT THE ADVENTURE, THOUGH..
BOOM!
WHAT WAS THAT?!
SNEAK ATTACK!
...IT WAS WHAT WAS MEANT TO BE.

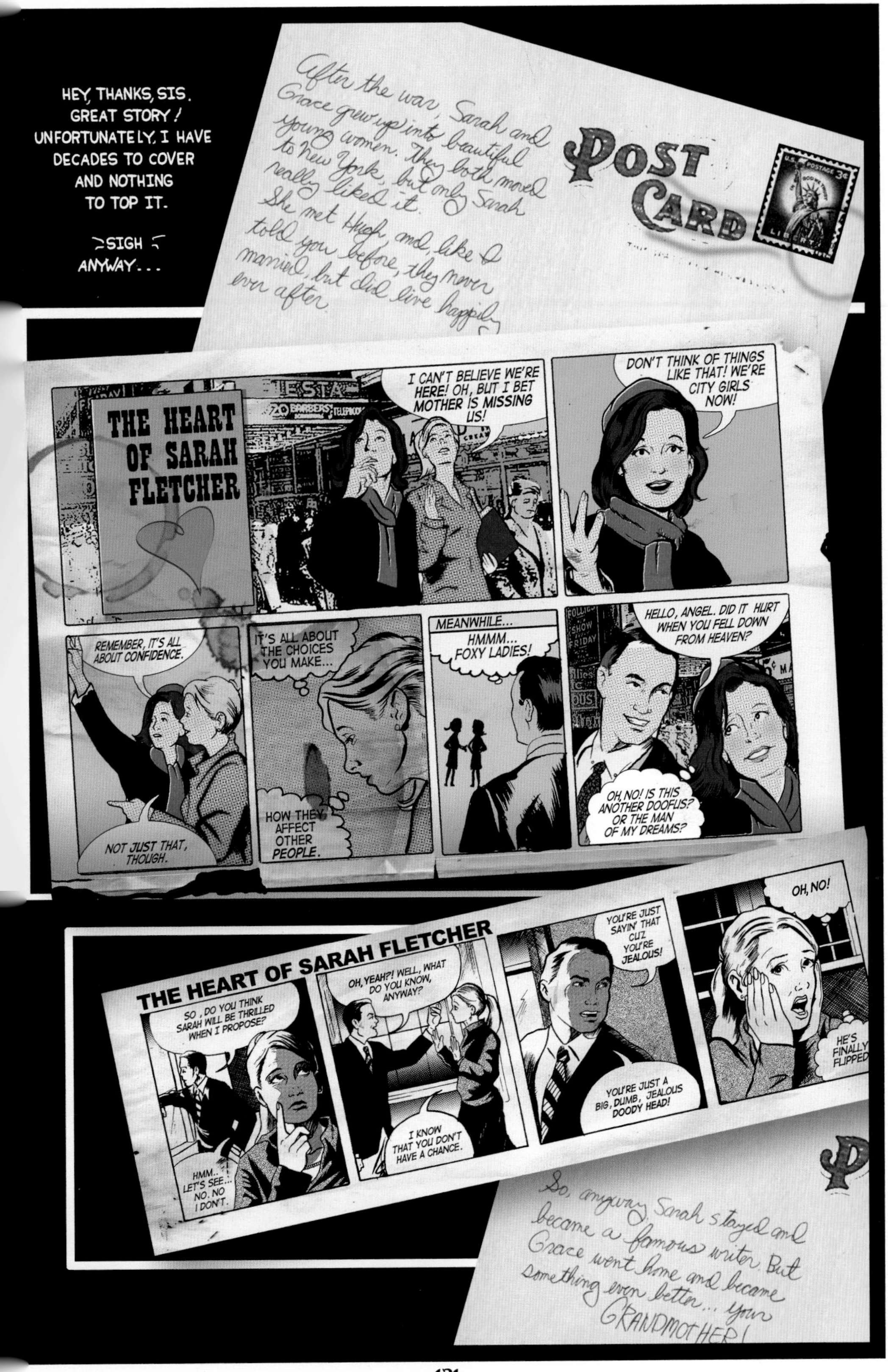
HEY, THANKS, SIS. GREAT STORY! UNFORTUNATELY, I HAVE DECADES TO COVER AND NOTHING TO TOP IT.
>SIGH<
ANYWAY...
After the war, Sarah and Grace grew up into beautiful young women. They both moved to New York, but only Sarah really liked it. She met Hugh, and, like I told you before, they never married, but did live happily ever after
POST CARD
THE HEART OF SARAH FLETCHER
I CAN'T BELIEVE WE'RE HERE! OH, BUT I BET MOTHER IS MISSING US!
DON'T THINK OF THINGS LIKE THAT! WE'RE CITY GIRLS NOW!
REMEMBER, IT'S ALL ABOUT CONFIDENCE.
NOT JUST THAT, THOUGH.
IT'S ALL ABOUT THE CHOICES YOU MAKE...
HOW THEY AFFECT OTHER PEOPLE.
MEANWHILE...
HMMM... FOXY LADIES!
HELLO, ANGEL. DID IT HURT WHEN YOU FELL DOWN FROM HEAVEN?
OH, NO! IS THIS ANOTHER DOOFUS? OR THE MAN OF MY DREAMS?
THE HEART OF SARAH FLETCHER
SO, DO YOU THINK SARAH WILL BE THRILLED WHEN I PROPOSE?
HMM.. LET'S SEE... NO. NO I DON'T.
OH, YEAH?! WELL, WHAT DO YOU KNOW, ANYWAY?
I KNOW THAT YOU DON'T HAVE A CHANCE.
YOU'RE JUST SAYIN' THAT CUZ YOU'RE JEALOUS!
YOU'RE JUST A BIG, DUMB, JEALOUS DOODY HEAD!
OH, NO!
HE'S FINALLY FLIPPED
So, anyway Sarah stayed and became a famous writer. But Grace went home and became something even better... your GRANDMOTHER!

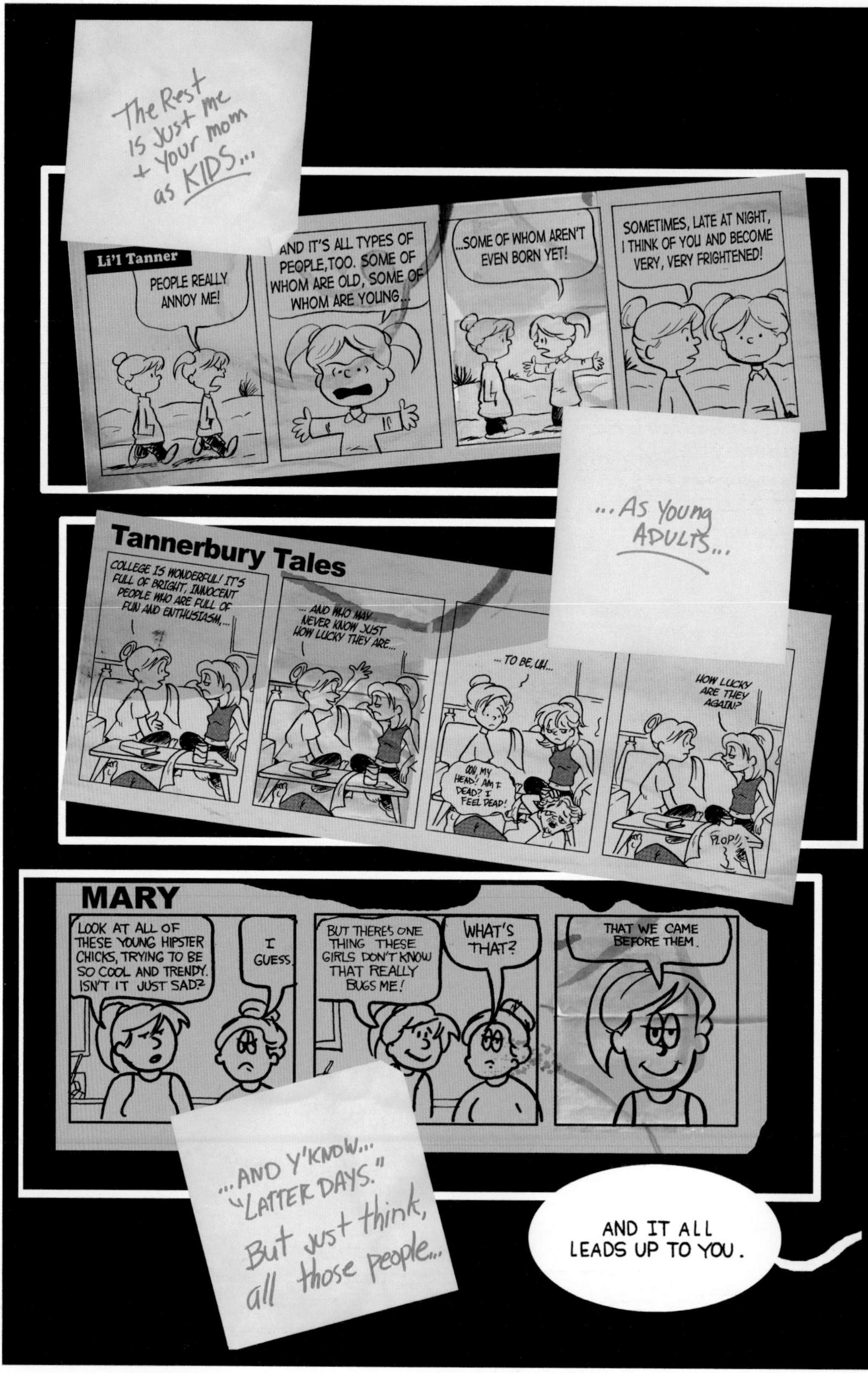
The Rest is just me + your mom as KIDS...
Li'l Tanner
PEOPLE REALLY ANNOY ME!
AND IT'S ALL TYPES OF PEOPLE, TOO. SOME OF WHOM ARE OLD, SOME OF WHOM ARE YOUNG...
...SOME OF WHOM AREN'T EVEN BORN YET!
SOMETIMES, LATE AT NIGHT, I THINK OF YOU AND BECOME VERY, VERY FRIGHTENED!
...As Young ADULTS...
Tannerbury Tales
COLLEGE IS WONDERFUL! IT'S FULL OF BRIGHT, INNOCENT PEOPLE WHO ARE FULL OF FUN AND ENTHUSIASM,...
... AND WHO MAY NEVER KNOW JUST HOW LUCKY THEY ARE...
... TO BE, UH...
OOU, MY HEAD! AM I DEAD? I FEEL DEAD!
HOW LUCKY ARE THEY AGAIN?
FLOP!
MARY
LOOK AT ALL OF THESE YOUNG HIPSTER CHICKS, TRYING TO BE SO COOL AND TRENDY. ISN'T IT JUST SAD?
I GUESS.
BUT THERE'S ONE THING THESE GIRLS DON'T KNOW THAT REALLY BUGS ME!
WHAT'S THAT?
THAT WE CAME BEFORE THEM.
...AND Y'KNOW... "LATTER DAYS." But just think, all those people...
AND IT ALL LEADS UP TO YOU.

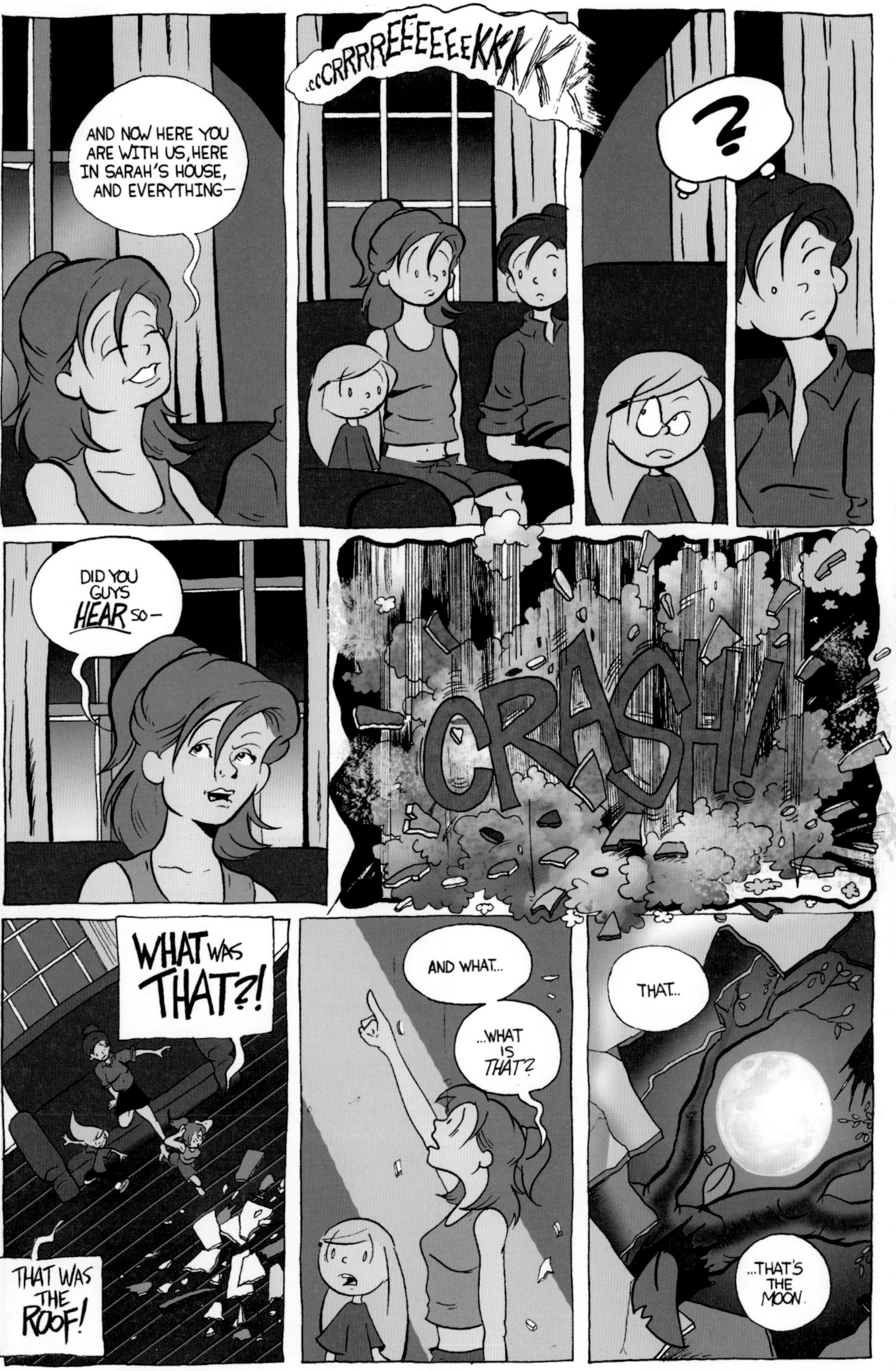
AND NOW HERE YOU ARE WITH US, HERE IN SARAH'S HOUSE, AND EVERYTHING—
...CCCRRRRREEEEEEEEKKKKK
?
DID YOU GUYS HEAR SO—
CRASH!
WHAT WAS THAT?!
THAT WAS THE ROOF!
AND WHAT...
...WHAT IS THAT?
THAT...
...THAT'S THE MOON.

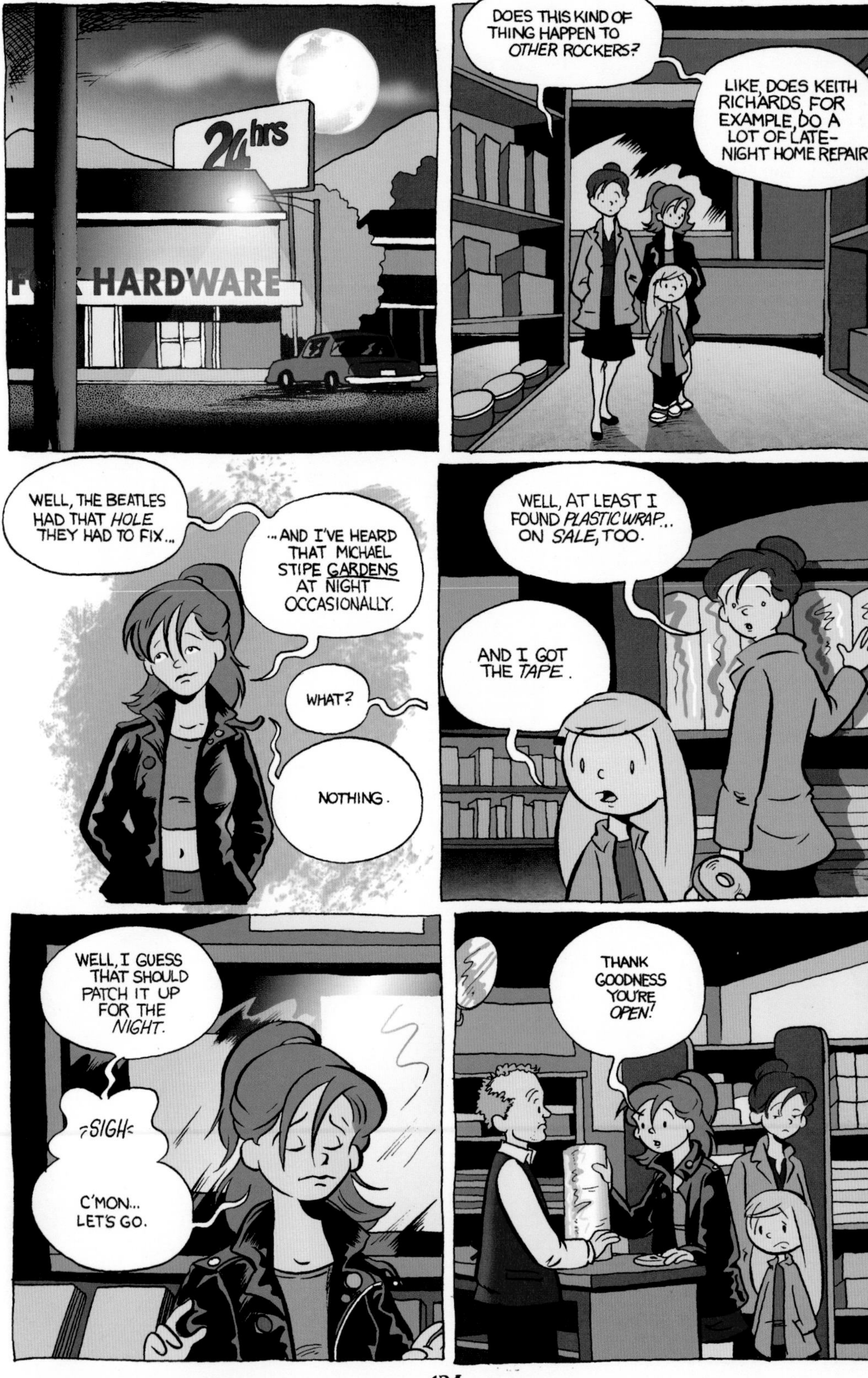
24 hrs
HARDWARE
DOES THIS KIND OF THING HAPPEN TO OTHER ROCKERS?
LIKE, DOES KEITH RICHARDS, FOR EXAMPLE, DO A LOT OF LATE-NIGHT HOME REPAIR?
WELL, THE BEATLES HAD THAT HOLE THEY HAD TO FIX...
...AND I'VE HEARD THAT MICHAEL STIPE GARDENS AT NIGHT OCCASIONALLY.
WHAT?
NOTHING.
WELL, AT LEAST I FOUND PLASTIC WRAP... ON SALE, TOO.
AND I GOT THE TAPE.
WELL, I GUESS THAT SHOULD PATCH IT UP FOR THE NIGHT.
SIGH
C'MON... LET'S GO.
THANK GOODNESS YOU'RE OPEN!

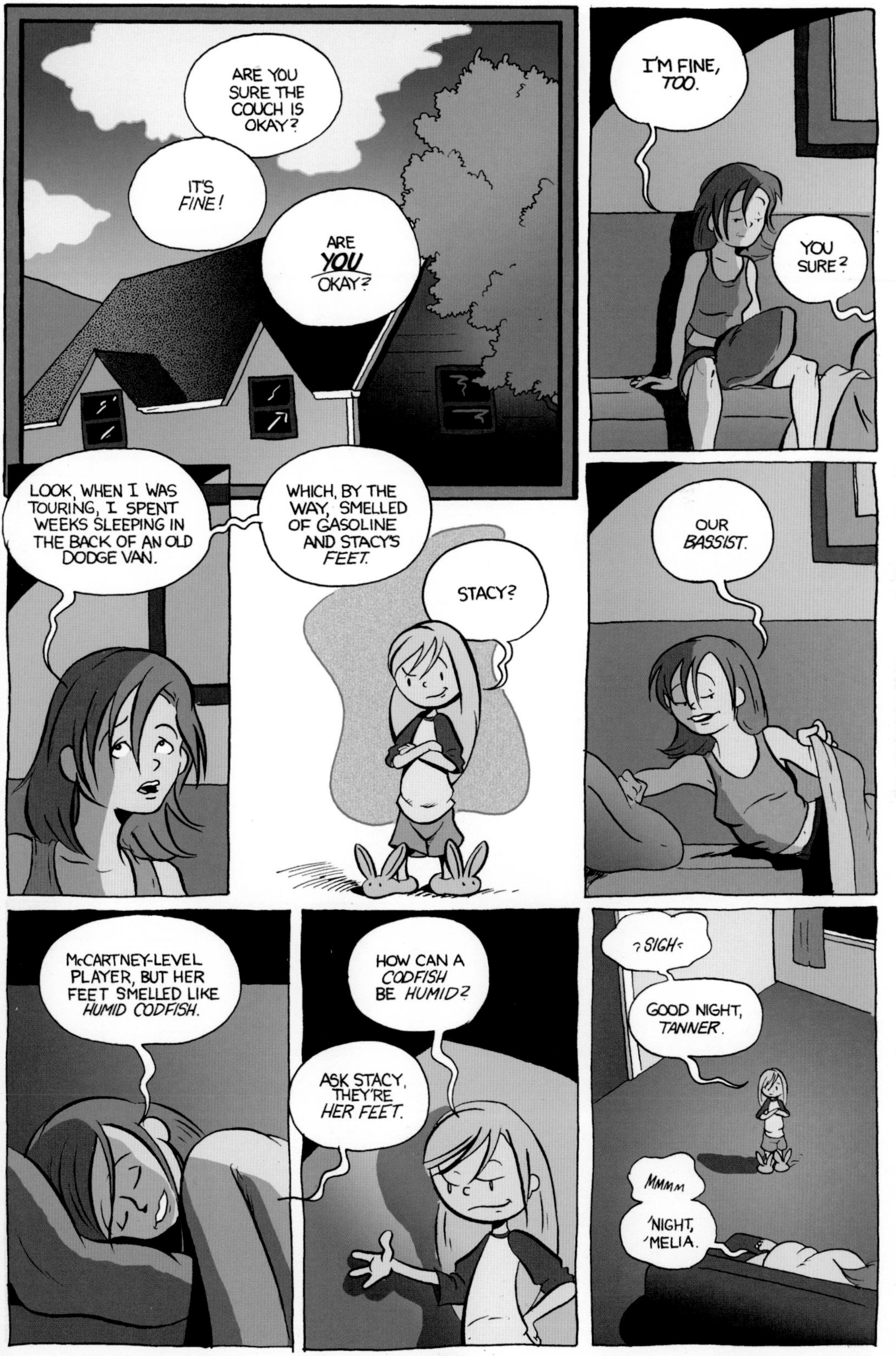
ARE YOU SURE THE COUCH IS OKAY?
IT'S FINE!
ARE YOU OKAY?
I'M FINE, TOO.
YOU SURE?
LOOK, WHEN I WAS TOURING, I SPENT WEEKS SLEEPING IN THE BACK OF AN OLD DODGE VAN.
WHICH, BY THE WAY, SMELLED OF GASOLINE AND STACY'S FEET.
STACY?
OUR BASSIST.
McCARTNEY-LEVEL PLAYER, BUT HER FEET SMELLED LIKE HUMID CODFISH.
HOW CAN A CODFISH BE HUMID?
ASK STACY, THEY'RE HER FEET.
SIGH
GOOD NIGHT, TANNER.
MMMM
'NIGHT, 'MELIA.

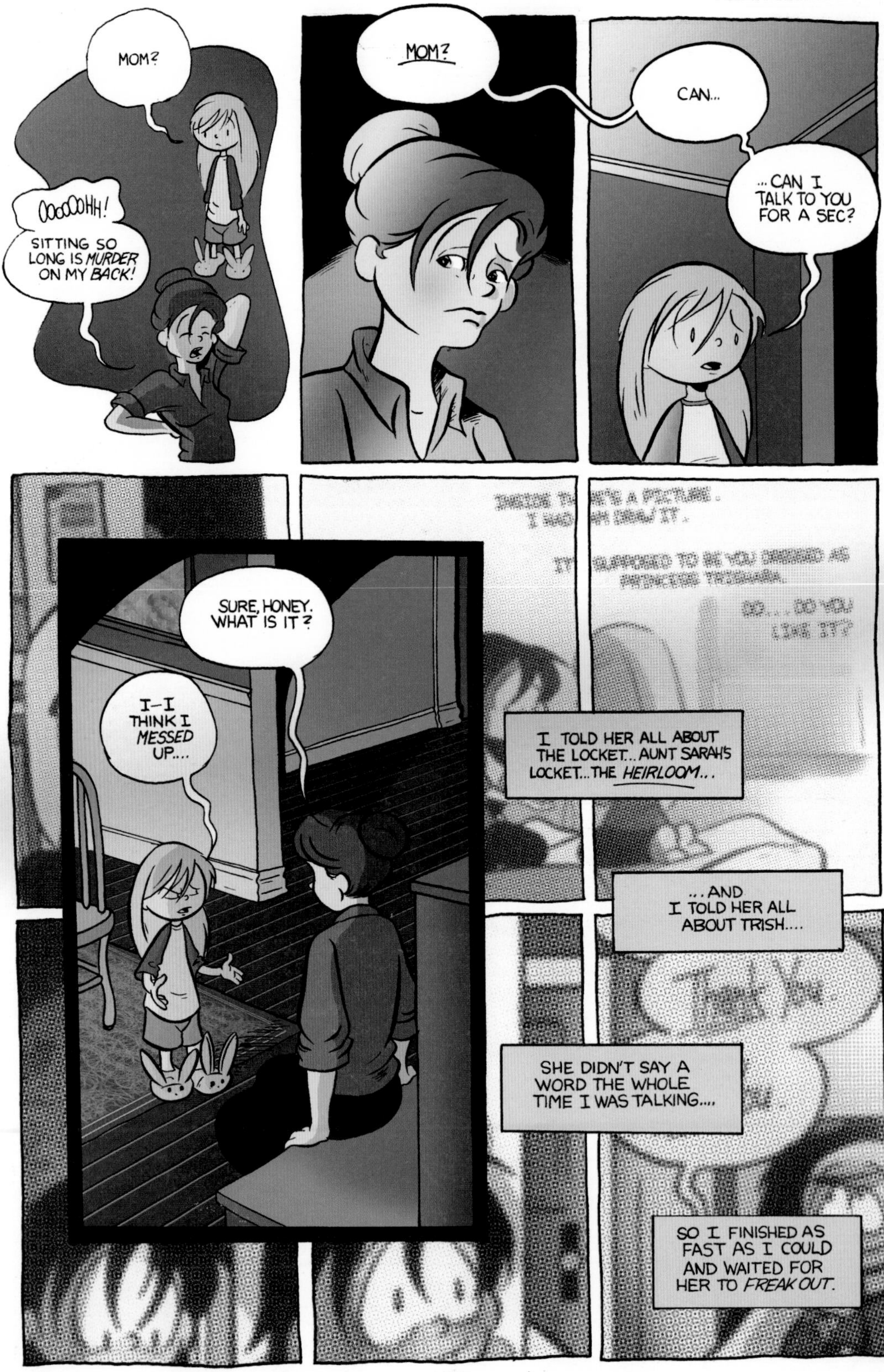
MOM?
OOOOOOHH!
SITTING SO LONG IS MURDER ON MY BACK!
MOM?
CAN...
...CAN I TALK TO YOU FOR A SEC?
SURE, HONEY. WHAT IS IT?
I-I THINK I MESSED UP....
I TOLD HER ALL ABOUT THE LOCKET... AUNT SARAH'S LOCKET... THE HEIRLOOM...
...AND I TOLD HER ALL ABOUT TRISH....
SHE DIDN'T SAY A WORD THE WHOLE TIME I WAS TALKING....
SO I FINISHED AS FAST AS I COULD AND WAITED FOR HER TO FREAK OUT.

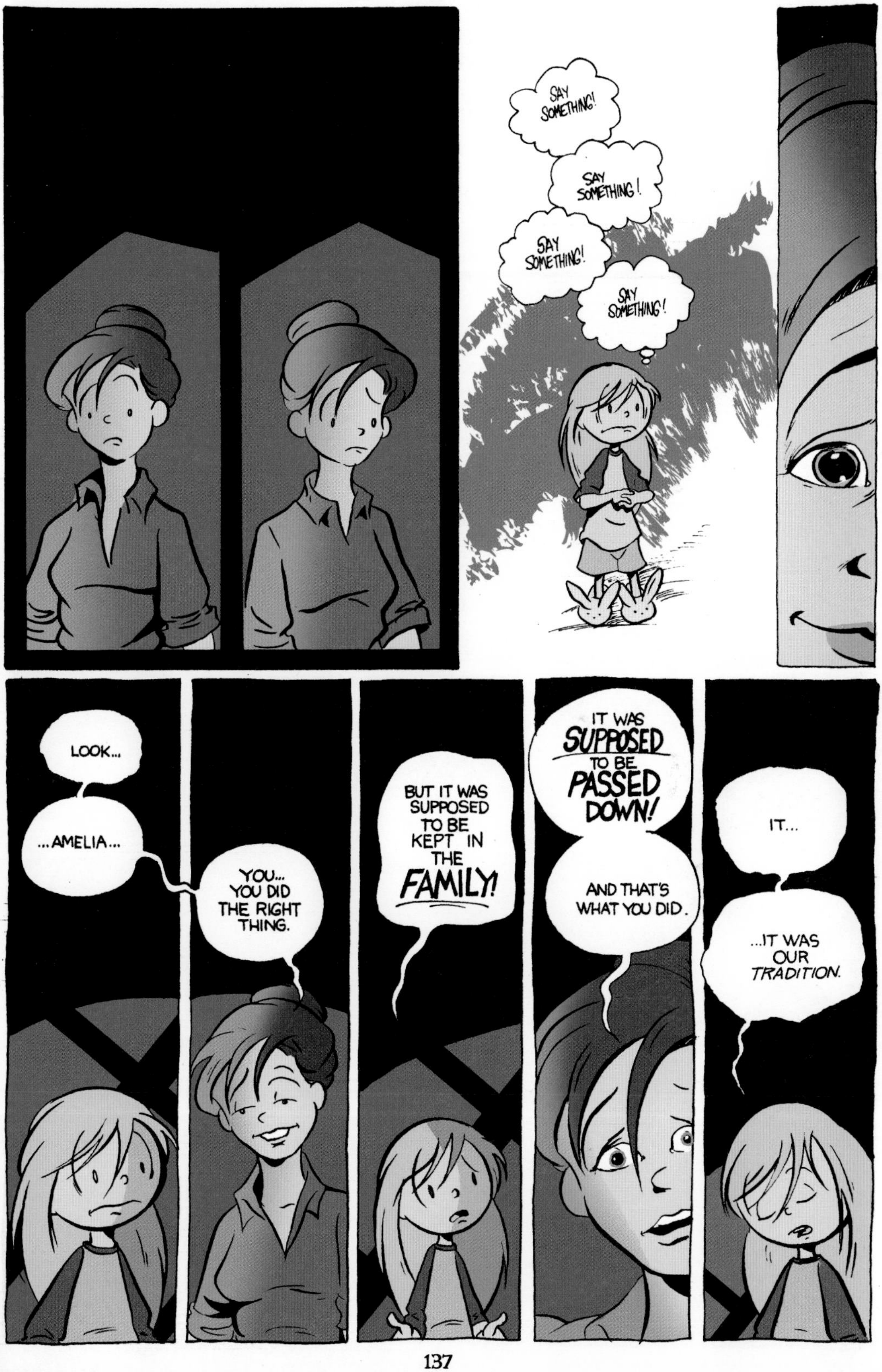
SAY SOMETHING!
SAY SOMETHING!
SAY SOMETHING!
SAY SOMETHING!
LOOK...
...AMELIA...
YOU... YOU DID THE RIGHT THING.
BUT IT WAS SUPPOSED TO BE KEPT IN THE FAMILY!
IT WAS SUPPOSED TO BE PASSED DOWN!
AND THAT'S WHAT YOU DID.
IT...
...IT WAS OUR TRADITION.

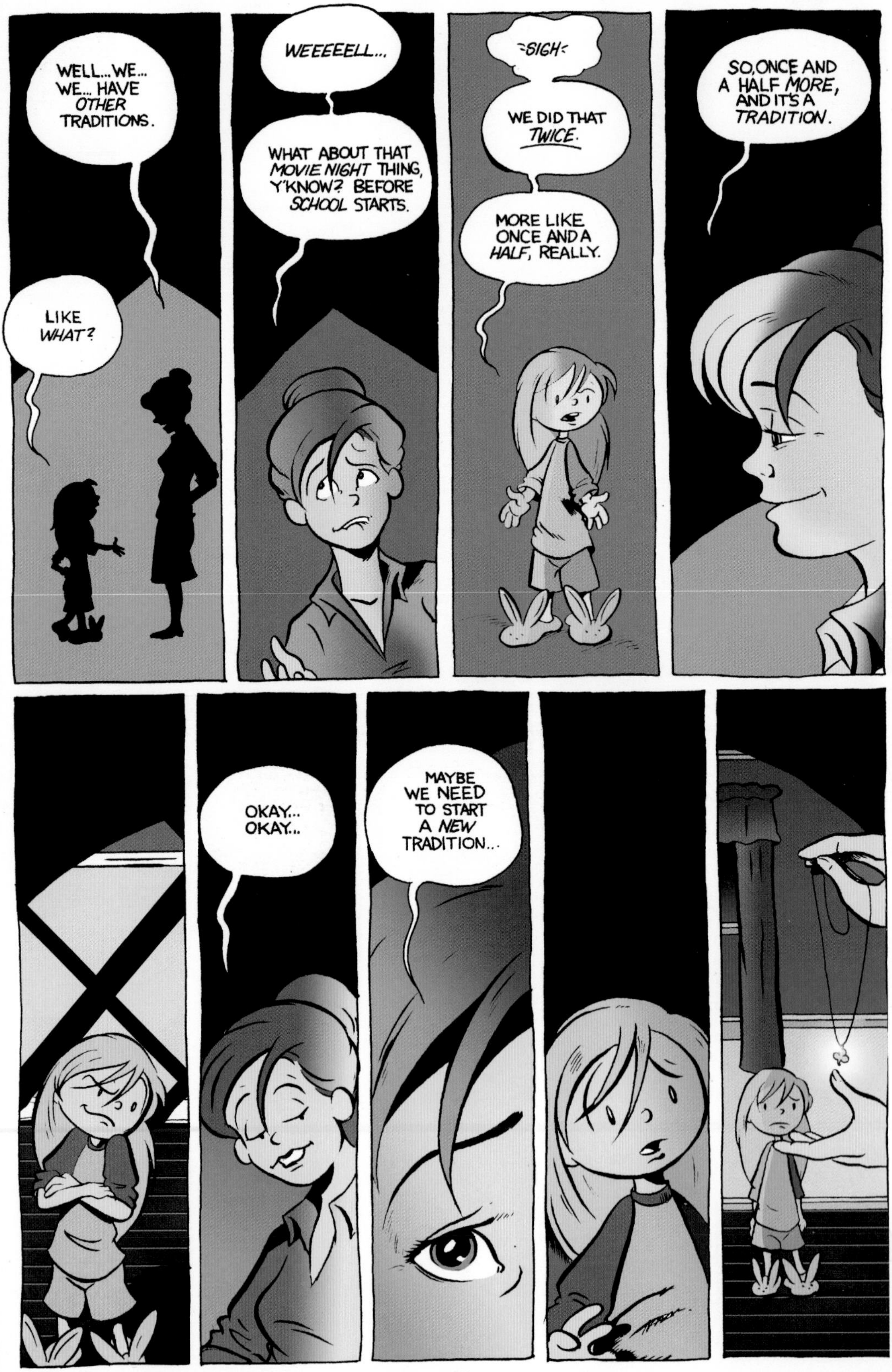
WELL...WE... WE... HAVE OTHER TRADITIONS.
LIKE WHAT?
WEEEEELL...
WHAT ABOUT THAT MOVIE NIGHT THING, Y'KNOW? BEFORE SCHOOL STARTS.
=SIGH=
WE DID THAT TWICE.
MORE LIKE ONCE AND A HALF, REALLY.
SO, ONCE AND A HALF MORE, AND IT'S A TRADITION.
OKAY... OKAY...
MAYBE WE NEED TO START A NEW TRADITION...

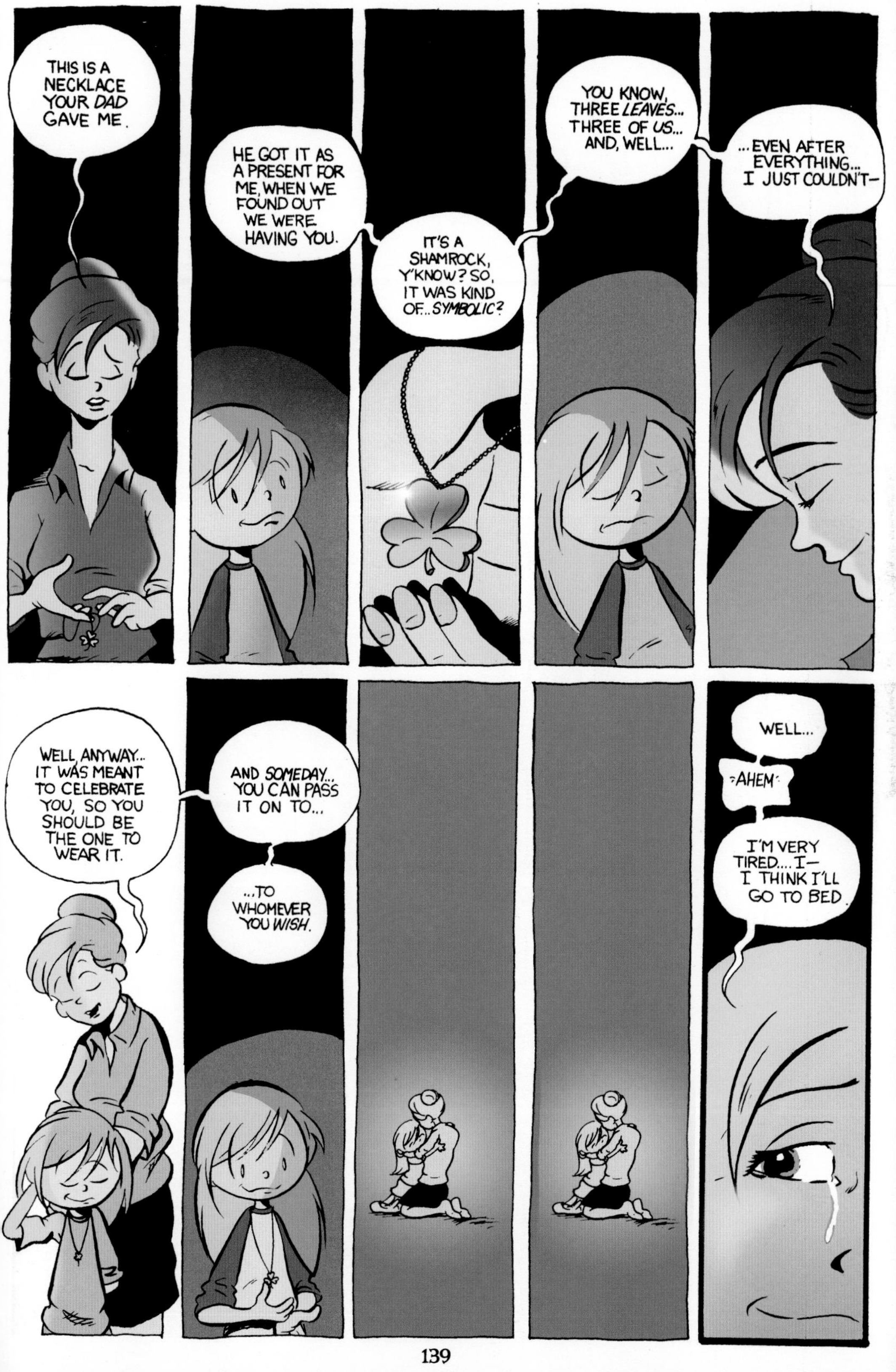
THIS IS A NECKLACE YOUR DAD GAVE ME.
HE GOT IT AS A PRESENT FOR ME, WHEN WE FOUND OUT WE WERE HAVING YOU.
IT'S A SHAMROCK, Y'KNOW? SO, IT WAS KIND OF... SYMBOLIC?
YOU KNOW, THREE LEAVES... THREE OF US... AND, WELL...
...EVEN AFTER EVERYTHING... I JUST COULDN'T–
WELL, ANYWAY... IT WAS MEANT TO CELEBRATE YOU, SO YOU SHOULD BE THE ONE TO WEAR IT.
AND SOMEDAY... YOU CAN PASS IT ON TO...
...TO WHOMEVER YOU WISH.
WELL...
AHEM
I'M VERY TIRED.... I– I THINK I'LL GO TO BED.

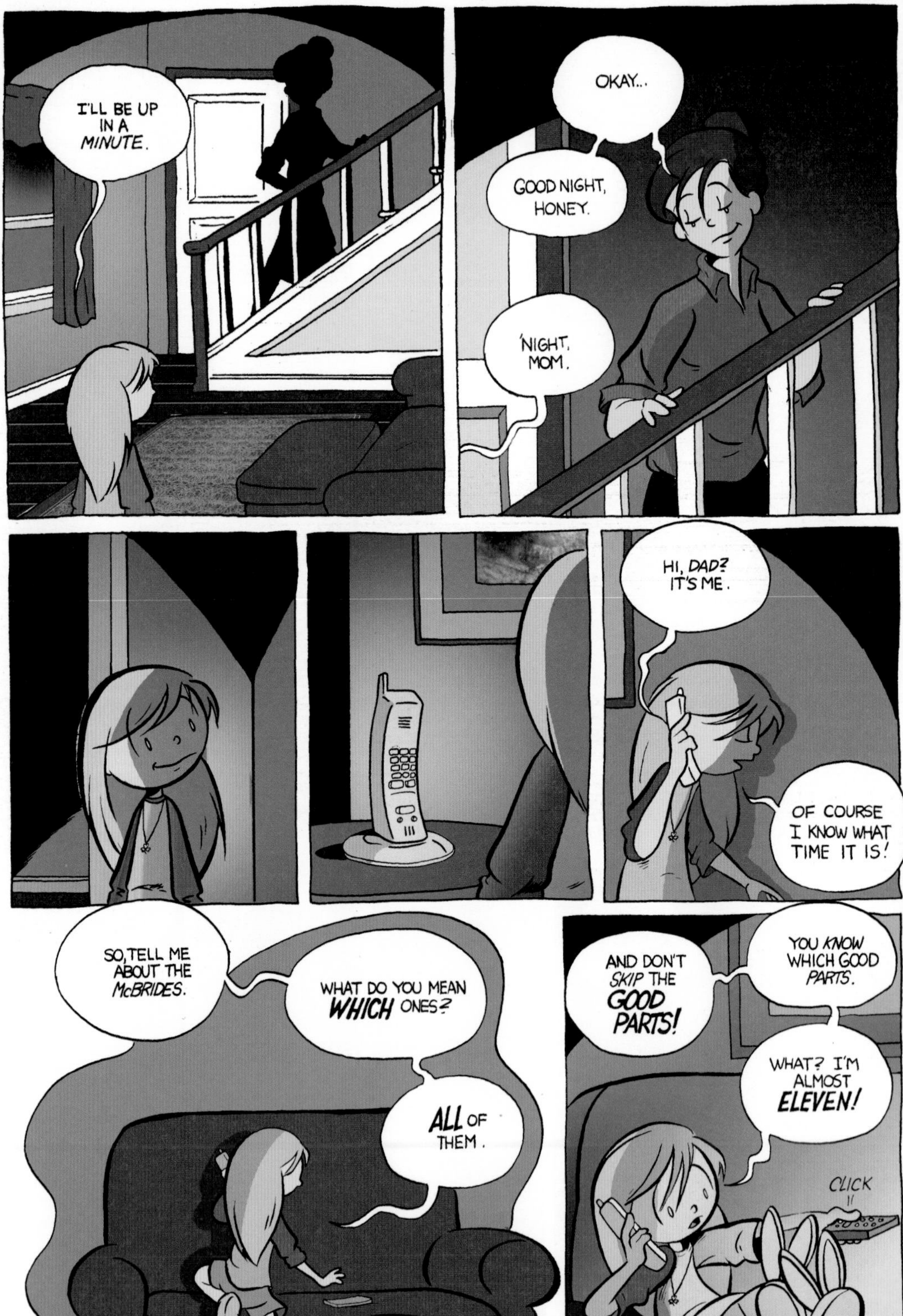
I'LL BE UP IN A *MINUTE*.
OKAY...
GOOD NIGHT, HONEY.
'NIGHT, MOM.
HI, *DAD?* IT'S ME.
OF COURSE I KNOW WHAT TIME IT IS!
SO, TELL ME ABOUT THE *McBRIDES*.
WHAT DO YOU MEAN **WHICH** ONES?
ALL OF THEM.
AND DON'T *SKIP* THE **GOOD PARTS!**
YOU *KNOW* WHICH GOOD *PARTS*.
WHAT? I'M ALMOST **ELEVEN!**
CLICK

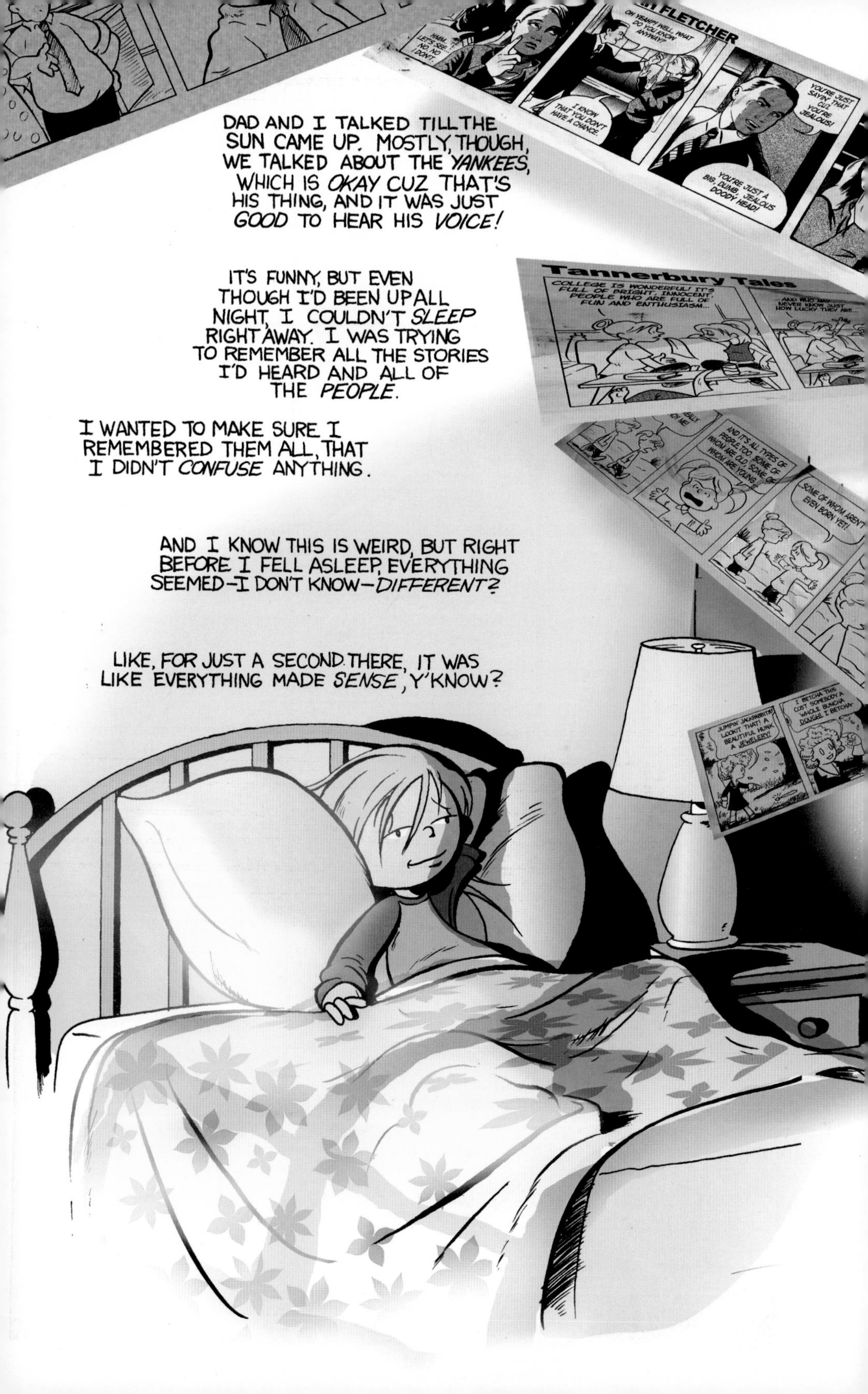
HMM, LET'S SEE... NO, NO I DON'T.
OH YEAH?! WELL, WHAT DO YOU KNOW ANYWAY?
I KNOW THAT YOU DON'T HAVE A CHANCE.
YOU'RE JUST SAYIN' THAT CUZ YOU'RE JEALOUS!
YOU'RE JUST A BIG, DUMB, JEALOUS DOODY HEAD!
DAD AND I TALKED TILL THE SUN CAME UP. MOSTLY, THOUGH, WE TALKED ABOUT THE YANKEES, WHICH IS OKAY CUZ THAT'S HIS THING, AND IT WAS JUST GOOD TO HEAR HIS VOICE!
Tannerbury Tales
COLLEGE IS WONDERFUL! IT'S FULL OF BRIGHT, INNOCENT PEOPLE WHO ARE FULL OF FUN AND ENTHUSIASM...
...AND WHO MAY NEVER KNOW JUST HOW LUCKY THEY ARE...
IT'S FUNNY, BUT EVEN THOUGH I'D BEEN UP ALL NIGHT, I COULDN'T SLEEP RIGHT AWAY. I WAS TRYING TO REMEMBER ALL THE STORIES I'D HEARD AND ALL OF THE PEOPLE.
I WANTED TO MAKE SURE I REMEMBERED THEM ALL, THAT I DIDN'T CONFUSE ANYTHING.
AND IT'S ALL TYPES OF PEOPLE TOO. SOME OF WHOM ARE OLD, SOME OF WHOM ARE YOUNG!
SOME OF WHOM AREN'T EVEN BORN YET!
AND I KNOW THIS IS WEIRD, BUT RIGHT BEFORE I FELL ASLEEP, EVERYTHING SEEMED—I DON'T KNOW—DIFFERENT?
LIKE, FOR JUST A SECOND THERE, IT WAS LIKE EVERYTHING MADE SENSE, Y'KNOW?
JUMPIN' JACKRABBITS! LOOKIT THAT! A BEAUTIFUL HUNK A JEWELERY!
I BETCHA THIS COST SOMEBODY A WHOLE BUNCHA DOUGH! I BETCHA.

LIKE EVERYTHING FIT.

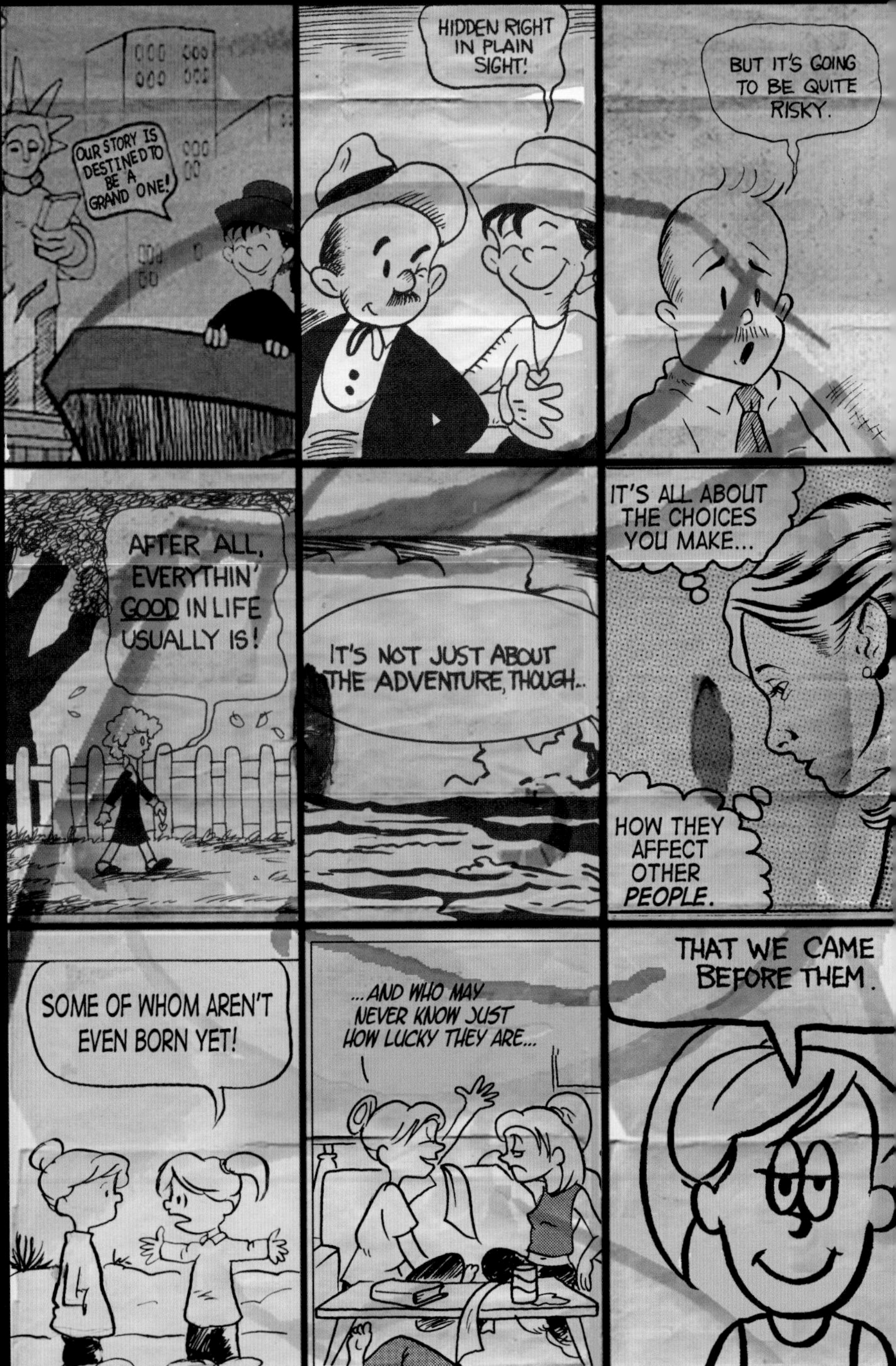
OUR STORY IS DESTINED TO BE A GRAND ONE!
HIDDEN RIGHT IN PLAIN SIGHT!
BUT IT'S GOING TO BE QUITE RISKY.
AFTER ALL, EVERYTHIN' GOOD IN LIFE USUALLY IS!
IT'S NOT JUST ABOUT THE ADVENTURE, THOUGH...
IT'S ALL ABOUT THE CHOICES YOU MAKE...
HOW THEY AFFECT OTHER PEOPLE.
SOME OF WHOM AREN'T EVEN BORN YET!
...AND WHO MAY NEVER KNOW JUST HOW LUCKY THEY ARE...
THAT WE CAME BEFORE THEM.

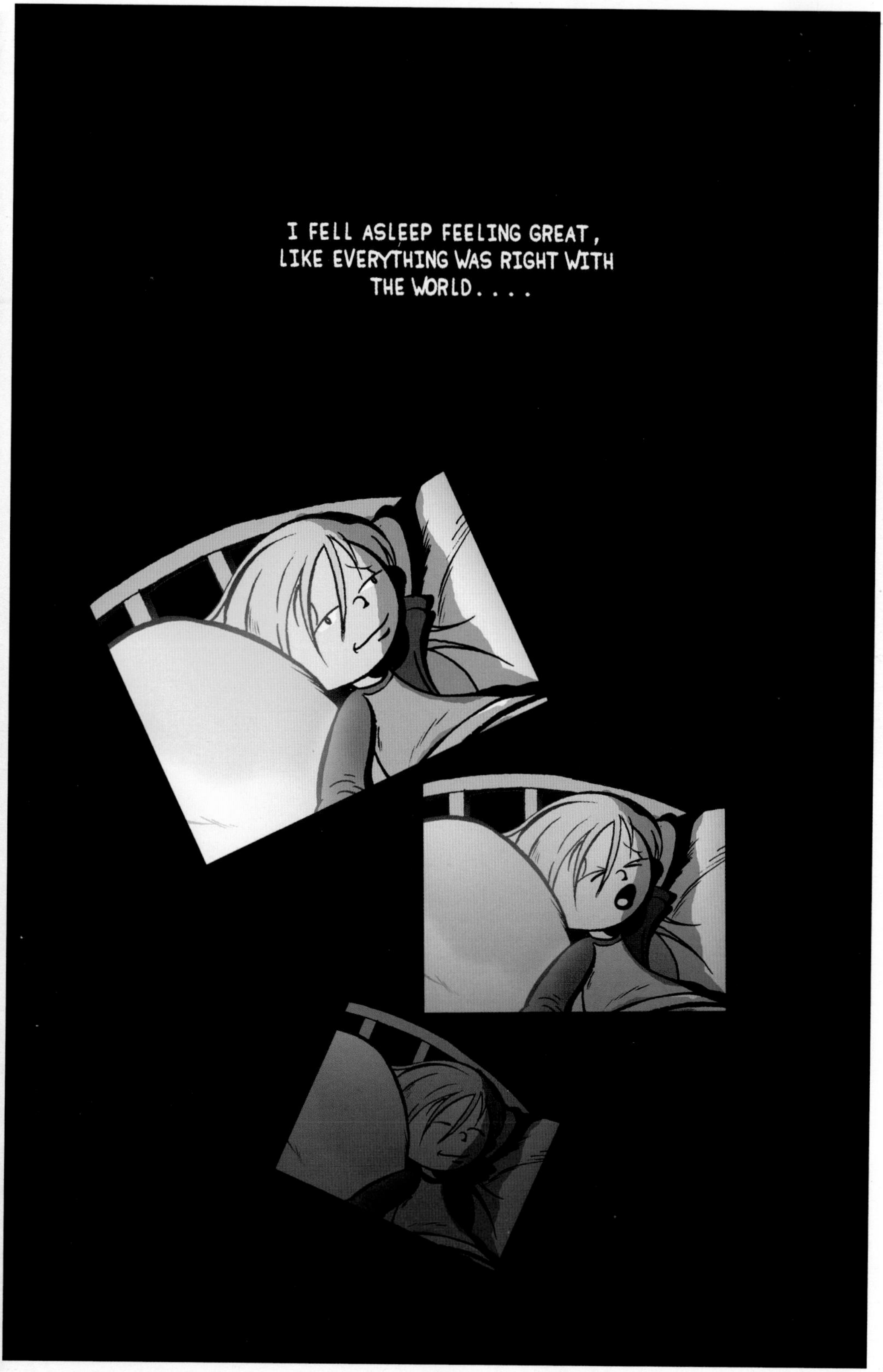
I FELL ASLEEP FEELING GREAT, LIKE EVERYTHING WAS RIGHT WITH THE WORLD. . . .

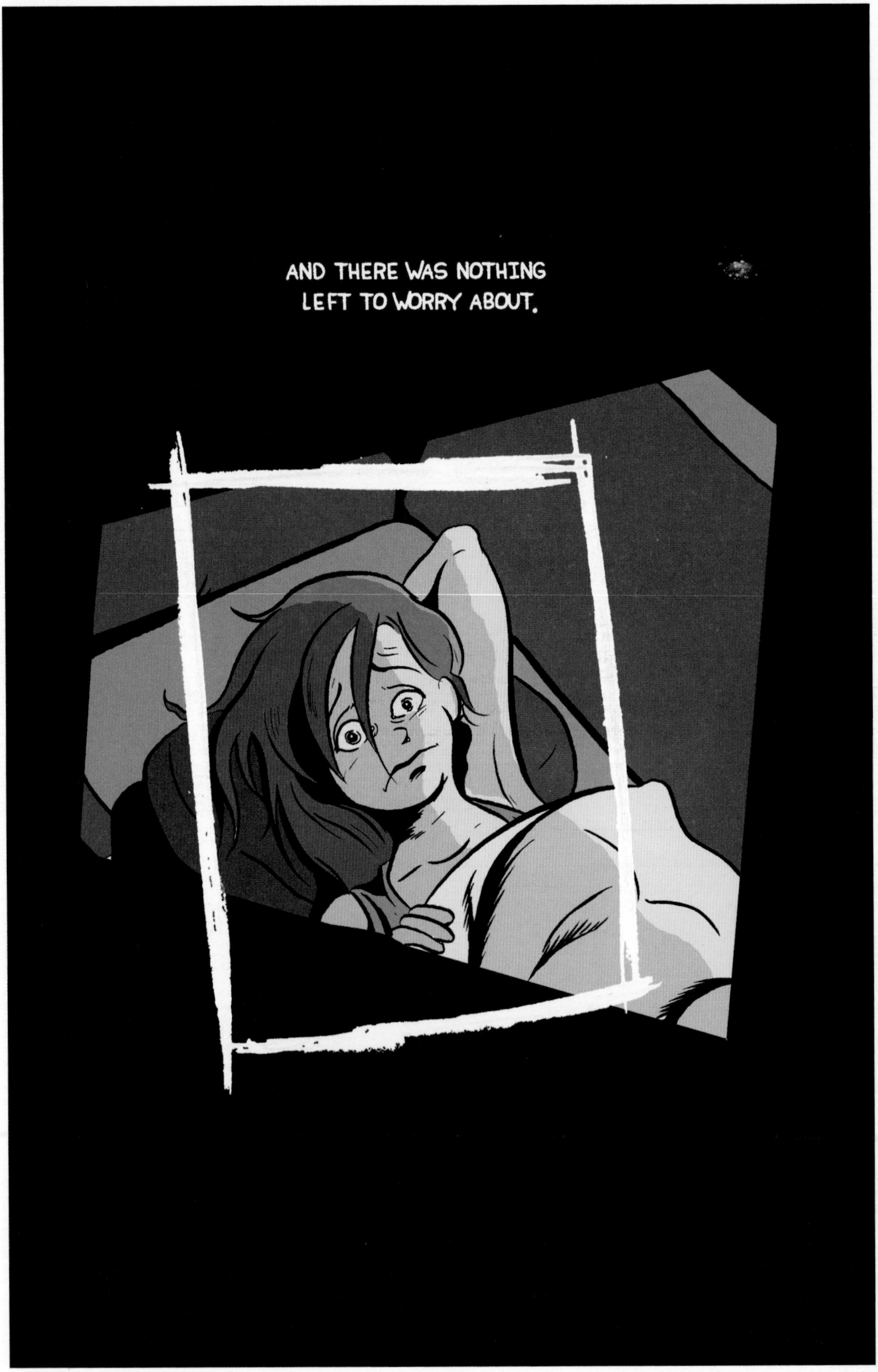
AND THERE WAS NOTHING LEFT TO WORRY ABOUT.

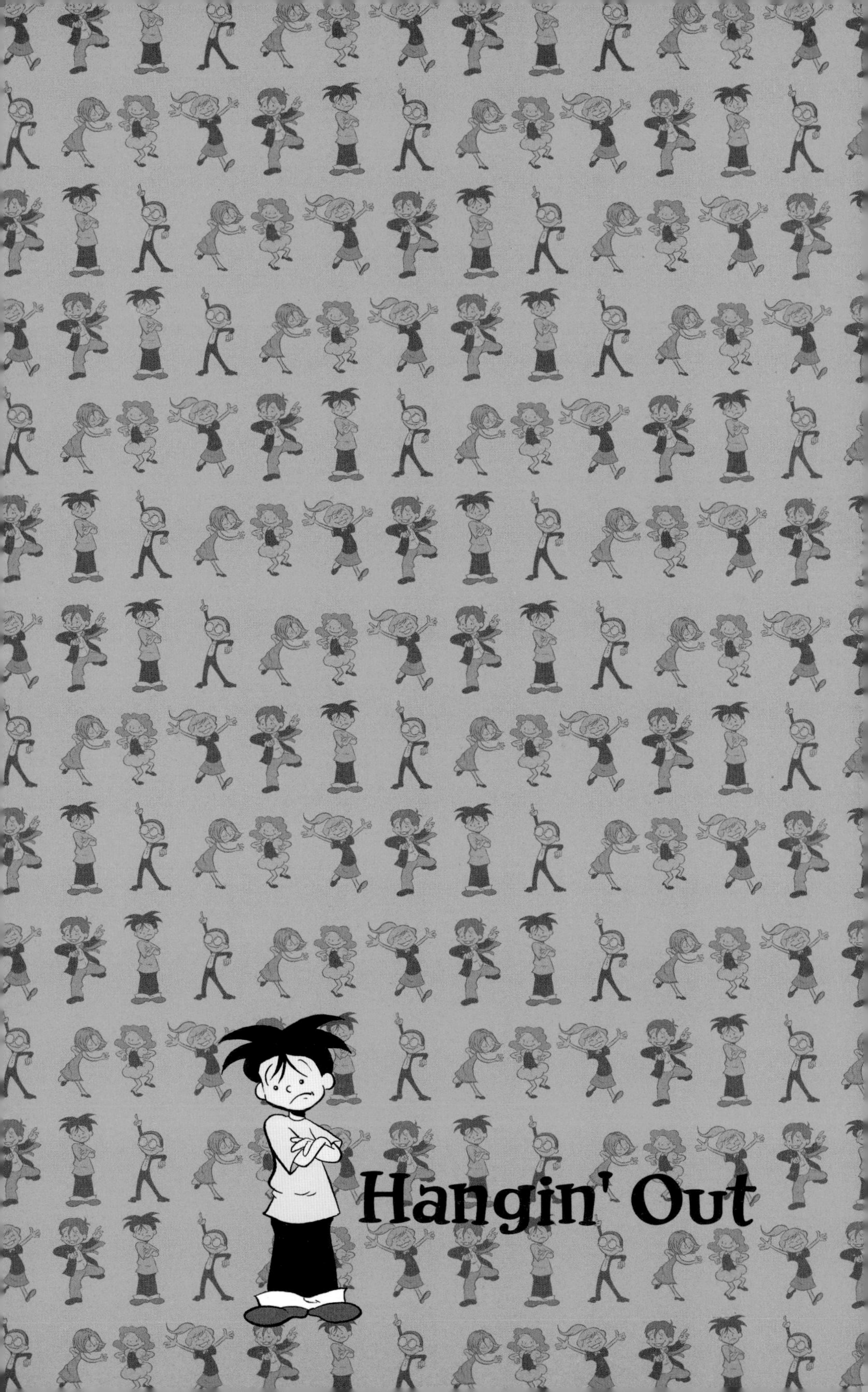

Hangin' Out

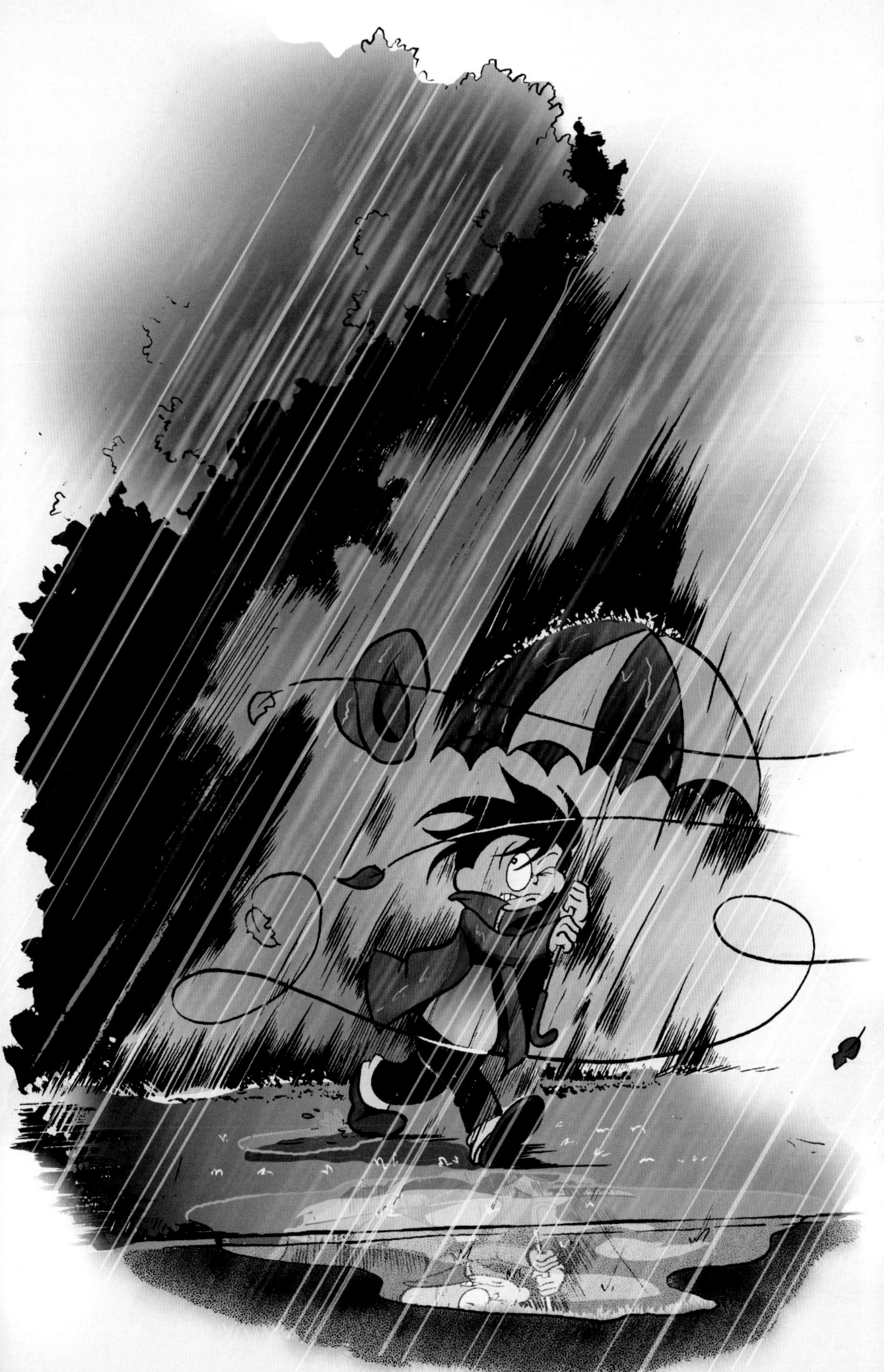

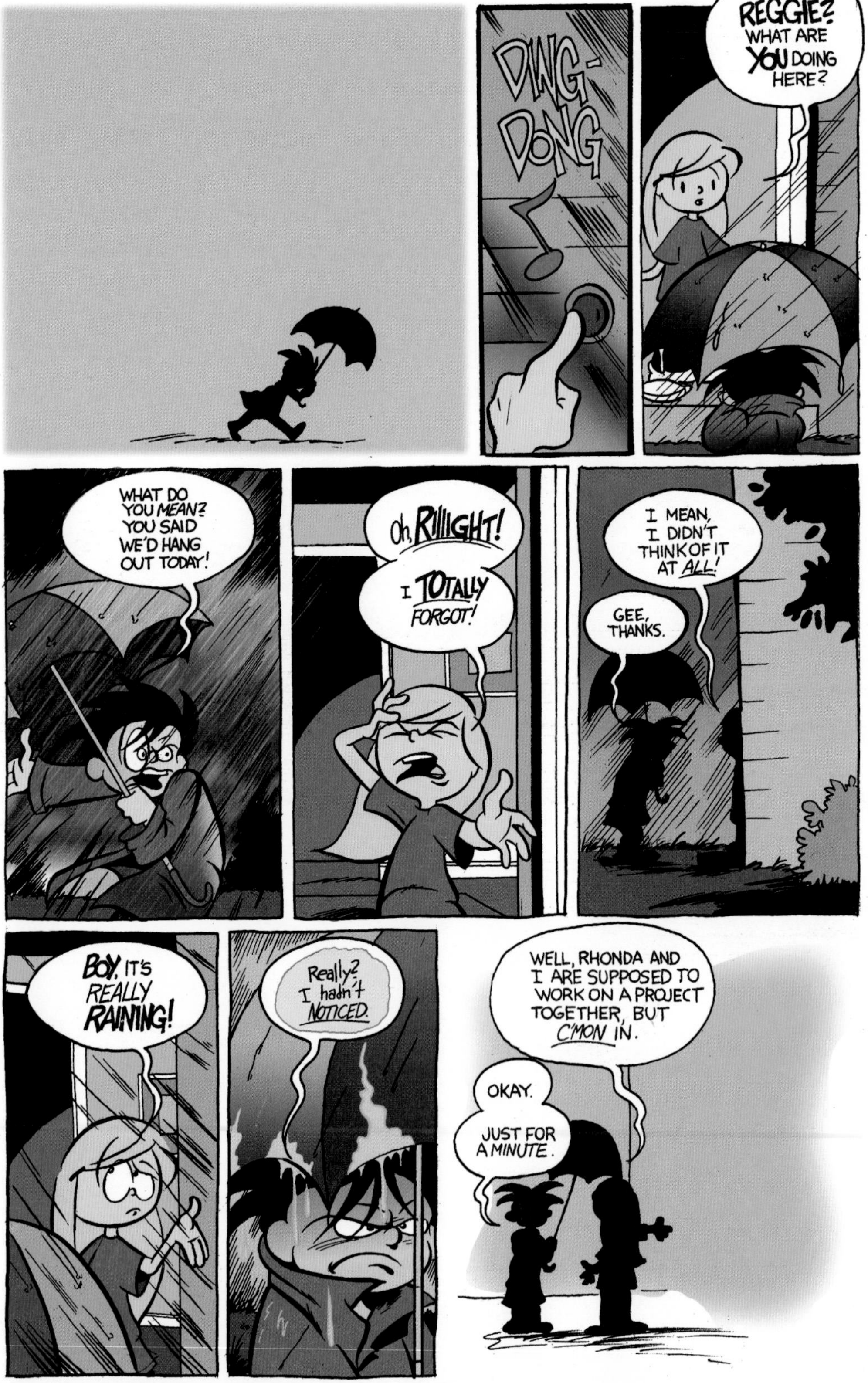
DING-DONG
REGGIE? WHAT ARE YOU DOING HERE?
WHAT DO YOU MEAN? YOU SAID WE'D HANG OUT TODAY!
Oh, RIIIIGHT!
I TOTALLY FORGOT!
I MEAN, I DIDN'T THINK OF IT AT ALL!
GEE, THANKS.
BOY, IT'S REALLY RAINING!
Really? I hadn't NOTICED.
WELL, RHONDA AND I ARE SUPPOSED TO WORK ON A PROJECT TOGETHER, BUT C'MON IN.
OKAY.
JUST FOR A MINUTE.

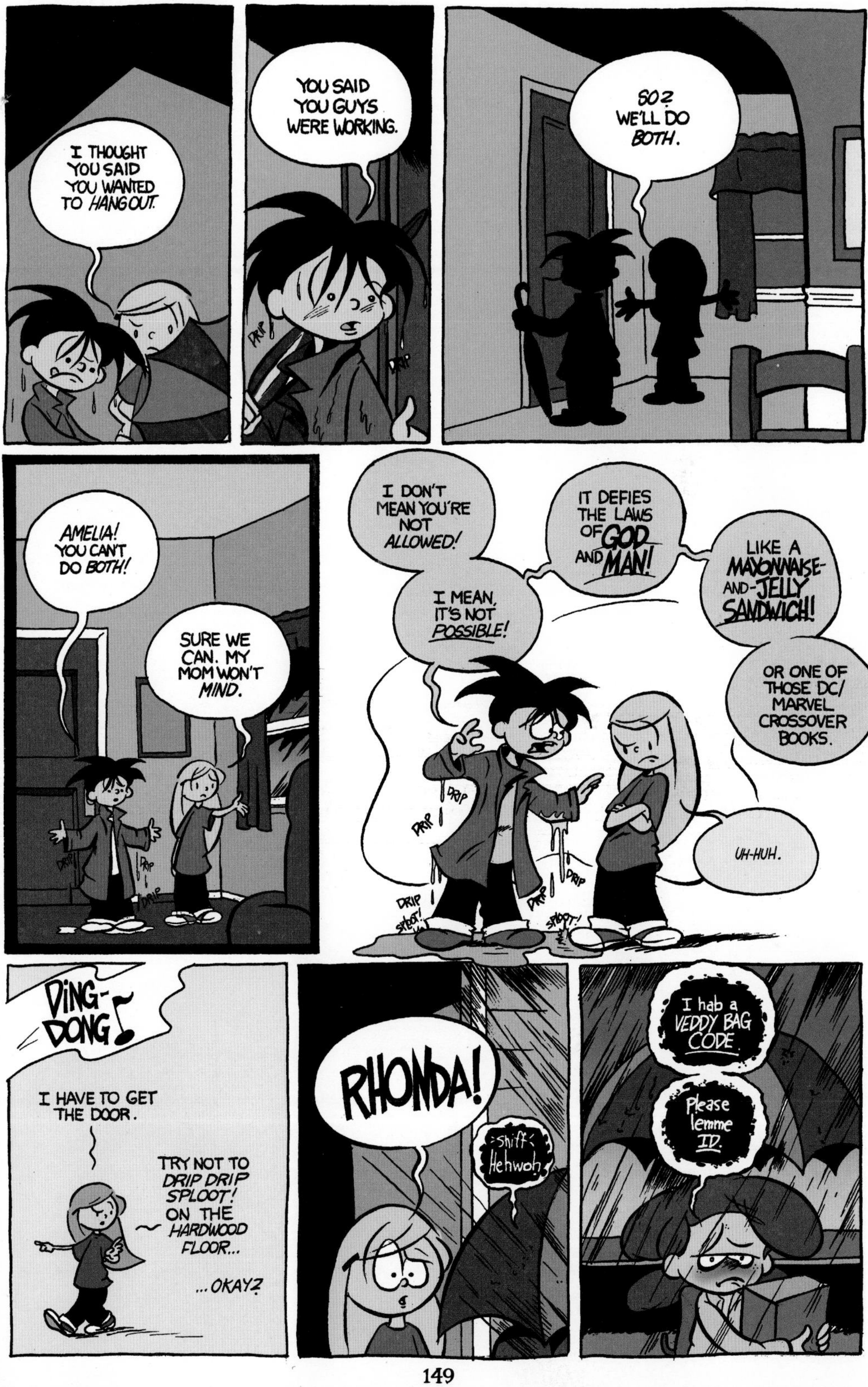
I THOUGHT YOU SAID YOU WANTED TO HANGOUT.
YOU SAID YOU GUYS WERE WORKING.
DRIP
DRIP
SO? WE'LL DO BOTH.
AMELIA! YOU CAN'T DO BOTH!
SURE WE CAN. MY MOM WON'T MIND.
DRIP
DRIP
DRIP
I DON'T MEAN YOU'RE NOT ALLOWED!
I MEAN, IT'S NOT POSSIBLE!
IT DEFIES THE LAWS OF GOD AND MAN!
LIKE A MAYONNAISE-AND-JELLY SANDWICH!
OR ONE OF THOSE DC/ MARVEL CROSSOVER BOOKS.
UH-HUH.
DRIP
DRIP
DRIP
SPLOOT!
DRIP
DRIP
SPLOOT!
DING-DONG
I HAVE TO GET THE DOOR.
TRY NOT TO DRIP DRIP SPLOOT! ON THE HARDWOOD FLOOR...
...OKAY?
RHONDA!
:sniff: Hehwoh
I hab a VEDDY BAG CODE.
Please lemme IN.

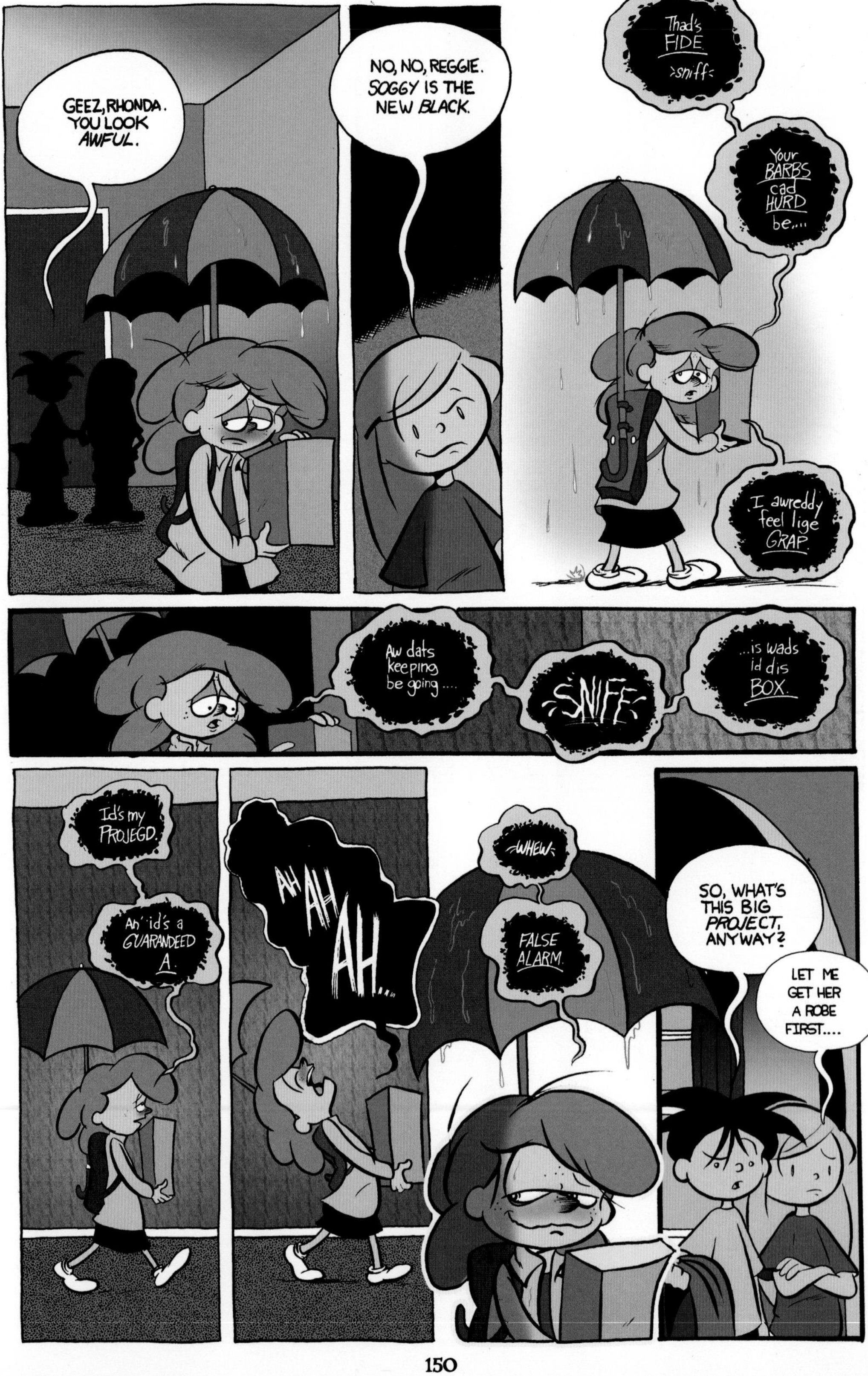
GEEZ, RHONDA. YOU LOOK AWFUL.
NO, NO, REGGIE. SOGGY IS THE NEW BLACK.
Thad's FIDE. >sniff<
Your BARBS cad HURD be....
I awreddy feel lige GRAP.
Aw dats keeping be going....
SNIFF
...is wads id dis BOX.
Id's my PROJEGD.
Ah' id's a GUARANDEED A.
AH AH AH...
WHEW
FALSE ALARM.
SO, WHAT'S THIS BIG PROJECT, ANYWAY?
LET ME GET HER A ROBE FIRST....

SHE'S DRIPPIER THAN YOU ARE.

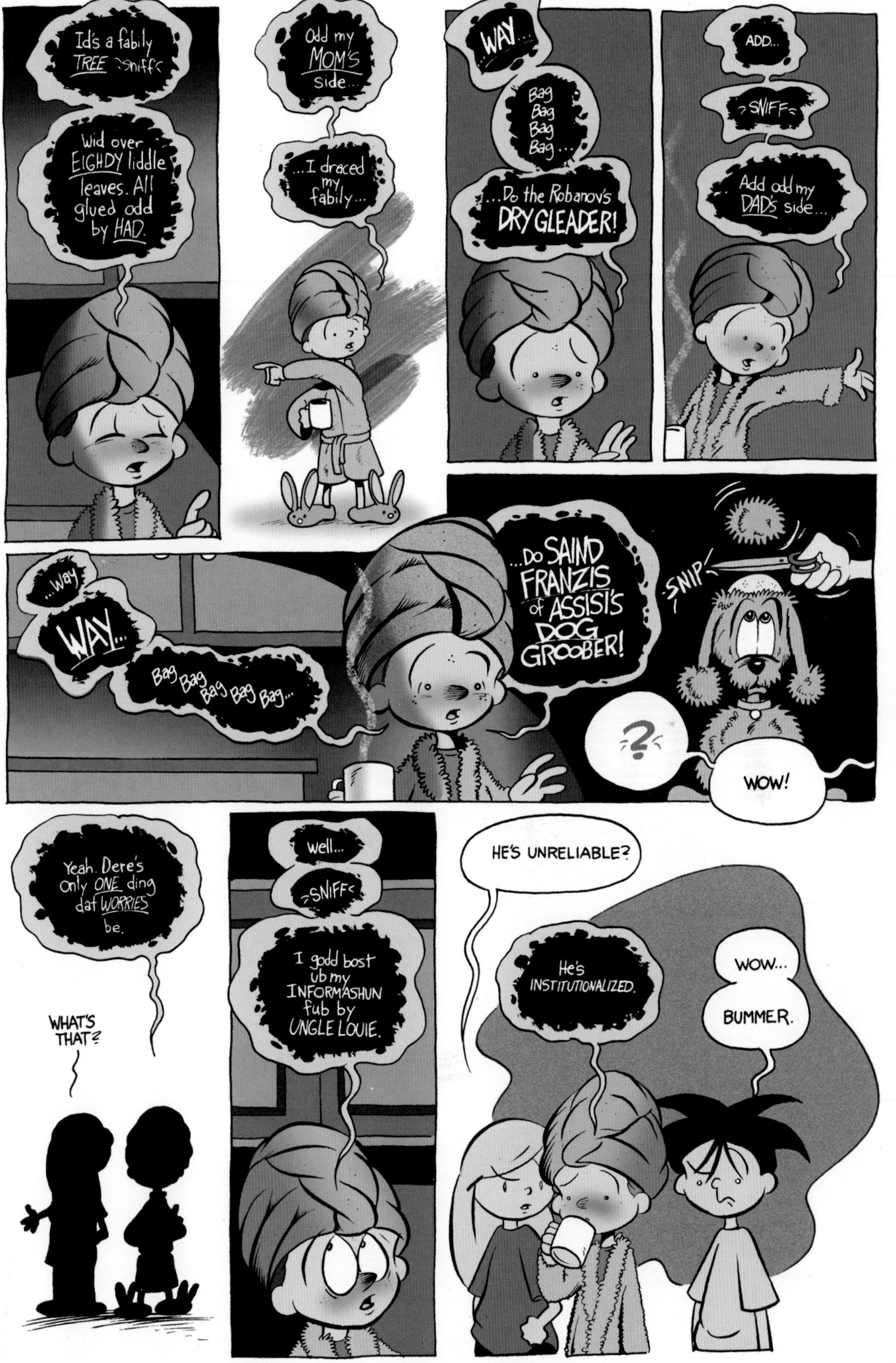

Id's a fabily TREE ≈sniff≈
Wid over EIGHDY liddle leaves. All glued odd by HAD.
Odd my MOM'S side...
...I draced my fabily...
WAY...
Bag Bag Bag Bag...
...Do the Robanov's DRY GLEADER!
ADD...
≈SNIFF≈
Add odd my DAD'S side...
...Way
WAY...
Bag Bag Bag Bag Bag...
...Do SAIND FRANZIS of ASSISI'S DOG GROOBER!
SNIP!
?
WOW!
Yeah. Dere's only ONE ding daf WORRIES be.
WHAT'S THAT?
well...
≈SNIFF≈
I godd bost ub my INFORMASHUN fub by UNGLE LOUIE.
HE'S UNRELIABLE?
He's INSTITUTIONALIZED.
WOW...
BUMMER.

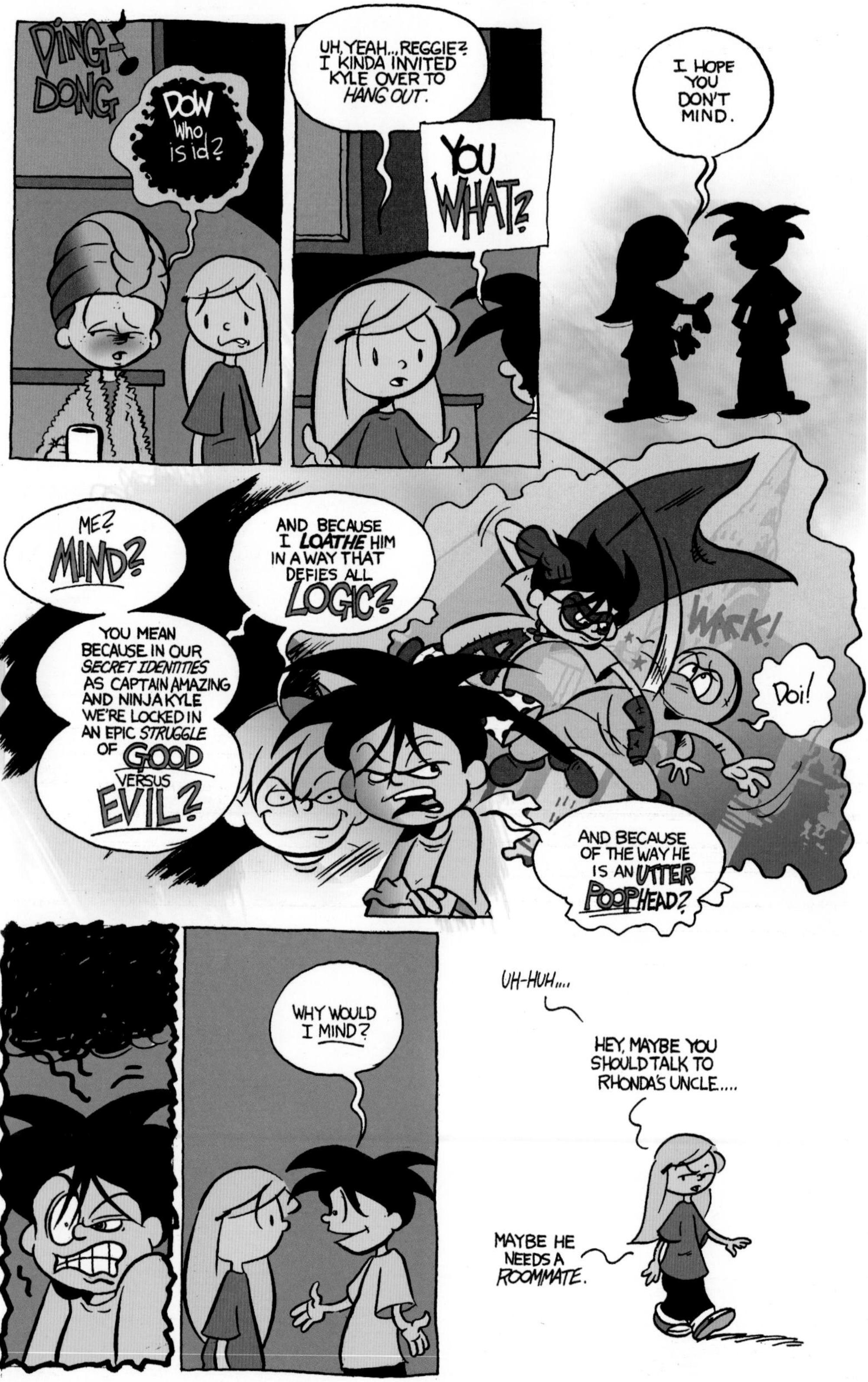
DING-DONG
DOW Who is id?
UH, YEAH... REGGIE? I KINDA INVITED KYLE OVER TO HANG OUT.
YOU WHAT?
I HOPE YOU DON'T MIND.
ME? MIND?
YOU MEAN BECAUSE IN OUR SECRET IDENTITIES AS CAPTAIN AMAZING AND NINJA KYLE WE'RE LOCKED IN AN EPIC STRUGGLE OF GOOD VERSUS EVIL?
AND BECAUSE I LOATHE HIM IN A WAY THAT DEFIES ALL LOGIC?
WACK!
Doi!
AND BECAUSE OF THE WAY HE IS AN UTTER POOPHEAD?
WHY WOULD I MIND?
UH-HUH....
HEY, MAYBE YOU SHOULD TALK TO RHONDA'S UNCLE....
MAYBE HE NEEDS A ROOMMATE.

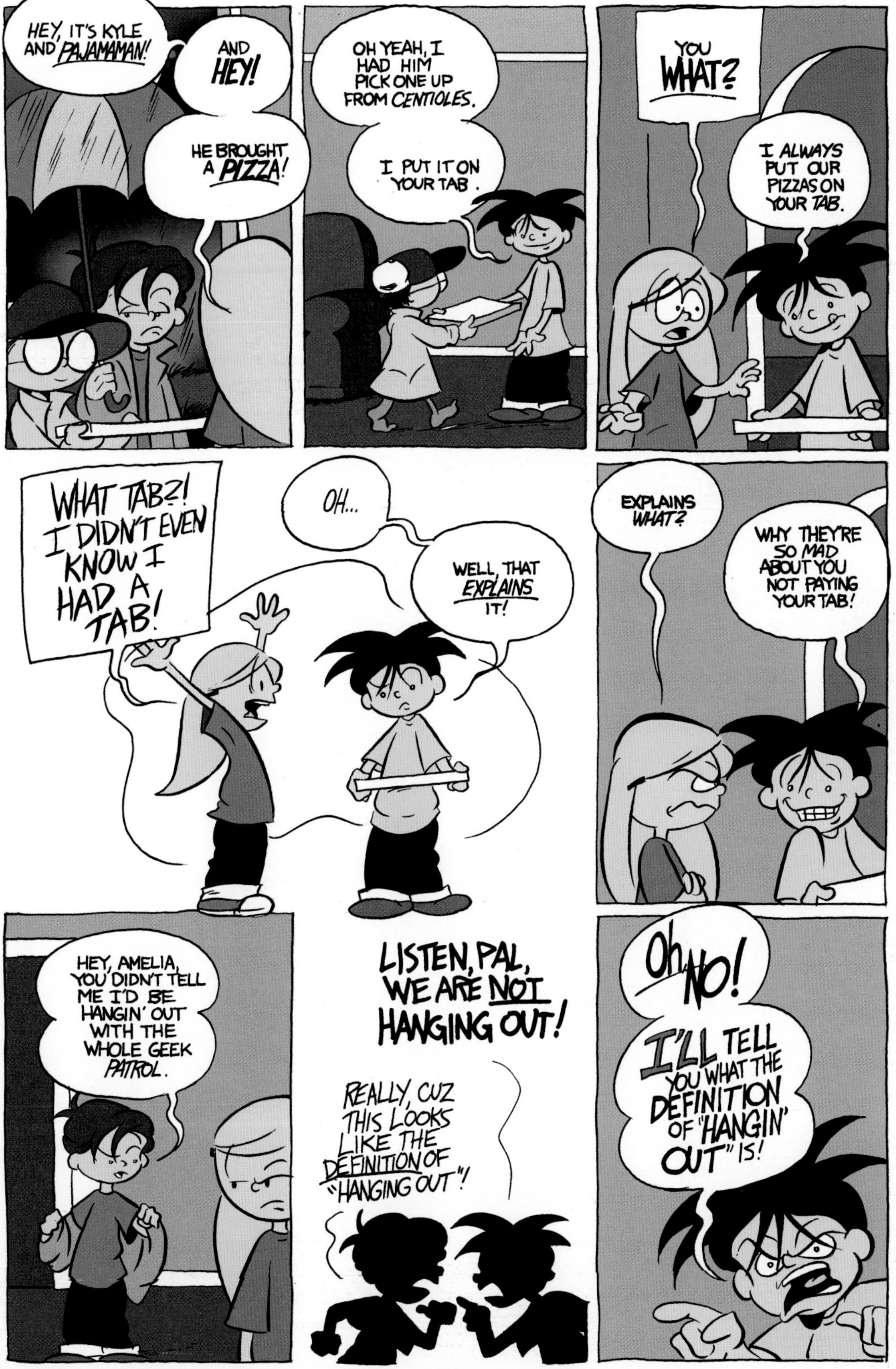
HEY, IT'S KYLE AND PAJAMAMAN!
AND HEY!
HE BROUGHT A PIZZA!
OH YEAH, I HAD HIM PICK ONE UP FROM CENTIOLES.
I PUT IT ON YOUR TAB.
YOU WHAT?
I ALWAYS PUT OUR PIZZAS ON YOUR TAB.
WHAT TAB?! I DIDN'T EVEN KNOW I HAD A TAB!
OH...
WELL, THAT EXPLAINS IT!
EXPLAINS WHAT?
WHY THEY'RE SO MAD ABOUT YOU NOT PAYING YOUR TAB!
HEY, AMELIA, YOU DIDN'T TELL ME I'D BE HANGIN' OUT WITH THE WHOLE GEEK PATROL.
LISTEN, PAL, WE ARE NOT HANGING OUT!
REALLY, CUZ THIS LOOKS LIKE THE DEFINITION OF "HANGING OUT"!
Oh NO!
I'LL TELL YOU WHAT THE DEFINITION OF "HANGIN' OUT" IS!

Hangin' Out

Hangtavious Outacus–More commonly known as "hanging out" is a twentieth-century American invention, in the vein of "bummin' around" or "chillin'." Although hanging out at first appears rather simple, in fact, its rules are myriad.

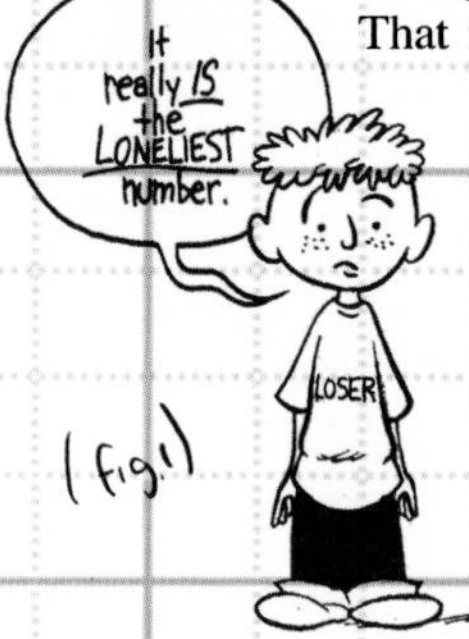
It really IS the LONELIEST number.
LOSER
(fig.1)

Hanging out cannot be done alone. That is called "moping" or "being a pariah," and neither one is particularly attractive (fig. 1).

Any group containing two to five people may engage in hanging out, so long as doing nothing is the primary activity. For example, "hanging out and talking" is acceptable while "hanging out and building shelters for Habitat for Humanity" is not. Snacks are not required, but are highly recommended (fig. 2).

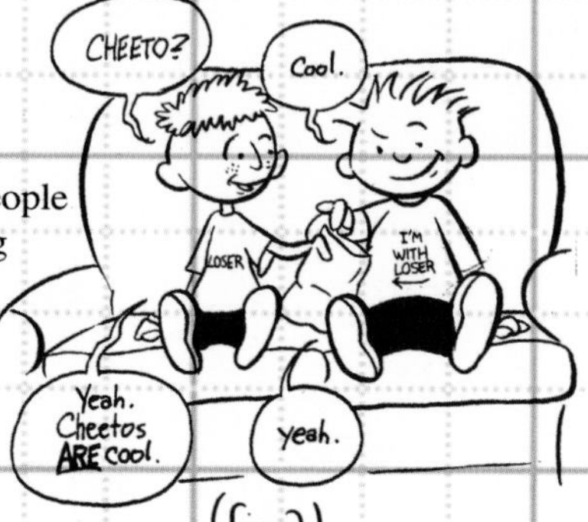
CHEETO?
Cool.
LOSER
I'M WITH LOSER
Yeah. Cheetos ARE cool.
yeah.
(fig.2)

There are strict restrictions on how many people may hang out and how often the hanging may occur. For example, more than five people is now a party, and while it may seem like you can hang out at a party, you can't because the music is too loud, and let's face it, there's no way you like more than five people anyway (fig. 3).

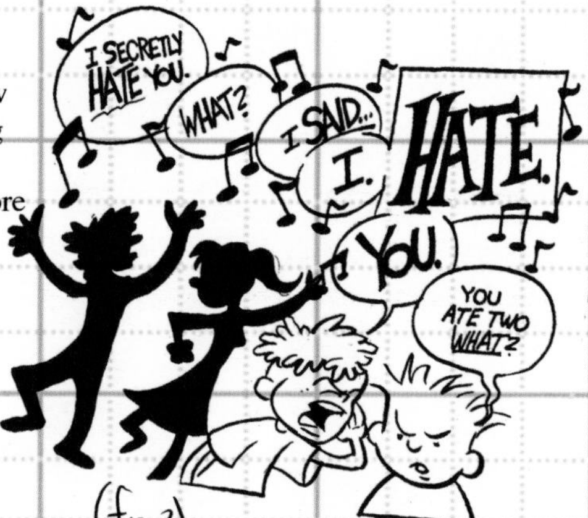
I SECRETLY HATE YOU.
WHAT?
I SAID...
I.
HATE.
YOU.
YOU ATE TWO WHAT?
(fig.3)

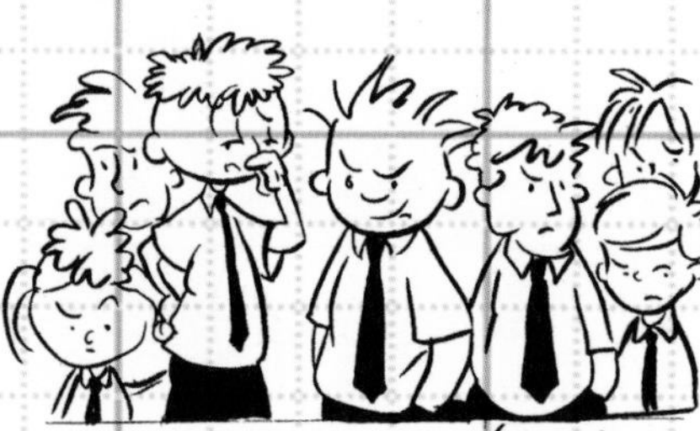
(fig.4)

Here is where the slippery slope gets even slipperier.

More than five people who meet more than once a month is no longer a party but a club (fig. 4). This is fine, but you may be expected to pay dues or pretend to be interested in other people's boats and/or record collections. More than once a WEEK, and it becomes a cult. It is definitely advisable NOT to join a cult, but if you feel you must, remember that it is better to be the leader than the guy who collects the fingers (fig. 5).

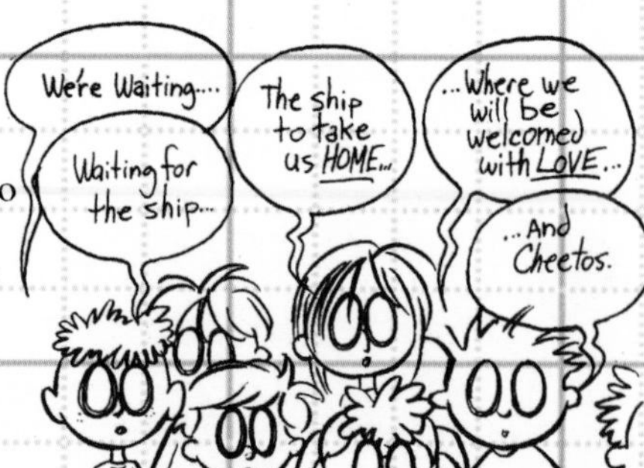
We're Waiting...
Waiting for the ship...
The ship to take us HOME...
...Where we will be welcomed with LOVE...
...And Cheetos.
(fig5)

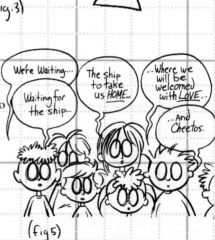

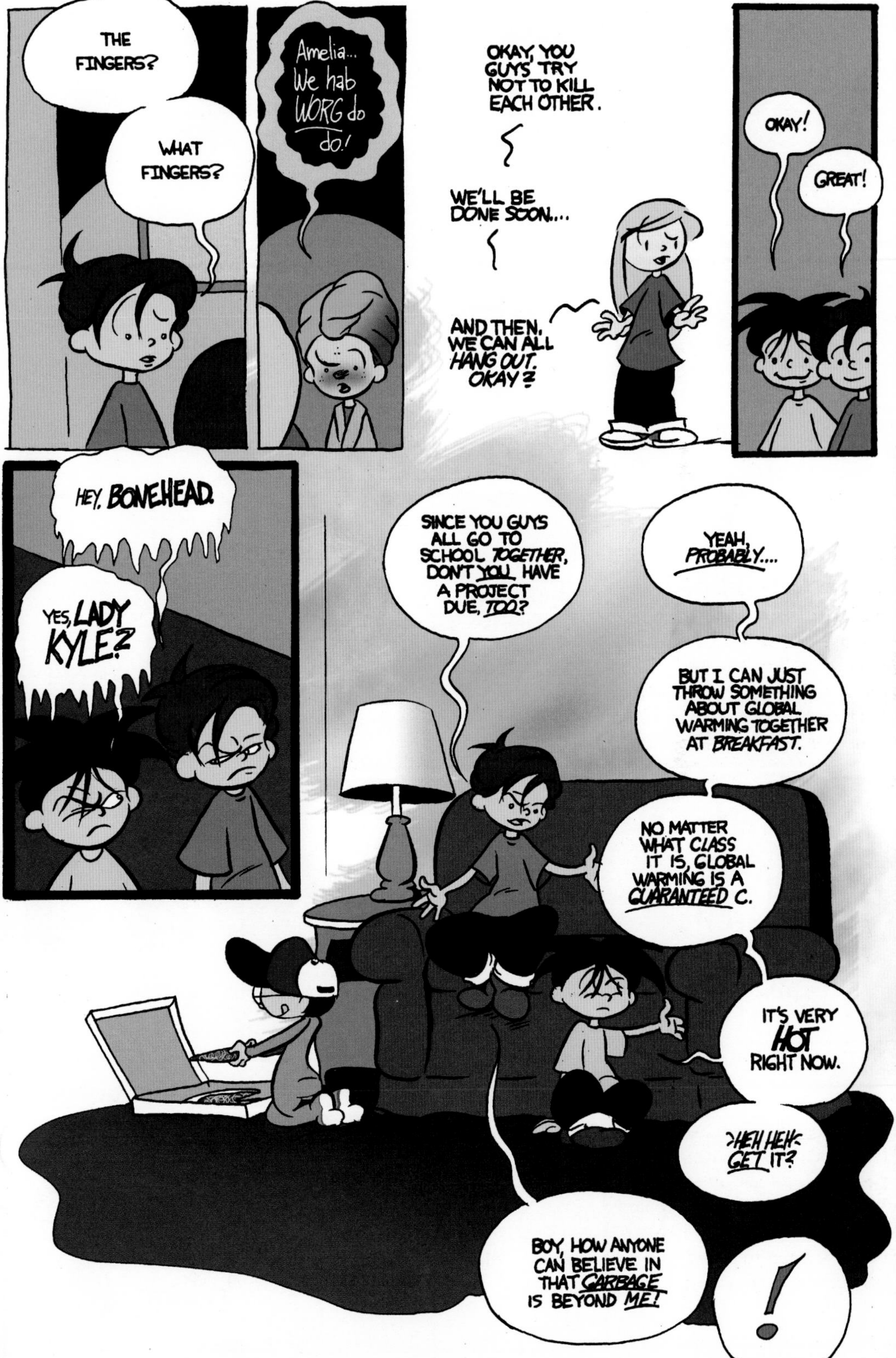
THE FINGERS?
WHAT FINGERS?
Amelia... We hab WORG do do!
OKAY, YOU GUYS TRY NOT TO KILL EACH OTHER.
WE'LL BE DONE SOON....
AND THEN, WE CAN ALL HANG OUT. OKAY?
OKAY!
GREAT!
HEY, BONEHEAD.
YES, LADY KYLE?
SINCE YOU GUYS ALL GO TO SCHOOL TOGETHER, DON'T YOU HAVE A PROJECT DUE, TOO?
YEAH, PROBABLY....
BUT I CAN JUST THROW SOMETHING ABOUT GLOBAL WARMING TOGETHER AT BREAKFAST.
NO MATTER WHAT CLASS IT IS, GLOBAL WARMING IS A GUARANTEED C.
IT'S VERY HOT RIGHT NOW.
HEH HEH GET IT?
BOY, HOW ANYONE CAN BELIEVE IN THAT GARBAGE IS BEYOND ME!
!

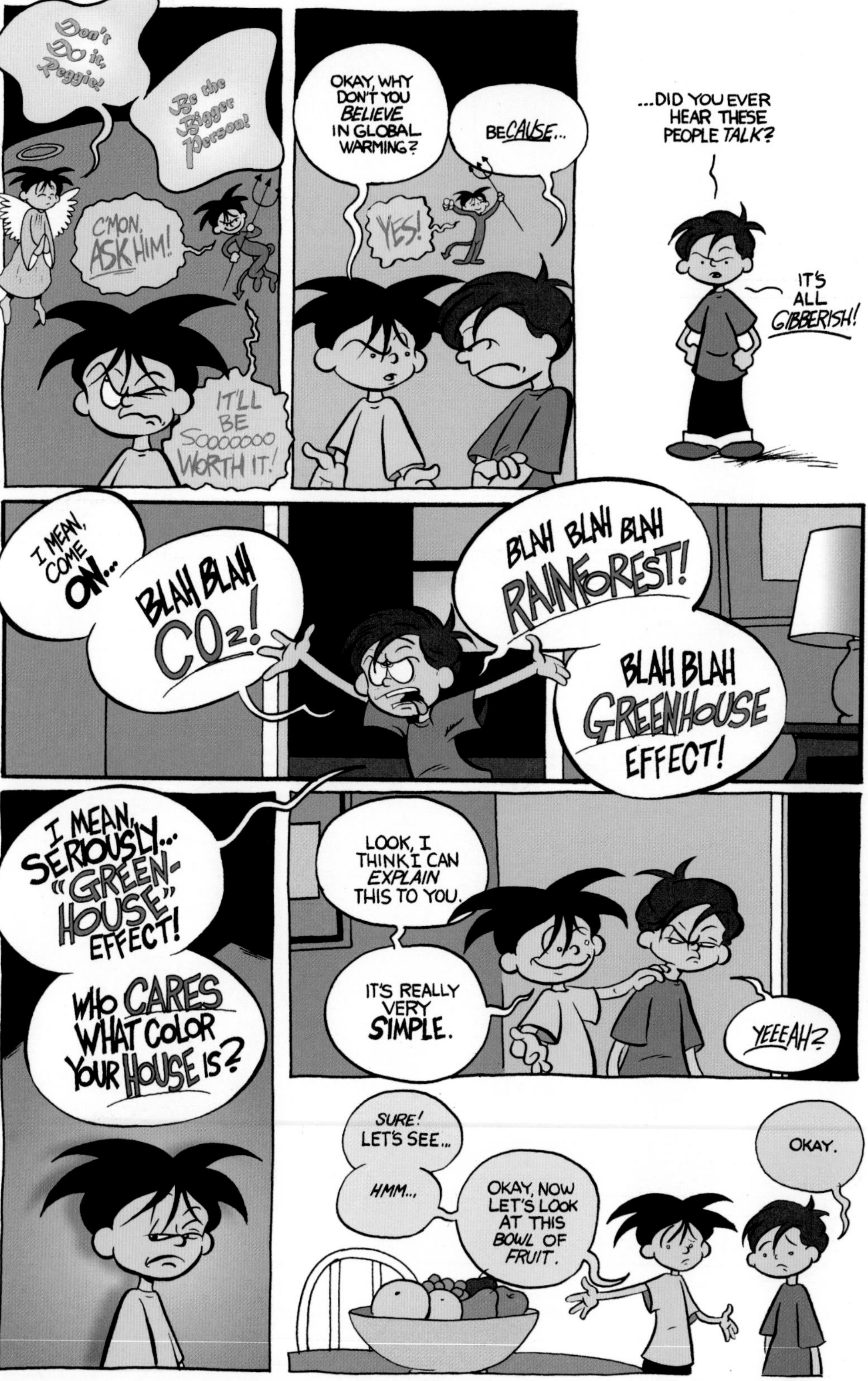
Don't DO it, Peggie!
Be the Bigger Person!
C'MON, ASK HIM!
IT'LL BE SOOOOOOO WORTH IT!
OKAY, WHY DON'T YOU BELIEVE IN GLOBAL WARMING?
YES!
BECAUSE...
...DID YOU EVER HEAR THESE PEOPLE TALK?
IT'S ALL GIBBERISH!
I MEAN, COME ON...
BLAH BLAH CO_2!
BLAH BLAH BLAH RAINFOREST!
BLAH BLAH GREENHOUSE EFFECT!
I MEAN, SERIOUSLY... "GREEN-HOUSE" EFFECT!
WHO CARES WHAT COLOR YOUR HOUSE IS?
LOOK, I THINK I CAN EXPLAIN THIS TO YOU.
IT'S REALLY VERY SIMPLE.
YEEEAH?
SURE! LET'S SEE...
HMM...
OKAY, NOW LET'S LOOK AT THIS BOWL OF FRUIT.
OKAY.

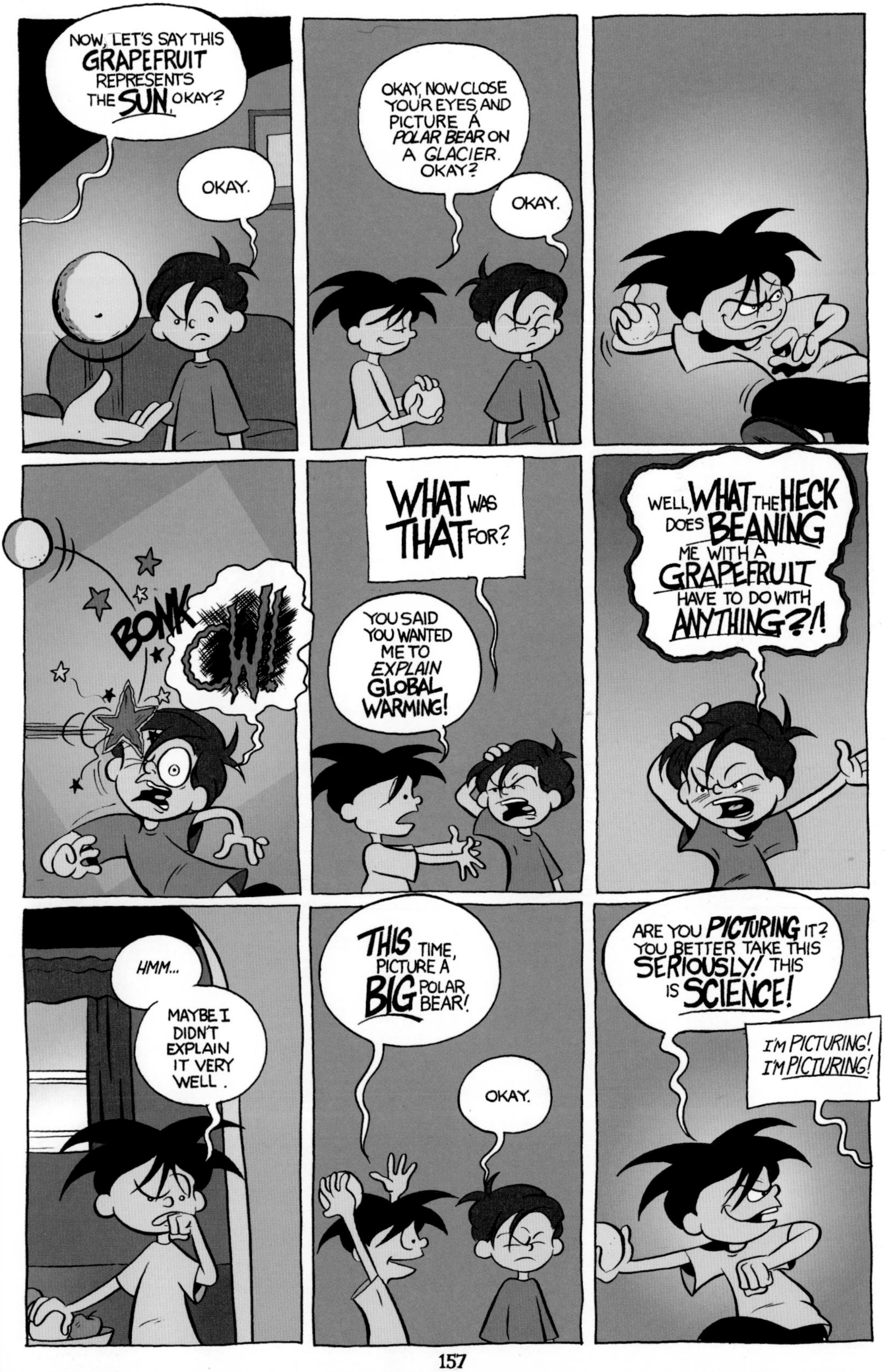
NOW, LET'S SAY THIS GRAPEFRUIT REPRESENTS THE SUN, OKAY?
OKAY.
OKAY, NOW CLOSE YOUR EYES, AND PICTURE A POLAR BEAR ON A GLACIER. OKAY?
OKAY.
BONK
OW!!
WHAT WAS THAT FOR?
YOU SAID YOU WANTED ME TO EXPLAIN GLOBAL WARMING!
WELL, WHAT THE HECK DOES BEANING ME WITH A GRAPEFRUIT HAVE TO DO WITH ANYTHING?!!
HMM...
MAYBE I DIDN'T EXPLAIN IT VERY WELL.
THIS TIME, PICTURE A BIG POLAR BEAR!
OKAY.
ARE YOU PICTURING IT? YOU BETTER TAKE THIS SERIOUSLY! THIS IS SCIENCE!
I'M PICTURING! I'M PICTURING!

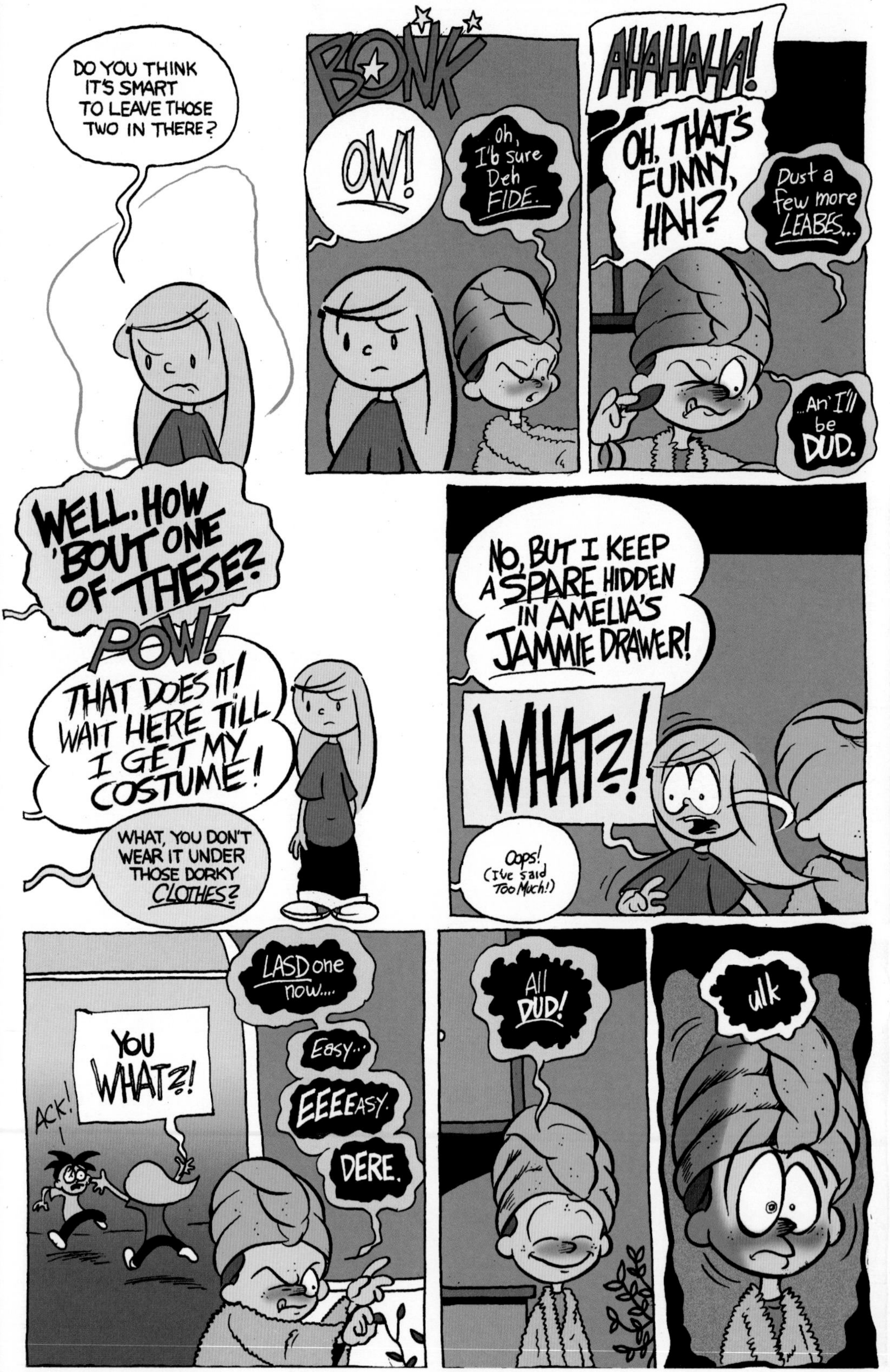
DO YOU THINK IT'S SMART TO LEAVE THOSE TWO IN THERE?
BONK
OW!
Oh, I'b sure Deh FIDE.
AHAHAHA!
OH, THAT'S FUNNY, HAH?
Dust a few more LEABES...
...An' I'll be DUD.
WELL, HOW 'BOUT ONE OF THESE?
POW!
THAT DOES IT! WAIT HERE TILL I GET MY COSTUME!
WHAT, YOU DON'T WEAR IT UNDER THOSE DORKY CLOTHES?
NO, BUT I KEEP A SPARE HIDDEN IN AMELIA'S JAMMIE DRAWER!
WHAT?!
Oops! (I've said Too Much!)
YOU WHAT?!
ACK!
LASD one now....
Easy...
EEEEasy.
DERE.
All DUD!
ulk

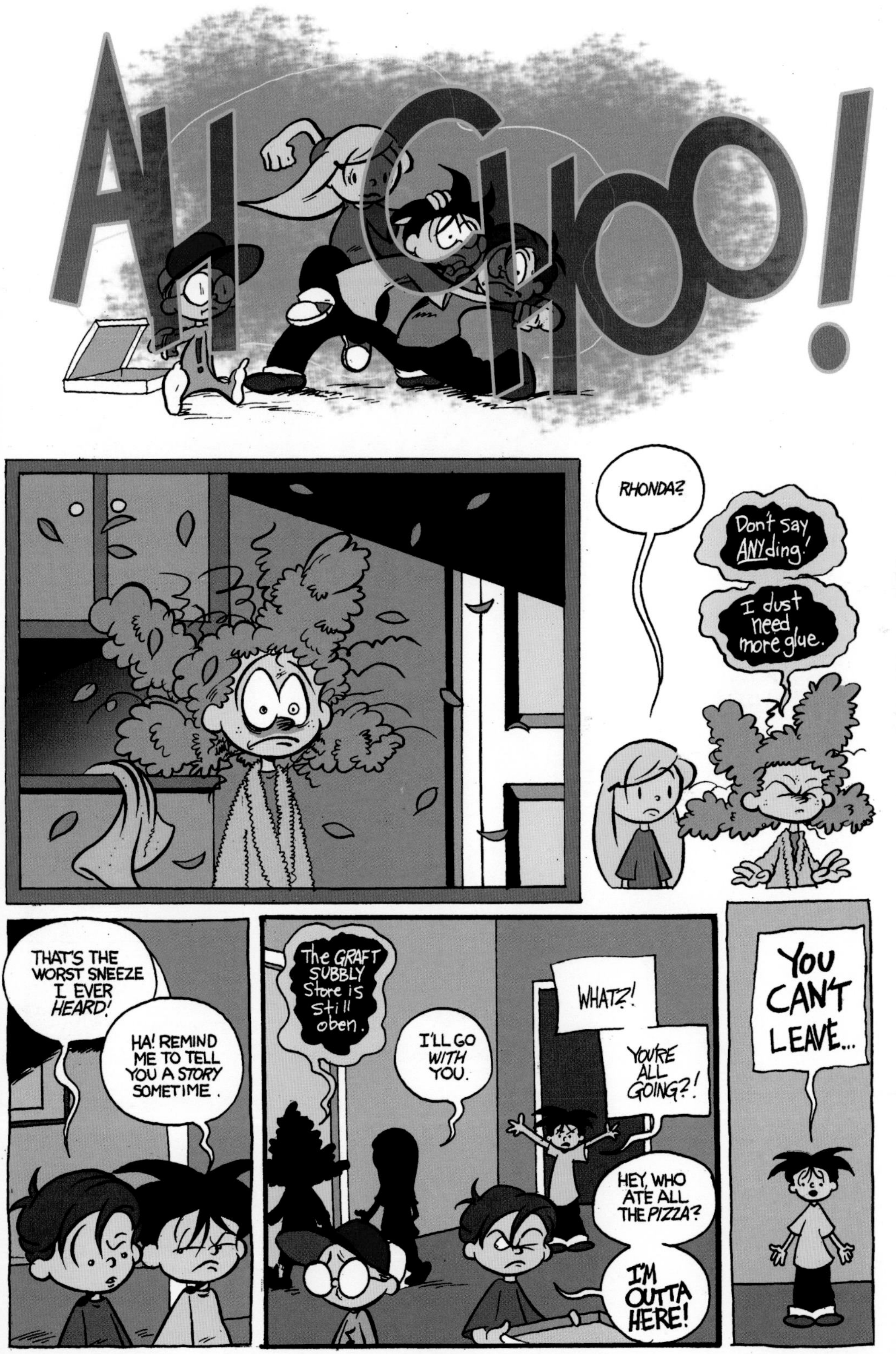
AH CHOO!
RHONDA?
Don't say ANYding!
I dust need more glue.
THAT'S THE WORST SNEEZE I EVER HEARD!
HA! REMIND ME TO TELL YOU A STORY SOMETIME.
The GRAFT SUBBLY Store is still oben.
I'LL GO WITH YOU.
WHAT?!
YOU'RE ALL GOING?!
HEY, WHO ATE ALL THE PIZZA?
I'M OUTTA HERE!
YOU CAN'T LEAVE...

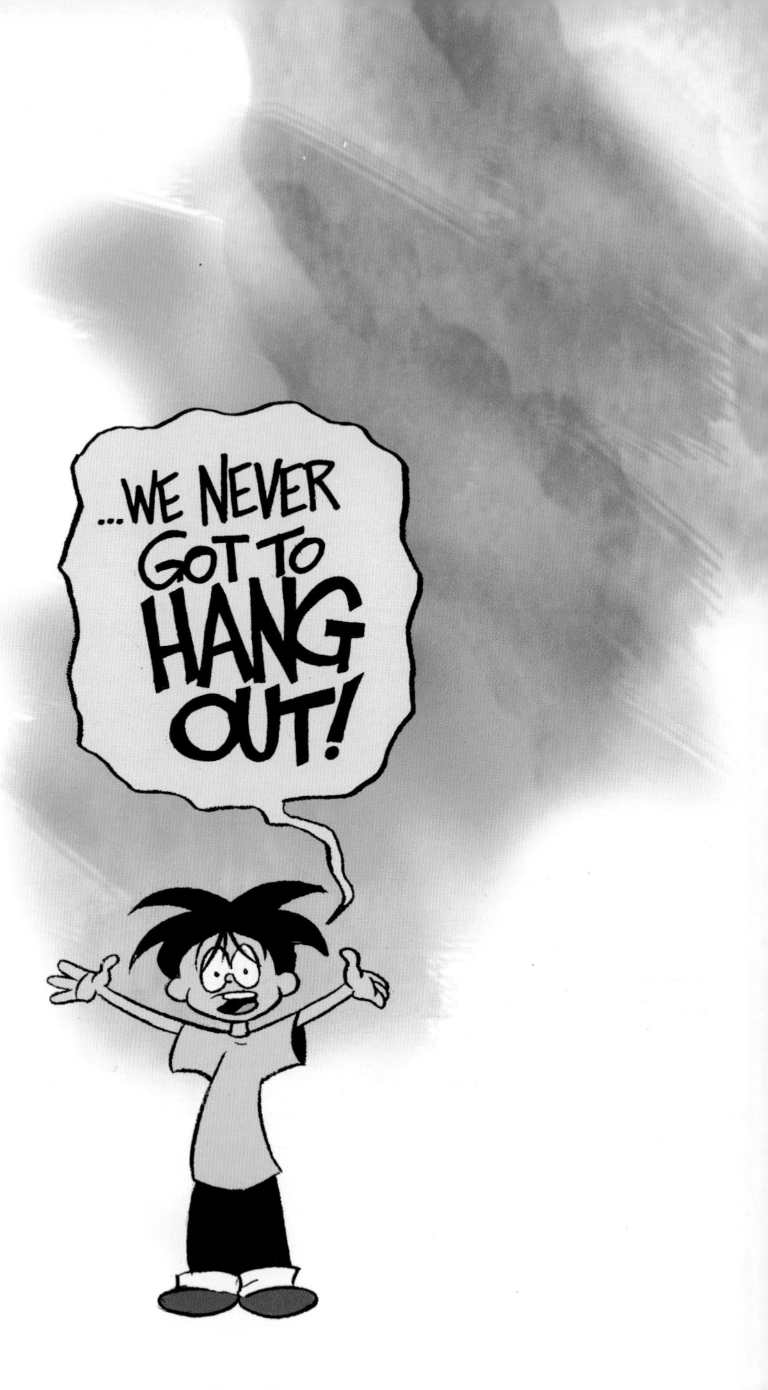
...WE NEVER GOT TO HANG OUT!

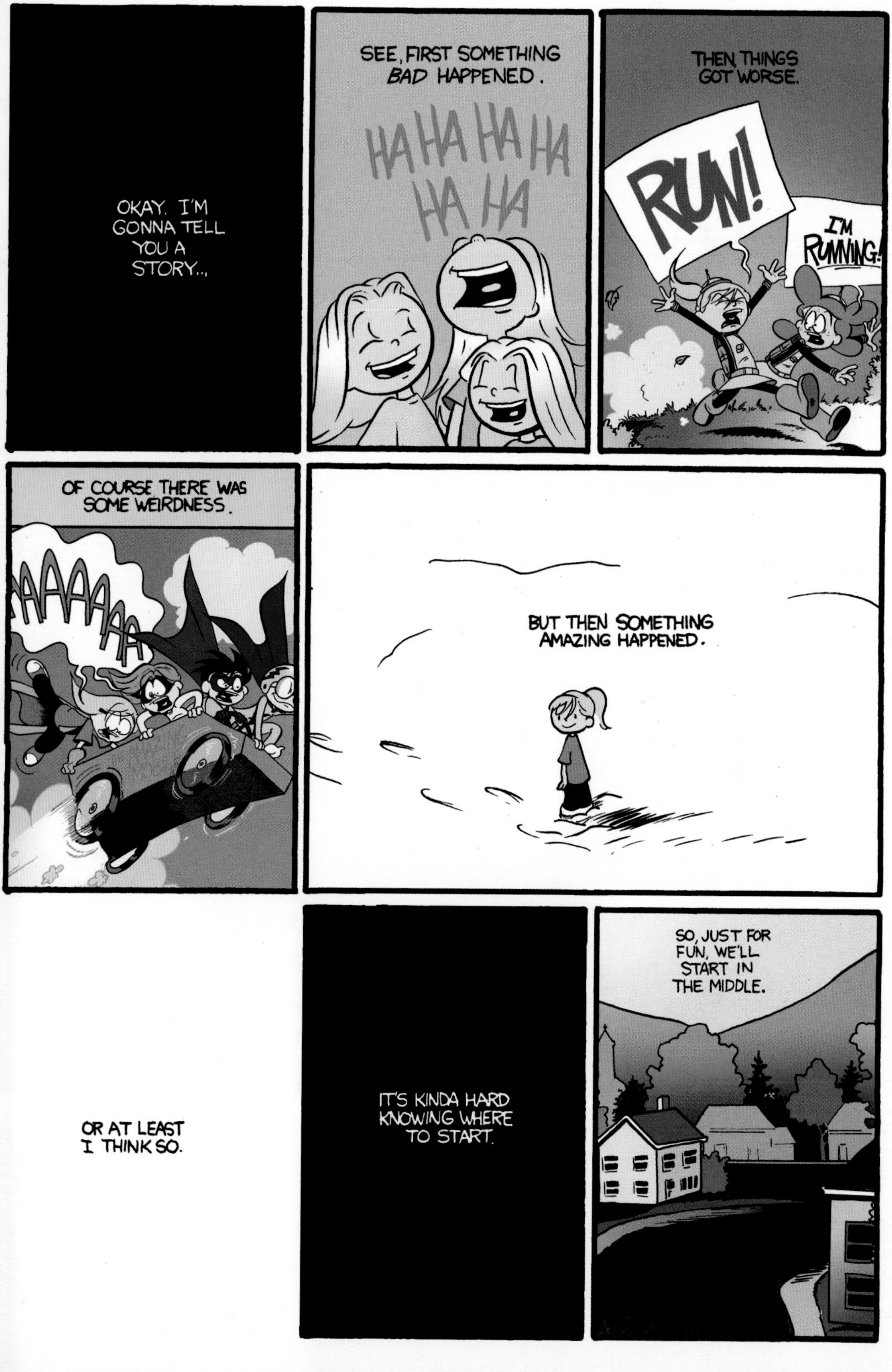

OKAY. I'M GONNA TELL YOU A STORY...
SEE, FIRST SOMETHING *BAD* HAPPENED.
HA HA HA HA HA HA
THEN, THINGS GOT WORSE.
RUN!
I'M RUNNING!
OF COURSE THERE WAS SOME WEIRDNESS.
AAAAAAAA
BUT THEN SOMETHING AMAZING HAPPENED.
OR AT LEAST I THINK SO.
IT'S KINDA HARD KNOWING WHERE TO START.
SO, JUST FOR FUN, WE'LL START IN THE MIDDLE.

Turn the page for a sneak peek
of the next Amelia Rules! book

THE TWEENAGE GUIDE TO NOT BEING UNPOPULAR
"A character to rival Ramona."
–School Library Journal
An AMELIA RULES! Book
WRITTEN AND ILLUSTRATED BY
Jimmy Gownley

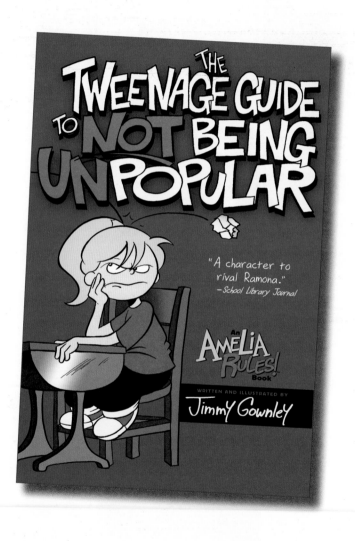

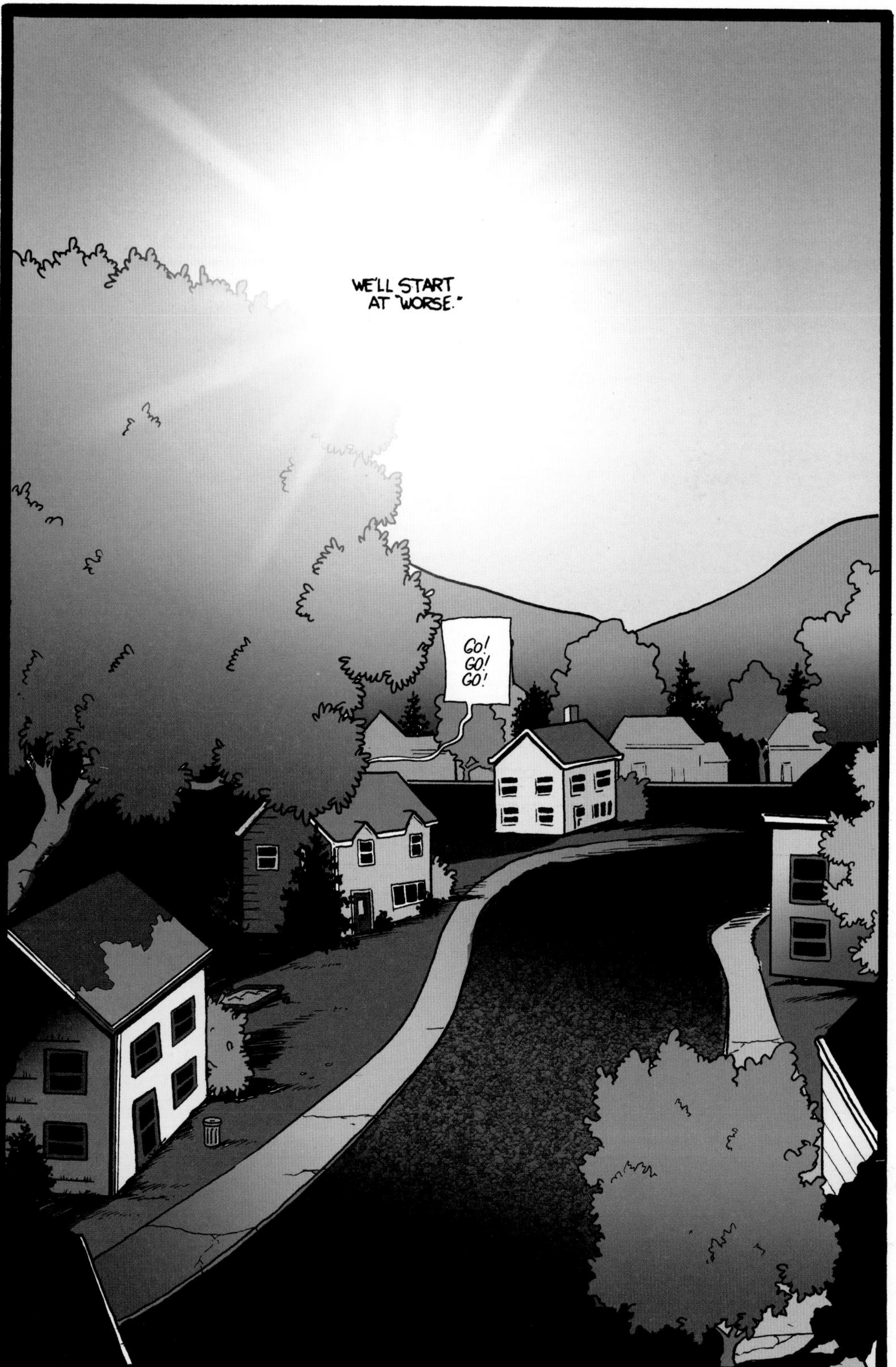
WE'LL START AT "WORSE."
GO! GO! GO!

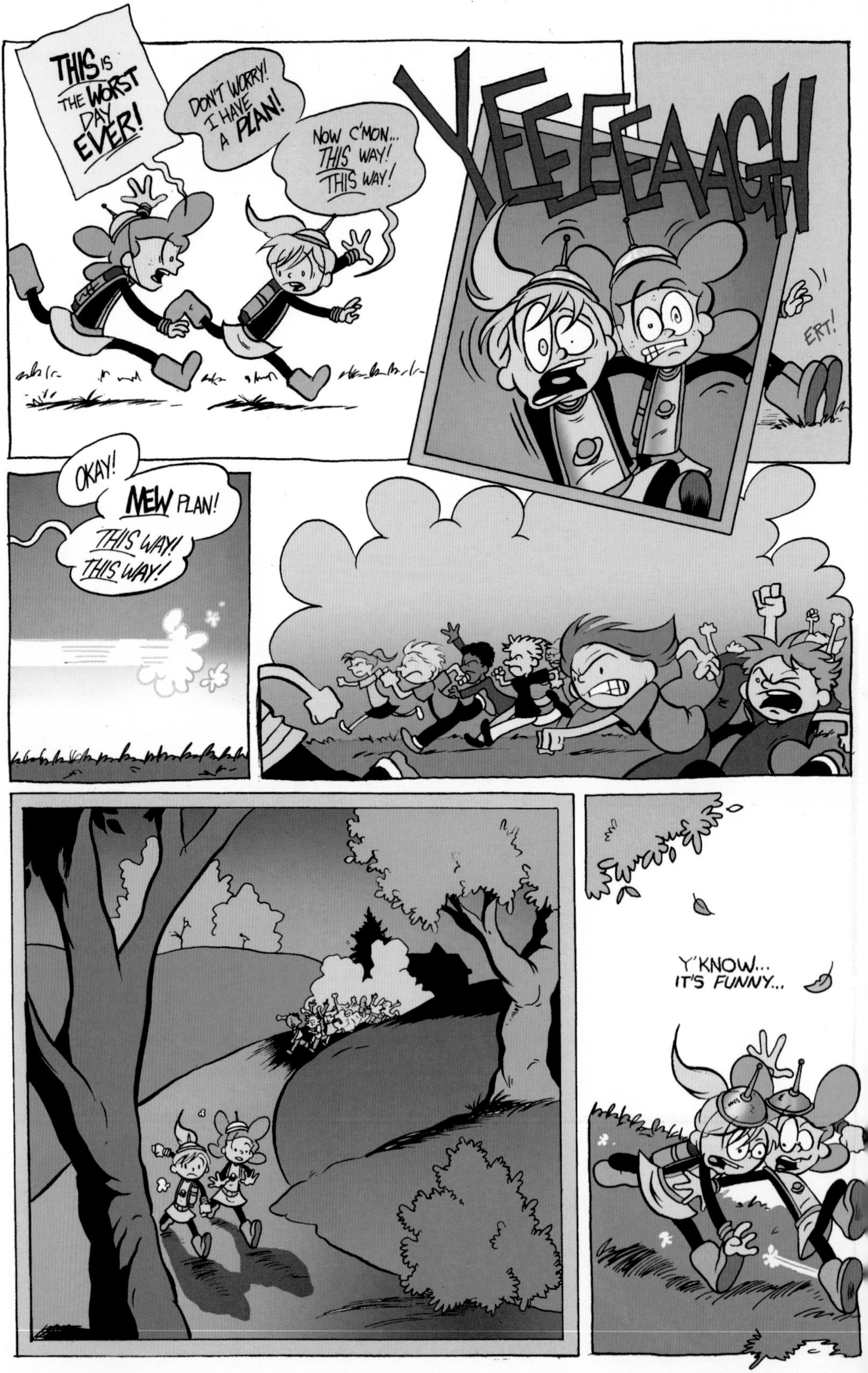
THIS IS THE WORST DAY EVER!
DON'T WORRY! I HAVE A PLAN!
NOW C'MON... THIS WAY! THIS WAY!
YEEEEAAGH
ERT!
OKAY!
NEW PLAN!
THIS WAY! THIS WAY!
Y'KNOW... IT'S FUNNY...

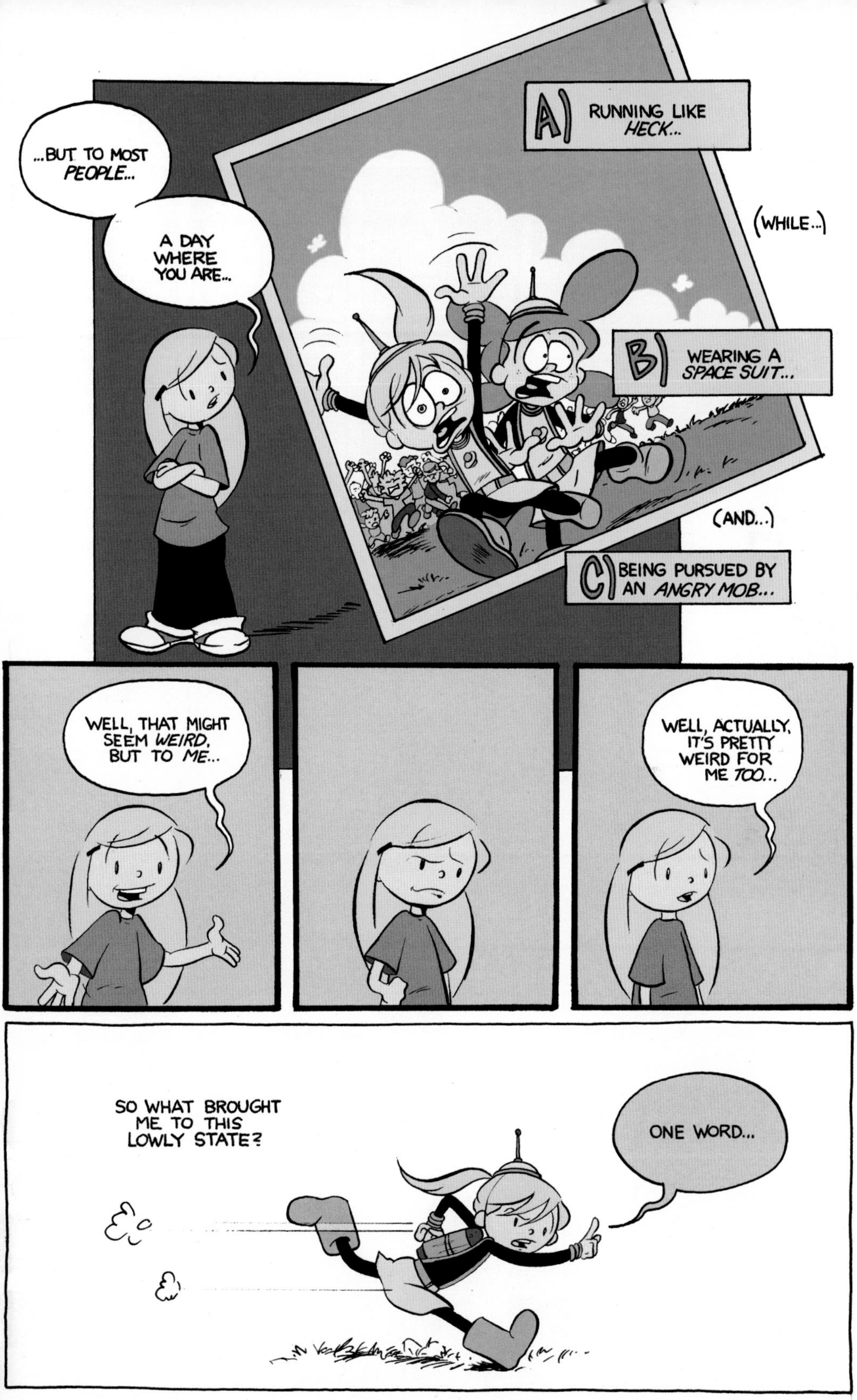
...BUT TO MOST PEOPLE...
A DAY WHERE YOU ARE...
A) RUNNING LIKE HECK...
(WHILE...)
B) WEARING A SPACE SUIT...
(AND...)
C) BEING PURSUED BY AN ANGRY MOB...
WELL, THAT MIGHT SEEM WEIRD, BUT TO ME...
WELL, ACTUALLY, IT'S PRETTY WEIRD FOR ME TOO...
SO WHAT BROUGHT ME TO THIS LOWLY STATE?
ONE WORD...

POPULARITY...

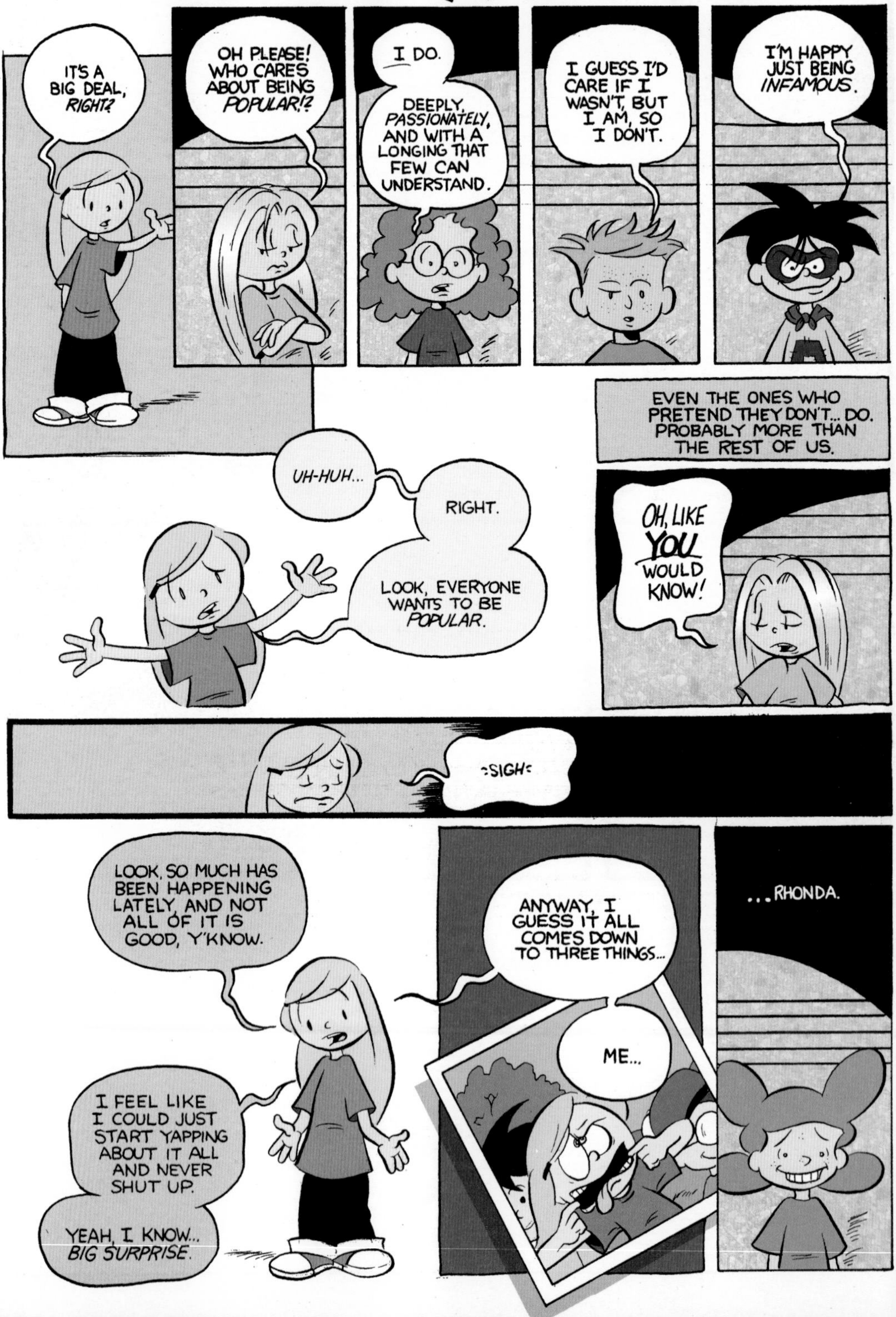

IT'S A BIG DEAL, RIGHT?
OH PLEASE! WHO CARES ABOUT BEING POPULAR!?
I DO.
DEEPLY, PASSIONATELY, AND WITH A LONGING THAT FEW CAN UNDERSTAND.
I GUESS I'D CARE IF I WASN'T, BUT I AM, SO I DON'T.
I'M HAPPY JUST BEING INFAMOUS.
EVEN THE ONES WHO PRETEND THEY DON'T... DO. PROBABLY MORE THAN THE REST OF US.
UH-HUH...
RIGHT.
LOOK, EVERYONE WANTS TO BE POPULAR.
OH, LIKE YOU WOULD KNOW!
:SIGH:
LOOK, SO MUCH HAS BEEN HAPPENING LATELY, AND NOT ALL OF IT IS GOOD, Y'KNOW.
I FEEL LIKE I COULD JUST START YAPPING ABOUT IT ALL AND NEVER SHUT UP.
YEAH, I KNOW... BIG SURPRISE.
ANYWAY, I GUESS IT ALL COMES DOWN TO THREE THINGS...
ME...
...RHONDA.

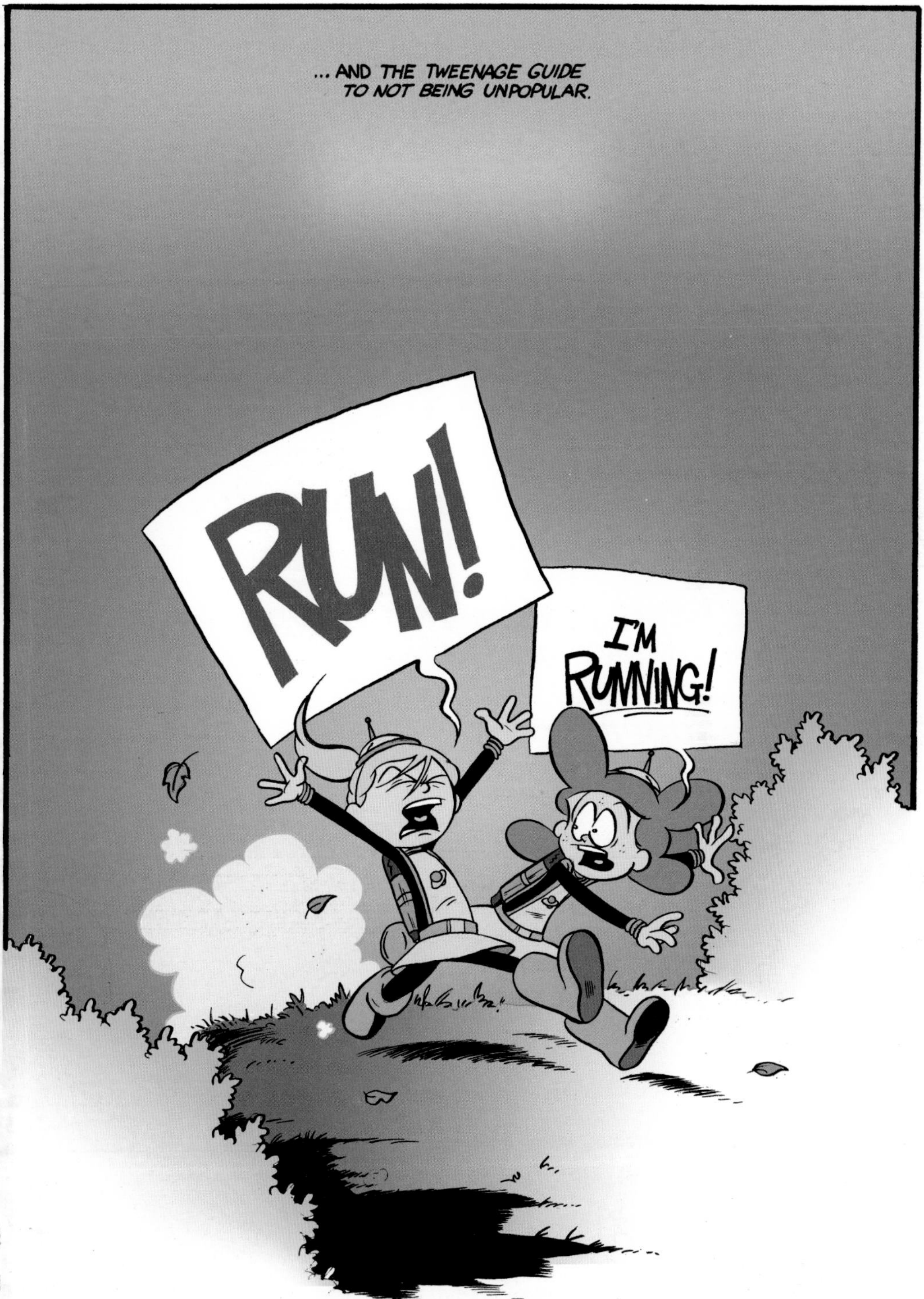

... AND THE TWEENAGE GUIDE TO NOT BEING UNPOPULAR.
RUN!
I'M RUNNING!

Jimmy Gownley's **AMELIA RULES!**™

Join Amelia and the gang for adventures, mishaps, and homework.

Collect them all!

☐ **#1:** *The Whole World's Crazy*
ISBN: 978-1-4169-8604-1

☐ **#2:** *What Makes You Happy*
ISBN: 978-1-4169-8605-8

☐ **#3:** *Superheroes*
ISBN: 978-1-4169-8606-5

☐ **#4:** *When the Past Is a Present*
ISBN: 978-1-4169-8607-2

☐ *A Very Ninja Christmas*
ISBN: 978-1-4169-8959-2

#5 The Tweenage Guide to Not Being Unpopular

ISBN: 978-1-4169-8610-2 (hc)
ISBN: 978-1-4169-8608-9 (pbk)

THE TWEENAGE GUIDE TO NOT BEING UNPOPULAR

"A character to rival Ramona."
—School Library Journal

AMELIA RULES!
Jimmy Gownley